# GUARDIANS

# GUARDIANS

### THE PROPHECY FULFILLED

## LINDA COLE

iUniverse, Inc.
Bloomington

**GUARDIANS**
**The Prophecy Fulfilled**

*iUniverse books may be ordered through booksellers or by contacting:*

*iUniverse*
*1663 Liberty Drive*
*Bloomington, IN 47403*
*www.iuniverse.com*
*1-800-Authors (1-800-288-4677)*

*ISBN: 978-1-4759-7225-2 (sc)*
*ISBN: 978-1-4759-7227-6 (hc)*
*ISBN: 978-1-4759-7226-9 (ebk)*

*Printed in the United States of America*

*iUniverse rev. date: 01/24/2013*

# Acknowledgements

I'D LIKE TO GIVE A huge thank you to:

My editor Paul Carlos for a fantastic job you did and for putting up with me. Without you this story would not be readable and I am looking forward to working with you in the future.

Linda Frazer, for your help with getting my web site up and running, you are amazing! Check it out at www.lindacole.ca

Kimberly Lake, Kim White and Norm Pederson for believing in me and gently pushing me to believe in myself.

Family and friends, thank you for always being there with strong shoulders, kind words and lots of hugs!

For excepting and loving me as I am. Thank you Kevin, Samantha and Tom.

And to my readers, I thank you for your interest in reading my favorite story, I hope you will like as much as I do.

# The Prophecy

There are seven times two, who guard the life force,
One will rise to alter the course.
Against the one seven stand
Balance tipped on Taysia's land.
Until from seven there is one.

Seven to one through time and space,
The power of four the one shall face.
When one and one make three,
Pleased are the power that be.
The balance restored, the course is set.

Out of the light the dark descends,
Beware the foe who is a friend.
The one thought dead to be alive.
Nature divided, only one will survive,
All will be as before

~Deia

Starian words and phrases used in the story:

Ayena kad linear lye ent. Zawwa tar ze tar vax zif, keylie zrefia ze decia avada benwa.—lightening streaks across the sky, from star to star he flies giving hope to those who cry.

Da! Ish, Link, ish—No! Stop, Link, stop.

Zekon vol ty airon—They come in peace.

Sta Tia?—What Tia?

Fetca.—Please.

Maya—Mother

Ne fent, sek en meriad!—Yes father, I am home

Zo fentera—My son

Thayia de mar!—Powers that be!

Sek kytar ak—I love you.

Ne, da—Yes, no

Tarine lye thayia de mar—Thank the powers that be.

Rayla vinex ce—Look forward

Laymar van zyon—Walk with courage

Tarine-ak—thank-you

# Prologue: Taysia

"Beautiful isn't it? Just like I always imagined paradise would look." Keyla said taking a seat beside her sister on the large rock by the lake. The blue sky was reflected in the clear water and beyond the lake stood the woods. Sunbeams reached through the tall trees touching the smaller bushes loaded with flowers and ripened fruit, given them just a hint of golden shine. The green and blue hues of the grass on the other side of the lake blended together looking as soft as a painters brush stroke; colorful flowers sat on top of the grass as though they were floating, bobbing in the gentle breeze that blew across the water. The wind lifted several long strands of her blond hair waving them out behind her like golden ribbons.

"Yes, it is." Kittana answered absently, putting a hand lovingly on her extended belly when she felt the baby kick, caressing it as she continued to stare out over the lake.

Keyla studied her sister's face—it was the same face Keyla had—smooth even skin, high cheek bones, perky nose and full lips. Judging from the sad expression on her twin`s face Keyla knew she wasn`t really seeing the beauty of Taysia and she couldn't really blame her. It was hard being pregnant and having the love of her life ripped from her for some unknown reason, and now, living on the strings of hope that he'd come back someday. It was hard on all of them.

"I just . . . I wish Reace was here. I know Timelana said he'd return, but that was eight months ago! You'd think being the Guardian of Time, she would have been able to tell us *when* he'd return. This waiting and wondering is driving me *CRAZY!*" Kittana's eyes flashed as she vented her frustration. "Having a baby is supposed to be one of the most amazing things to ever happen to a person. I want Reace to be here. It's his baby too."

Keyla could see the tears shimmering in Kittana's dark blue eyes when she turned to her.

"Keyla, I need to know how he feels about this. I know it sounds silly but having a baby is a huge responsibility and . . ."

"And balancing the life forces wasn't?" Keyla interrupted her. "Kit, I think he is acquainted with responsibility—very well."

"I know but this is different." Kittana insisted.

"When he gets back I'm sure he'll be fine with being a daddy." Keyla caught herself just in time; she had almost said 'if' he comes back. She hadn't believed Timelana when she had told them that he would return. Reace would not have left them alone to battle Malic—not willingly. As hard as it was to except, he was dead. Pushing down her heartache and the tears that came close to the surface, she plastered a smile on her lips. Her sister didn't need any more stress and worry, not with her baby due any day.

"I hope your right and I hope it's soon," Kittana said turning back to look at the vibrant colors of the landscape.

"Hey, did I tell you what Arron found in the library?" Keyla's voice broke the silence that had fallen between them.

"No, what did he find?" Kittana swung her blue gaze into the green gaze of her twin. Their eye color was the only difference; well, that and the powers they wielded she was the Guardian of the Mind while Keyla was the Guardian of Magic.

"He found a book of Deia's prophecies apparently she had more than one." Keyla told her trying to put some excitement into her voice before she added with a tilt of her head. "Do you want to go take a look?"

Kittana smiled sadly and shook her head, "Thanks Key, but I think I need to be alone right now."

"Are you sure?" Keyla asked wishing she could help her sister to feel better but there was nothing she could do to erase the sadness in her eyes.

"Yeah," Kittana sighed. "I'm sure."

"Okay then," Keyla stood and dusted herself off. "I guess I'll go back and tell Arron he's on his own, he'll have to translate it himself." Keyla turned starting to leave the lake area when she looked up and saw the dark clouds hanging in the sky. Glancing at her sister's back worried lines etched her brow, she shouldn't be surprised by the clouds she supposed, her sister was upset and carrying the Guardian of Nature—well this wouldn't be the first time Kittana tapped into his powers.

"Don't stay out here too long Kit, it looks like it may rain." She called before leaving her sister alone.

Kittana heard, but she didn't turn around, she continued to watch the wind play in the trees and over the lake. It was hard to believe that this was the same place the four of them had entered eight months ago. Taysia had changed so much.

When they had first come here from Earth the whole place was dark. No sunlight could push its way through the thickness of the grey clouds that had covered the sky. The trees that stood tall and proud now, were withered, gnarled and shrunken with evil. There were no bushes; no berries; no food. The lush grasses were all yellowed, no flowers bloomed. Even the clear water of the lake had looked like black tar. Taysia had been a haven for death and evil. Even the air had stood still as if holding its breath, waiting for them.

Coming here, her, Arron, Reace and Keyla had opposed Malic, the dark Guardian, and balanced the life forces of Taysia; saving the planet Vanishtar from suffering the same fate as Staria had. The four of them had brought spring to this place. Today everything was alive and fragrant, a lush paradise.

She should be happy, proud of what they had accomplished but what is paradise without the one you love? She sighed, if only he were here.

Shortly after losing Reace, the Guardian of Time appeared to them and along with the wonderful news that she was carrying a baby—a fact that Arron confirmed—Timelana had told them Reace would return, but that seemed so long ago that Kittana was starting to give up hope.

Even Arron had stopped believing. He was having a hard time, Kittana thought; he and Reace had been close friends for so long that without him Arron seemed lost. Losing Reace had affected them all. She looked down at her expanded belly, feeling the child kick Kittana smiled sadly. She had hoped Reace would return before their child was born but time was running out and so was her belief. Maybe Timelana was wrong. Perhaps she'd just have to except that he was gone. Kittana looked up as clouds moved over the sun.

*Keyla was right about the rain.* She thought, struggling to move her bulky body into a standing position. Looking out over the lake she took a deep breath, smelling the rain in the air. Closing her eyes, she started to concentrate on teleporting herself home.

Kittana didn't pay attention to the rumble of thunder or notice the deep vibrating laughter that filled the air around her seconds before lightning stuck behind her. She screamed struggling to free herself as strong arms encircled her from behind.

"Hey, it's me." Reace breathed in her ear.

At the sound of his voice, a voice she thought she'd never hear again, Kittana sagged in his arms, relief flooded into her veins.

"Reace," she whispered. Hearing his voice again and feeling his arms around her was like something out of a dream.

"I'm finally back." He laughed turning her around. His smiling face changed into a look of incredibility as he stared at her belly.

"A b . . . b . . . baby?" His electric blue eyes flew to her face for confirmation.

"Yes," Kittana nodded. Reaching out her hands to touch his chiseled face, ran them through his shaggy black hair and over the broad shoulders of his six foot frame reveling in the feel of him—solid in front of her.

"You're here! You're really here!" She whispered hugging him tightly. "I've missed you so much. What happened to you? We thought you were dead. Where have you been?" She demanded pulling away from him and looking up into his face.

"A baby?" He repeated trying to wrap his mind around that fact.

Having heard Kittana scream, Keyla and Arron materialized into the clearing beside the lake. After a moment of shock Keyla squealed in delight and launched herself at Reace.

"OH MY GOD! Reace you're alive! Timelana was right, you're back!" She said as she hugged him her legs going around his waist forcing him to hold her up.

"Yeah, I'm finally back." Reace said stumbling backwards as he caught Keyla in a hug.

Glancing past Keyla's hair he noticed Arron still standing a few feet away a look of surprised disbelief on his face. Reace put Keyla down when he saw Arron still hadn't moved then walked over to him. Being similar in height, himself just slightly lankier then Arron's athletic build, they stood eye to eye.

"Comrade, it's me. I'm home!" Reace smiled his blue eyes twinkling.

"You're back." Arron said on a breath. A grin slowly spread over his face bringing out both of his dimples. Arron swallowed back his tears of joy at seeing a face he had thought he'd never see again to tell Reace. "If you ever do that again I will personally beat you to a bloody pulp then kill you myself."

"That bad, huh?" Reace asked putting a hand on Arron's shoulder.

"Yeah." Arron whispered nodding, a lock of blond hair falling across his forehead as he pulled Reace into a hug. When the two boys broke apart Arron demanded, "What happened to you? Why did you leave?"

"Where did you go?" Keyla asked as she and her sister came up beside them.

Kittana put her arm around Reace's waist, she had to keep touching him, the small shocks she received from him helped to remind her that this was real. He was finally here with them.

"I didn't mean to leave . . . it just happened." Reace put an arm around Kittana's shoulders hugging her too him as he thought of the answers they wanted. "I want you to know that I would never have left if I had a choice, if I knew . . . I have been trying to get back here all this time." He glanced up from the women in his arms towards Keyla and Arron. "I guess you and Key were right, I was too much in control. When Malic blasted me with that water it forced me to lose control. That first time I didn't know what happened one minute I was with you and the next I was in another place." He paused, remembering.

"It took me a while but I discovered that if I let myself go and relax I can blend in with the electrons in the air and rematerialize in another place. When I left here I was zipped all over the galaxy helping who ever called me. At first it was like I didn't have a choice," his face took on a look of amazement. "I have been to amazing worlds. I have helped all kinds of creatures from every walk of life imaginable. It's incredible all the worlds and the vast differences out there in the universe but the most amazing thing is that we are all similar. We all have the same feelings and desires it's . . ." Reace shook his head unable to describe it in words.

"There are so many people out there; so many that need help. I felt . . . compelled to help. Even now if I concentrated I can hear them calling and asking for aid."

"And you should help them Reace, that's what Guardians do." Kittana said and when she saw the expression on his face she explained further. "It was my favorite line at the end of the legend dad told me as a child 'the Guardians help those in need, those who call upon their name."

"We've had a visit from Timelana too," Arron told Reace. "Guess we were chosen to do double duty as Guardians of the life forces: not only do we have to balance the forces of good of evil but we also have to help people in need. When we are ready we will feel the call as you did, to help." His brown eyes lit up as a thought hit him, and as Arron recited in Starian a pleased grin spread over his features. "Ayena kad linear lye ent, zawwa tar ze tar vax zif, keylie zrefia ze decia avada benwa."

At Reace's quizzical expression Kittana translated.

"Lightning streaks across the sky, from star to star he flies, giving hope to those who cry." Turning to Arron she grinned before adding, "You're right it is about him."

"Huh?" Reace was still confused. What were they talking about?

It was Keyla who took pity on Reace and explained, "Arron's been learning the language and he found a book of Deia's prophecies. Apparently she had more than one and we think that one is about you."

Reace repeated the phrase in his mind and nodded. He could accept that, he had been from star to star, planet to planet and the many people he had helped . . . Reace pushed them from his mind, he was home now.

"Who is Timelana?" Reace asked after clearing his throat. He remembered Keyla had spoken of her too, he wondered who she was and what she had to do with them? Looking at his surroundings for the first time he noticed that everything was different, beautiful, like paradise. He wondered at that too.

"What happened after I left? You must have defeated Malic, this place is amazing." He stated with a smile that didn't quite reach his eyes he still couldn't shake the feeling that defeating Malic was wrong, that somehow there was another way.

"Timelana is the Guardian of Time. After you disappeared we thought you had died," Keyla took a deep breath before continuing, "and we were a mess. Kit did a physic blast on Malic but it only hurt him, it didn't kill him."

"It hurt both of us," Kittana added she still felt weak and she knew in her mind that it would be a while before she would feel like her old self again. "But it did weaken his control over Taysia and destroyed the shades."

"Balance, we figured out after you disappeared, means you have to have both good and evil to live." Arron added.

Reace's smile broadened this time reaching his eyes. He was glad that they figured it out. It was what he was thinking too but he had been too scared then to voice his thoughts. Now he wondered if he had spoken up what would have happened. Would he have been here to watch Kittana grow large with his child? Would he have been here to feel its first kick?

"How do you feel about the baby? Reace, how do you feel about being a father?" Kittana asked him seeing the way he was looking at her belly. It was nice to have his presence back in her mind again but she was reluctant to reach out through their bond and read his mind, scared of what she might find.

"I . . . I think it's incredible." He said with honesty shining in his eyes.

"Incredible but . . . I feel there is a 'but' coming." Keyla interrupted, Kittana nodded in agreement with her sister's intuitive statement then held her breath as she waited for Reace to open up.

"Is there a but?" Arron demanded, narrowing accusing eyes at his best friend.

"Yes, there is" Reace admitted slowly. Turning his attention to Kittana he said, "I don't know if I'll be a good father, what if . . ." he lowered his gaze for a second trying to find the words to explain the way he felt, the fear he felt. "On Earth people talked of abuse running in cycles with the abused becoming an abuser, it happened to John, what if it'll happen to me? God, Kit, I don't want to hurt you or our child."

The anguish on his face brought fresh tears to Kittana's eyes. "Do you love me Reace?"

"Yes, I love you with everything that I am." He spoke honestly. "But that isn't enough. John loved my mother too and he still hit her . . . I . . . I can't . . ." he trailed off.

"I love you too. That's all our baby needs. You won't hurt me. Reace, you are nothing like John, if you were then I don't think you'd be a Guardian, at least not one on our side."

"You wouldn't hurt anyone Reace, but if it makes you feel any better, Arron and I will be here to help out." Keyla added.

"Yeah," Arron agreed. "You're not alone anymore."

Reace looked at his friends then turned back to Kittana speaking without words through the link they shared. *"I'm scared Kit, I've never been a father before."*

She smiled at him and replied with telepathy. *"I've never been a mother before but I think we'll be okay. We'll learn together."*

He nodded and hugged her too him, "I'M GOING TO BE A DAD!" He shouted, then turned serious again as a thought stuck him. "You know I didn't stay with John all those years because of fear, I mean fear helped, but that wasn't the main reason."

"You have another reason—blackmail." Keyla pointed out. "He would have told about your abilities."

A humorless smile flashed across his face. "Yeah, but the real reason I stayed and took his abuse was out of guilt. I felt like it was my fault; my mother died and I couldn't save her . . . John made me feel that way. I know that now, but then I didn't. I thought I had lost his love that night too . . . all those years I tried so hard to gain it back. Doing everything I thought he wanted, trying to be perfect." Reace's eyes darkened in memory. "But it didn't matter, he hated me anyway."

Kittana felt a chill run up her spine when he turned those eyes on her.

"What I am trying to say, Kittana, is that if I ever die promise me that you'll never make our child feel like that, like it's his fault. Promise me that you'll never make him feel guilty," he stared at her demanding a response. "Promise me!"

"Alright, I promise. You know I'd never do anything like that."

"I know." He whispered, relieved as he hugged her again. "Thank-you," he muttered against her hair as he kissed her head.

Keyla was watching her sister and Reace share a moment when the ground beneath her feet trembled slightly; she looked at Arron, her face asking the silent question: *Did you feel that too?*

Arron didn't have time to answer as the ground beneath their feet shifted violently again.

"What the hell was that?" Keyla demanded when the trembling stopped.

"How the hell should I know?" Arron snapped when he saw the way Reace and Keyla were looking at him.

"You're the expert in biology." Reace reply trying to keep himself and Kittana upright as the ground moved again.

"Biology. Not geology!" Arron retorted back at him just as the ground stopped shaking and a round shimmering disc of golden light appeared in front of them and grew until it was a little taller than they were.

"Arron," Reace spoke staring at the golden circle.

"That isn't from me, man." He replied just as surprised as Reace to see it.

"It's not from the baby, me or Malic." Kittana told them after checking on Malic's location with her mind.

"Portal," Keyla said. She had seen that before, in her spell to show Reace's real father.

Arron heard Keyla and was ready to use his powers if they were needed. Both he and Reace moved in front of the girls as though they planned it, protecting them just as three people emerged from the portal which closed behind them and disappeared as quickly as it came.

"Arron shield!" Reace barked when he saw the mark flash on one of the new Guardian's wrist seconds before fire erupted from his hand.

"Ahead of you," Arron shot back. He too had seen the mark glow and put up a hand, palm outward, his yellow tinted shield ready to block the fire power of the stranger.

"Da! Ish, Link, ish," The smaller of the two women who stood on either side of the Fire Guardian said in a pleading voice as she tugged on his arm. "Zekon vol ty airon."

"No! Stop, Link, stop . . . they come in . . . me?" Arron translated most of what she said but, hearing his name threw him for a loop so he turned to Kittana with a questioning look.

"Not you Arron, airon it means peace." Kittana explained.

Arron repeated the word committing it into memory. He smiled when he thought how closely it resembled his name and how it meant peace, funny how his parents named him that—after all they had been through and he ended up being the Guardian of Life. His smile turned into a frown when he remembered that he was also the Guardian of Death.

"Sta Tia?" Looking at the girl tugging on his right arm, Link spoke to her in a voice that was deep and commanding, yet gentle. He was handsome with curling brown hair streaked with red and gold highlights, smoldering eyes the color of flame and a body that must have been carved out of years of hard work. His mark stopped glowing as he lowered his hand, the fire dissipating into nothing.

She answered him in rapid speed, too fast for Arron who was just learning the language to grasp. With Link's fire arm down and the mark no longer glowing Arron no longer felt in danger and lowered his shield as he dropped his arm.

Kittana seemed to understand what was being said so Arron, Reace and Keyla watched with interest as she spoke to them, at the same time she used her mental powers to reveal what was being said.

"Yes, we come in peace; we are not here to fight but to live together in harmony. You must be Guardians too, from Staria?" Kittana asked hopefully as she shouldered her way past Reace and Arron to stand in front of the strangers.

"Staria? Staria is dead. We come from Vanishtar and Volairon." Link motioned to himself and Tia being from Vanishtar and Awkwade being from Volairon. "I am Link, the Guardian of Fire." As if to accent his words the mark of a flame on his left inside wrist pulsed with light.

The women on Link's left stepped forward, a little taller than Kittana's and Keyla's five foot nine inches, she was beautiful in an exotic way with long pale blue hair mixed with darker blue highlights that matched the color of her eyes perfectly and her skin was so pale it almost glowed, a soft white, but instead of making her look pasty it made you think she was beautiful water nymph straight from a fairytale. Reace and Arron couldn't help but stare at her. She spoke in a voice that was strong and musical, almost hypnotic. "I am the Guardian of Water. My name is Awkwade"

"I guess all those tales about sirens in the sea really are true." Keyla mumbled as she punched Reace in the arm.

Reace frowned at Keyla before returning his gaze back to the new comers, avoiding the bewitching women of water. He focused his eyes on the shorter woman still standing on Link's right side.

She paled in comparison to the beauty of the other two Guardians with her short, pixie-cut brown hair, streaked with light purple and wide lilac colored eyes, her features were plain yet Reace thought she had something that the others lacked . . . something that he understood.

"And you are?" Arron demanded when she hadn't stepped forward to introduce herself.

"I am Tia." She simply said staring deep into Arron's eyes.

# Chapter one

Taysia, sixteen years later:

Nature, a care-free boy of sixteen with inky black hair and bright green eyes, was playing a game of hide and seek with three wood nymphs, several tree frogs and a furry little creature called a Nex. An easy smile curved the tanned skin of his lips upward and he laughed as he turned from one tree to another searching for his friends when a fairy flew up to him in such a panicked rush that he almost hit Nature in the face.

"Hey, watch it!" Nature called out throwing his hands in the air as he dodged the crazy flying fairy then recognizing him held up a hand in invitation.

"Sorry Nate." Flynn said as he landed in Nature's outstretched hand, huffing and puffing from flying so fast.

"Flynn? What's wrong? Why are you in such a hurry?"

"It's Zarrick, Nate you have to help, he's at it again and this time I don't think he's playing. Foxy and Bark are going to kill each other!" Flynn exclaimed.

"Calm down, that's not going to happen even Zarrick won't go that far." Nate said with more assurance then he felt. Zarrick was Arron and Tia's son. Nate didn't want to believe that the fifteen year old would actually kill anyone but then again, Zarrick was the Guardian of War, maybe that was . . .

"Hurry, Nate, come on! We have to hurry, you have to stop it." Flynn's worried voice broke through Nate's thoughts bringing him to the problem at hand: Zarrick.

Speaking to the hiding creatures Nate called off the game they were playing then he followed Flynn through the forest. The fairies expected him to somehow stop Zarrick from using their friends in his sick idea of testing his powers, but how could he stop Zarrick?

*What could he do?* Nate asked himself as he ran behind Flynn.

He had been born with the expectation that he was supposed to be this powerful Guardian but all he could really do was grow plants and make it rain. Zarrick had real power, being Guardian of War he could change people's emotions; make them angry enough to fight to the death or scared enough to run away and he could blow things up.

Nature was no match for him and Zarrick knew it.

Nate pushed his helpless feelings aside; he had to do something Flynn was counting on him. The fairies had this unshakable belief that he was a powerful being; it was only Zarrick and the chosen seven that knew the truth. Going to their parents was out of the question: Zarrick would only get into trouble and later take it out on him. He had to think of something on his own. Besides he wanted to prove himself capable so his parents and Uncle Arron could be proud of him. He was tired of feeling like a failure.

When they burst into the clearing Nate stopped, appalled by the scene in front of him: two fairies were fighting each other with such intent, with such hatred toward each other that their auras were black instead of the bright colors they should have been, but even more disturbing was the bloody mess both of them were. Nature could see why Flynn was so upset. Usually fairies were happy creatures, even at the worst of times. This kind of rage—the kind *war*s were started by—wasn't in their emotional range.

"ZARRICK!" Nate bellowed narrowing his green eyes as he surveyed the area around him looking for the Guardian that was responsible for this. He could hear him laughing and his anger increased. When he spotted Zarrick high up in a tree he demanded. "STOP IT! Let them be. It isn't fair to use your powers like this."

Zarrick jumped down to stand face to face with Nate, they were about the same height, but that was where their similarities ended. Zarrick had long light brown hair swinging just above his shoulders as he moved. It was streaked with the same yellow color of his eyes. His pale face held the look of hostility (even when he was in a good mood.). No matter how hard Nate tried he just couldn't see Arron in Zarrick at all.

"How else are we to practice using them?" Zarrick demanded then with a smirk he continued. "Oh! That's right, I forgot. You, the most powerful Guardian ever to be born, don't have any powers to practice with." Zarrick taunted enjoying the look of anger that crossed Nature's face. "Not any real powers anyway." His smirk changed into a smug smile as he mockingly challenged "Who's going to stop me . . . you? What are you going to do, grow a flower? Make it rain?"

Nate stood there listening to Zarrick's words, getting angrier at each one, and at himself for not being able to live up to the expectations placed on him at birth. The wind picked up, lifting the hair on the two boy's heads as thunder rumbled overhead and lightning streaked across the sky, the flash of chain lightning landing inches from Zarrick's feet, scorching the ground.

"Okay, okay, I'll stop." Thinking Reace, the Guardian of Electricity was nearby, Zarrick decided to end his little game and he released the fairies from the pull of his powers. Sulking he turned to Nate and said. "You didn't have to call your father I was only having a little fun."

Nature didn't bother to deny that statement he was just relieved that Zarrick had stopped. He stood there watching as Zarrick left. He hardly noticed the fairies thanking him and leaving too.

*Why does my father always have to come to my rescue? I could have handled that,* Nate thought bitterly, *I would have thought of something.* He told himself, no longer glad that his father had come to his rescue once again. Why didn't anyone think he was strong enough to handle things on his own? He angrily kicked at the grass on the ground, not liking the answer that echoed in his mind. The voice that told him that he was weak and his parents knew that. Nate's shoulders slumped a little in defeat. Heck! Everyone knew that, everyone but the fairies.

"Poor, weak little Nature, standing here feeling sorry for yourself are you? You are not as weak as everyone seems to think you are. They just do not realize your true potential." The voice came from behind him.

Startled Nate turned and saw him. He was dressed entirely in black robes. The only thing Nate could see was the lower half of his pale face and the knowing smile that curved his thin lips—it was the smile that caught Nate off guard for a moment.

"Who are you? And how do you know me?" Nate demanded, he knew everyone on Taysia, everyone except . . . Malic!

"I see you have figured it out. Your parents raised you well: Smart, quick and foolish not to be afraid!"

"Why should I be afraid of you?" Nate countered. "My parents over came your evil before I was born, you are no threat to me."

"I did not come here to threaten you, I came to help." Malic purred in a voice so hypnotically sweet that Nature felt himself wanting to hear him out. "You are the Guardian of Nature and yet you do not fully understand the strength of your power."

"Why would you want to help me? What do you know of my powers?" Nate demanded.

"A great deal more then you," Malic pointed out. "But, if you don't want my help then I shall leave you to your belly aching." He slowly turned to go.

"Wait! Malic, Please, tell me what you know." Nate knew he shouldn't be accepting help from his parent's enemy but his desire to have powers overrode the warning he was brought up with.

Malic hid his triumphant smile behind a mask of kindness as he turned back toward the boy.

"Very well you have the power over nature correct?"

At Nature's nod he continued.

"Nature is not just growing flowers and planting trees."

"I know," Nate interrupted "I can make it rain." He shouldn't be here listening to Malic, he should go talk to his parents or one of the others but looking at the older Guardian he didn't think he was dangerous.

"You can do more than that; you are not as weak as you think you are. With your powers you could be great, my son."

"I am NOT your son!" Nature frowned, suddenly he wanted to leave.

"Of course you're not *MY* son," Malic used his powers of emotion to sooth the young Guardian before him. "*My* son would have full Starian blood running through his body. *My* son would know of his full potential but you are not *my* son. You are the son of Reace and Kittana. Earth runs through your veins." At those words he held up a round smooth crystal about the size of a cantaloupe.

Nature stared at the dark swirling crystal, unable to tear his gaze away—he was seeing scenes from Earth. It was like watching TV(his father once explained the concept to him) but somehow Nature knew this wasn't pretend these scenes were real life images; Malic had the power to see life on Earth. The crystal showed pictures of a teenage boy about his age walking in, what Nature assumed, was a school(again from his father's description) laughing with friends, holding hands with a girl and playing sports. He reached out his hands to touch what he had only dreamt about. He couldn't help himself; it was what he wanted his whole life: to go Earth and experience all the wonders of a normal life—like his parents had.

"That could be you," Malic's voice slithered around Nate's body fanning the taste of desire in his mouth. "You do not belong here. You feel useless on Taysia because you belong on Earth, but your parents trapped you here." He paused for a moment, "It is not fair is it? There is so much for you to do on Earth, they *NEED* you there."

Malic was right! Nature admitted to himself. He did feel useless here; he wasn't a chosen like his parents were—to balance the life forces. He could grow flowers and trees but the fairies could do that too. He could make it rain, but again on Taysia it wasn't necessary.

*Earth,* Nate thought, he would be needed there, and he would feel needed there. Earth had pollution and huge environmental problems like draughts and forest depletion maybe the Guardian of Nature could help, on Earth he could make a difference.

Deep in thought Nature didn't notice the crystal grow dark again or that Malic, satisfied that he had put his plan into motion, slipped away.

\*

Back inside of Stone Mountain, seated on his throne, Malic cursed the powers that be that forced him to play this game of weak old man when he knew he was about to finally win. He flinched at the memory of that retched brat, Nature telling him—Him! The great Sartay of Staria, where for centuries the mere mention of his name had struck fear in the bravest of warriors—that he wasn't scared. Malic would show Nature the meaning of the word fear. He'd show them all . . . soon. He just had to wait a little longer and then he'd have his revenge.

\*

5

Nate was still standing there thinking about what Malic had told him when Keyla touched his shoulder.

"Hey, Nate, you okay? You're doing some pretty deep thinking, anything you want to share?" She asked.

He looked around him wondering where Malic had gone and when? Not having an answer, Nate shrugged figuring Malic had probably left as quickly and as quietly as he had come. How long had he stood there thinking? Suddenly, he looked at Keyla as if he just remembered that she was standing there and answering her question he replied, "Nothing much, Aunt Key."

"Took you long enough to answer. You sure you're okay?"

"Of-course I'm okay." He grinned at her. "Why wouldn't I be?"

"Zarrick came home and told us that you got mad at him again and stormed off. What was it about this time?" Keyla pushed for an answer hoping for the truth, she could tell that Zarrick had been withholding information, information she hoped Nate would be more forthcoming with.

"Are you sure Zarrick is related to Arron? I mean Arron is so nice and cool, but Zarrick? We-ell . . . he's not."

Keyla couldn't help the half laugh that came from her as she reached over to ruffle Nate's thick black hair. It was getting harder to do now that he had grown taller than her, she figured when he was finished growing he'd be about as tall as Reace's six feet, maybe taller.

"Yeah, funny how different people can be huh?" She said then added "But I think Zarrick has a lot of Tia in him too, maybe more Tia then Arron. So what really happened?"

Nate sighed he didn't want to be a tattletale so he chose his words carefully.

"He's right, Aunt Keyla, I did get mad at him and I needed time alone to think."

"Okay," Keyla paused then pressed "So what made you so mad?"

Nature frowned as he thought of how to answer her question. For a second he thought of not answering, then he remembered that this was Keyla and if you didn't answer her the first time she'd just keep asking until you did, but he knew he could trust her.

"Zarrick was showing off his powers." Nate grimaced as he remembered seeing the fairies fighting. The look on their faces, he shuddered, closing his eyes tightly to clear the images from his mind. Taking a deep breath he let it go in a resigned sigh before adding. "He just made me so mad." Nate opened his eyes but he didn't look at his Aunt, he couldn't. "Then I got to thinking and well maybe he is right . . . I don't belong here." He didn't tell her who he was talking about now, it really didn't matter who anyway the result was the same: he didn't belong here.

"That's crazy! Of course you belong here. The powers that be wouldn't have created you if you didn't belong here." Keyla tried to reassure him, surprised to hear this coming from him she briefly wondered if she'd been missing the signs of depression, something to tell he was considering suicide.

"No, Aunt Keyla, I didn't mean it that way, I do belong somewhere. Just not here." He rushed on before she could object and voice the thoughts he saw on her face. "I am half Earthling, the powers that be made me that way for a reason and I think that reason is on Earth. You can't argue with me, you were my age when you and mom, Arron and dad came here."

"True," she began but Nate continued before she could say anything more.

"And it was the right thing for you. I'm not saying I am going to Earth right now . . . I'm not sure if that is even possible. I don't know if I could survive there, but I am thinking, turning it over in my mind." He refused to look at her, choosing to look at the ground at his feet instead, he didn't want to see the worry and disappointment on her face.

"All this because Zarrick made you mad?" Keyla asked quietly relieved that Nate wasn't talking about suicide, but going away?

"It was a little more than that but yeah; Zarrick could make an angel angry." Nate said honestly and Keyla nodded in agreement.

"Are you sure you're not just trying to get as far away from Zarrick as you can?"

Nature smiled. "That would be a plus for going, huh?"

"Yeah," she put an arm around her nephew as she reminded him. "Just remember, Nature, there are people here who love you."

"Speaking of them, Aunt Key, this stays between you and me, okay?"

"Do you even have to ask?" Keyla had never betrayed any of Nature's secrets even though her and Kittana and Reace were very close, what she and Nature talked about stayed between them and she was a little hurt that he had to ask.

"Not really," He gave her an impish grin and put his arm around her, she squeezed him in a half hug.

"Speaking of loved ones, your mother's waiting for you at the crystal mount." Keyla finally told him the reason she had come looking for him in the first place.

"Lesson time again?" He groaned.

"Hey, education is important, Guardian or not."

"Yeah, yeah, yeah." Nate rolled his eyes, and laughed when Keyla playfully swatted him. Turning serious, Keyla held onto Nate as she started her spell:

> "Magic I contain,
> Take us home again."

She finished with a flick of her wrist and a swirl of magical sparks. Seconds later both she and Nate were standing in front of his mother, Kittana, in the highest room inside the crystal mountain. Sunlight came in through the thinner walls of the crystal ceiling lighting up the interior. Like a library, six foot high bookshelves lined the walls and in between the shelves at evenly spaced intervals hung large oval crystals, each a different color. The center of the large room held several tables and chairs. Zarrick sat at the far end of the room quietly working on his report. Just beyond Zarrick was another smaller room filled with artifacts encased in the walls of the crystal mountain, like a museum of sorts.

"What took you so long?" Kittana demanded. Being the Guardian of the Mind she could have found out by reading their minds but she refused to invade someone's privacy unless invited or an emergency.

"Zarrick is almost finished his work and you have yet to start!" Kittana had to bite her lip to keep from smiling at him, he looked so much like his father—the same square jaw line, black unruly hair, the only real difference was their eye color; Nature's eyes were a brilliant green while Reace's were electric blue—that she really had to work at sounding mad.

"Sorry mom," Nate's voice held an apologetic tone that turned hopeful as he asked, "Does that mean I'll be working mostly by myself?"

"Don't sound so happy about it, Nate, you're supposed to work together, you know that." Kittana reminded him in a whisper.

"Yeah," he agreed then in a lower voice he added, "but sometimes mom, he gets on my nerves."

"Go easy on him, Kit. He's had a hard day already." Keyla said, meeting her sister's gaze with one of her own.

"It'll be an even harder night." Kittana replied turning her attention to her son she continued, "You're going to stay up until all your work is done and I don't want to hear any complaints out of you! Nate, you brought this on yourself."

Kittana turned him and gently shoving him toward a chair beside a table loaded down with books and crystals. She watched as he sat before turning to her sister and quietly the two of them left the room.

Nate stared at the small mountain of books on the table in front of him. Zarrick and he were systemically learning the history, languages and social protocol of every known populated planet in the universe. Today it was Earth, Nate smiled to himself maybe this wouldn't be so bad. Picking up a book off the top of the pile Nate opened it and started to read.

So involved in the book, taking in all the information he could about the place he most wanted to go, that he didn't notice Zarrick had moved from his table to stand beside him until he spoke.

"Everyone expected you to be so powerful—the first born to the Guardians on Taysia—but look at you." Zarrick sneered down at him. "You're pathetic." He snorted, before continuing to insult Nate. "Maybe you're not a Guardian after all; maybe you're too *earthling* to be Guardian. No wonder you're such a disappointment to everyone."

Satisfied that his words hit a nerve, Zarrick with a smug smile, turned and left.

Nature seethed in anger, glaring at the younger, stronger boy's back as he walked away already finished with his work.

Zarrick was right—Nate couldn't deny it—he was pathetic.

Disgusted with himself he looked back at the book. He tried to focus on the task at hand but his mind kept returning to Zarrick's words replaying them over and over until Nate could no longer concentrate. Throwing the book across the room in frustration, he enjoyed the dull thud it made when it hit the floor then he ran a hand through his hair in an effort to calm down. He wasn't sure why he was letting Zarrick get to him he had heard things like that all his life from the younger Guardian and he'd never let it bother him before so why was Zarrick suddenly getting under his skin?

Determined to forget Zarrick and concentrate on the school work he had to do. Nate grabbed another book off the pile stacked in front of him and opened it, but his mind wouldn't co-operate, remembering instead what Malic had said about nature being more than just growing flowers.

What did that mean? Having no answer for himself Nate sighed. Glancing back at the writing on the page of the book he still held. *It was going to be a long night.* He thought as his eyes scanned the page again. He was almost ready to give up when a phrase caught his attention.

"Force of nature," Nate read out loud. The wheels in his mind turning, could he use this force? Wasn't he Nature? Reading on he discovered that earthquakes, volcanoes, tidal waves and floods were all part of nature, as were snow storms, blizzards, tornadoes and whirlwinds. He knew he could make it rain but could he create a flood?

Putting the book aside Nate allowed his thoughts free reign. Maybe if he could use this power—this force of nature—he might be able to stop Zarrick then maybe his parents would be proud of him and they'd stop trying to protect him. More importantly, he'd be proud of himself. Arron wouldn't be happy though, he didn't like to see creatures getting hurt and these powers, this force of nature could hurt a lot of people and innocent creatures.

Suddenly, pinpoints of colored light swirled in front of his eyes. He blinked as he watched her materialize in few feet in front of him. She was the most beautiful women he had ever seen and living in a paradise he had seen lots of exotic creatures but she had topped them all.

She was dressed in a long white gown fastened at the shoulders by two golden brooches. The gown draped over her generous curves like a waterfall. She wore a golden belt that held all manner of gems, in all colors. A chain hung from her belt and attached to the chain was a weird looking round thing that looked like a crystal sphere covered in numbers. Finally when Nature looked into her face it was like looking into the face of timeless perfection. Her skin was smooth and flawless, her eyes were as dark as her shiny black hair loosely piled on top of her head and tied with golden ribbons. A few tendrils of hair escaped and framed her lovely heart shaped face. When she spoke her voice sounded like she looked—all feminine.

"Nature, I am Timelana, the Guardian of Time." Her skin glowed and pulsed with her inner power, he knew she spoke the truth even without looking at the hourglass shape on her left wrist that pulsed and shined with light. "And your future friend," She added with a smile, holding out her hand to him. "I came to show you that you are indeed the most powerful of all Guardians ever to be born. Come Nature, it is time to learn to use that power."

Almost before he knew what he was doing he got up and walked to her, placing his hand trustingly in hers.

She thudded her staff on the floor three times in rhythm. It was the first time Nate even noticed that she had the thing in her hand but he barely had time to look at it before cringing as a loud noise filled the air around them, making his ears ring with a tune of some strange music. Music he was sure he never wanted to hear again. As suddenly as the music came, it stopped and Nate found himself standing on a strange planet that looked as far as he could tell, devoid of life. He turned to the Guardian at his side with a questioning look.

She laughed a melody of sound. "I brought you here, Nature, at the infancy of a planet, so you could learn how to use some of your abilities without hurting anyone or anything. There is only you and I here. Now let us begin your training."

Nate looked at the vast landscape before him: a raw land, ripe with volcanoes, raging seas in the distance and wild winds playing through the rocky terrain. Chewing on his lower lip he wondered what he could do. Where to start? And why was this Guardian of Time helping him? He swallowed hard summoning his courage to ask her when she spoke first. Turning to look at her he forgot all his questions.

"No living thing is here, yet. No one will be hurt. Come Nate, it is time for you to begin your destiny." She held out her hand to him.

He found himself trusting her. He took her hand and she guided him. Showing him how to use the different forces of nature to his advantage, teaching him in the ways he could help and in how he could harm.

# Chapter two

Nature returned to the library he had left and as Timelana had promised it seemed like only moments had passed. It was a weird feeling knowing he had been gone days—learned so much about his powers and himself—yet only a few minutes had passed for everyone else. Standing there in the middle of the room he reflected on his trip.

At first, on the new planet, he'd been nervous wondering what to do but with Timelana's encouragement he'd soon lost that awkward feeling. At first he exploded volcanoes playing with the lava that flowed down its sides then he learned he could move the ground. Shifting and rolling it to form mountains and valleys, flatlands and hills which he covered in abundant vegetation. He grew whole forest in one day filled with plants of every shape and color. He reveled in the feel of the wind over his skin, playing with it through the tops of the trees and over the seas. Whipping the water into crashing waves then calming it taught him about control. He created mists and fogs that ghosted along the water's edge and over the land. Lastly he learned how he could change the air he breathed.

Timelana had watched him during the days sometimes offering advice but mostly letting him learn on his own. At night they talked sitting on the lush grass watching the sun go down and the three moons rise. The stars winked at them, as he and Timelana formed the bond of friendship that she had been waiting centuries for.

He had left here seconds ago, a weak person who had no clue about himself and while he had been away he had pushed himself to the limit gaining the confidence he had lacked before.

Pulling himself up to his full height, and puffing out his chest, he walked with new found pride toward the table then his shoulders slumped and he groaned out loud as he looked at the pile of books in front of him, he still had to finish that report. Lowering himself into a chair, he grabbed the book on top and opened it. He was just starting to read when his mother appeared.

He wanted to run to her and throw his arms around her in a hug, telling her how much he missed her. He wanted to share with her all the things he had learned but one look at the expression on her face made him back down. She was mad.

He gulped, putting his book down. He wondered what he had done to make her mad this time. Could she have somehow known he'd left Taysia?

"OF COURSE I KNOW YOU LEFT TAYSIA!" she shrieked, reading his mind. "I am a telepath; I knew the minute you left and the second you came back. And being a telepath I also know you needed to go but knowing that and not being able to sense you in my mind are two different things." Her son had gone missing, even if just for a few moments. She didn't know exactly how to express her fear of having him ripped from her like she had her father and Reace (once in the past) but she continued to try. "I am not just a Guardian, Nate, I am your mother and you scared the hell out of me!" She gave him a look before pulling him into a tight hug.

Nate hugged her back and mumbled a heartfelt apology he really hadn't thought anyone would know he had left, in truth it never even crossed his mind to think of anyone but himself. He was drawn out of his thoughts as his mother continued to talk.

"I hope you learned what you needed to because if you ever do that again . . ." She let her words trail off not sure what she would actually do.

Nature pushed her away from him as he stood up. "Mom, I am not a child anymore, I am a Guardian too and someday I will feel the call like you and everyone else and I will have to go to help those in need." To himself he added: *If you didn't stop treating me like a child I'll scream!*

"I know, I know that you'll grow up someday and that you will be a great Guardian, however, right now you are still my son and you are still a child . . ."

"I am sixteen! That was the age you were when you decided that you were old enough to be a Guardian and come here. IT IS THE SAME AGE YOU WERE WHEN YOU HAD ME!" Nate exploded letting his anger wash over him. He heard the thunder rumble in the distance and rolled his eyes. "You didn't call dad too did you?" He accused. As much as he knew his parents loved him, he couldn't help but feel as though he was a disappointment to them.

Kittana didn't bother to tell Nate that Reace wasn't on Taysia, he was away seeing to a call on Dicot, instead she focused on his thoughts. "Neither I nor your father are disappointed in you. Why would you even think that?"

"I . . . wait a minute. I didn't say that . . . you read my mind! MOM! THAT'S NOT FAIR! YOU PROMISED YOU WOULDN'T DO THAT." Nate yelled.

"I believe I promised not to read you unless it was an emergency and I think having my son disappear for two minutes qualifies." She countered.

"I've been back for at least ten minutes now so you can stop. I'm fine and I promise I won't do it again." Nate's anger evaporated when he saw the look on his mother's face. "I'm sorry I scared you. I . . . . I guess I just didn't think before I left, I went with Timelana. She said you knew her. I just really needed to learn what I can do." He spoke honestly, his eyes searching her face for signs that she forgave him.

"I know Nature. I know you needed to go. I know you need to grow up but I am your mother and it isn't easy to let you go, to let you make your own mistakes. It's hard to watch you struggle and not help." Her eyes held a far away look as she thought of Nate's baby days. How he used to cuddle into her shoulder when he was tired; the way he looked up at her when he was four—so proud that he had tied his own shoe.

She sighed, now he was a teenager who was fighting her every step of the way.

"Someday you will understand—when you have kids of your own." Kittana continued, as her eyes focused back on Nature and the pile of books on the table in front of them. She inclined her head silently directing Nate's attention toward the table and back to his school work.

"But for now you are still my child and you have a lot of work to finish before tomorrow."

"Aw, mom!" Nate groaned as he sat.

Kittana smiled and leaned down to kiss the top of his head before using her powers to teleport herself from the room.

# CHAPTER THREE

"Tia, have you heard what our son did?" Arron demanded, walking into their bedroom. "The fairies are very upset about it and I agree that they should be. What Zarrick did was wrong and he knows better! He's not five anymore, we have to do something about this. We can't let it happen again." Glancing across the room to where his wife sat.

She had her head down, her eyes staring at the scar on her left wrist, where her mark should have been—the scar he couldn't heal, she wouldn't let him. It was a reminder, she had told him once, a reminder of where she came from. Although he had asked her what she meant by that she wouldn't tell him. Now when he saw her staring at it with that far away look on her face he knew she wasn't listening to him she was in a place he couldn't follow—in her past.

*Her father held nothing but anger and hatred for her since the day she was born a girl instead of the boy he had so desperately wanted. His anger grew towards her when he discovered his stupid girl was different, that she was a chosen, a Guardian.*

*She had been eight years old when the mark of a diamond had formed on her left wrist. Scared of what it might mean she showed her father.*

16

*In his twisted mind a Guardian was an evil thing, the Dark Lord in the legend had been a Guardian. It didn't matter that 'The Seven' who defeated the Dark Lord were also Guardians in his mind they were all evil. Her father was scared that if people ever found out she was one of them that they'd . . .*

*She wasn't exactly sure what he was scared that they would do, but it was this fear that made him grab the arm of a terrified eight year old child and drag her toward the sink, picking up a knife on the way. The blade was cold on her skin . . .*

"Tia? Are you okay?" Arron asked touching her shoulder gently, his touch and gentle voice brought her out of her dark memories and into the bright sunshine of her life now, her life with Arron, but it was all a lie.

Crouching in front of her, Arron watched the emotions play across her face, "Hey, what is it? Talk to me, whatever it is you can tell me."

"I . . . ah, Arron . . ." Tia croaked out her throat suddenly gone dry. The concern in his voice weighed on her, making the guilt she felt double. She should have told him years ago but she didn't know where to start. She really had made a mess of things. Could Arron forgive her? Would he understand why she had done what she did? She hated fooling him but she had been fooling him for so long it was almost too late to go back.

Tia sighed with relief when her son walked into the room and Arron's attention turned from her toward Zarrick. She didn't have to tell him . . . yet.

"Zarrick, we need to talk." Arron declared as he watched his son enter the room. Standing he faced the young teen who seemed to think that life—other people's lives—could be played with like a toy. Arron thought he had taught his son that it was wrong to use their powers to hurt others. '*Where had I gone wrong?*' He wondered, shaking his head, he was disappointed in himself feeling like he had failed his son in some way.

"I guess you heard what happened with the fairies huh? Nate just couldn't keep his damn month shut could he? He probably ran home and told you all with a smile on his face." Zarrick sneered, glaring at his parents waiting for them to hate him, ready for them to hate him.

"Nate didn't tell us." Arron told him with a frown wondering where this hostility was coming from.

"Yeah, cover for him like you always do." Zarrick snorted then tossed his head of yellow and brown hair as he yelled "ADMIT IT! Why don't you just admit it, you like him better than me. You always did! You wish that I was him!" Zarrick accused his father with hot eyes.

"I have never put Nate before you, you're my son . . ."

"STOP IT! STOP LYING TO ME!." Zarrick yelled at Arron. "I know. I know you're not my father."

Those words hit Arron like a ton of bricks square in the chest. His heart restricted, he couldn't breathe and his head spun. Even though he suspected the truth ever since he first looked into Zarrick's eyes—eyes so much like Malic's—golden yellow, he hadn't wanted to believe it. Arron closed his eyes for a second as he tried to regain control over his emotions. His son needed him right now and he would be there for him.

"Who told you that?" Tia questioned. Her world falling apart before her eyes as her past came up to meet the present. She swallowed hard keeping her gaze carefully on the wall behind Arron and her son, she couldn't look at them yet, she wasn't ready for this and she couldn't face the ugly truth.

"No one told me, maya," Zarrick said using the Starian word for mother, his eyes fastened to Arron as he spoke, "Malic showed me the truth." Zarrick watched his face for signs of horror and shock but he was surprised by the look of pity, pity mixed with love and understanding.

*Understanding?!* Zarrick thought, in surprise. He didn't want Arron to understand, how could he? Arron wasn't evil like he was. Zarrick needed to stay angry at him. He needed to be angry or else he'd end up crying and he didn't want to cry in front of anyone. He was too old for tears. Why did they lie to him? Why did they let him believe all his life that he was good when he wasn't? Why did they make him conform to what they wanted. Was Malic right? Was it because of Arron? Was it Arron's fault that he always felt like an outsider?

"Christ!" Arron muttered. Compassion welled up inside of Arron for the boy he had raised. Malic would have been brutal in his showing of the truth, like he had been when he had shown Arron the truth of his parentage, the rape of his mother. Arron glanced at Tia and wondered if Malic had raped her or if she had . . .

"Listen to me Zarrick," Arron began startling himself out of his thoughts.

"Listen to you? Why the hell should I? You've *LIED* to me my whole life and now you're going to tell me what I can and can't do. NO! No, you're not my father. My father wouldn't lie to me."

Arron paled at those words. No, Malic wouldn't have to lie not when the truth was more painful. Just because the truth was evil didn't mean Zarrick was. Arron briefly wondered why Tia wasn't helping him, but he couldn't look at her right now he had to focus on Zarrick. Swallowing hard the lump of emotion in his throat he forced the words out.

"I didn't lie to you, you are my son. The blood that runs in your veins may not be mine but I have raised you and *loved* you from day one and that gives me the right to call you mine. That makes you MY SON. Zarrick, torturing other beings is wrong. You know that!"

"You can't tell me what to do and you can't . . ." Zarrick broke off desperately trying to get his emotions under control. "You don't . . . you don't understand, YOU'RE NOT MY FATHER!" Zarrick shouted before running from the room.

Arron started after him but Tia's hand on his arm stopped him, "Let him go."

Arron looked down at her, she was right Zarrick needed to have some time to come to terms with this, the two of them could talk later after Arron had the truth from Tia. How did he let this happen? How could he have let Malic get to Zarrick?

Arron's eyes searched her face. "Tia. It's time we had a talk."

*

Zarrick stormed off away from Arron and Tia and anything or anyone that had to do with them. His anger exploding inside of him and the more he walked the more he thought about Arron's look of pity, he flicked his fingers toward a rock that was in his path but he was too angry to be satisfied at the sound of the explosion. He just walked past and flicked his fingers again and again, not caring if he blew up a flower or a rock or some fairy's home. He was just trying to expel some of the anger that flowed through him.

Looking up he found his angry strides had quickly brought him toward the Stone Mountain, hardly pausing before he walked through the door which appeared before him, he found his way to a father who had never lied to him—Malic.

As he entered the throne room he heard Malic whisper in his mind. *"Welcome home my son!"*

"Ne fent, sek en meraid," The young Guardian used the language of his ancestors to say: 'Yes father, I am home.'

Malic smiled as he lounged in his throne, while Zarrick paced before the dais in an angry adolescent rage as he ranted.

"They lied to me . . . for years. I was their kid, how could they do that? Then they think they have the right to tell me what to do! Okay, so maybe I was wrong to practice my powers on the fairies but . . . KANDA LYE THAYIA DE MAR! It's not fair, Nate gets to practice his powers, why can't I?"

"You can . . . just not here. Come Zarrick and I will show you." Malic stood, moving toward the huge crystal sphere that sat on a pedestal of the same black stone the rest of the mountain was made of. The sphere pulsed with a light all its own casting eerie shadows across Malic's face.

Zarrick followed and Malic waved a hand over the smooth surface, for a second Zarrick saw nothing then slowly as he thought of what he wanted to see, to do, images appeared.

"Zarrick, zo fentera," Malic smiled a true smile that made his yellow eyes glow golden when he called Zarrick his son, so he repeated it. "Zo fentera, you are the Guardian of War, your powers are so much more then turning fairies into fighters. You can use your power to direct outcomes on other worlds. Let Dicot be your playground."

"No, not Dicot," Zarrick said with a twisted smile, turning his features to look so much like his father's, "Earth." The mark of two swords crossed on his left wrist pulsed with unleashed power.

Malic laughed in pleasure at how like him his true son was.

# CHAPTER FOUR

TIA MOVED DEEPER INTO THE room and sat in the same chair she had used before. Arron followed behind her but was too restless to sit. As the silence stretched between them he began to pace the length of the room like a caged animal.

Tia watched him wondering where to begin. Finally she decided she had to say something, anything before Arron's pacing drove her nuts. She opened her mouth to speak but Arron beat her to it.

"Zarrick's not mine. I know that. I have suspected since he was a baby, but why Tia? Why didn't you tell me?" His eyes pierced her from across the room.

His words surprised her, "You knew? You have known for all these years, why did you not say anything?"

"I was waiting for you to tell me . . . to trust me that much, I guess." He stopped pacing and watched her face for a moment before asking again, "Why didn't you tell me?"

"I was afraid," she whispered looking down at her hands folded in her lap. "Afraid that you would hate me, Arron, that is something I cannot bare . . . to see that look of hatred on your face."

"How could I ever hate you, Tia? Sek kytar ak." Arron knelt down at her feet his eyes level with hers as he told her he loved her.

The honest emotion shining in the depths of Arron's warm brown eyes was too much for Tia, she looked away. Tears fell from her eyes and she wiped them away with her hand.

"Arron, you do not love me. When I first came here, I saw you and . . ." she sighed heavily, "I did what I did out of love. Please, you have to believe that." She pleaded briefly making eye contact before looking away again in shame.

Arron frowned trying to understand what she was telling him the growing apprehension inside of him came through in his voice "What did you do, Tia?"

"When I first came here, I saw you and for once in my life I took what I wanted . . . I wanted to be on the receiving end of the love that Reace and Kittana, Link and Awkwade have. I wanted someone to love me so badly that I . . ."

"What? What did you do" Arron prompted.

Taking a deep breath she continued "That I made you love me."

She spoke so quietly that Arron had to lean in to hear her.

"You made me love you?" He repeated a confused look on his face as he stood up.

"I am not the women of your heart, Arron. I know you care for me and that you think you love me but you really do not."

"What are you saying Tia? I have loved you for sixteen years." Arron demanded as he began to pace the room again. He didn't understand how their love could be such a bad thing and she had yet to look him in the face and tell him.

"THAYIA DE MAR! ARRON." Tia exploded in frustration before finally glaring at him, angry that he was making this harder for her. "DO I HAVE TO SPELL IT OUT FOR YOU?" she half shouted. "I am the Guardian of Emotions I MADE you love me!"

"You've used your powers on me? For sixteen years?" Arron asked, trying but not quite succeeding in grasping the horrifying idea.

"Ne. Da." Tia closed her eyes at the pain and disbelief on her beloved's face.

"Well which is it, yes or no?" Arron whirled on her.

"DAMN IT, TIA! I need an answer." He demanded when she hadn't answered him.

"No." Tia said then continued, "In the beginning yes, but after a while I felt guilty and stopped using them on you . . ."

"When did you stop, after a year, two, ten, yesterday?" Arron voice broke at the end of his sentence as emotion swamped him. How could she do this to him? Was anything he had felt since he first met her his true feelings?

"Shortly after Zarrick was born," She answered looking at him with a pleading look that begged him to hear her out. "I just could not keep living a lie."

Relief flooded Arron his whole life hadn't been a lie, he still felt cheap and used but at least he knew that everything he had felt in the past fifteen years was his.

He stared into her face from across the room. What would he feel in the future? He was angry with her . . . hurt, but he knew that his anger would cool and his heart would heal—in time. He just couldn't see his life without her. He loved her and he still wanted to be with her.

"Say something? Arron, get mad at me, hit me, something! Fitca." Tia begged breaking the silence that fell between them.

It was the Starian word 'fitca' that caught his attention 'please' his mind translated it and spurred him into saying. "That was fifteen years ago, Tia. I love you and I am still standing here as your miteon, your life mate."

"Yes, but Arron if I had not changed your emotions then you would be with who you were meant to be with—the women of your heart." Tia looked at Arron and sadly shook her head. "She is not me . . . never was." She whispered and looked meaningfully at the door behind Arron.

The way Tia kept looking at the door Arron racked his brain to guess who she was talking about.

"Keyla?! You think she's the women I want?" Arron almost laughed at that—almost—but settled on shaking his head. "After all these years, Tia and for all your emotional insight, I can't believe you could be that stupid." He paused for a second. "Okay, maybe a long, long time ago I did desire her but she made it clear right from the start that we'd never be anything more than friends." He came to her then crouching down and taking her hands in his and looking into her eyes he continued "I moved on. Tia, it's you who owns my heart. It's you who I love all on my own."

Tia stared at him hardly believing what she was hearing, what she had so long waited to hear, someone truly loved her!

"Believe it." He said flashing both dimples as he grinned at her.

"But will you still love me after I tell you . . ." She broke off.

"You can tell me anything and I'd still love you." He countered then asked. "Tell me about Malic. What happened?"

"Love, I did it for love. Please try and understand Arron, all my life I have just wanted to be loved. To feel what it was like to be hugged, and cherished. My mother gave up her life force shortly after I was born and my father . . ." She made a sound in her throat that was half sob, half laugh and shook her head. Her eyes burned with anger, pain and unshed tears but her voice was steady. "He never loved me; he could not stand the thought that I was not the boy he wanted."

He didn't want to think of anyone hurting her but something about her body language and the way she talked about her father reminded him of Reace. Arron swallowed hard trying to get his words past a throat that had suddenly gone dry. "Did . . . did he abuse you?"

Tia shrugged her reply, "Only when I deserved it, that I could live with and even understand but it was the look in his eyes—the hatred—that hurt."

"I'm sorry, Tia. I . . ." Arron began but stopped when she gaped at him.

"Why are you sorry? You did not hurt me, you have never hit me and if you had been there you could not have stopped him."

Arron dropped his gaze to the floor knowing she was right, standing he began to pace the room. He couldn't have helped her just like he wasn't able to help Reace, back on Earth. Christ! He hated this helpless feeling! Arron's hands turned to fists at his sides and a muscle worked in his jaw as he clenched his teeth tight together.

Tia could feel his emotions building, the frustration, and the helpless anger. She hadn't meant for him to feel that way, not about her past. Wanting to fix it, to sooth him she raised her left hand to him.

Arron saw her intent and his shield came up fast between them.

"Don't!" He choked out. "Don't use anymore of your powers on me." He held her gaze steady for a few minutes. At her crumbled look, at the hurt in her eyes he added in a softer voice, "Let me handle my own emotions, okay?"

She nodded lowering her hand, her voice breaking a little when she spoke.

"I did not tell you this to make you mad or for you to feel sorry for me. I do not want pity, Arron, I just want you to understand why I did it out of love. I just wanted to own that feeling. Just once," she whispered, "I wanted to know what it felt like to be loved. When I first met you, when

I first came here, I felt that love between you . . ." she paused leveling her gaze at him, "And Keyla. No . . . just let me finish okay," she said when he would have interrupted her. At his nod she continued, "But you two were denying your feelings for each other and I wanted that feeling so badly . . . that I made you . . . love me."

Arron didn't say anything, so she continued her story.

"I knew what I was doing was wrong and I was miserable and lonelier than ever. Malic seemed so nice, so sincere and friendly. He came to me by the lake. We talked and he really seemed interested in what I was saying. I thought he enjoyed my company." She shook her head at her own stupidity. "I thought he truly loved me, for me. I thought that we were soul mates, but he was only using me. He used his powers on me—my own power of emotion turned against me!" She paused, ashamed of how foolish and naive she had been. "When I found out what he was doing, I stopped seeing him. I have not talked to him in over fifteen years."

She looked at Arron then, her eyes pleading with him to forgive her.

"When you found out I was pregnant, you were so happy that I did not have the heart to tell you that it may not be yours. Arron, I am sorry." She covered her mouth with her hands, her eyes floated with unshed tears as she repeated. "I am so sorry," she took a few moments to collect herself before adding. "It was after Zarrick was born that I stopped using my powers on you. I just could not keep living a lie, no matter how beautiful it was."

"Did . . . did Malic rape you?" Arron asked as the scenes flashed in his mind, scenes Malic had forced him to witness seventeen years ago, scenes of his mother rape by his shade father, Yentar.

"Da! No! He used me, used his powers of emotion and mind control but it was not rape . . . not like your thinking, not like your mother." She finished quietly.

Arron let a pent up sigh escape him, he was relieved that it hadn't been rape; he couldn't take seeing her face replaced his mothers in his nightmares, but still, she was willing with another man and not just any other man, his enemy.

"Tia, you've lied to me, slept with another man and used your powers on me; I . . . I'm going to need some time to get over this. I do love you." He covered his face with his hands than ran them down and added "I know this happened in the past, but right now I need . . . I need to go . . . I have to go get some air, sort this out in my head. Okay?"

Relieved that she had finally told him the whole truth, the huge weight of guilt had been lifted off her shoulders. Tia chewed her bottom lip and nodded silently letting him know that she understood and that she was willing to give him the time to forgive her, but she couldn't stop that little voice in the back of her head that whispered. *He says he loves you but does he really? You stole his heart, his love from another so how can it truly be yours.*

Arron hadn't waited to see her nod he just left, just turned after he had spoken and left, needing to get outside. He started jogging to clear his head; he found speed always helped him to think. He didn't know if he could ever look at Tia in the same light as before.

Arron breathed heavily, she had been with Malic willingly! He shuddered to think it. Damn it! He cursed. He could understand why she had gone to him and why Malic had so easily fooled her, Malic could be very persuasive when he needed to be. He used his powers to find out all your desires, then turn them against you. No, Arron didn't blame Tia, she was opened and hurting and to trusting for her own good.

Christ! He wished she had told him all this years ago then he'd be able to do something to help Zarrick. He should have confronted Tia years ago when he first suspected, but he hadn't wanted to believe it then, and a part of him, even now, still wanted to be in denial but you can't ignore the truth when it's slapping you in the face.

He shook his head, right now, his son needed him more than ever and Arron wondered how he could be there to help Zarrick when he felt like he was drowning himself?

Arron slowed to a walk when found himself close to the lake beside Stone Mountain.

Zarrick was there sitting on the large flat rock beside the lake, he turned his head toward Arron when he approached.

# Chapter five

Nature looked around carefully in the early morning light making sure he was alone. Relieved, he felt free to think about the place Malic showed him—the place he had always longed to see—Earth. As a child he had grown up listening to the stories his father and Arron told of the planet they grew up on and Nate had dreamt of it, of someday going there. He wasn't sure if this dream had been a premonition of things to come or a longing to experience something different. He only knew that he had to go. He had to see for himself the wondrous things he had heard and dreamt about—the places Malic had shown him.

He remembered promising his mother, only last night, that he'd never just leave again without telling her first and he felt guilty breaking that promise but, he just couldn't tell her of this desire, this need that was growing inside of him. He felt consumed by it. He was worried that if he told her or any of the adults they'd try to stop him somehow and he couldn't let that happen. This was something he had to do, so taking a deep breath he called her name.

"Timelana." Nate spoke softly, hoping she'd hear him. Even though he was expecting her he was startled when she appeared before him, as beautiful as the day she had become the Guardian of Time more than two thousand years before. Nature didn't see her beauty in the way a man sees a women but in the way a friend recognizes a friend.

"Yes, Nature, what is on your mind?" she asked with a beaming smile on her lips.

"I . . . I was wondering, you can go anywhere in time and open a portal into any place in the universe, right? That is your power isn't it?"

She nodded knowing what he was asking her.

"I was just thinking, hoping really . . . Could you let me see Earth, maybe even let me go there?" He raised hope filled eyes to hers.

She met his eyes with a confident stare, "Yes Nate, I can. It is fate that you feel drawn to Earth, your future lies there."

"M . . . my future? Tell me—no don't! I don't want to know."

"You are learning well the rules of time." Pride was evident in her voice and her smile widened.

"Not really," a quick grin flashed on his face. "I just figured that if I know what is to happen then instead of making it happen I'd just wait for it to and that would somehow change what is meant to be," He let out a breath, "I'm afraid it'll make me into someone I don't want to be."

"You have a better understanding of time then most others. I am proud of you, Nate."

"Thanks Timelana."

His face grew hot under her praise. She was one person he didn't want to disappoint, it was strange the way their relationship had formed or rather how it was forming now. She had been waiting since well before he was born but he had only met her a few weeks ago, at least it seemed like a few weeks, it had really only been a matter of hours. It helped, he guessed, having her know him so well from the future. It was weird, to say the least, talking to someone who already knew you better then you knew yourself. Then again, what was normal in his life anyway? And that thought brought him full circle as to why he longed so badly to go to Earth, a place where he could experience normal and all the fun and excitement that went along with it.

"Where and when do you want to go?" Timelana spoke bringing Nate out of his thoughts and back into their conversation.

"I want to go to the city my dad grew up in—to the place they all left behind—Springfield. I want to go seventeen years from when they left so it'll be as if I was born on Earth." He looked at her, his bright green eyes pleading with hers. "I want to go now, before mom realizes what I'm planning. I know what I'm doing and I don't need to be talked out of it or reasoned with. Please, Timelana, take me to Earth."

Giving him a look he didn't understand she nodded once then reached out her hand to take his as she tapped her staff on the ground three times. In a swirl of bright jeweled colors and ringing music, they vanished.

*

## Earth 2007:

Stepping into the world he had always dreamed of, he could hardly contain his excitement, he moved forward looking around in awe.

"Nate," Timelana's voice sounded behind him and he turned to her. "You are in the backyard of your father's old house. This is your destiny, embrace it! I will always be a call away." She banged her staff on the soft ground and with an encouraging smile she disappeared, leaving the young man alone in a strange land.

Nate looked at his surroundings, like Timelana had said, he was in the backyard of the house his father grew up in, glancing at the house in front of him he expected to feel some of the horror that his father had lived through—that still gave Reace nightmares—but all Nature saw was a large white square building with a triangle top.

Shrugging, he looked past the house to the road where he heard the noise from the engines of cars that whizzed past at incredible speeds. In excitement he stood wide-eyed watching, taking in every detail, every smell, and breathing deeply Nate gagged at the bitter taste of polluted air.

He decided to fix that first so he could enjoy himself, but not really sure how to fix the entire planet or even if he should, Nate concentrated on the air around him. Raising his arms he called on the powers given to him at his conception, he waved his hands in the air as he slowly turned in a circle. Creating a large bubble of clean air around himself and inhaling deeply, Nate smiled before exhaling.

Feeling very pleased with himself, he ventured forward toward the noisy street, coming up with a plan as he walked. Turning left when he reached the sidewalk, in his childhood he had asked so many questions about Earth—about this city—that he thought he knew his way around. Right now he was heading toward Arron's old house.

For a moment the sight before Nate made him miss a step and falter. His eyes widened in alarm, coming toward him was Arron! Had they found out that fast? He hoped to have more time on Earth before they had found out he'd left but he never thought they'd have so little faith in his ability to come searching for him like some wayward child.

Nature was even more surprised when Arron walked right by him, not even glancing at him as he passed. A little confused Nate turned and caught up with him.

"Arron, I know . . . ," he began but broke off when he touched Arron's arm. Nate gasped in shock when Arron turned to face him with blank eyes, eyes that didn't know him. "You're not Arron." Nate stated the obvious then demanded. "Who are you?"

"Dude, take your fucking hands off me! What are you some kind of freak?"

"I . . . I'm sorry," Nate mumbled trying to understand how this person could look so much like the Guardian he had known his whole life yet be so different. "I thought you were someone else."

Looking into the face of the boy who had just grabbed him, Jake was surprised to find it looked familiar and even more surprising was the guilt that welled up inside of him when he saw the confused frown appear. He felt like he had just kicked a puppy which he told himself was stupid even as he heard himself ask.

"Are you okay? You look a little sick."

"Yeah, I'm fine, confused, relieved, but I'm okay." Nate glanced at the Arron-look-alike in front of him then added, "You really do look a lot like someone I know." As an idea stuck him he continued, "He used to live around here, maybe you could help me find his address?"

"Sure," Jake replied with a small smile as he inhaled, at least the guy was clean and anyone who smelled that good couldn't be too crazy, he thought. Now that Jake had gotten a good look at the fellow in front of him, he wondered where he came from. He had an odd way about him, not strange odd, just odd in that he was somehow different. Not from around here. Jake again wondered why he looked so familiar.

It was the name he used that shook Jake out of his thoughts, making him pay attention to what the stranger was saying.

"His name is Arron Price. I was told he used to live around here, a few houses away from where my father, Reace Stelmen, grew up." Nate explained.

Reace! That's why this kid looked so familiar. When Jake was little, his nanny, Mrs. White had given him a picture of Arron and Reace. It was the only picture he had ever seen of the two of them together. There was something in Reace's eyes, something personal and secret that intrigued him, and as a child he had turned Reace into an imagery friend, someone who was always there to talk too. Someone he could share things with, secrets he wasn't allowed to tell other people. Maybe it was why he felt more like a long lost friend then stranger to the guy in front of him, he looked like Reace.

"The Price's house is over there." Jake pointed behind him to the house he had just left. Wondering what this kid wanted with Arron, Jake added, "But Arron Price has been dead for seventeen years. I'm Jake . . . his son."

# CHAPTER SIX

NATURE'S HEAD SPUN, *ARRON'S SON?!* Had he heard that right?

"Arron's son? You are Arron Dean Price's son? That's impossible!" Nate challenged, although the evidence was in front of him: Jake was the spitting image of Arron, yet Nate had a hard time believing it.

He had idolized Arron all his life, Arron had always been his favorite Guardian, the very model of what was good and right. How could he have sired a child and left it behind? All the stories he had heard, all the questions he had asked and no one had ever even hinted at this? It didn't make any sense unless . . . Could it be that even Arron didn't know? Nate's eyes darted back to Jake's.

"Want a sample of my DNA?" Jake snapped "I know who my fucking father was!" His eyes glittered with hurt and angry defiance. "Why is that so hard to believe?"

"B . . . because Arron . . . he just . . . he wouldn't . . ." He trailed off unable to finish any of the sentences he started.

"You talk like he's still alive, like you know him. HE'S DEAD! DEAD! OKAY? SO STOP IT! THIS ISN'T FUNNY!" Jake yelled then turned on his heel and walked away.

"Shit!" Nate had forgotten that Arron had left a suicide note behind before they went to Taysia, so of course everyone here would think that

Arron had died. Nate cursed again, meeting Jake had certainly complicated things and Nate needed to talk to him.

Running to catch up to Jake, Nate again grabbed his arm spinning him around until they were face to face.

"Look, Jake, there's a lot you don't know about Arron, your father, that I do." Hoping he was doing the right thing Nate asked, "Please can we go somewhere and talk? Just talk."

Jake looked into Nate's face wondering why he was even considering talking to him, the guy was obviously crazy. Everyone knew that Arron was dead, just because no bodies were ever recovered didn't mean that they could be alive, that was just some twisted fantasy Jake had always played in his mind. Yet, here was this guy—about the same age as him—the very image of Reace, talking as if his dad, Arron, were alive. How could that be?

"What's your name?" Jake suddenly asked, stalling, hoping that with time and a little more information he'd suddenly know what to do.

"Nature, but everyone calls me Nate."

"Okay, Nate it is." Jake tried not to smirk but couldn't help himself, Nature was a funny name. Suddenly turning serious, Jake spoke, his honey brown eyes staring into Nate's bright green ones. "Can I ask you something?"

Nate nodded.

"This may sound funny but I have to ask, I have to know. I mean . . . you sound so . . ." Jake took a deep breath, "Is my father, is Arron Price alive?" and let it out slowly as he waited for Nate's reply.

"Yes," Nate answered honestly, looking into Jake's face. "He's a Guardian, of course he's alive."

Jake stared at him wondering why he believed him, was it because he wanted to? Was it because Nate looked so much like Reace? Or maybe it was because the guy talked like he knew Arron? Then again it could be just something in Nate's eyes, something honest and trustworthy, almost noble.

"I'm supposed to be on my way to school, but okay, let's go somewhere and talk. I know a place—it's private"

At Nate's nod, Jake turned and led them back the way they had come. He stole a glance at Nate, wondering if he was doing the right thing. "Where are you from?"

"Taysia," Nate replied as though it were a place around the corner but Jake had never heard of it.

"Taysia," Jake repeated the word, liking the exotic way it sounded. "Must be somewhere I've never been." He muttered as he began walking across the lawn. Making their way behind Mr. Stelmen's house they walked over the hill and into the ditch that led the way to an old nuclear fallout shelter built in the nineteen fifties.

"Hey, is this the shelter?" Nate asked as he walked in front of Jake, parted the branches of a bush and crawled into the pipe that led to the door of the shelter, leaving a stunned Jake to follow.

*How had he known about the shelter?* Jake wondered. It was impossible to see with the bushes in front of it unless you knew exactly where to look. Besides that, it looked like a large drainage pipe in a ditch. It wasn't until you were about fifteen feet in the drainage pipe that it opened up into the roomy shelter, complete with a bathroom, and running water.

Jake had stumbled onto it by accident when he was about ten. He had gone looking for Max—he'd been a puppy then. Max was scared of thunder so when thunder boomed overhead Max ran into the pipe and refused to come out. Worried, Jake was forced to go in after him and he was surprised to find the shelter. Ever since it had been his secret hideout, even his neighbor, Mr. Stelmen and his kids didn't know it existed. No one did. So why, how did Nate?

Following, Jake was about to demand an explanation but stopped short when he saw the expression on Nate's face.

Nate stood in the center of the main room, looking around, seeing memories he had only heard about.

"Dad and Arron used to come here and hang out, sometimes dad would spend days here." Nate pointed to one of the two metal doors on the left of him. "He slept on the bottom bunk in there when things with John got bad." Embarrassed, Nate glanced at Jake he probably shouldn't have said that.

Jake gaped at Nate, stunned for a second, he had found that bunk made up with blankets and a pillow covered in a thick layer of dust and he had always wondered who had used it. He was pleased that it had been Reace, that they both had used the same place as a secret hideout. Then the rest of what Nate said slammed into him and he frowned in confusion.

"Mr. Stelmen and Reace didn't get along?" That he knew, but the way Nate said it was a surprise. It sounded like Mr. Stelmen was the problem not Reace and he had always been told it was Reace who was the trouble maker, besides, Mr. Stelmen had a wife and other children now and they had no problems.

"Forget I said anything, dad wouldn't want anyone to know."

Jake shrugged and sat on the lumpy sofa.

"So tell me what you know that I don't about my father. What's he like? Where does he live? What does he do?" Jake tried to sound as if the answers didn't matter to him, but the truth was evident in his eyes. These questions were hard to ask, they were things that he should know about his father not things he should have to ask a stranger.

"How much do you already know?" Nate countered as he sat on the over turned crate in front of Jake. He wondered where to start, he didn't want to scare Jake with more than he could handle.

"I know Arron disappeared along with Reace Stelmen and two girls seventeen years ago. The bodies were never found but everyone believes that Reace murdered them."

"What? Dad? Murder?" Nate gasped in shock. "Why would anyone believe that?"

"Evidence," Jake told Nate then he elaborated, "First there was the fact that Reace brought a stun gun to school about a week before they disappeared. Some guys testified they saw him pull it out and threaten Arron with it at his locker. Then there was the stabbing incident. Rumor had it that Reace was involved with a bad bunch—drug dealers and he owed them a lot of money, it went sour and he got stabbed. Some guy named Ryan Summers became a hero out of it for saving Reace's life and he even got a medal, now Ryan's a doctor, one of the best cancer doctors in the state." Jake had done a lot of research on the topic he obsessed over and was excited to have someone who he could talk too about it. His mother or really anyone he knew didn't want to even hear Arron or Reace's name let alone talk about what took place before Jake was born.

"Anyway," Jake continued, "the day before they disappeared, neighbors say they heard John and Reace fighting then they saw Reace and another girl leave the house seconds before the ambulance showed up. The police believe Reace used the stun gun on his father—a few times. After that the police speculate that he went to Arron's demanded money from him and when Arron said no, Reace killed him and the two girls, twins, one of them was Kittana Messer. She was the foster daughter of Dave and Nancy MacDonald. The police later found Arron's car out of town in a wooded area but no bodies were ever recovered. There were also some unfounded rumors that the occult was involved, guess they found a circle of melted candles or something. You know how old folks get: anything that has to do with kids' dying they always try to link it with cult rituals and shit like that." Jake leaned forward resting his elbows on his knees. He looked into Nate's eyes and added "That's all I could find out."

"What about Arron's suicide note?" Nate asked confused. How could anyone think his father could kill people? Why would people accuse his dad of killing Arron when his note said that he took his own life?

"Suicide . . . what are you talking about? There wasn't any note." Jake spoke then added. "Look, I don't believe that Reace killed anyone. I have no proof . . . it's just a feeling I have, really." He got up and moved to the corner, where he searched through the small wooden trunk he had brought it in years ago to hold his personal things, withdrawing something he handed it to Nate before returning to his seat on the couch.

Nate stared down at the worn picture in his hands and smiled. It was easy to pick out his father's piercing stare and Arron's easy smile. Their looks really hadn't changed much, living on the timeless plain of Taysia probably helped.

"It's a picture of Reace and my dad taken over twenty years ago." Jake stated the obvious. "There is something in that picture, at the way they seem so close, almost protective of each other, that made me think Reace couldn't do it. He couldn't have killed Arron over money anymore then I could kill my mother over burnt toast. It just doesn't make sense, besides that, almost everyone that I talked too played down their friendship until it seemed like they were merely neighbors but I know they were more." Jake sighed. "I can't explain it . . . I just know."

"You're right," Nate said quietly. "They were and still are more than neighbors, they were like brothers. Fentra! Arron is so much like my Uncle that sometimes I do call him that—Uncle Arron." Nate's bright smile faded into a look of puzzlement as he asked. "What's a stun gun?"

"What's a stun gun? Dude, where have you been? A stun gun is like a Taser, it uses electricity to make you faint so the police can cuff you easier, it shocks people. I don't know if it could actually kill someone but I suppose it could if you shocked them enough, maybe several times in a row . . . What's so funny?"

"Dad doesn't own one. He doesn't need too." Nate said with a laugh and a shake of his head. At Jake's confused frown Nate didn't elaborate; he didn't think this was the time to go into all that, not yet. So instead, he decided to say: "Kittana Messer, and her twin sister, Keyla were the two girls with them that night. Kittana is my mother. I can tell you they are very much alive and are probably on their way to getting very mad at me." Nate grimaced, a twinge of regret and guilt at the way his mother and father would be feeling right now rose inside of him, pushing that away he glanced at Jake and this time gave an explanation. "I didn't exactly let anyone know I was coming here."

"Shit! You ran away from home?" Jake raised his eyebrows at Nate who shrugged.

"I wouldn't call it running away, I'm embracing my destiny." Nate raised his chin a notch as he borrowed Timelana's words. "Seeing where I fit, besides, they don't need me there." His eyes were a little sad he lowered them so Jake wouldn't see. "I'm going to stay around here, maybe go to school . . . experience life."

"Nate, you are one of a kind." Jake shook his head but he couldn't help the smile that tugged at his lips. Rummaging through the box in the corner again, he put away the picture Nate handed him and pulling out an old silver flask.

"I am going to need this." He muttered taking the cap off and raising it to his lips, he took a long swallow then lowering the flask he added. "I got it from the house no one there drinks so it won't be missed. I've been saving it for . . ." Jake trailed off as he stood and turned back to Nate, taking another swig before he had the guts to ask. "Okay. Why did my father leave? Where did he go?" Jake looked down at the flask in his hands then to Nate before handing the bottle to him as he sat again saying, "Here have a drink, good for the nerves."

"Sure," Nate said taking the flask and bringing it to his lips he took several big gulps thinking it was water then choked as his throat burned and his eyes watered. Nate handed the flask back to Jake as he leaned forward his hand gripping his stomach as the liquid reached there and pooled.

"Dude, are you okay?" Jake asked when he saw Nate's face pale and his body tremble. Glancing back into Nate's face he saw his eyes drifted shut, panic rose inside of Jake.

"Fuck! Why didn't you tell me you were allergic? Do you want me to call 911?" He stood ready to assist.

Nate was beyond hearing as his stomach turned against him and pain was everywhere in his body running side by side with his powers that suddenly he couldn't control.

Knowing his phone didn't work down here, Jake chewed on his bottom lip, should he leave and get help or stay and do . . . something? He didn't have time to do anything as the ground shook beneath them.

"Okay, that's just an earthquake." Jake's voice cracked a bit as he wondered what was happening, they usually didn't get earthquakes here.

"Don't worry we're safe in here, it's a bomb shelter." Jake talked more to reassure himself then to Nate as he steadied himself to keep from falling.

Violently, the heavy steel door swung open as a strong wind whipped through the interior of the shelter, picking up old papers, soda cans and other debris scattered about, whirling them faster and faster around Nate, who was now on his hands and knees on the floor.

Jake stumbled backward onto the couch; wide-eyed as the air surrounding Nate crackled and sparked with electricity.

Nate's wrist glowed pulsating with a strange inner light and his skin shone with unleashed power as he slowly stood up, oblivious to the strong wind, electricity and the ground that still heaved and shuttered under their feet. Slowly the wind died down almost creasing him now and as much as Nate reveled in the feel of it, he knew this wasn't normal here and he had to stop it. Nate pointed to the door, the wind picked up again and with a forlorn moan it rushed to the door slamming it shut before dying down again into nothing.

To Jake it seemed as if the wind had come in say hello but left angry slamming the door behind itself and to Jake's surprise, when Nate looked down at the floor, the ground stopped shaking as though Nate could control it. The look on Nate's face when he finally looked at Jake was one of guilt, as though he were to blame for the weird weather and the earthquake.

"I can explain." Nate's voice seemed loud in the now quiet room.

Jake visibly swallowed, his eyes never leaving Nate's face, "That would be good. What the hell was that? Who . . . who the fuck are you?"

# CHAPTER SEVEN

"I AM NATURE, GUARDIAN OF Nature." After Nate said those words the shape of a leaf on his left wrist glowed, pulsating in time with his heart, with his inner power, a power that this time he was in control of. He raised his head proudly as the strength of his life force flowed through him.

"You're a freak!" Jake accused in a half whisper, his brown eyes opened wide.

"So are you," Nate spoke as his grass green eyes stared into Jake's. "What was that drink?"

"How did you know?" Jake whispered in a horrified gasp. Wondering how Nate—this stranger—could know things about him that he had never told anyone.

"Who told you?" Jake demanded, for a moment he thought his mother may have said something but he dismissed that idea as soon as he thought it. His mother would never betray him like that. It was she that cautioned him against telling anyone, even his own grandparents, about his special ability. So how could Nate know?

"You're Arron's child. You're half Starian, just like me." Nate replied then asked again "What was in that drink?" he suspected it was alcohol but he wasn't sure.

"It was just Vodka. You know, alcohol." Jake answered still staring at Nate.

"Poison." Nate muttered then suddenly laughed, "That's what happened to dad that night at Arron's party. That's how Aunt Keyla found out he was a Guardian. Wow! It hurt. Dad never said it hurt." Nate shook his head then explained, "Alcohol is like a poison to Guardians it makes our powers go . . . well uncontrollably crazy."

"Guardian; you've said that before, you said Arron, my dad was one. What is it, some kind of cult? And what does Starian mean?" Jake asked he had never heard the word before and it sounded weird to him. This whole thing was weird. It seemed so unreal, like he had just stepped into a sci-fi movie. The worst part was that he was just sitting here calmly asking questions.

"What's a cult?"

Nate's question and honest bewilderment that showed on his face made Jake pause. How can anyone not know what a cult was?

"A cult is a group of wacked out religious people who brainwash others into joining their religion in order to control them." He turned a questioning face to Nate "Where have you been living? Underground? Don't you watch the news or read the paper? Listen to the radio, go on the internet? It's been the top news story for more than a week now. 500 cult members from two different, normally peaceful religious sects suddenly erupted into violence. It was quite a blood bath. Not one surviving member. Creepy, huh?"

Nate gave a shudder, all those people, all that life gone, and over what? An idea? Was it worth it? Something about the story reminded Nate of the fairies and the fight he had helped to stop yesterday morning. He was glad they hadn't ended up dead.

"Guardians are not a cult. We are appointed by the powers that be to guard the life forces. Some, like our parents, are chosen above the rest to influence the forces of good and evil which affect the balance on other worlds. My father, Reace, is the Guardian of Electricity which is why he doesn't need a stun gun. He controls lightning and he can shoot electricity from his hands. My mother, Kittana is the Guardian of the Mind and you already know that I am Nature. Your father, Arron, is the Guardian of Life and Death. He has these really cool powers. He can heal any creature and he can protect life with his golden shield. He is also the only Guardian—the only Starian—who can kill with a touch but, Arron doesn't use that power, he . . ."

Nate trailed off when he saw the look on Jake's face.

"Jake, I get that this is hard to understand. Arron left Earth seventeen years ago with Reace, Kittana and Keyla because they had to fulfill their destiny. Your father is a Guardian chosen to be part of the power of four, part of the prophecy. They were heroes. They saved the lives of countless peoples; whole planets would have died if they hadn't gone to Taysia."

Nate's look was compelling and full of honesty. Jake found himself wanting to believe him and he listened with interest as Nate continued.

"Me, my dad, mom, Aunt Keyla, Arron, his wife Tia and their son, plus countless others have been living on Taysia, the world of the Guardians for the past seventeen years, but I swear to you Jake, Arron couldn't have known about you . . . he'd never have just left you behind."

"I have a brother? What's his name? Is . . . is he like you? Is he a . . . a Guardian?" Jake asked curiously. He still wasn't sure if he believed everything Nate said but it did explain a lot of things Jake had wondered about all his life, like where his ability had come from and why?

"Yes, he's a Guardian, the Guardian of War. His name is Zarrick, he's a year younger than me, I'm sixteen and he's fifteen." Nate tried to keep his voice even and his face devoid of emotion. He didn't want any of his feelings to show for his honorary cousin. He didn't want Jake to think badly of his own brother or to meet him with preconceived ideas.

Holding out his hand, Nate changed the subject when he asked, "Let me see your wrist."

Jake thought this was a strange request and it must have shown on his face because Nate added. "I promise I won't bite."

With a shrug he put his right hand in Nate's.

"The other one, your left arm," Nate instructed and Jake changed arms letting Nate examine his left wrist up to his elbow. It was clear, no mark upon it, Nate's frown deepened maybe Jake wasn't a Guardian after all. Sometimes it didn't follow bloodlines, Nate thought as he let go of the arm he held.

*'How did you know?'* Jake's whispered words came back to Nature making him wonder what Jake was talking about if not powers. Raising confused eyes to him, Nate questioned. "Do you have any powers? Can you do things others can't?"

Jake swallowed the lump of surprise and fear. He glanced away from Nate's questioning gaze, wondering if he should tell him. Nate had been honest with him so far, even showing him his powers maybe he should be honest too.

"I ah . . . I have never told anyone, not even my grandparents."

*Maybe it would be easier to show him?* Jake thought, as he stood and walked over to the wooden trunk, he bent for a second then straightened pulling something that was made of metal and about a foot long out of it. Turning he showed Nature the dagger he held.

"I bought this a few months ago, at the pawn shop. Mom doesn't know about it yet," he shrugged before adding, "Not that she'd worry I'd get hurt playing with it . . . that was something she has never had to worry about."

"What are you going to do with that?" Nate asked watching Jake sit on the couch with the knife. Alarm made his eyes wide as Jake pulled his sleeve up pass his elbow.

Gritting his teeth, Jake made a fist and deeply slashed his arm from elbow to wrist with the knife. He flinched at the pain of the deep cut and watched mesmerized for a second by the bright red blood that instantly swelled to the surface before dripping down his arm onto his hand.

"Holy shit! What the hell did you do that for? I can't heal you, we need Arron for that and he's . . ." Nate stopped mid sentence when Jake directed his attention back to the cut on his arm. The skin that had been deeply cut seconds before fused itself together as though it had never been cut; growing smaller and smaller until it completely disappeared leaving Jake's arm with only a smear of blood.

"You're healed! You can heal yourself!" Nate exclaimed with a smile that quickly turned into a frown. He noted that no mark flashed on Jake's wrist, and there was always a feeling—a spark or a tingle, a rush of energy—something whenever Guardians touched but he hadn't received anything like that with Jake.

"You're not a Guardian." Nate stated then gesturing towards the now healed arm as he asked one of the thousands of questions that crowded into his mind: "How . . . When did you discover this?"

"It was something I was born with, something my body was always able to do." Jake shrugged his shoulders as he wiped the blood off his arm with his hand then wiped his hand on his pants before he rolled down his sleeve and put the knife away.

"I guess it must have been hard on my mom when I was little, you know how kids are always getting hurt: cuts, scrapes and bruises. She'd always have to make some excuse as to why they'd heal so fast and she was always ready with a bandage to hide it. She's good about it though." He grinned, feeling relieved that he had told Nate and Nate wasn't freaking out; it was comforting to know that someone else knew. "She's a little overprotective sometimes, but she's cool, you'll like her when you meet her. She's the only person besides you that knows about this . . . that knows I can heal myself. I guess that's the reason I'm not that freaked out about all this." Jake gestured to Nate then lowering his voice he continued, "I know what's it like to be different and it's not so bad. You just don't tell anyone, blend in and act natural, normal." Jake's gaze caught Nate's and held it. "Normal is easier then you think . . . I could help you."

Nate nodded accepting Jakes offer for help to fit in but he was only half listening to him. The wheels were turning in his mind, remembering what his mother had told him about his grandfather, Kade who was Starian—not Guardian and didn't have a mark or the powers his children and their friends possessed but Kade did have two abilities: with the help of a Theyan crystal he was able to move things with his mind and Starians couldn't die unless they wished it. Their bodies would just keep healing, however, like Earthlings it took time but Jake healed instantly.

"Must be your Starian side." Nate said thoughtfully.

"Starian? What's that? How am I Starian?"

The sound of Jake's confused voice brought Nate out of his thoughts and back to reality.

"Starian? You're one quarter Starian because Arron is half Starian, Arron's dad; Yentar was from a planet called Staria the second planet in the Fentra solar system, five galaxies away from Earth. I think that's why you are able to heal yourself." Nate tried to explain the thoughts that were forming in his head, hoping it sounded better then he thought it did. He glanced at Jake to see him nod, excepting what he told him.

The two boys talked for the rest of the day learning things about each other and themselves, sharing stories of their childhood, tightening the bonds of friendship that started with their parents and now continued with themselves. By late afternoon they left the shelter going into Jake's house in search of food.

*

Nate and Jake were sitting at the breakfast bar in the kitchen of Jake's house talking as they ate left over pizza and drank cans of coke when Jake's mother walked in carrying a purse and two bags of groceries. She was a slender woman standing five feet seven inches in high heels, dressed in an expensive dark blue pant suit paired with the light pink blouse that complemented her peaches and cream complexion. Her blond hair was short and curled about her head in soft waves.

Seeing the two of them sitting there Heather dropped the bags from arms that suddenly went numb and her hands flew to her face, covering her mouth as a startled gasp escaped her lips.

Jake whirled around and was off his stool in seconds, concern written on his face "Mom! Are you okay? You look like you've seen a ghost. Come sit. I'll get you some water."

He turned, after making sure his mother sat on a stool, to get a bottle of water from the fridge.

Nate wondered why she dropped the bags when she entered the room from Jake's reaction it wasn't normal. Wanting to be helpful Nate gathered up the food that fell but not sure where anything went he placed it all on the counter.

"Thanks," Heather said, a shaky smile curved her painted lips then as she took the cold bottle from Jake's hand she asked, "Who's your friend?"

"Oh right! Mom this is Nate, the guy I told you about on the phone. Nate this is my mother, Heather." Jake looked back at his mother, "It is still okay that he stays here for a few days, right?"

"Yes, yes of course." Heather nodded, then looked at Nate and said, "Thanks—Nathan is it?—for picking up my groceries . . ."

"Nature," Nate corrected, "My name is Nature but please call me Nate." He spoke gently, an easy smile on his lips.

"Well Nate, I don't know what happened, guess old age is setting in, arthritis." She mumbled going over the truth in her mind. Seeing them there looking so much like Reace and Arron, her mind had done a quick time travel. How many times in her youth had she come in here to see Arron and Reace sitting there, eating pizza and drinking cans of coke. What she wouldn't give to go back to those days. She'd do so many things differently. Heather closed her eyes as tears gathered behind them. She sighed opening them again letting her gaze fall on her son, Jake. If she did do things differently would she still have him?

She loved her son with all her heart. No, she decided, she wouldn't have changed a thing about him or her past. She smiled; a look of love crossed her face, softening the beginning lines of old age. She sighed again as she told Jake. "You look so much like your father—so young and handsome."

Heather patted his cheek as she rose from her seat and started toward the bags on the counter. "Well I should get these groceries put away and then I'll let you boys be."

"No mom," Jake firmly said. "We can put the groceries away, you go and rest." He had never seen his mother so pale and shaken; he hoped that with rest she'd feel better. With his ability he knew would always be healthy, but he couldn't say the same for his mother and that scared him. She had been there his whole life and he wanted to make sure she was there for the rest of it, or at least a good part of it.

"You want to put away the groceries? Did I hear that right?" she looked from one to the other. Nate was the spitting image of Reace except for the green eyes and the easy smile on his face she'd swear it was him. Shaking her head, she must be seeing things. Reace was dead or at least long gone from here.

"Yes! Now go and rest." Jake smiled at her and Heather understood her son didn't want his mother hanging around. She turned to walk toward the doorway that led to the rest of the house but Nate's words made her turn back to face them.

"It was nice to meet you and thanks for letting me stay here, I really appreciate it." When a smile lit her features again Nate enjoyed the way it made her look younger, happier. Her brown eyes seemed so sad a few moments ago that Nate had wondered what she was thinking. He was glad to see her smiling now.

"No problem," Heather waved a hand in the air. "Any friend of Jake's is welcome here." She paused in the doorway to turn back to Nate and ask, "Who did you say your parents were?"

"No one you know mom, Nate's from out of town." Jake hurriedly spoke worried that Nate may say something strange about Guardians or worse . . . his parent's names.

Nate frowned at Jake as he answered for him, Heather noticed that frown and again it struck her how much he resembled Reace.

"Have a good rest." Jake added to hurry her from the room.

"Sure, thanks." Heather muttered as she continued out of the kitchen toward the steps, seeing Mrs. White coming down, Heather smiled at the old housekeeper.

"Jake has a friend who will be staying with us for a few days, could you make up the spare bedroom beside Jake's, please and he'll probably be staying for supper." Her voice was kind as she spoke with Mrs. White, the women who practically raised Arron and her own son too. Mrs. White was more like a grandmother or an old family friend then an employee.

"Already done and supper is on the way. Why don't you go have a nap, you look like you need it. You work too much for a girl your age; too much work and not enough fun." Mrs. White gently prodded the younger women up the stairs.

She was fond of Heather, that girl sure straightened out just fine to become a wonderful mother. She had to hand it to her, Heather sure was tough. Having to grow up fast when she found herself pregnant and alone at the tender age of sixteen, the father of her child missing and presumed dead even before Jake was born, anyone else would have cracked under the pressure but not Heather, Mrs. White thought with a proud smile, Heather was strong, she was a survivor. Arron had chosen well the mother of his child. Heather had even managed to endear herself to the Prices (a feat that Mrs. White had thought impossible), raise her baby and climb the corporate ladder all on her own.

Mrs. White sighed and shook her head, but at what cost to herself? That girl hadn't been out on a date since . . . well, since forever. And she looked so tired. Damn, but Heather was too young to be so tired, the old house keeper thought as she made her way into the laundry room to check on the clothes in the dryer before heading into the kitchen to fix supper.

# Chapter eight

Taysia

"ZARRICK," ARRON BEGAN AS HE walked toward the angry teen—who had gotten up and had started to walk away from him.

"Zarrick, listen to me!"

Zarrick stopped but didn't turn to face him.

"I know what you're going through. No don't," Arron quickly added when Zarrick whirled around ready to comment but Arron rushed on not giving him a chance. "Just listen, besides I know what you're going to say, 'How could I know' right?" Arron took a deep breath and let it out before continuing. "When I first came here, when I first met Malic . . . he seemed to know more about me then I did. It threw me off guard." Arron was lost in past memories for a moment before he returned his honey brown gaze to meet Zarrick's hostile yellow ones and spoke knowingly, "Malic can be very persuasive. He showed me the man I had always thought of as my dad wasn't. My father was Yentar, a shade that . . ." Arron closed his eyes tight fighting against the images that swam before them, "that raped my mother."

Zarrick could see that telling him this was hard for Arron and his resolve softened towards him. The anger he held toward the older man slowly ebbed as he realized that they had a lot in common and maybe, just maybe Arron could understand.

He raised questioning eyes to the man who raised him, and asked the question he had wondered about ever since Malic had first contacted him. "Am I evil?"

"No!" Arron quickly replied his eyes snapping open to stare honestly at Zarrick. No, he repeated in Starian. "Da."

"But I am Malic's son and he's evil and I am the Guardian of War." Zarrick didn't add the with Malic's help he had used his powers to hurt people on other planets, it wasn't something he was proud of, he swallowed hard.

"I am the Guardian of Life and Death. I was conceived out of the horrible act of rape, by a shade. Does that make me evil?" Arron asked his son.

He was surprised that Arron was the son of a shade, he had heard about those creatures and he shuttered in memory of those stories. He had always thought that Arron and Reace were brothers or something, nobody ever really talked about Arron's parents. Zarrick shook his head and almost sneered as he said, "Nothing could make you evil, Dad. You and Reace are prefect."

"Far from it!" Arron countered with a huff. "It's not our blood that makes us evil but our choices. War can be used for good, Zarrick . . ."

A flash of light interrupted them. Reace materialized beside them, the frantic, worried expression on his face made Arron demand.

"What's wrong?" He knew there was no immediate danger because he wasn't feeling the tingle at the back of his neck that told him to put up a shield, even knowing that, didn't lesson the dread that pooled in his stomach as he waited for Reace to tell him what had him so upset.

"Arron, have you seen Nate?" At the negative shake of his head Reace turned to Zarrick, "Zarrick you? When was the last time you saw him? Did he say anything about going anywhere?"

"No." Zarrick said honestly meeting Reace's bright blue eyes.

"What's going on? What's happened to Nate?" Arron demanded bringing Reace's piercing gaze swinging back to his.

"He's missing. Kit can't sense him anywhere. Arron, she's frantic, says this happened before—yesterday, he disappeared for a few minutes afterward he said he'd not do it again—but this time he's been gone for hours." Reace turned his worried gaze to Zarrick and pleaded. "Please,

Zarrick if you have any idea where he went or what happened to him, please tell me."

Zarrick's eyes widened he had never heard Reace beg before and he wished he could help but the truth was that he was the last person Nate would confide in. Zarrick's gaze slid to the ground suddenly ashamed of the way he had teased and bullied Reace's son. "Sorry, Reace I wish I could help but Nate didn't say anything to me."

"Will you help us look for him?" Reace asked bringing Zarrick's head up. "Yeah,"

"Of-course, we'll help." Arron's voice over topped Zarrick's soft reply and looking at Reace Arron didn't see the younger Guardian's eyes narrow in irritation at being spoken for.

\*

*"KEYLA!"* Kittana telepathically screamed her sister's name as worry got the better of her; she had searched through the entire mountain and surrounding areas—twice. She had asked all the Guardian friends that she could think of but none of them had seemed to know anything about her son's disappearance and for the past twenty minutes she had used her mind to try and find him. Kittana was starting to get really scared. What if something happened to him? Kittana worried her bottom lip as she watched her sister appear in a swirl of magical sparks.

"You didn't have to shout." Keyla grumbled as she put a hand to her still throbbing temples. Seeing the expression on her twin's face alarmed her. "What's the matter?"

"It's Nate," Kittana sobbed giving into the tears that were shining in her eyes, tears that had been building since she first felt Nate's presence leave her mind. Keyla wrapped her in a hug. "He's disappeared. I can't sense him. I can't find him anywhere."

"Malic?" she asked in a scared whisper.

"No." Kittana said quickly dispelling Keyla's fears as she pulled herself away from the comforting embrace, sniffing before adding. "He's done this before last night he disappeared for about a minute. This time he's been gone for hours."

"Do you suppose he's growing into a new power?" Keyla suggested remembering how Reace had disappeared after gaining a new power. "Maybe he's just discovered a way to open portals?"

"What are you talking about . . . portals to where?" Kittana demanded, if Keyla was right then her son could be anywhere in the universe. What if he was in trouble? What if he got hurt and needed them? What if they couldn't find him in time, images of Nature hurt, broken and dead floated into her mind and she pushed them away to focus on her sister.

"Calm down Kit, you're getting irrational!" Keyla told her sister as some of her twins thoughts leaked into her mind.

"Calm down?! My son is missing he could be anywhere hurt, bleeding, dead! And you want me to calm down?"

"Yeah. He can't die, Kittana, he's a Guardian." Keyla reminded her.

"But he barely knows his powers, or what he's capable of?"

"Neither do we. Maybe he has grown into a new power." Keyla suggested again.

"Opening portals?" Kittana asked feeling herself calm down.

Keyla nodded. She had never betrayed Nate's confidence and she hoped he would forgive her now. Pushing away the nagging twinge of guilt she told her sister. "The other day Nate and I were talking and he mentioned feeling drawn to Earth. He said he was thinking about going there."

"To Earth?!" Kittana was stunned. She hadn't thought about Earth, the planet of her birth in a long while. "Oh god! Anything could happen to him on Earth, he doesn't know anything about life there or how to fit in, how not to use his powers in public. Why did he have to go to Earth?"

Kittana didn't expect an answer and Keyla didn't give her one. By the look on her sister's face Keyla guessed her worry just tripled. She imagined her sister was picturing Nature strapped to a table and being dissected by a curious team of scientists. Suddenly nauseated Keyla suggested, "Let's go find Reace and Arron. We'll need the power of four to get back."

*

Reace, Arron and Zarrick turned toward Kittana and Keyla as they materialized to the left of them in the clearing by the lake.

"Have you found him?" Reace asked, the hope in his voice was reflected in his eyes.

"No, but Keyla thinks he's on Earth. We have to follow him! We need to go to Earth make sure he's okay." Kittana's anguished eyes implored him.

Reace nodded. "Let's do it."

"Wait! Wait a minute," Arron demanded his mind working fast to figure out what everyone else seemed to already know. "You want us to go back, to Earth? We are not even sure that's possible. How did Nate get there?"

"It's the best lead we have. Keyla said he mentioned feeling drawn there and that he was thinking of going." Kittana chewed her bottom lip with worry. "Arron, he doesn't know Earth or the dangers of using his powers in public. Please, we have to go back, we have to save my son."

"Okay, we'll find him." He agreed looking into Kittana's sapphire blue eyes, shining with raw fear. What it would be like on Earth after seventeen years? How would people react to him coming back from the dead?

# Chapter nine

The four Guardians stood in a circle, hands clasped, in the exact spot where they had first entered the world of the Guardians. This time they didn't have to worry about Malic taking over or tipping the balance of good and evil, they were leaving Tia, Link, Awkwade and Zarrick here to oppose him and they planned to return very soon with Nature.

Kittana nodded to Reace to begin Keyla's spell. Her sister had reworded it but it was basically the same spell that brought them here seventeen years ago. She saw him hesitate and knew he was remembering the last time they had done this and how she had been hurt. *"It won't be like that this time,"* she mentally reassured him, *"There are no more shades and besides, Malic doesn't know we are going."*

Pushing his fears aside, Reace swallowed hard and began.

"I am the Guardian of Electricity." He was unable to stop the grin that covered his face as his power erupted from him. The blue energy ached high into the sky above them. His gaze found and held Keyla's as he waited for her words next.

"I am the Guardian of Magic." She laughed as her power turned the sky pink.

"I am the Guardian of Life." Arron's voice was loud with command and his eyes lit up with an inner light, an inner happiness as his power shined a bright yellow beside Keyla's and Reace's high above their heads.

"I am the Guardian of the Mind." Kittana's voice rang out next sending her brilliantly white power above her head to mingle with the rainbow of colors already there. She watched, feeling an incredible high as her sister continued the rhyme.

"Together let our powers combine."

The colors above them swirled together at a dizzying speed as they all chanted the beginning line of the spell:

"The power of four,
Will open the door;
Through time and space,
Earth is the place."

They continued to chant as Keyla's voice rose above them.

"Powers that be, heed our plea
Nature's trail we wish to sail
Through time and space,
Earth is the place.
The power of four will open the door."

Keyla finished chanting with the rest of them then closed her eyes as silver sparks rained down on them, bright and cold they touched the flesh of the ones who held the power to open the portal. A thick fog rolled around them created by their spinning powers high above their heads, enclosing them in. When the fog dissipated they were gone.

\*

Malic knew the second the chosen four left, he felt it. A slow smile spread on his face, he was pleased that his plan was working. Now, he had to act fast before they found the brat and returned. If they returned to soon then he would have lost and *that* was something Malic wasn't about to let happen.

The dark figure sat cross-legged on the cold stone floor, surrounded by candles but Malic didn't see any of the light his eyes were closed. A twisted grin curved his lips as they moved over the words to a spell that would finally give him his revenge. He had waited centuries for this moment and now that it was upon him, Malic relished it, savoring the sweet taste of revenge.

"Son of my bone,
Son of my blood,
Soul to soul,
Make us whole.
His body, my mind,
Our powers combined!"

\*

After seeing their friends off, Link walked beside Tia and Zarrick as they slowly made their way back to the crystal mountain where Awkwade waited for them.

Zarrick suddenly stumbled then fell to the ground as a ball of light slammed into him from behind.

"Zarrick! What happened? Are you alright?" Tia fell to the ground beside her son, worry making her voice sharp.

Link scanned the area, wondering where the attack had come from and why? A fireball resting in his hand ready to launch at the unknown enemy, but finding nothing he closed his fist drawing the fire power back within himself. Turning his attention back to his friends he spoke. "Judging from the direction, it came from Stone Mountain."

"Malic?" Zarrick gasped trying to overcome the pain in his head and in his arm as it started to claw its' way up from his left wrist burning like liquid fire a path to his elbow. Breathing through the pain Zarrick questioned. "Why . . . would he . . . attack us?"

"Maybe he knows the chosen four have left Taysia?" Tia suggested.

"I'll go and check it out." Link said moving behind them toward the direction the attack came from. His eyes carefully scanned the area, his body ready to erupt in flame defending those he cared about.

"We'll come with you." Tia spoke quickly making Link look at her with a puzzled frown.

"Are you sure? Zarrick is hurt."

"I'm fine." Zarrick announced standing and trying not to show how much pain he was in. "We'll be fine, lead the way."

Link nodded then turned and made his way toward the black mountain.

As the three of them walked closer to the Stone Mountain—Malic's fortress of solitude, Zarrick noticed something, perhaps it was just his imagination, but the closer they got to Malic's the better he felt, stronger and somehow . . . more alive.

When they entered Malic's Mountain home, Tia used her power of emotion to feel where he was.

"He's not here," Zarrick heard himself tell his mother and Link. The certainty in his voice made him frown.

"Not here?" Link repeated looking strangely at Zarrick with an expression that asked: *How could you possibly know that?*

"Not here unless he's somehow gained the ability to cloak himself," Tia confirmed with a frown wondering where or how Malic suddenly left. She raised scared eyes to Link, silently asking him if they should be worried.

"I don't trust Malic." Link answered her unasked question. "So until we know otherwise let's proceed with caution and continue to check out this place."

Link cautiously went in front of them again making sure the way was safe for Tia and her son.

Zarrick brought up the rear, sauntering lazily through the dim interior of the Stone Mountain. Remembering things that happened in every room they entered—things he wasn't sure he should know.

Link suddenly stopped and at the motion of his hand, Tia and Zarrick stopped too. With an inclination of his head Link silently brought their attention to the body sprawled out on the floor of the throne room.

The three of them crept forward until they were standing within the circle of melted candles.

Malic hadn't moved.

Tia knelt down next to Malic, when she touched him her eyes closed in concentration, seconds later, she was filled with feelings—emotions that were not her own. Delving into these emotions seeking his last feelings, anything that would give them some insight as to what happened here.

"He had a strong desire to leave this body and a sense of excitement and happiness." She told them then looked up at Link as she added in a whisper. "He is dead."

Link frowned at the strangeness of this: Starians don't die unless they wish it and then their body's combust—always.

Tia glanced down looking at Malic's left wrist; all of the marks he had before, the marks of the powers he held were gone, only a fading imprint remained. The final sign that somehow the Malic they feared had really died.

"Are you sure?" Link demanded.

"Yes, his spirit left this body, he wanted to."

"Then let's finish it! Let's make sure he can't return." The Guardian of Fire lifted his hand and doing what came naturally to him, released a stream of flame and watched as it melted and burned Malic's body.

*"There is no way to stop me now!"* The words echoed in Zarrick's mind and he smirked as he watched the body burn. The newly formed diamond shaped mark on his left arm flashed as he slid his golden gaze to Tia.

# CHAPTER TEN

## Earth

IN SCHOOL, NATE WAS ONLY half listening to Jake again explain the do's and don'ts of high school life mostly how not to attract attention as he looked around in excitement.

Jake took one glance at Nate's face and shook his head as he led them toward the main office; if Nate was crazy enough to *want* to enroll in school then they had to start there: filling out papers, faking enrollment sheets. Jake had come up with a good excuse as to why they didn't have Nate's past transcripts. He just hoped Nate would go along with it and not screw this up by saying something weird. Yawning, he remembered how late the two of them had stayed up the night before just talking. It was nice, really nice to have someone—other than his mother—who knew about his ability. With Nate, he could be totally honest. It was surprising how much they had in common. Lost in his own thoughts Jake kept walking toward their destination not noticing that Nature was no longer beside him.

As Nate walked beside Jake he took everything in, it was so exciting to be walking the same halls his father had. To be in school, surrounded by other kids . . . Girls!

Nate stopped walking as his gaze settled on a group of girls standing and talking beside their lockers. The tall red haired girl in the middle of them caught his attention and he couldn't look away. He sucked in a breath when his body threatened to pass out from lack of oxygen.

"Who is she?" Nate asked Jake when he suddenly appeared beside him again, grabbing Nate's jacket trying to get him to move, but Nate resisted.

"Who?" Jake demanded glancing around. He had wondered why Nate had stopped in the middle of the hallway and seeing Anna-Maria Macdonald he understood then inwardly groaned. "Anna? She's way out of our league and she's got a boyfriend . . . with big friends."

"Is that her boyfriend?" Nate questioned never taking his eyes off Anna. He watched her expression as a guy came up to her.

"She doesn't look very happy to see him." Nate commented, frowning, just as her irritated voice reached his ears.

"Get lost, Cody! I said we were over and I meant it. Stop it! Cody, leave me alone!" Anna snapped swatting at her ex-boyfriend's hands when they grasped at her.

"Yeah," Jake said with a snort. He didn't like the way Cody was treating the girl but what could he do? "That's Cody Marshal, he's the captain of the football team . . ." Jake trailed off as Nate walked away from him toward Cody and Anna. *Shit!* Jake thought as he called after him. "Wait, Nate! You just can't . . ."

But it was too late Nate was already beside them. In a steady voice Nature demanded that Cody let Anna go, both turned toward Nate with surprised expressions.

"Hey, do you mind? I'm talking to my girl here." Cody said his eyes narrowed on Nate, sizing him up. Nate was about the same height as his own six feet and Cody figured that they were about equal in body weight judging by the frame—they were evenly matched. Anna's hissed words brought Cody back to the realization that they were in a hallway not the gym.

"I'm not your girl! Not anymore."

Nate raised an eyebrow and smirked at Cody before firmly repeating, "Let her go."

At Nate's smug look Cody narrowed his eyes in anger.

"And whose gonna make me, you?" Cody challenged, his hazel eyes daring as they held Nate's bright green gaze steady.

Jake decided he needed to get Nate away before something happened that they'd later regret. Placing himself in between the two would be fighters he clamped an arm around Nate, pulling him back a step as he spoke.

"Hey, Cody!" An uneasy smile on his face as he continued, "I see you have met Nate Stelmen, he's new to the school . . . ah . . . from Canada. He's just being a boy scout. No hard feelings okay. We don't want any trouble."

Anna playing off Jake's lead grabbed Cody's arm and plastering a smile on her face she demanded. "Come on Cody, walk me to class."

Glancing at the boy, sweet enough to try and stand up for her. She didn't want to see anything bad happen to him so she'd go with Cody . . . for now. Hopefully the new comer could handle himself because he had just made an enemy of Cody and an enemy of Cody was an enemy of the entire school, everyone here thought that the Marshal's hung the moon and stars; she smirked and mentally shook her head, everybody but her.

Cody grunted throwing Nate a triumphant glare before walking away, his arm wrapped tightly around his prize.

"Rain?" A voice in the hallway exclaimed.

"There wasn't a cloud in the sky a second ago?" Someone else answered looking out the window.

"I thought it was supposed to be sunny today, guess you really can't trust the weather man."

"Oh shit! It's pouring outside and my tops down in my convertible!" A teen yelled as he dashed for the door.

Nate heard the voices in the hallway and he tightened his fists, gritted his teeth in an effort to gain control over his powers.

"What the hell's the matter with you?" Jake demanded turning to face Nate. "Didn't you listen to a word I said? If you want to fit in here there are some rules to follow and number one is Anna-Maria Macdonald is off limits. Number two, don't make Cody your enemy, he'll make your life hell!" Jake lowered his voice and leaned in closer to Nate's ear, "but most importantly . . . no powers!"

Nate glared at Jake for a second before nodding his consent. Jake was right this wasn't Taysia it was Earth and no one had powers here. He had to learn to control his emotions better, taking a calming breath he let it out slowly relaxing as the rain outside diminished but the clouds still hung in the sky.

DING! The bell rang loudly in the hallway signaling the beginning of morning classes.

"Come on, we're late." Jake said as he turned and tugged Nate in the direction of the main office.

\*

"Did it work? Are we back?" Keyla asked cracking open one eye to peer around her, opening them both when Arron spoke.

"Yeah, we're back." Arron frowned as he let go of Reace's and Kittana's hand and stuffed his hands in the pockets of his worn jeans. "Looks like the same place we left seventeen years ago."

"It worked. Nate's here! I can sense him." Kittana said with a relieved smile on her face.

"Great! Where is he? Can you tell?" Keyla asked.

"No," Kittana groaned in frustration after a moment's concentration. "There are too many other people I can't get a clear reading. We're too far away. And no, Reace, I can't risk teleportation, not with so many people around."

"It was just a thought." Reace muttered then sighed heavily before adding, "I guess we should start walking then, it's a long way into the city and I doubt Arron's car is where we left it."

"I agree, let's go. The quicker we find Nate the quicker we can get back." Arron snapped moving forward.

Reace frowned briefly as he fell into step beside Kittana wondering what was up with his comrade he wasn't usually so snappy and impatient.

Arron, Keyla, Kittana and Reace walked the long way to Arron's house and because no one would be living there they figured they would use it as a base, from there they would figure out their next move, or rather, Nate's next move. Entering the spacious front yard they were surprised to see a car parked in the driveway and the front door was unlocked. Arron shrugged muttering something about a housekeeper.

Suddenly, Reace and Arron were anxious to see her again. Mrs. White had been more of a mother to the boys, who were practically abandoned, than an employee. Rushing in the front door, Arron came to an abrupt halt.

Reace slammed into him from behind, looking around Arron with confusion as to why he had stopped so suddenly, Reace's eyes widened in surprise. Coming down the steps into the front entry way was Arron's old girlfriend Heather.

"Jake? Nate? What happened? I thought you two went to school?" Heather demanded not realizing her mistake until Arron spoke.

"Heather! What are you doing here?" Arron spoke with a puzzled look of confusion spreading across his face.

"Did you say Nate? Where is he? Have you seen him?" Reace shot the questions at her as his blue gaze pierced hers in a demanding search for answers.

Both boys were surprised when Heather's eyes rolled back into her head and she fainted.

Kittana coming in behind Reace and Arron used her quick reflexes, calling on her telekinetic ability to stop Heather from falling down the stairs and hitting her head of the hard floor. She floated her into the living room where Kittana gently lowered Heather until she was laying on the sofa, her head resting on a pillow. Turning she noticed the rest of the group had followed her.

Arron stared at Heather's sleeping form as his mind whirled. What could Heather be doing here? If he didn't know better he'd have wondered if his parents had sold the house but that was impossible, there was a saying in the Price's household that went back generations—as long as you owned land, you had something of value. No one in his family had ever, ever sold land. It was the reason they had about fifteen houses in seven different countries around the world. Arron was startled out of his thoughts when Reace nudged him.

"Hey look," Reace pointed to a portrait above the fireplace, a portrait of Arron that hadn't been there before, one that Arron hadn't posed for.

Arron's frown deepened as he briefly considered Heather's sanity.

"I don't think it's a picture of you." Keyla stated. She'd been looking at the family photos that graced the mantel below the portrait, photos that hadn't been part of the crisp décor before. Photos that showed Heather with a small child that looked surprising like Arron. Keyla's eyes turned to the plague on the bottom of the picture frame.

"Jacob Arron Price." She read out loud then turned to stare at Arron as the realization hit her.

"You have a son with Heather." Kittana said as she too stared wide eyed at Arron.

Arron staggered backward as if he'd been physically hit.

"A son . . . but that's impossible." He muttered but his mind took him back seventeen years ago to a party, held here. He remembered.

"Yes, he's your son." Heather's weak voice came from behind them and the four Guardians turned as one to look at her.

"Is it really you, Arron? Kittana? Reace? God! I must be dreaming. You are all dead." Heather shook her head as she tried to move into a seated position.

Arron came forward sitting on the coffee table, facing her he ran a head over his face trying to wrap his mind around the fact that he's been a horrible father to not just one kid but two. "Christ Heather! A son, why didn't you tell me?"

"Why didn't I . . . ?" she repeated in a stunned whisper, surprised by that question and all the emotion behind it. Anger crept up into her face but before she could utter any of the phrases that clouded her mind, Mrs. White entered the room.

"Nate? Jake? Didn't I already chase you boys off to school? What are you doing back here and you had better not be bothering your mother, she's not feeling well and took the day off to rest"

The housekeeper's warmly stern voice washed over Reace and Arron. They shared a look that spoke volumes before turning toward their beloved Mrs. White.

"Arron? Reace?" Mrs. White's eyes shone with unshed tears as she realized who she was talking too. "You've come home!" She stared at the boys she hadn't seen in years then she opened her arms wide and welcomed them both in a hug.

"Oh, lord! I've always known they had it wrong. I could feel it in my bones and you know these old bones are never wrong! I knew you were alive." Her voice was muffled but happy. When she released them she turned to Heather and said. "Heather, they've come home. My boys have come home!"

Mrs. White turned twinkling eyes from Heather to take in her boys. Looking carefully at Arron first then at Reace she shook her head and said to Reace, "Boy, what are they feeding you? Come on I'll fix you a lunch and you can tell me where you've been and what trouble you've gotten yourself into now." Mrs. White gently scolded as she firmly led Reace, Keyla and Kittana into the kitchen. "Come on, you girls too. By the looks of you, you all could use some home cooking."

"Man, it's good to see her again." Arron said with a grin as he watched his old housekeeper herd everyone from the room. Slowly he turned back to Heather, his smile disappearing when he realized he was alone with her.

"Why didn't I tell you?" Heather's eyes were angry and they blazed at Arron as she repeated his question reminding him of the last thing he said to her. "You didn't exactly leave a forwarding address. Besides I was barely pregnant when you disappeared—we all thought you had died but obviously you didn't . . ." she turned an accusing expression to him as she demanded. "How could you just leave like that? How could you let us all think you had died? How could you do that to your parents? Not one call, not one note, not one WORD from you for seventeen years, not even to tell us you're alive."

"I'm sorry for any hurt I may have caused you or my son but you can't tell me my parents were sad at my suicide, inconvenienced maybe, but they have never cared one bit about me." He said surprised at the bitterness in his voice. He had thought he had gotten over it. Arron sighed and ran a hand over his blond hair as he added more to himself then to her. "And I can't blame them."

"Suicide?" Heather frowned, "Arron, I don't know what problems you've had in the past with your parents but they are good people. They have really been there for Jake and me."

Being here with Arron looking so much like he did when they were sixteen, it was like all those years fell away and she was sixteen again too . . . *Sixteen and pregnant*, she told herself. *And alone*, she mentally added. She had grown up a lot having a baby and she had clawed her way to the top of the company. She wasn't a naïve teenager anymore but a women; fully grown and powerful in her own right. Squaring her shoulders, putting steel in her spine she sat up straighter, took a deep breath forcing her voice to be steady and to act like the professional she had become.

"Your son's name is Jake, Jacob Arron Price, named after your grandfather, like your parents asked. If you have any doubts that he is yours, they will fade when you meet him. Jake is the very image of you." She took another deep breath. "That's why I called you Jake when you first came in, I thought . . ." she trailed off, gave her head a shake.

"Your parents, Arron, have been very kind to us over the years. They gave us this house and they have transferred your trust fund into Jake's name, so if you came here looking for money—there isn't any here for you. But if you need a place to stay . . ." She didn't finish her sentence but let her meaning hang in the air as she stood and walked to the doorway of the living room then turned back to him. "Your parents will be here tomorrow, they visit Jake every second weekend, I'm sure they'd like to see you too."

"Are you finished?" Arron asked turning to her his jaw tight with anger. He stood slowly watching Heather with narrowed eyes. He wasn't angry at her, but he couldn't help taking out his feelings on her, she had just told him that his parents cared more for his son then for him. That hurt!

His emotions were already at the breaking point, in the last twenty four hours his worst fears were founded: the son he had raised was really the son of his enemy; his wife had had an affair with Malic and had used her powers to twist his emotions to suit her; then he'd found out that Nate was missing and coming here he learned he had abandoned a son. Now hearing that his parents loved their grandchild enough to actually visit Jake every two weeks when they could hardly stand to see him at Christmas, Arron was ready to explode and his voice was harsher than it should have been when he spoke.

"First of all, I didn't come back here looking for money so you can stop guarding your bank account. Second, I didn't come back here for you or a son I didn't even know I had." Arron paused, realizing that he was being unfair he tried to push past his feelings, taking a deep calming breath he let it out slowly before continuing in a softer voice. "I came to help Reace and Kit fined their son Nature. If you have any information about Nate, we'd like to hear it," he glanced at her then and added, "and lastly, I do want to see my son but I won't lie to him or you . . . I can't stay in Springfield." He shook his head sadly suddenly he knew leaving this time would be harder, this time he would have no anger to spur him onward and no unknown threat to make going easier. This time he would be leaving a lot behind. "Like you, Heather, I have grown up too and I . . ."

Arron broke off at an ahem from Reace as he stepped into the room.

"Nate's in school with . . . Jake." Reace's eyes were full of expression when he spoke the name of Arron's son for the first time. "He'll be back here around two-thirty, three, according to Mrs. White. She went to fix up the guest rooms, hope it's okay if we stay here, Heather? I tried to talk her out of it but she was pretty insistent."

Reace glanced at Heather seeing her nod in agreement he was surprised, but hid it quickly, as he continued. "Kit decided to go pay a visit to her foster parents, let them know she's alright and Keyla went with her." Reace paused shifting his gaze as he shuffled his feet. "I'm going to go for a walk." He told Arron before turning and walking quickly toward the kitchen and the back door.

"Oh, no," Arron muttered with a cock of his head before he strode from the living room. They had seen the car parked in the driveway before they entered Arron's old house and both boy's knew that John was home.

"Reace!" Arron barked walking into the kitchen behind Reace.

At the sound of Arron's voice behind him Reace stopped just before opening the door.

"You're not thinking of going over there, are you?" Arron demanded as he placed a hand on Reace's shoulder, glancing out the window embedded in the backdoor, Arron's gaze fell on the same thing that Reace's did . . . John's house.

Reace colored when Arron correctly guessed what he was thinking he nodded biting his lip before he said in a quiet voice. "I have too, Arron."

"I can't believe it! You're actually going to go over there." Arron shook his head as he swung away from Reace to pace the length of the kitchen. At the other side of the room he spun on his heel and glared at Reace demanding, "Why? You don't owe him anything."

"Yes I do." Reace replied quietly, calm in the face of Arron's anger. "I owe him an apology. Look, I know you don't understand, but he's the only father I had and I . . . I don't like the way I left it."

"What about the way he treated you? Man, he hates you, you even admitted it. Damn it, Reace! He tried to kill you!" Arron's face was a mask of anguish and worry.

"He didn't try to kill me, we both know that. Besides, this isn't for him, it's for me." Reace said then almost sighed in relief when Heather entered the room effectively stopping Arron from saying more. Reace had never thought he'd ever be happy to see her but right now he could hug her . . . almost.

"Okay, well I have to be going, I'm sure you two have a lot to talk about and I have something I have to do . . . excuse me." He turned back to the door, then glanced back at Heather and with a sincere smile he added, "It was nice to see you again, Heather, really."

With a slight nod of his head, he opened the door and left ignoring Arron's cry.

"Reace wait!"

# CHAPTER ELEVEN

REACE HESITATED AT THE INVISIBLE line between the two properties wondering if he should go in the back door or around to the front, part of him wondered if Arron was right maybe he shouldn't do this. He glanced back toward Arron's house. No, he thought with a shake of his head, he needed to do this. With sure steps he moved to the front of the house deciding against going in through the kitchen.

He had just walked up the front steps and was trying to decide if he should knock or just go right in, when two police officers approached him from behind.

"Reace Stelmen?"

Reace turned at the sound of his name, a confused expression on his face to see the two officers. One he recognized as Officer Riley, he was older and maybe a bit heavier, but Reace was sure he was one of the cops who visited him in the hospital—questioning him about the knife wound he'd received years ago. Apprehension slowly built inside of Reace, as they advanced to stand in front of him; he answered their question. "Yes?"

"You are under arrest," Officer Riley said as he grabbed Reace's wrist, turned him around shoving him face first against the door and cuffed his hands behind his back. His partner patted him down making sure Reace had no weapons before they continued reading him his rights. "for the murders of Arron Price, Kittana and Keyla Messer and the attempted murder of John Stelmen. You have the right to remain silent . . ."

The officer's voice droned on as Reace's head reeled with the information—murder? His gaze caught someone's in the window of the house seconds before the curtain was dropped. Reace didn't have time to wonder who it was, but he knew that it wasn't John, before his attention was forced back to one of the officers who was shoving him toward the police cruiser.

"I knew you were in trouble back when you were a kid but I never thought it was of your own making." Officer Riley spoke then added as he helped Reace into the back seat of the car. "Guess I was wrong."

"No! You weren't wrong. I didn't murder anybody." Reace finally found his voice as the door was slammed shut in his face. His words falling on deaf ears Reace remained silent the rest of the way to the police station. His mind was still trying to take in the events that happened, Murder?! He was being accused of murder? How? Why? And who was that peeking out of the curtain at John's house? He asked himself hoping the answers would come to him, frowning when they didn't. He cursed his rotten luck! How would he ever find Nate and get back to Taysia now? He briefly wondered if he could use his 'talents' to break out but decided against it, too many questions. Why did Nate want to come here? For himself it was like returning to hell.

*

In the high school cafeteria he saw her again, Anna-Maria. Nate's heart soared with hope when she glanced at him but plummeted again as he smiled at her and her look soured before she turned away to laugh and giggle with her friends.

As Jake talked to his friends surrounding them, Nate sat there thinking of her. She was the girl of his dreams, he had often wondered if she was somewhere in the universe waiting and dreaming of him too. He had hoped so and he had hoped that somehow, sometime they'd meet. He just didn't think that when they had she'd be with another guy and think him a total loser.

He shook his head at the irony of life as he toyed with the idea of asking Timelana to rewind time so the whole incident never happened. He sighed, that would be unfair his conscious told him, he had to be his own person and learn from his mistakes. He had to figure this out on his own, besides he told himself he could almost hear Timelana's voice now: '*Nate, you cannot just erase your mistakes you have to find your own way to fix them, that way you learn not to make them*' and she'd be right. Nate sighed again, she'd be right.

Looking down at his tray of odd looking food, odd to him at least, he picked up his fork and started to lift some of the reddish goop to his mouth but stopped mid way; he paled lowering his loaded utensil when a familiar tingle nudged his brain.

Jake had noticed how quiet Nate had been during lunch but he figured that Nate was just nervous being around strangers, he himself was shy sometimes, so Jake hadn't given it much thought. But, now when it was just the two of them and Nate still didn't respond plus seeing the spooked paleness of his expression, Jake wondered if something else was going on. "Hey, dude, are you okay? What's wrong?"

"They're here," Nate stated. The tingling nudge was the familiar feel of his mother's telepathic probe. He mentally pushed against it, not wanting to be found just yet.

"They're here?" Jake repeated then asked, almost scared of the answer but needing to be sure. "Who's they?"

"Mom and I . . . I can't tell who is with her." Nate said glancing at Jake and rubbing his head where it suddenly began to ache.

"But there is someone right? And that someone could be Arron, right? I mean . . . my dad, he could be here." Jake swallowed not sure how he felt about that just yet. One part of him was excited to finally get the chance to meet the father he had only heard about but the other part of him was scared. What if Arron didn't want him; didn't like him or worse, was disappointed in him?

Nate watched as Jake glanced around nervously as if he half expected Arron to suddenly pop out from behind a chair. Then he noticed that the room was practically empty which meant only one thing . . . time to move on to the next class. Bringing his gaze back to Jakes he nodded before speaking.

"Yeah, it's possible." Nate sounded slightly distracted as he thought about it. If they used the power of four, then yeah, Arron, Keyla and his parents would be here but that would mean leaving Taysia and putting the balance at risk or could Link, Awkwade and Tia balance Malic? Where they strong enough? Would his mother really put the balance at risk just to find him? Maybe she asked Timelana for help? No, he thought, giving his head a shake, he couldn't see the Guardian of Time betraying him like that.

Sooner or later he'd meet up with them and he had to figure out what to say to them to explain his actions. They would want to know how and why he left Taysia and in order for them to except that he was an adult he had to act like one and give them an answer. What would he tell them?

The ringing of the bell interrupted his thoughts and spurred him and Jake into moving. First they had to get through the school day then he'd face whatever came next.

*

Arron sighed, turning toward Heather who stood in the kitchen behind him.

"Why are you so worried if he goes for a walk? Are you scared he'll meet up with a drug dealer?" she asked after seeing the way he and Reace interacted.

"What?" Arron exclaimed, looking at her in confusion for a moment then answered, "No, Reace can't do drugs." He stated as if it were obvious then added under his breath. "None of us can."

"Then what's the big deal if he takes a walk?" Heather pushed.

"He's NOT taking a walk." Arron informed her as he glanced out the window but he couldn't see Reace, he was already gone from sight.

"If he's not taking a walk then where did he go . . . Oh no! Not over to see his father? What if he tries to murder him again? I've got to call and . . ."

"Murder?" Arron's head snapped back to gap at her. The look on his face made her pause in the act of reaching for the phone. "Reace would never do that!"

"But he did electrocute Mr. Stelmen the night you all disappeared." Heather stated a widely known fact.

"He was protecting Keyla and himself." Arron snapped back before he realized he shouldn't have as he remembered the way Reace had said he shocked John before they left. Could John have told people that Reace tried to murder him? It wouldn't have surprised Arron if he had.

"Protecting himself?" Heather repeated in a whisper trying to figure out how or why or who Reace was protecting himself from?

"Look, Heather, I can't explain. Just trust me—I have never lied to you." He couldn't remember but he hoped it was the truth. "Reace would never, NEVER hurt anyone who was innocent."

"You're talking in riddles, Arron. Are you saying that Mr. Stelmen wasn't innocent?"

Arron slammed his hand down hard on the counter making Heather jump at his sudden show of temper. "Christ! Heather! Would you just drop it?" Arron ran a hand through his hair in frustration as he gritted out between clenched teeth, "I don't want to talk about this right now. Okay?"

"Okay." she drew out the word.

Arron look at her in surprise, he hadn't expected the sudden compliance. He could see that Heather had changed. Where he had expected catty comments and nasty words, he got understanding and comfort. Motherhood agreed with her, he thought. Even Reace would like this Heather.

"Seems you have picked up some anger issues over the years," Heather stated after a few minutes of silence.

"I'm sorry." He offered as he sat down on one of the bar stools leaning his arms on the island counter and resting his head in his hands. "I've had a really bad day!" he gave a soft humorless chuckle, "A really bad day." He repeated then turned his honey brown eyes on her and said. "Tell me about you, what are you doing now? Tell me about our son . . . Jake." It was the first time he said the name out loud and a wave of tenderness overwhelmed his heart for the child he didn't even know—for a face he had never seen.

She Ignored the 'tell me about you' part of Arron's question because there wasn't a lot to tell about her life. She was still single—still alone. Becoming pregnant at an early age had pretty much ruined her—her high school self that is. Her friends left her one by one, not that she blamed them, she had heard the whispers, and the rumors being said about her behind her back. Jen and Marsha had tried to keep in touch but with her having a baby, they just didn't have anything in common anymore and drifted apart. She had something other than boys and clothes to care about, she had her son and seventeen years later she still had her son and not much else. So instead of talking about herself she focused on her son—their son.

"Jake's a good kid," Heather started. "He loves animals, we had a dog when he was younger but it died, got hit by a car a few years ago. Jake took it pretty hard and he didn't want another. He still loves them, but now it's more from afar."

Heather stopped talking for a few seconds replaying in her mind her son's tear stained face and the questions Jake had asked, the ones she couldn't answer: *"Why mom, why can I heal myself but not other's? Why did god give me this gift if I can't help people with it?"*

Arron frowned at Heather's story if he had been there he could have saved Jake's dog.

"um . . . he's smart, a straight A student." Lost in her memories she didn't notice Arron's frown and continued talking, "Jake's not as social as we were at that age . . . no wild parties here anymore." She gave a little laugh and looked at Arron before continuing. "He can talk his way out of getting into trouble too, he just turns these big puppy dog eyes on you and you melt." Her expression was soft for a moment before turning worried as she glanced at Arron and asked. "You are planning to stay for a few days, get to know him, aren't you? It'll break his heart if you don't. He's always wanted to meet you . . ."

"And Reace." She added grudgingly she never understood her son's fascination with Reace Stelmen, she, herself, wanted to forget him.

Arron nodded, opening his mouth to speak when Mrs. White entered the kitchen wringing her hands.

"Lord, that boy's got himself into a peck of trouble now. You know, Arron, I have never believed what everyone said about him. They just didn't know him . . . Reace was always such a sweet boy!"

"What are you talking about?" Arron asked after looking from Heather to Mrs. White, a puzzled frown on his face.

"Reace has just been arrested." Mrs. White clarified.

"WHAT?" the word exploded from Arron.

# CHAPTER TWELVE

As KITTANA AND KEYLA WALKED to Kittana's old house they reminisced about Earth, all the things they liked and didn't like and what they missed over the years. Living on Taysia neither had really thought much about Earth in the last seventeen years.

Her son, Kittana thought, was here going to school and soon she'd be able to see for herself that he was alright then, somehow, she had to make him understand that Earth wasn't all fun and adventures like he had heard from Arron and Reace. Some of the stories they told Nate were fond memories but there were other memories. Ones Kittana didn't even want to think about!

Earth was a dangerous place and her son, the Guardian of Nature, didn't belong here—none of them did. Not anymore. She sighed, but being here now she had to admit it was nice, like visiting your parent's home after living for years on your own.

Reaching the front door of the Macdonald's house, Keyla glanced at her sister. She had been quiet for the last few minutes and Keyla wondered what she was feeling. It must be hard to come see the people you had been away from for so long. She thought in sympathy.

For herself she was starting to feel like a third wheel on a bicycle she had no one to revisit, no one in this world cared about her. She hadn't wanted to stay at Arron's house not with Heather there—a reminder of Arron's past and her own inadequacy. Reace, she noticed, had changed becoming more like his old brooding self the closer they got to Arron's, next door to the house he grew up in. She hoped Reace wouldn't go over there, seventeen years was a long time . . . anything could have happened maybe John wasn't even living there anymore.

Keyla had left Arron's with Kittana thinking her sister would need her support and now looking at her, seeing her freeze with emotion on the door step to her foster parent's house, she had been right. Giving her sister's shoulder an encouraging pat Keyla knocked on the door for her and stepped back behind her twin.

The years had been kind to Nancy; she looked almost the same—only older with maybe a hint of sadness in her eyes, but it was hard to tell because when she saw them standing there they lit up with surprise and pleasure and a list of other emotions that Keyla didn't take the time to analyze.

"Oh my, Kittana? Oh Kittana! You're alive!" Nancy sobbed tears freely streaming down her checks as she beheld the daughter she thought long gone. Nancy pulled her into a hug. "Kittana, I've always known you weren't dead, that you'd come back someday and here you are . . ." She pulled back to look at Kittana, her eyes taking in every detail of her face. "It is you, isn't it? I am not dreaming?" She asked then smiled when she saw Kittana nod and enveloped her into a tight hug again. "Of-course it is, oh. Kittana!"

Nancy looked past Kittana's hair to see the person standing behind her daughter then Nancy grabbed her in a hug too at the same time as she said her name. "Keyla!"

Keyla's eyes widened in surprise and pleasure at the contact, she was surprised to be remembered. The hug was over with quickly then Nancy took Kittana's hand and led them into the house.

"Mom, it's so nice to see you, I've missed you, I didn't realize how much until now." Kittana said as she and her sister were led into the living room where she and Nancy took a seat on the coach while Keyla choose to sit facing them on the lazy boy chair.

Glancing around the room Kittana could tell Nancy had been sad, it showed in the pictures that graced the surfaces and the walls. The time after she had left had been hard on her foster mother, it was evident in the way she clutched at her hand but Kittana didn't mind as she held on just as tightly.

Nancy took a moment to look at Kittana and Keyla, just staring at them, reassuring herself that they were real and they were here . . . alive. After a few moments she asked the questions that were crowding in her mind.

"Tell me everything; where you've been, what you're doing, what you have done? My, but you haven't changed a bit! Both of you still look the same, so young. Maybe I've just gotten older." she gave a nervous laugh. "Tell me, have you met anyone special? Do I have grandkids?" Nancy asked her foster daughter questions she had wondered about all these years but she didn't ask the one burning question: why did you leave? She couldn't, not yet, she wasn't sure she was strong enough to handle the answer. "Wait until Dave and Anna-Maria see you. They'll be so excited. You are staying for supper right?"

Her voice sounded panicky and it twisted a knife in Kittana's heart.

"I mean, will you stay for supper?" Nancy forced herself to calm down and ask politely. She didn't want to scare them off.

"Of-course we'll be here for supper but we do have an errand to run shortly." Keyla commented with a bright smile. She couldn't help but feel sorry for this woman who had lost so much or her sister who had to leave such great people behind, people who truly loved her.

"Yes," Kittana confirmed nodding, she found herself looking forward to a home cooked meal.

"Great, as I was saying they'll be so excited! I've never stopped believing that you'd come back to us someday. I just couldn't believe that you were dead. I'd have felt it in my heart if you were. Besides, without a body how could there be a murder? I just knew there was hope that you'd still be alive." Nancy's voice broke a little and there were fresh tears in her eyes as she spoke. "And I was right. Here you are . . . alive and well, both of you!"

Keyla frowned at the mention of her and Kittana being thought of as dead. It was the third time she'd heard that and she had a feeling that it couldn't be good. She was about to question Nancy about it when her sister spoke first and Keyla's question was temporarily forgotten in the wake of curiosity.

"Anna-Maria, who is she?" Kittana asked curious if Arron was successful in healing Nancy and allowing her to have what she always wanted—a child of her own.

"Anna-Maria is my daughter. Oh, Kittana the doctors, they were all wrong! A few months after you . . . disappeared we found out that we were expecting, the doctors said it was a miracle but I know . . ." she trailed off.

Kittana glanced at her in surprise holding her breath. Had her mother known about her and Arron? Did she remember them being here that night and healing her?

Keyla noticed the way her sister tensed and suspicion entered her mind, she wondered if her sister and Arron had something to do with Nancy's miracles healing?

"I know," Nancy continued not noticing how her guest's body language had changed, "I know they made a mistake and were just covering up that fact."

Kittana relaxed at those words and let her breath out with a mixture of relief and disappointment that she covered with an overly bright smile as Nancy continued talking.

"I am glad for the mistake though, it brought you into our lives and that was never, NEVER, a mistake." She patted Kittana's knee reassuringly. "Anna-Maria just turned sixteen a few months ago. You'll like her when you meet her; she's smart, beautiful and a very talented artist."

"She's the same age as Nate." Keyla added giving her sister a knowing glance.

"Who's Nate?" Nancy inquired.

"He's my son." Kittana answered as her worry came rushing back to her—the reason they were there in the first place.

"Oh, good god! You were pregnant!" Nancy exclaimed. "Is that why you left? You didn't want to tell us, you thought we'd be disappointed?"

"No! No, we left because we had too, I found out I was pregnant later, after . . . Err! I can't explain it mom. But, I never meant to hurt you or David." Kittana tried to make her foster mother understand.

"Then why? Why did you leave without a note or a call in seventeen years?" Nancy demanded finally voicing the question she had been aching to ask.

"Don't you see, I couldn't call, not even to tell you that I was alright, it would have left you with questions that I couldn't . . . can't answer . . ." Kittana sighed heavily. "But you had Anna-Maria right? She's your real daughter—one you can love and who'll never leave you like I did . . . like I will. She made you happy, she made you forget me."

"Never Kittana, I have never forgotten about you and I have never stopped loving or thinking of you as my daughter. I've been through *HELL* thinking you were murdered by that boy, both of you. Hoping against hope that somehow you'd still be alive," Nancy took a deep breath about to continue when Keyla interrupted her.

"Murdered by who?" Keyla asked, not sure now that she asked, that she wanted to know the answer.

Nancy's gaze swung to Keyla's briefly before returning to Kittana's face before she spoke, "That Stelmen boy. The one you told me about, but I have to say after hearing what you said about him before . . . I . . . I wondered if he did do it or if like you said people just thought the worst about him without giving him a chance."

The phone rang then and Nancy got up to answer it, with her back to her guests she didn't see the girl's mirror faces whiten in shock.

# CHAPTER THIRTEEN

AFTER GETTING OFF THE PHONE with Arron, and learning about Reace's predicament, Keyla and Kittana bid a hasty good-bye to Nancy, promising to be back for supper. Ten minutes later they meet Arron at the police station and together they entered the public building. Standing at the front desk they wondered where to start, what to do when a nasally sounding voice startled them.

"Can I help you?" The clerk behind the enclosed desk asked not really looking at them.

"Hi," Arron said speaking for them. "We heard a friend of ours had been arrested for murder and we would like . . ."

"Name please."

"Name?" Arron asked startled by her abruptness.

"Yes, the name of your friend, I'll get his file and then I may be able to help you." The clerk answered slowly in a condescending tone as if she was talking to a child.

"Oh, right. Ah Reace . . . Reace Stelmen." Arron supplied his face reddening in embarrassment as he mentally berated himself.

The office women glanced up sharply at the sound of the name and hardly paused a moment before saying, "Sorry, can't help you."

"But . . ." Arron started but was pushed aside by Keyla so she could talk to the women.

"Hey! Reace was arrested for the murders of Arron Price, Keyla and Kittana Messer and we're here to show you that the charges are false." Keyla told her with determination flashing in her eyes. "We are right here and we are very much alive, obviously."

"And who are you? What evidence do you have?" The clerk's eyes hardened.

"We are Arron Price and Kittana and Keyla Messer the supposed victims." Kittana's voice was just as icy as the women behind the desk.

"You're Kittana and Keyla Messer and Arron Price? Really? Do you have any proof, any identification?" The women's eyes showed her disbelief that they were who they said they were.

Showing the needed identification that they withdrew from their pockets after Keyla muttered a few words to produce the proof. They were taken to the officer in charge of the case, Officer Riley. After an hour of verifying who they were, Reace was cleared of the murder charges.

"So he can go free right?" Kittana asked already knowing the answer and dreading it.

"No," Riley replied.

"WHAT? WHY? YOU HAVE NO REASON TO KEEP HIM NOW!" Keyla shouted unable to control her frustration.

"I'm sorry, I'd like to help, really, but my hands are tied. He's still has a warrant out for his arrest." The officer said, amazed by the fact that Reace really didn't murder these people and he briefly wondered why they had not come forward before, the case did achieve some state wide media and television coverage, especially since the Prices were a very rich and influential family.

"On what grounds?"

Arron's question forced the officer away from his thoughts as he answered: "Assault and Attempted murder."

"Who? How?" Keyla sputtered.

"John Stelmen," Officer Riley replied after looking down at the open case file in front of him, "His father, look, I shouldn't be telling you this but since it is information that you could find online or in any of the archived news articles, we don't have much other then what the news reported anyway, the weapon used was a stun gun."

"Wait a minute," Keyla argued, "by law you can't be charged with murder by a stun gun"

"True, however in this case Reace used excessive force, the wounds on the victim's body were evidence that Reace had stunned him more than once and that is an attempt on someone's life." Riley looked up at the group and offered, "Off the record, it was only the miracle of science that John Stelmen survived and unless he drops the charges I'm afraid your friend can't be released." The officer said with a shake of his head then added. "Not until the bail hearing anyway and the date hasn't even been set yet, that could take anywhere from two hours to six months, though."

"Thank you, officer." Arron nodded curtly forcing a smile as he ushered himself and the girls out of the office and down the hallway then out the door of the police department building leaving the stunned officer shaking his head in bewilderment at the abruptness with which they left.

"John drop the charges?" Keyla echoed the officers' earlier words. Her mind already thinking of a spell she could use to change one of them into looking like John.

"No!" Kittana told her reading her mind, "We can't do that what if the real John comes in? No, it's too risky; it'll raise to many questions."

"Okay, then what if you go to John and force him to drop the charges using your mental control?" Keyla asked her sister.

"No!" Arron spoke firmly, "I'll go talk to him. I'm sure with a little pressure he'll see things our way and none of us will get exposed by using our powers."

"And if that doesn't work?" Kittana demanded.

"Then we'll use Keyla's idea." He told her with a grin.

"Great, I'm plan B." Keyla grumbled. Kittana laughed and laying an arm over her twin's shoulders she urged her to follow Arron.

\*

"Mr. Stelmen, there's someone here to see you."

"Send them in Joanne." John's voice came back to his secretary through the intercom.

Arron nodded and walked into the office. He took a deep breath and looked at the man he had secretly hated for years, the person responsible for his best friend's pain. How many times had Arron seen a bloody and beaten Reace? How many times had he talked to, smiled and been coolly polite to Mr. Stelmen when all along he wanted to punch the son of a bitch who had hurt his friend? He sighed, now was no different, he admitted. He still had to be nice and not kill the man but this time, Arron smiled wickedly, this time he could let the bastard know he knew.

"I suppose by now you've heard that Reace was arrested." Arron began as soon as the door closed. Standing he watched the man seated behind the desk.

"Yes, Jake I heard. We can all rest easier knowing that bastard is behind bars. It's not often that you come in here to see me so what came I do for you?"

Arron frowned when John called him by son's name, his subconscious picking up details that Arron didn't want to notice, like how calm the man before him seemed, softer, older and . . . happier. Then Arron's gaze fell to a framed photo on the desk. A picture of John, with his arms around a woman and standing in front of the smiling couple were a few children—neither of them Reace. How dare this monster find happiness while Reace was rotting in jail, like some criminal!

"It's Arron, Arron Price." He gritted out between clenched teeth. Arron had to really work at calming himself down, but he took satisfaction in seeing the older man pale.

"Arron? Thank god! We thought you were . . ."

"Dead?" Arron finished for him smirking as he sat down in the chair across from John, with the desk between them it made it easier not to kill the man. "Nope, I'm not dead after all. Surprising isn't it? I'll tell you what else is surprising, I was just on my way back from visiting a good friend you remember him, don't you? Reace—your son. Turns out that he's in jail and here's the funny part for the murder of me, his wife and his sister-in-law. Now since we are obviously still alive, we paid him a visit, seems they can't release him yet, on account of some attempted murder charges—charges you can drop if you wanted to . . ."

"Why would I want to? That bastard tried to murder me. He . . ." John trailed off when Arron shook his head.

"Was it murder or self-defense?" Arron asked jumping up from his chair and leaning across the desk, Arron carefully put his hands on the smooth polished wood, half afraid that if he touched the bastard right now he'll kill him.

"I know," he growled staring into John eyes. "I know all about how you beat the crap out of him time and time again and that stab wound—I know it was you too. You sick bag of shit." Arron had the pleasure of seeing fear enter John's eyes as the man paled further and his eyes widened in surprise. Arron continued. "And I am willing to testify in court . . . if you want to take it that far." Then Arron added, "Imagine how you'd be perceived if Reace's abilities were to accidentally come out during the trial too. Do you really want someone picking you apart under a microscope just to make sure you and he aren't related? Do you really want your loving wife" Arron cocked his head toward the picture of John's new family, "and your colleagues knowing what you did to your son?" Arron picked up the phone and held it out to John. "Do you want the truth to come out or are you willing to make that call?"

Giving Arron an unreadable glare John grabbed the phone out of his hand and dialed.

"Good choice," Arron smiled coldly as he straightened, not leaving until he heard the end of the conversation, making sure that John really dropped the charges against Reace before going toward the door.

"Arron, I've changed . . . I'm a different man now. I . . ." John began, hanging up the phone as Arron moved toward the door.

"Save it for someone who cares!" Arron told him with a sneer before shutting the door behind him.

*

Thirty minutes later, John found himself standing in front of the police station. He had made the call as Arron requested and now he had to sign the papers that would formally release Reace and drop the charges against him.

He had to see Reace again and the emotions just the idea stirred within him were enough to make him pause, to make him want a drink. He had been sober, not even craving a drop of alcohol for fifteen years. Ever since Reace had left, his life had changed . . . he had changed. John breathed deeply trying to screw up his failing courage. For the sake of his new life, his wife and their children he had to do this. John squared his shoulders and walked into the building.

After signing the papers John went to the holding cell where he saw him, laying on the bench staring at the ceiling.

"So it's true, you really did come back." John said taking small pleasure in the way Reace reacted to his voice. Maybe just maybe, he'd be able to keep Reace away and the truth hidden.

Hearing John's voice outside of his head after so many years, Reace bolted upright swinging his legs over the side of the bench before he paused, realizing then that he didn't feel any fear maybe it was because they were in a public place. Nodding he replied slowly, "Yeah, I came back."

"I don't have any money for you to steal so why did you come back?" John demanded.

Reace gave him an odd look as he stood and walked closer, standing face to face, the bars of the cell the only thing between them. "I am not after your money. I came back because my son is missing and I want to find him."

"You have a son? Is he . . ."

"Like me?" Reace finished John's question with a smirk, John hadn't changed. "Yeah, he's like me and I am damn proud of him too."

John nodded, "Don't come by the house there is nothing there for you."

"There never was." Reace replied his eyes hardened, "Are you going to drop the charges against me or do I have to find my own way out?"

"I've dropped the charges but, you stay away from me, the house and my wife, got that?"

"You're w . . . wife?" Reace echoed in disbelief.

"Yeah, got married a couple of years after you left, she doesn't know much about you and what she has heard . . . well." John looked embarrassed for a second then his face hardened as he glared at Reace before adding in a threatening voice. "If you know what's good for you, you'll stay away and call off your watch dog. I don't like to be threatened," John leaned in closer to growl, "Got that . . . bastard?"

Reace swallowed at the look in his step father's eyes, John still hated him, Reace could see that and he knew from past experiences what John was physically capable of. Not trusting himself to speak as the fear he had only experienced in his nightmares for the past seventeen years took hold of him, he only nodded letting John know he'd keep his distance.

John called an officer to unlock the door, he waited for his stepson as the officer told Reace that he was a free man. When Reace left the cell John grabbed his arm, in such a way that it looked like Reace had grabbed John, forcing him to turn and face him. John's voice was only loud enough for Reace to hear. "I meant what I said . . . stay away."

Reace yanked his arm out of John's hold, John unbalanced fell back a step.

"You okay, John? This thug bothering you?" The officer butted in with a worried expression on his face he didn't know John Stelmen very well but he had heard of him and he was more than willing to protect one of their own against scum like this kid.

"Thanks Frank, but I'm fine. This young man isn't going to be bothering me anymore," John said with a confident smile before walking ahead of Reace and talking to the cop as they left the holding cell.

Reace just shook his head in wonder at the way people kept treating him—like a criminal when he had done nothing but get attacked and tried to defend himself. Reace collected his things at the front desk and left the police station a free man.

He saw Arron, Kittana and Keyla on the sidewalk just outside the building and he walked toward them.

"Hi beautiful, you're a sight for sore eyes!" Reace hugged his wife and kissed her check then turned to Arron and Keyla flipping a thumb over his shoulder at the building behind them he questioned. "I never thought I'd ever see the day when John would help me. You have something to do with that?"

"What are friends for?" Arron's dimples flashed as he grinned, admitting, "I had a little chat with John today and I may have mentioned something about telling the court of law what I know and I guess he didn't like that idea very well." Arron shrugged then added, "Oh, by the way, did you know he has a new wife?"

"I know and she's scared of me," Reace admitted quietly.

"What? Why? She doesn't even know you!" Keyla exclaimed.

"I can imagine what John tells her," Kittana said with anger behind her words.

"Let's just leave it alone, it doesn't matter who, what or why because I am never going to meet her and I am never going over there again," Reace said with a firm voice.

"Glad to hear that you've finally come to your senses," Arron clapped him on the back as they started walking down the street heading towards Arron's old house.

Kittana's expression soured, being a telepath she knew why Reace decided to never met his new step-mother—John had threatened him.

# CHAPTER FOURTEEN

ARRON, REACE, KITTANA AND KEYLA walked through the door into the Price's house. The place didn't seem to fit him anymore, Arron thought as they walked into the kitchen, stopping short when they saw Nate sitting on a bar stool at the counter.

"Nate!" Kittana exclaimed. Pleased and relieved to see him she engulfed her son in a hug and at the same time she mentally checked him over.

He pushed away from her in annoyance at being treated like a child. "I'm okay, mom."

Satisfied that he was okay she sighed with relief and then loudly scolded him with her mind.

*"WE ARE SO GOING TO TALK NATURE!"*

Nate winched at the volume of her power in his mind and the pounding headache that accompanied it.

Reace who stood beside his wife laid a hand on Nate's shoulder, giving Nature a familiar light shock at the touch. Emotion clogged Reace's throat making his voice sound rough as he said, "You made us worry, Nature."

"We're all glad to see you're okay." Arron added with a smile as he hugged Nate healing his headache at the touch.

"Arron," Nate breathed, almost unable to believe it was really him but the healing and the peaceful feeling that settled over him at the Guardian of Life's touch told him that yes, this was Uncle Arron.

"Thanks" Nate mumbled, feeling sheepish under Arron's steady gaze. "I can't believe your all here! You left Taysia and the balance . . . for me . . . why?"

"Because we love you, you dolt!" Keyla told him with a grin. "Now give your Aunt a big hug before I cry."

Nate smiled at Keyla as he complied.

They were all hugging and talking and laughing when Jake entered the room. Arron saw him first and went still, his eyes fastened on the younger version of himself. Arron's smile slowly disappeared to be replaced by an odd combination of awe and curiosity.

Keyla noticed Arron's reaction and following the direction of his eyes she saw the young man hovering at the entrance to the room. Stepping forward with her hand held out she said, "You must be Jake, we've heard so much about you . . . don't worry it's all been good." She added with a cheeky grin.

Jake tore his gaze away from his fathers' as he took her outstretched hand in his and shook it, coming more fully into the room. His eyes must have showed his confusion because she added, letting go of his hand at the same time she spoke.

"I'm Keyla, Nate's Aunt and this is my sister, Kittana and Reace, Nate's parents. You already know Nate and . . ."

Jakes' eyes widened and grew warm with recognition when they beheld Reace—he was really here, he was real! Jake forced his eyes to move with Keyla's voice as she finished with the introductions.

"And this is Arron. I'm sure you know who he is." She muttered under her breath that last sentence but Jake still heard. "Everybody," Keyla continued in a voice loud enough to catch everyone's attention. "This is Jake."

"Hi Jake," came a chorus of voices but Jakes eyes didn't move, they stared at Arron. A man he didn't know but desperately wanted too.

"Well, I, ah, I think we should go and have that talk now, Nate." Kittana said after a few moments of awkward silence. Nate nodded his consent and the two of them left the kitchen, Reace followed them into the living room, closing the pocket doors for added privacy.

Back in the kitchen Keyla stood glancing from Arron who was still staring at Jake, to Jake who was starring at the floor. Probably wondering what to say or where to start, Keyla thought and decided they needed some time alone.

"Well, I have to go . . . um . . . use the bathroom." Keyla departed glad to get out of the kitchen away from the mounting tension. She hoped they'd talk like father and son should be able to.

"Hi," Arron mumbled thinking it was a lame way to start a conversation with his son. A son he didn't know he reminded himself hoping it would make it easier, somehow, but that fact only made things worse.

Arron got angry with himself for not being here, for not knowing. He was the Guardian of Life, for Christ sake! *Damn it, I should have known!*

"Hi," Jake replied lifting his eyes to Arron's, "You're really my dad, you're alive and . . . here." The words spilled out of Jake's mouth.

Arron winced at the 'you're alive and here' part as it twisted a knife in his guilt filled heart.

"Yeah, I'm alive and here." He repeated not knowing what else to say. He ran a hand over his hair and took a deep breath before adding, "Look, I'm sorry, I wasn't here before I . . . I . . ." Arron trailed off unsure of how to finish. This wasn't going as he hoped it would. Trying to break the awkward silence that filled the room he offered, "I, ah, hey, do you want a coke?"

"Sure, I'll get it." Jake jumped on Arron's suggestion and almost sprinted to the fridge. Arron was taken back for a moment, reminded that this wasn't his home anymore—it belonged to Heather and Jake.

Arron popped the top of his can of coke when Jake handed it to him before getting himself one. They sat in silence for a while each very interested in the drinks in front of them until Jake finally spoke.

"Listen . . . Arron," he didn't feel comfortable yet calling him dad, "Ah, Nate told me that you had to leave before, to fulfill a destiny. He said you were a Guardian and you have . . . special abilities." Jake seemed uncomfortable saying it out loud, his shoulders squirmed a bit before he added quietly. "I understand."

Arron's head came up quick when he heard that, "You do?"

"Yeah, I just wanted you to know that you don't have to pretend or lie to me . . . I understand."

"Jake, I would never, *never*, lie to you." Arron assured him.

"Okay," Jake said then continued, "I know what it's like to have to pretend your normal when you're not." Jake let out the breath he had been holding hoping his father would understand what he was really saying without Jake having to actually say it.

As what Jake said washed over him Arron wondered *Could Jake be a Guardian?* The thought hadn't occurred to him before but it was possible. And did that mean Heather knew about them? This opened up a whole new set of possibilities and a possible threat to the five of them. He had to find out.

"What special abilities do you have?" Arron asked watching Jake closely.

Jake breathed a sigh of relief. Arron got it, his hidden message. Now maybe he'd get some real answers. Jake opened his mouth to start but before he could say a word his mother breezed into the room, with a light floral scent that seemed to lessen the tension in the air.

"Arron, there you are! I wanted to tell you that your parents are coming home tonight instead of waiting until the weekend. Apparently they heard that Reace was cleared of all charges because you were alive and back in Springfield."

"Nana and papa are coming tonight?" Jake interrupted his voice tinged with regret because not only would he have to share his time with his dad but now he'd have to be careful what he said and what he did and that meant he may not be able to get all the information he craved out of his father especially if they had to pretend to be normal.

"Hey, I thought you'd be happy to see them." Heather turned her attention toward her son with a confused expression on her pretty face. Why suddenly, was he not excited to see his grandparents? Suddenly, her eyes widened and moved to catch Arron's face before going back to her son's with an accusing glare.

"What did I interrupt?" She tried to sound light hearted but it was hard with her heart in her throat, what if Jake had said something to Arron about his ability to self heal? Her gaze moved from one to the other, they looked so much alike and both avoided her gaze like the plague, which only increased her anxiety and forced her to ask. "Jake, can I speak to you privately?"

"No," he answered her, "Whatever you want to say you can say in front of him."

"Jake, I . . ." Heather began but Jake cut her off.

"He knows mom. He's the reason I have it in the first place." Jake informed her.

"What special ability does Jake have?" Arron asked again.

Heather sighed, Jake was right. Arron did need to know. She wondered why Jake said it was Arron's fault, did he have this ability too? If he did, why didn't his parents ever say anything about it?

The answer came to her, Arron didn't have it. He was normal. She knew because when she had been intimate with Arron, in high school, she had asked him about the different scars from his childhood. Ignoring Arron's question, she shook her head and spoke to Jake instead.

"No Jake. You're wrong. I'm sorry but I know him better then you do." It hurt to say that to her son and watch his face crumble as her words hit him like a slap in the face. "Arron is not like you."

"What do you mean, what is Jake like?" Arron demanded reminding everyone of his presence in the room.

"Arron," Heather began turning her attention back to him but Jake's voice kept her focused on her son.

"There are a lot of things you don't know, mom. Nate told me that Arron . . ."

"Nate? Jake, I hope you didn't say or do anything stupid!" Heather jumped on the name, interrupting Jake's words much to Arron's relief.

"I am not stupid!" Jake snapped then added in a quieter voice, "and yeah I told Nate, he's like me. Mom, he can do things others can't."

"Nate's been real chatty, hasn't he?" Arron grumbled but no one paid any attention to him.

"Oh, Jake, are you sure? He could . . ." Heather swallowed unable to voice her fears.

"Mom! I saw him, okay, there was no way it was rigged or anything. It happened because of an accident." Jake tried to explain.

"What accident?" Arron said in alarm. His frustration was growing at being ignored and having his questions go unanswered.

"Arron, I'm sorry about all this . . ." Heather began, turning her attention to him but not sure of what to say, what not to say she trailed off.

"It's okay," Arron reassured her with a smile then looked to Jake. "Just tell me what's going on."

"I . . . I was born with the ability to heal myself . . . immediately." Jake blurted out staring into his father eyes, waiting for his reaction.

"Really?" Arron finally said as the questions and possibilities ran through his mind at dizzying speeds.

Heather paled as her son revealed the truth. She watched Arron like a hawk to see how this shocking news would affect him. She was ready to jump in to defend her child if need be.

She was surprised, when most people would have freaked out and demanded an explanation or proof . . . something, Arron remained calm. He seemed to understand what Jake was talking about, even asking if he had any other abilities. When Jake shook his head Arron preceded to ask as he showed his left inside wrist.

"Do you have a mark like this—only different on your left wrist" Arron held his breath as he waited for Jake's answer.

"Oh my god! What the hell happened?" Heather's shrill voice reminded Arron that she was still in the room and he winced as she continued to demand, gasping in horror when she saw the way Arron's skin was disfigured by a piece of sparkling glass imbedded in his flesh, like some kind of weird tattoo. "Who did that to you and why would you think my son would mutilate himself like that?" Looking at it again before turning away in disgust, she didn't even know what the symbol meant, it was one she had never seen before—a plus sign with a solid circle in the middle of it.

Ignoring her and a little embarrassed Arron turned his wrist over hiding that mark of a Guardian from her gaze as he waited, watching Jake.

"No," Jake replied, shaking his head. Not wanting to meet Arron's gaze he stared at the floor as he added, "I'm not a Guardian, just half-Starian."

"Guardian? Starian? What are you guys talking about?" Heather demanded glancing from one to the other.

Arron sighed heavily, he wanted to reassure Jake. Let him know that it didn't matter to him if his son was a Guardian of not. Arron wanted to tell Jake . . . so much. But first he had to explain to Heather, make them both understand who he was and where he came from.

"I'll explain everything," Arron finally said, "It may take some time so why don't we all just sit?"

*

"I guess everybody's pretty mad at me huh?" Nate's voice seemed loud in the quiet room. He stood by the windows watching as his father leaned against the pocket doors he had just shut. Nate's gaze then swung to his mother, who sat on the sofa as she answered his question.

"Yes, Nature, at first we were too worried to be angry but now that you're okay . . ." She trailed off and took a heavy breath before demanding. "What were you thinking? And how did you even get here?"

"Mom, stop treating me like a child! I'M SIXTEEN!" Nate yelled.

"And you are still my child." Kittana countered matching her volume and tone with her sons.

Nate sighed this argument was getting old, he thought in frustration. "I'm the same age as you were when you decided to go to Taysia and when you had me."

"We are not talking about us, we are talking about you." Reace calmly pointed out.

Nate sat in the chair closest to him, deflated.

"Yeah, me," he huffed and rolled his eyes. At this moment he wished he were anyone else, he hated being him. "If I were Zarrick you'd all be thrilled that he was an adult, responsible for his own actions, you would never have left the balance at risk to go find him like some child. You'd trust his ability to handle things." Nature looked at his parents and asked, "Why can't you trust me?"

"It's not that we don't trust your capabilities but you don't know the things that can happen to you here, Nate, terrible things." Kittana was unprepared for the on-slot of memories that bombarded her, clouding her mind as she tried to reason with her son.

"I know more about earth, about Springfield, than you think. Besides Jake is helping me fit in and I have my powers if anything bad happens. Mom, I'll be okay." Nate pressed.

"Jake knows about you?" Reace stated more than questioned.

"Nate! How could you tell someone about your powers? You don't even know him," Kittana insisted even though Jake was Arron's son. Arron and Heather's, she reminded herself, and if memory served Heather wasn't exactly someone she could trust.

Nate squirmed in his chair as he admitted, "I didn't exactly tell him, I . . . I showed him . . . it was an accident."

"ACCIDENT?!" Kittana and Reace shouted in alarm.

"What kind of accident?" Reace demanded.

Nate glanced sheepishly at them before returning his gaze to the floor, his cheeks reddened as he confessed, "well, I, ah, drank some vodka . . . by accident." he hastily added, "I thought it was water."

"Alcohol?" Reace responded in disbelief.

Nate leveled his gaze at his father, "yup," he answered, than his look changed becoming more quizzical as he asked, "why didn't you ever say it hurt?"

Reace frowned in memory, and shrugged his shoulders as he replied, "I never said it was a walk in the park. Why did you think I avoided it?"

"Because it made your powers crazy," Nate answered.

"Yeah that, and it hurt like hell." Reace added.

Kittana glared at Reace with a look that clearly said to watch his language before she turned to her son and spoke.

"This wasn't in a public place, I hope?" Kittana's worried voice brought Nate's attention back to her.

"No," Nate told her. "It happened in the shelter."

"Thank God!" Reace sighed in relief. They really had to explain to Nate about the dangers of showing his powers in public. The boy had no idea what people were capable of, Reace thought with a mixture of pride and dread. He was glad that his son had grown up with everything that he never had—love, affection, acceptance and understanding. But now they had to show him the other side of life and Reace wasn't looking forward to it.

*"Kit,"* Reace said in his head knowing that his telepathic wife would hear him.

Kittana nodded, *"I know,"* she telepathed back to him reading his thoughts, *"You're right, he needs to be shown."*

She sighed, this wouldn't be easy, but Nature needed to understand where they were coming from. He needed to know that not everyone was tolerant and accepting here. She stood coming closer to Nate, about to touch him and use her powers of the mind to take him through her experiences with the government, show him how Kade, his grandfather was hunted down and forced to give up his life because he was different. She was prepared to show Nate her past and Reace's when the clock on the mantle chimed the hour reminding her that this would have to wait.

"It's four o'clock." she stated "We have to go."

Reace frowned in confusion, "Go? Go where? What about showing Nature?"

"Showing me what?" Nate asked not liking the sound of that.

"That will have to wait until later, right now we to go; we're having a family dinner with my foster parents, and their daughter."

Reace rolled his eyes and groaned as his son's voice echoed his thoughts exactly.

"Aw! Do we have too?" Nate whined.

"Yes, we have too . . . both of you," Kittana told them in a firm voice before turning to leave the room, with a flash of her mark and a wave of her hand the heavy oak doors slid silently opened, then to Reace she silently added *"It won't be that bad, you may even enjoy yourself."*

To which he thought back, *"It'll be real fun sitting and eating with people who hate me."*

In the doorway Kittana paused, she wanted to tell Reace that her parents didn't hate him but she had a suspicion that he'd not believe her so she figured she'd let him find out on his own. Sparing him a sideways glance she continued moving towards the front door.

# CHAPTER FIFTEEN

"KITTANA! HI, I'M SO GLAD you could make it and you brought your family." Nancy welcomed them, hugging Kittana after opening the door to their knock. Reluctantly she let go of her foster daughter, stepping backward so they could enter her home.

"Where is Keyla?" Nancy inquired, noticing her absence.

"Keyla decided not to come tonight, she was really tired and needed to have a nap, I hope that's okay," Kittana answered.

"Yes, of-course, I hope she'll be alright, not coming down with the flu or anything," Nancy asked genuine concern written on her face.

"I'm sure she'll be fine, the trip probably just tired her out," Kittana didn't mention that Keyla couldn't get the flu, as Guardians they never got sick, nor did she add that if they did get hurt Arron could heal. Instead Kittana started introducing her family to the woman who had become a second mother to her. "Ah, mom, this is Reace, my husband."

"Reace, I am glad to finally meet you. We've heard lots of great things about you," Nancy said with a radiant smile and a quick hug.

"Glad to see you're out of jail and I hear you've been cleared of all charges, that must make you happy." David spoke, coming up behind his wife in the foray and glaring at Reace, totally ignoring Nancy's disapproving frown.

"Ah, yes sir," Reace answered in a clipped voice. He watched as David ignored him to hug Kittana.

"Being arrested this afternoon must have been horrible for you we are relieved that you're out and were able to clear your name, now that's all behind you." Nancy tried to smooth over David's harsh tone.

"Jail? You were arrested?" Nate turned inquisitive eyes on his father.

"Mom, dad, this is Nate, our son." Kittana said forcing the conversation away from Reace and focusing it on her son, Nature.

Nate inwardly sighed with relief and sent his mother a silent thank-you for using his nickname instead of his full name—Nature. He'd learnt enough about this planet to know that Nature was a weird name. Nate smiled at Nancy and David, saying a quick "Hi," before Nancy engulfed him in a hug, her eyes shining with love and unshed tears.

Moving to look into Nate's face but keeping her hands on his shoulders Nancy made eye contact as she spoke to him, "Nate, we would be honored if you'd think of us as your grandparents, you could even call us granny and gramps if you like. After all, your mother is a daughter to us and that makes you part of our family."

Nate nodded unsure of what to say, he just returned Nancy's warm gaze.

"We have someone for you to meet," Nancy told Nature. "She's about your age, I hope you two will get along," Nancy added before letting him go and turning to lead the way into the living room.

Following behind her and his mother, Nate looked around at his surroundings as he walked beside his father with David bringing up the rear.

The group walked into the living room and sat. Nate was busy looking around, this place was beautiful and so homey feeling that he started to relax. Glancing at his father who sat beside him on the sofa, Nate wondered if he was ever going to tell him about being in jail.

Reace sat so still, tense and quiet—so unlike the dad he knew. Caught up in curiosity, he watched his father, studying him so intently that he failed to notice a new person entered the room. It wasn't until Reace elbowed him that Nate realized that someone was even talking to him.

"Nate, Kittana and Reace, I'd like you to meet my daughter, Anna-Maria." Nancy graciously introduced her to everyone when she came into the room.

"Kittana?" Anna's gaze flashed to her mother's for confirmation.

Nancy nodded with a beaming smile.

Anna's eyes were angry as they accosted Kittana's.

"Your alive?" She half questioned-half accused before her gaze moved to Reace and hardened. "You're out of jail. You got off Scott free after everything you've put our family, the Prices' and your father through!"

"Anna-Maria!" Nancy exclaimed in outrage at how her daughter was acting.

"I'm not sorry, mom, I can't hide my feelings and they need to know how their careless actions effected others, nice innocent people got hurt because of them; people that didn't deserve that kind of PAIN!" Anna finished with a shout.

Before anyone could respond, Nate jumped up coming face to face with Anna—the girl he's made a fool of himself in front of earlier at school, but at this moment he didn't care who she was—she had just insulted his parents and he couldn't just sit there and take it . . . he wouldn't! He had to say something in their defense. It was obvious that his parents weren't going to defend themselves. "Not everyone is as innocent as you think. My fath . . ."

"Nate!" Reace growled in a voice that held a note of warning.

Nature immediately shut his mouth but his eyes glared back at Anna's. He was tired of people thinking the worst of his dad. He wanted to tell everyone the truth—that Reace was innocent, he wanted to tell Anna that his parents were hero's, their actions before he was born were not careless, they weren't being selfish when they left Earth. His parents and Arron and Keyla, they saved . . .

Nate sighed. It didn't matter because he wasn't allowed to tell anyone, the injustice of it all made him angry, apparently it made his dad angry too because in the silence that followed his outburst, everyone heard the rumble of thunder that boomed overhead. Nate smirked, just knowing that his father was angry at the unfairness of it too, somehow, in some twisted way, satisfied him and he sat back on the sofa.

Kittana cocked her head at Reace, silently asking him if that thunder was from him, she frowned when he shook his head and both of them glanced at Nate briefly before turning their attention back to the young women standing before them.

Kittana wished that Tia were here, she could use some insight into Anna's emotions and perhaps help from the Guardian of Emotions to melt away some of that anger but Tia wasn't here. She was on her own and in front of her parents the only powers she could use on the girl were words. Inwardly sighing, Kittana cleared her throat and began.

"Anna, I can understand that you're upset, perhaps we were careless when we left but please believe we had a valid reason for leaving . . . I can't tell you what it was—that's private. However, I can tell you we never meant to hurt any innocent people." Glancing at Reace and Nate before turning back to Anna, she continued. "We are sorry for any pain we caused," She turned her gaze to her parents and repeated, "really sorry."

Nancy nodded tears in her eyes matching those in Kittana's.

"We are just happy that you're here now, alive and well," David told Kittana, his eyes warm with love, a love that he extended to her son, Nate, but when David's eyes fell on Reace, they turned cold.

"Well, dinner is ready. Why don't we all move into the dining area and eat." Nancy announced, jumping up, glad to have dinner as an excuse to compose herself.

*

Dinner was an awkward affair for everyone except Nancy and Kittana, the two of them were happy to be together, chatting about everything.

Reace had warmed up to Nancy quickly, she was so full of genuine love for everyone, it was easy to see why Kittana loved her and how hard it must have been for his wife to leave them behind seventeen years ago when they had to go to Taysia to balance the forces of good and evil, saving the planet of Vanishtar and others from suffering the same fate as Staria.

Reace's thoughts turned to David as his gaze fell on him. David had glared at Reace all through the meal making him feel like he was on trial, being judged to see if he was good enough for his daughter. Reace had to admit that he admired the man, Kittana wasn't even his real child yet he loved her and wanted to protect her that was something Reace respected and if their places were reversed he knew that he'd feel the same way.

They treated Nate nicely and it was obvious that Nancy and David's love extended to Kittana's child, if not her husband, and Reace appreciated that. His gaze fell to the person seated across from his son at the table, Anna-Maria.

Was she the reason Kittana asked Arron to heal Nancy before they went to Taysia? Had Kittana wanted to give Nancy the gift of another child? Anna had been quiet during the whole meal. Reace noticed her eyes didn't reflect as much hostility as before and her face had softened a bit.

He could tell she was thinking, mauling over what Kittana and Nature had said earlier, Reace's eyes narrowed wondering what she had decided when she suddenly smiled at Nate and suggested getting away from the "stuffy adults" after dinner.

\*

"And this was Kittana's room," Anna announced, ending the tour of the house when she and Nate entered her foster sister's old bedroom.

Nate glanced around, curious to see where his mother had spent her teen years. He was surprised by the way the room looked—like his mother had been gone ten minutes not seventeen years.

As if reading his thoughts Anna explained, "It's exactly the way Kittana left it—mom didn't have the heart to change anything and I guess she was right in her belief that Kittana would one day come back." Anna smiled slightly in memory as she continued talking. "When I was younger, I used to spend hours in here, I guess I wanted to get to know her, I even read all of her father's diaries . . . what I could make out anyway—they were pretty screwed up. I guess that's why she ended up in foster care . . ." Anna's voice trailed off and she blushed in embarrassment at what she'd just said out loud. She looked at Nate, "oh! I'm sorry, I . . ."

"That's okay," Nate told her, holding up a hand. To himself he added, *you don't know the truth and you don't understand.*

Part of him wanted to tell her everything, make her understand but he knew if he did his parents would never let him stay here. Hell, they were already mad enough with him for letting Jake know which made no sense to Nate at all. Jake was Arron's son and Starian. Raising his eyes to hers, Nate changed the subject.

"Kade's journals?" he asked, "Are they still here? Can I see them?"

"Yeah, there's a whole box in here," Anna turned going into the closet and coming out again holding a storage box, "with everything that Kittana had from her old life—her life before she came here."

Putting the box on the floor, she and Nate sat on either side of it. Nate lifted the dusty cover on the expensive cardboard box and set it aside, glancing in the box a rush of excitement filled him; these things belonged to his grandfather. With reverence he reached in and pulled out a leather jacket, after inspecting it he placed it on the floor, smiling at Anna, he peered into the box again.

"Aren't you even going to try it on? It looks like it'd fit you."

Anna's words halted him.

Smiling encouragingly she added, "I think it'll look good on you."

Nate shrugged but picked up the jacket and put it on. As the jacket settled on his shoulders, a sense of warmth spread through him like an invisible hug, closing his eyes he sighed.

With his eyes closed Anna took the opportunity to appraise him. He was tall, with the body of an athlete. The tan color of his skin went well with his inky black hair giving him an exotic look and when he opened his eyes, she lost her breath. His eyes were the most amazing shade of green, fringed with thick black eyelashes.

Nate stared at Anna wondering why she was looking at him with such a strange expression on her face,

"You have the nicest eyes, they're so green, are they contacts?" Anna spoke her voice husky and breathless sounding.

"N . . . no, they're my eyes," Nate answered frowning in confusion he didn't understand what she was talking about, what were contacts? Hiding his embarrassment, Nate looked down turning his attention on what else the box held.

Inside a nylon backpack they found twelve books, 11 handwritten journals and one homemade fairytale book. Nature pulled them out and flipped through them, reading some parts out loud in his enthusiasm.

As Anna listened to Nate's voice reading passages from the journals out loud she became aware that maybe the weird writing in the books was another language—not just mumbo-jumbo. Nate was fluently reading, translating so easily that he hardly stumbled or paused. Hearing him she could almost believe the things he was saying as if it were all somehow . . . real—not just the crazed writings of some delusional guy.

"How do you know all this?" She questioned, interrupting him. "I mean, how can you read that?" She gestured toward the book in Nate's hands, the one he was reading from she knew had no English parts, just page after page of beautiful but meaningless symbols.

"It's written in Starian, the language of Staria, the language of my grandfather." Nate answered before he realized he shouldn't have.

"Staria?" Anna repeated she had read that word hundreds of times in the journals, the English parts, but she had never heard it spoken out loud before, it sounded beautiful coming from Nate, spoken with a soft accent that made her knees weaken, she was glad that she was already sitting down. Wanting to hear the language and the accent together she asked, "Can you read it in Starian?"

Nate stared at her for a second not sure what to do. Jake was always telling him not to say too much and he didn't want to make a fool of himself. She already had enough to laugh at after the fool he'd made of himself twice already today, once at school and again downstairs, a mistake he didn't want to repeat.

"Please Nate."

Hearing her speak his name was Nature's undoing, chewing his bottom lip nervously he nodded looking down at the open page of the book he held. He began to read in Starian, stumbling over the words finding them harder to get out then before, he was nervous wanting to impress her.

Anna was only half listening to him, fascinated by the sound of his voice and the way his lips moved over his words. She loved the way his eyes lit up whenever he said the word, "Taysia" she wondered what the word meant and was about to ask him when his mother's voice interrupted them.

"Nate!" Kittana called from the bottom of the stairs to her son, "Come on, it's time to go."

"Do you mind if I borrow these?" Nate asked Anna as he carefully placed the journals back into the nylon backpack.

"Yeah, sure, they belong to your mother anyway." Anna shrugged.

"Great! Thanks," Nate smiled at her as he stood up and hoisted the heavy bag onto his shoulder.

"Ah, Nate . . ." Anna said reluctant to let him go just yet. "You may not know, being new to the school and all, but there is a dance this Thursday, ah, tomorrow night, at the school. And I was wondering, um . . . unless you already have a date, of-course, if you'd like to go with me?" She sighed in relief at getting the words out, now she waited with hopeful eyes for Nate's answer.

Nate gapped at her for a second in surprise he had thought she didn't like him that she was only being nice to him to please her parents, yet here she was asking to spend more time with him.

"Ah, sure, yeah . . . I'd like that very much," he nodded, a slow smile turning his lips. They looked at each other in happy silence until Nate's expression changed when he heard his mother's voice in his head, *"Nate, come on we have to go! Arron's parents are coming home and we promised to be there for support."*

"I have to go, mom's waiting."

"Yeah, I'm really glad you came over, Nate. I'll see you tomorrow at school." She said watching him leave before turning to put the box away.

When she was younger and had read the journals she thought that Kade, Kittana's real father, had been crazy, the journals or the parts she could understand anyway read like something out of a science-fiction novel—describing fantastical worlds, made up fairytales and legends. But now, after meeting Nate and hearing him speak the language with a soft, sexy accent—she wasn't so sure anymore.

\*

As Nate descended the steps, Kittana gasped, half hidden in shadow, wearing his grandfather's jacket and carrying the backpack, Nate looked like Kade and the sight brought tears to her eyes.

Nate stepped off the steps into the well lit foray.

"Are you okay, mom?" He demanded in alarm when he saw the sheen of tears in her eyes.

His words brought everyone's attention to Kittana.

"Yes, it's just . . ." She trialed off then reached out a hand to touched the jacket Nate wore, she swallowed before trying again, "This is . . . was my father's jacket," She looked at Nate, the pained expression she wore on her face softened the instant she looked into her son's eyes. "You remind me of him. It looks good on you, Nate."

Kittana patted his shoulder before turning away to say good-bye to her foster parents.

Once outside, Nate spoke, "When I first put it on, it felt like a hug, warm and peaceful." Nate smiled in memory of the feeling. "I forgot I had it on or I would have taken it off . . . I'm sorry."

"Don't be sorry, Nature, it's yours now, a jacket like this is meant to be worn—not wasting away in some box." Kittana told him then inquired. "Did you get the journals too? I'd like to reread them."

Nate nodded hitching the book bag higher on his shoulder as the three of them walked back towards Arron's house.

# CHAPTER SIXTEEN

JUST AS THEY WALKED THROUGH the front door of the Price's home, Reace experienced a tightening around his heart and a weird feeling in the pit of his stomach, but he pushed it aside and focused his attention on his wife when Nate spoke.

"Mom, are you okay?" Concern and worry etched into his young face and carried through in his voice. Nature had noticed his mother's frown and heard her gasp of pain seconds before she stopped mid-stride and placed her hand over her heart as if in pain.

"Kit?!" Reace rushed forward, putting his arms around her, helping her to stand.

Kittana gave a nervous chuckle, patted Reace's hand nodding as she said, "I'm okay, I don't know what that was . . . maybe heartburn?" She guessed as the pain slowly eased and her stomach settled down.

Reace didn't think it was that easy to explain but before he could suggest anything a blood curdling scream was heard.

"Keyla!" Kittana's heart stopped for a second and her eyes rounded in alarm, her only thought; only instinct was to get to her sister as fast as she could. Grabbing Reace's arm she teleported them both into the room Keyla was staying in, leaving Nate to come up with some excuse in case they were seen.

Luckily they weren't seen by anyone other than Arron. He and Nate exchanged glances before sprinting for the stairs.

\*

"Keyla! What's wrong? What happened?" Kittana demanded seconds later as she and Reace appeared in front of her bed.

Keyla didn't say anything she just opened her arms and wrapped them tightly around her twin as Kittana rushed forward, climbing on the bed to sit beside her sister.

"Key! Answer us, are you alright?" Reace insisted just as they heard feet thumping up the stairs seconds before Arron and Nate burst into the room followed by Heather, Jake and Mrs. White.

"What happened?"

"What's wrong?"

"Keyla, are you okay?"

A chorus of voices said.

Keyla's eyes widened at the concern on everyone's faces and her cheeks reddened in embarrassment at having brought the whole household running, "I . . . it was just a dream." She began, looking from face to face, "I'm sorry to scare everyone . . . it was really just . . . just a dream."

"Just a dream, humph, more like a nightmare!" Mrs. White said, "Why child, you're as white as the sheet and still shaking! I'll go make you some nice hot chocolate, that'll calm you down and make you feel better." Mrs. White exited the room, making her way toward the kitchen muttering "poor child" as she went.

Jake and Heather followed the old housekeeper, relieved that their guest was all right—nothing more than a bad dream.

Heather decided it would be better if she left it up to Keyla's family to chase away her fears besides she didn't think Keyla or Kittana wanted her there anyway, not after the way she had treated them in the past, she wondered if perhaps, someday, they'd forgive her and see that she really had changed.

After making sure Keyla was alright Nate had followed Jake into the kitchen—the promise of hot chocolate and someone his own age to talk to was too tempting to ignore.

"Okay, that was more than just a bad dream." Kittana stated when it was just the four of them.

"Way more," Keyla breathed as she eased back out of Kittana's embrace.

"Tell us about it," Arron encouraged, as he sat on the bed beside Keyla, he put his arm around her shoulders as Kittana withdrew hers. "Was it a premonition?"

"Oh, God, I hope not, it was horrible. I felt . . . it was . . ." Keyla gave a shudder and took a deep breath trying again to put her dream—her nightmare—into words. "We were on our way back . . . we had gotten to Taysia, and there was this really thick fog, the kind you can't see through . . . I called and called for you, for anyone," she looked at her friends. "I couldn't see or hear anybody then I tripped."

Keyla remembered being on her hands and knees, she could still feel the moistness of the cool damp ground beneath her fingertips. In her dream she had looked down to see what she had tripped over. She closed her eyes tightly, she didn't want to recall the sight or the feel of the ice cold body, the lifeless eyes that stared upward, unseeing, but the scene was still vivid in her mind. She took a few calming breaths and opened her eyes. She had to finish telling them.

"I . . . I tripped over you," Keyla looked into Arron's concerned eyes she sighed with relief that they were warm with life. Holding his gaze steady, drawing strength from him, she continued, "You were dead." Her gaze flickered over Reace and Kittana, "All of you, the fog was gone then and when I looked around—all I could see everywhere were Guardians dead. All of them gone. Except me, I was the only one left and it was my turn. I felt it, my heart hurt. I . . . I was dying." Keyla clung to Arron as the feeling in her dream came rushing back to engulf her again.

"Shhh," Arron whispered in her ear as his hand stroked her hair and continued down her back, "It was just a dream."

"No!" Keyla shook her head, "It was more than just a dream. It felt so real. I . . . I heard laughter, it was as bone chilling as the voice," she paused. "It said 'everyone was dead, that it had finally won and now it was my turn.' That's when I felt it . . . death was coming for me."

"I won't let that happen," Arron's arms tightened around her, the thought of life without Keyla was something he didn't want to experience. "I promise."

Keyla lifted her head, turning in his arms to look at him in disbelief, "You were dead. How can you help me, protect me if you're already dead?"

"Was the voice, the laughter, was it like last time?" Reace asked referring to the dreams they had when they were last on Earth. "Was it from Malic?"

"Who else could it have been?" Kittana countered.

Arron agreed before they all turned confusing eyes on Keyla who was shaking her head, "No, it wasn't Malic . . . at least I don't think so. It couldn't have been because I saw his body . . . he was dead too."

"So, if it wasn't Malic, than who was it?" Kittana's voice demanded after a few moments of stunned silence.

"I don't know . . . I just don't know," Keyla raised scared eyes to Reace.

Reace remembered the feeling he had earlier, just before Keyla screamed and as a possibility stuck him, he asked. "Key, can you describe the feeling you had when . . . death was coming for you?"

"Reace!" Kittana began but Reace cut her off.

"It's important." He insisted, never breaking eye contact with Keyla. As much as he hated making her re-live it, he had to know.

"Okay," Keyla said slowly. "It felt like someone was squeezing my heart . . . and I had this feeling in my stomach . . ."

"Like you'd been too many times on a rollercoaster?" Arron asked.

They all stared at him for a few seconds until Reace stated. "You felt it too."

"Yeah, a few minutes before Key screamed. You?" Arron asked.

Keyla saw the look that passed between Reace and Kittana, "What?" She demanded, narrowing her eyes in suspicion at them. "I know what that look means. What's going on?"

Reace and Kittana exchanged glances again before Kittana sighed and confided. "We felt it too, at first I thought that I was channeling your experiences and passing them on to Reace, but now that Arron felt it too. I . . . we wonder . . . if maybe it has something to do with Taysia and the balance. I mean we are the balancing forces, right so, if something were to tip the balance we'd feel it. Nate was with us and he didn't feel anything." Kittana continued, "Just us four."

Reace nodded, it was what he was thinking.

"That makes sense but what . . . what could have tipped the scales?" Keyla asked, wondering what could happen that Link, Awkwade, Tia and Zarrick couldn't handle.

"I think we need to go back and soon." Reace said.

"Count me in, the sooner the better!" Arron agreed worried that Zarrick or Tia was hurt or worse.

"Wait! We can't go rushing back we can't leave everyone like we did last time." Kittana said, her emotions coloring her words. "It would crush David and Nancy, besides, what about Arron's son? We don't even know if he's a Guardian and . . ." she turned to Arron with a pleading look in her eyes, "Don't you want to spend a little time getting to know him? This could be our only chance. We may never see them again."

"Kit's right," Keyla stated then turned to Arron and continued, "Arron your parents are coming to see you, they haven't seen you in seventeen years. They thought you were dead. You have to talk to them and your son, Jake, he so desperately wants to know you; you can see it in his eyes." She moved her head to take in Reace and her twin before she added, "And Nate, he's not ready to go, then there is my dream . . . nightmare, warning—whatever you want to call it—we need to find out what it means. We need to be prepared. We need more time." Keyla finished, no one spoke for a few minutes, as they thought about what she said and the truth in her words.

"Alright, we'll stay for another day." Arron compromised.

"So, early Friday, just before dawn, we go back." Reace suggested and everyone nodded in agreement.

"Jake's not, by the way," Arron suddenly turned to Kittana and said.

"Not what?" she asked confused.

"Guardian . . . Jake's not a Guardian." Arron clarified.

"How do you know that?" Keyla asked.

Arron was about to answer when the doorbell sounded throughout the house shifting his focus away from her question to a new problem at hand.

"Great, my parents have just arrived." Arron groaned.

"Hey man, it's been a long time maybe they've changed?" Reace offered.

"Stranger things have happened." Arron mumbled.

Keyla patted his shoulder saying as he got up, "It may not be that bad, we'll be down in a few minutes to give you support."

"You mean you'll be in the kitchen drinking hot chocolate." Arron read the between the lines and found her true meaning.

Keyla grinned at him before retorting, "But, I'll be thinking of you the entire time."

Arron shook his head, grinning at her before he headed out the door. He wasn't ready to face his parents. He didn't think he'd ever be ready. Time had just run out.

Arron frowned as he walked down the steps, his feet like lead. He wondered if prisoners who were giving the death sentence felt the same way. Screwing up his courage as he rounded the corner, time to face the firing squad, he thought as he walked into the living room. Head held high he greeted the parents he hadn't seen in seventeen years.

\*

## Taysia:

Tia watched Arron and Keyla, it was Zarrick's idea to use the giant crystal in Malic's chamber to send a message to the four Guardians on Earth. She thought it was a great idea, at first, but now seeing them together, seeing Arron's concern for Keyla—the way he comforted her and the way she responded to him; like two halves of some whole—Tia knew what she had to do, a silent tear slipped down her face.

Zarrick, who stood at Tia's side, watched the tears well up in her eyes. He was frustrated, angry at himself for being a fool. He wanted to speak to her, to warn his mother about what was happening but he couldn't do anything more then watch—a silent prisoner inside his own body.

*"It's too easy!"* The words floated in Zarrick's mind as Malic's laughter echoed inside his head.

# CHAPTER SEVENTEEN

Earth:

"ARRON? IS THAT REALLY YOU?" Came a voice Arron hadn't heard in years; the voice of his mother.

His head jerked in her direction, as he came fully into the living room where his parents waited, with Heather, for him.

"Yeah, mom, it's me." Arron said, stopping a few feet away from her. He wanted to hug her but their relationship had never been a "hands on" one, instead he just stood there, watching her.

"Wh . . . where have you been? We thought you had died . . . committed suicide. How? Why would you make us believe that when you're alive? All these years not a call or a postcard to tell us . . . nothing." She looked hurt, crumpled.

Guilt overwhelmed Arron. He didn't know how to answer her he didn't know what to say. What could he say that she'd believe anyway? He couldn't tell the truth.

"Suicide?" Heather frowned, turning confused eyes to Margaret she demanded. "You told me he was missing. Reace was suspected of murdering him! So how, where does suicide come in?"

Arron smirked turning his attention to Heather. This was a question he knew how to answer. "I left a suicide note before I left. I knew it would be something they'd," he gestured to his parents, "be too embarrassed to dig into and it seems I was right." Arron returned his gaze to his mothers' as he put a question to her, "You didn't tell anyone about the note, did you?"

Heather reeled when Margaret gave a small nod, confirming what Arron had said. How could these people; people she had always thought of as nice, let an innocent man to go jail rather than tell people know their son commented suicide? And she had defended these people to Arron. She shook her head. He had been right all along.

"I'll tell you why he's never called, Marge." Arron's father's voice boomed. His eyes coolly stared at Arron as he sneered, "It's because he's a selfish bastard, always was!"

Arron just stared back at him in disbelief, this was the first time in years that he's seen his parents and this was the warm welcome that waited for him? Arron shook his head, even knowing the truth didn't stop the pain of neglect from entering his heart. Swallowing the pain he spoke.

"You want to know why I left?" His voice deceptively quiet, "It was because of this! I have been gone for years and this is the warm reunion I get? Thanks." he paused, shifting his feet like he was ready to turn and leave but changed his mind, running his hands through his hair, he told them. "I know . . . I know you've never loved me and I can even understand why. At least I thought I did." He looked at his mother with compassion, "I know that you were raped by Yentar, my biological father."

Heather gasped and both Howard and Margaret fell silent as they stared at Arron with wide eyes wondering how he could possibly know that? They had never told anyone.

Finally, Margaret regained her voice enough to demand. "How . . . how could you know that?"

Arron threw himself into a chair his long legs sprawled out in front of him, his palms digging into his eyes as if he could erase the images burned into his mind. "Never mind, it doesn't matter now anyway." He muttered than added, "I didn't come back for this."

"Why did you come back, after all this time?" Howard questioned, "Is it for money? Do you expect us to pay you to keep quiet? We won't be blackmailed!" He paled as a thought occurred to him and his face hardened even more as he glared at Arron, "Is it to take Jake away? We'll fight you on that, Heather has been a good mother and we will back her one hundred percent."

Arron groaned in frustration, pulling his hands away from his face as he turned his attention to Heather wanting to reassure her.

"No, I don't want to take Jake away from the people he loves, his mother and . . ." Arron trailed off, turning accusing eyes to his parents.

"I just want to know why? Why couldn't you love me, wasn't I good enough? God, damn it! Jake looks exactly like me and you love him so why not me?" Arron finished in a whisper. His eyes shining with tears he refused to shed, as he asked the question he had sworn never to ask.

"It's never been your fault, Arron, you were a good boy and a good son, but . . . it was just . . ." Margaret began but she couldn't continue that night was still too painful to think about. It was hard to even look at Arron and not remember—after all he was a constant reminder of that night, that horrible night he was conceived and the monster who conceived him.

"I know, I know, damn it! I was there,"

Margaret and Howard raised their eyes to him. How could he have been there? Their expressions demanded an explanation.

"Well, not there exactly, but Malic . . ." Arron paused unable or unwilling to explain. Looking at his mother, at the fear in her eyes compelled him to say. "I saw it mom, I saw what Yentar did to you. But that wasn't me! Why did you blame me for it?"

"We never set out to blame you . . ." Arron's mother bravely continued, "It was hard to hold you. To look at you, even as an innocent baby because every time I look at you I am reminded of that night . . . that creature! And what he did to me . . . I . . ." She broke down then and cried.

Howard moved to stand behind her, comforting her as he glared at Arron.

"Look what you did! You've made your mother cry. Are you happy now? I always knew you'd turn out to be like him! What kind of a sick person are you, getting your jollies out of someone else's pain?" Howard snapped at Arron and would have said more, but Margaret laid a hand on his arm stopping him without words.

Sniffing a few times and taking strength in her husband's comforting presence Margaret continued, "Yes, we have made some mistakes. We aren't perfect, but we gave you life and we gave you everything you have ever wanted," She paused to wipe her eyes and blow her nose on the tissue that Heather provided for her. "After we received your suicide note . . . and then we found out Heather was pregnant we thought maybe God had forgiven us and let us make a new start. We love Jake like we should have loved you and we won't let you take him away from us."

"You had wanted for nothing, your whole life. We had given you everything you have ever asked for and this is how our kindness is repaid by faking your own death? WHAT KIND OF MONSTER ARE YOU?" Howard's voice rose in volume as he gave his anger free range, "THEN YOU COME IN HERE, YEARS LATER THINKING NOTHING HAS CHANGED AND THAT WE'LL STILL HAND YOU WHATEVER YOU WANT, EXPECTING MONEY AND EVERYTHING ELSE TO BE HANDED TO YOU ON A SILVER PLATTER! DEMANDING TO SPEND TIME WITH YOUR SON—A BABY YOU ABANDONED . . ."

"I DIDN'T EVEN KNOW ABOUT HIM!" Arron's voice matched Howard's in force and volume as his frustration, hurt and guilt turned to anger. Howard didn't hear he just continued shouting at Arron. As he moved away from his wife, Arron stood facing Howard.

"YOU'D HAVE KNOWN IF YOU BOTHERED TO THINK ABOUT ANYONE BUT YOURSELF AND PICKED UP THE GOD DAMN PHONE YEARS AGO . . ."

Howard didn't see it coming; Arron's fist just flew into his face knocking the older man backward. Howard fell with a loud crash as his body collided with the coffee table that broke under his weight, carrying him to the floor.

Arron towered above him waiting for him to get up. Arron wanted Howard to get up and hit him back; he wanted another reason to hit the man. He wanted a fight.

Part of Arron was surprised by that, he'd never gotten angry enough to hit someone before, not without help anyway, he amended thinking back to the time when Malic had played with his emotions in high-school. Another part, a larger part of him, was telling him how good it felt to release some of his pent up anger—anger he wasn't even aware he held. It was this side Arron was listening to now, the side that whispered how nice to would feel to punch out his frustrations.

Everyone came running in after they heard the commotion. They all paused in surprise for a moment in the doorway at what they saw. It appeared that Arron had hit his father and it looked like he was willing to do it again.

Reace pushed his way through the crowded doorway and rushed to stand in front of Arron, giving him a little shove backward when Arron tried to step around Reace as Howard got to his feet with the help of Nate and Jake. Looking into Arron's face, Reace demanded, "What the hell is the matter with you?"

Arron wasn't looking at Reace, he's eyes were focused on Howard, as he struggled to get up.

"HOW COULD YOU?" Arron shouted at Howard, "HOW COULD YOU LOVE HIM AND HATE ME? I'M YOUR SON! I AM NOT THE BAD GUY HERE."

Reace held Arron back as he strained to get closer to his father. Finally Arron noticed Nate and Jake were in the room helping Howard to his feet and he stopped struggling with Reace. A crushed look crossed his face and Arron repeated in a softer voice, "I'm not the bad guy here."

Arron shrugged out of Reace's hold and spun away from him, going into another room. Reace and Keyla followed him, closing the door behind them.

Reace glanced at Keyla as she came to stand beside him. With one eyebrow raised his face asked her a silent question.

Keyla shook her head after studying Arron's aura. "He's not under any spell and as far as I can tell these are his own emotions." She answered concern for Arron showed on her face as she turned toward him.

Reace frowned and returned his attention to his friend, who was pacing the width of the room.

"If one more person calls me a rotten father, I swear . . ." Arron let the threat drop off not quite sure what he'd do.

"No one said you were a rotten father." Keyla told Arron hoping it was the truth.

Arron stopped mid-stride, twisted his body as he gestured wildly toward the other room and yelled. "THEY IMPLIED IT!"

"All right, what the hell's going on with you?" Reace was starting to get worried, he'd never seen Arron so mad, so full of anger in his life and trying to figure out what happened to change him was starting to give Reace a headache. "You've been acting strange ever since we got here."

"Let's just say I've had a rough twenty-four hours . . ." Arron gave an angry laugh, "No! Scratch that, the last forty-eight hours have been pure hell!" He turned after he said that and stared at the wall, not sure if he could elaborate or not.

"Tell us about it? What happened?"

Keyla's soft voice washed over him, it had a wonderful effect of calming his overly stretched nerves. Arron wanted to ask her to keep talking but he knew it was his turn, they were waiting. Taking a deep breath, he gathered his courage and began to speak.

"It started yesterday when Zarrick told me off. He said I wasn't his father so I had no right to tell him what to do." Arron shook his head. "Then Tia confirmed it." He turned back to face them, his eyes connected with Reace's.

"Wait! Zarrick isn't your kid?" Reace asked confused and blown away at the same time.

"Yeah," Arron broke eye contact and turned his head away, "Turns out he is Malic's son." He spat the name out with a bitter twist of his mouth. "Zarrick's not my son, not by blood anyway, but worse, Reace, and he knows . . . Malic showed him."

*Wow! This was big.* Reace thought. If Malic knew and he was close enough to show Zarrick then Reace could understand Arron's worry, his concern. The son Arron had raised, the boy he had loved as his own was at a crossroads.

Reace's gaze returned to Arron as his thoughts continued, if Malic was talking to Zarrick, seeking him out then he had a plan, away to use him somehow . . . *shit!* Reace silently cursed. Malic had been quiet lately . . . too quiet. They should have suspected something was up. Suddenly, Friday morning couldn't come fast enough.

"Arron," Reace spoke his name and when Arron looked at him unspoken messages were passed before Reace said, "Zarrick won't go to Malic's side. He's a good kid."

"Yeah, I know." Arron sighed. *But Malic can be so persuasive*, he added in his mind. Reace didn't understand how persuasive Malic really could be but Arron knew . . . Malic had almost succeeded in turning him evil years ago. Thankfully, he had Reace, Keyla and Kittana to help him find his way back from the edge. Arron glanced at Reace then Keyla. He just hoped he'd be able to do the same for his son. He hoped they got back in time to help Zarrick find his path.

"Are you sure Zarrick's not yours?" Keyla asked.

"Yeah." Arron replied unable to meet her eyes, shaking his head as the weight of guilt settled on his shoulders. Arron put his hands up to hold his head, "but the thing is I knew that." He pointed to himself, "I knew from the first moment I saw Zarrick's eyes—the same golden yellow as Malic's."

Arron's face crumpled into a pained frown, his eyes focused on the floor a few feet in front of him as he fought for the words to his feelings, for a way to put the past two days into words. "I don't know why I didn't confront Tia years ago."

Arron started pacing again. "I guess I was waiting for her to trust me with the truth, maybe I just didn't want to know . . . I don't know." He was quiet for a few seconds before bursting out with, "But Tia never trusted me, how could she?" He asked but since no one quite understood what he was talking about, no one answered. Arron didn't really care, he just continued talking, "She didn't even trust me to have my own feelings." He stopped pacing then and looked at his friends. "She told me I really didn't love her, that I should be in love with someone else . . . my soul mate or whatever."

Reace glanced briefly at Keyla, who raised her eyebrows at the news.

"She confessed to using her powers to make me fall in love with her." Arron continued.

"Oh my God!" Keyla exclaimed, horrified that one of their own, a trusted friend, could turn on them like that, how could Tia use her powers on them? Why? How could she have Malic's child and pass it off as Arron's?

"I know it sounds horrible, but Key," Arron raised his head to catch her gaze, "she had her reasons." Arron stated he didn't want anyone thinking badly of Tia, she had been through enough already.

"She manipulated you, for how long?" Reace needed to know, trying to control his raising anger toward Tia. There was an agreement between the seven Guardians—they wouldn't use their powers against each other. Tia had broken that.

"In the beginning, when we first met and until Zarrick was born." Arron answered his cheeks red in embarrassment at how he was fooled.

"Zarrick!? You're sure he's Malic's?" Keyla asked again not quite certain how any women could want Malic over Arron.

"Yes," Arron hissed then added, "Tia told me she had an . . . an affair with him."

"An affair?" Reace echoed, wondering if Malic had forced her, what he was thinking must have shown on his face because Arron shook his head.

"Malic used emotion and mind on her but it wasn't forced, it wasn't rape." Arron covered his eyes with his hands trying to dig out the images of his wife with Malic that his mind created, "God! Every time I think of it, of that monster putting his hands on . . . I get . . ." He trailed off.

"Man, you've got to calm down." Reace warned.

"CALM DOWN?!" Arron stared at Reace like he'd grown horns, "What the HELL do you think I've been trying to do for the past two days? My wife had an AFFAIR! My kid is in trouble because he blames me for not being his father. Reace, Zarrick asked me if he was evil, EVIL! Do you realize that one day I may have to fight my own child, and you want me to calm down?" Arron exploded taking a step toward Reace who backed away.

"Your mark, it's glowing." Reace explained at the confused look on his comrade's face.

"What? You're worried I'll accidentally heal someone?" Arron shot back.

At Reace's look Arron remembered that he was not only the Guardian of Life but also of Death, he was the only Guardian that could kill with a touch. He glared at his mark for a few minutes, willing himself to calm down. The last thing he needed was to start accidentally killing off his friends.

"Why would it do that? I didn't summon it." When his mark stopped pulsating with a soft light that came from inside of him, he raised honest eyes to Reace imploring him to believe him.

"Our powers are tied into our emotions so when we feel strong emotions like anger, fear, hurt, love, they take over in defense." Keyla tried to explain.

Reace nodded agreeing with Keyla remembering the times in his life when his powers had taken on a life of their own.

"Wonderful!" Arron muttered sarcastically before turning his gaze to Reace, "How do you do it? How do you keep it all in and stay so calm, so in control?"

"Look, Arron," Reace began, "I think our situations are totally different, I mean, if Kit ever . . . Ah, let's just say I'd have probably fried Malic by now or at least died trying."

"I wanted too," he admitted. "I was on my way to Stone Mountain when I came across Zarrick," Arron paused, "We were just coming to an understanding . . . of sorts when you told us Nate was missing and then to come here and find Heather . . ."

"That was a shock to all of us." Keyla added.

"And I have a son with her, one that I abandoned. How could I do that? How could I abandon my own child?" Horror and self disgust sounded in his voice.

"You didn't abandon him, you didn't know." Keyla let in the voice of reason.

"But I should have known!" Arron argued, "I'm the Guardian of Life. I knew Tia was pregnant even before she did. I should have known."

"How could you have known? You hardly had your powers then." Reace said, but Arron wasn't listening.

"And today hearing that my parents love Jake more than me . . . it was just . . . it was just the last straw." Arron continued talking, "Don't get me wrong, I'm glad that they do accept Jake, he's a great kid but I'm their son. Christ!" Arron slowly shook his head. "It's just too much!"

"You weren't kidding when you said *the past forty-eight hours have been pure hell.*" Reace agreed.

"But?" Arron interrupted, he could feel it coming and he inwardly groaned.

"But," Reace repeated with a slight nod, "We still have to deal with this one thing at a time and right now you've got to go back in there," Reace pointed in the general direction of the living room, "and talk to your parents."

"Without hitting anyone." Keyla added.

"Yeah, I know," Arron ran a hand down his face, then added, "Any ideas of what to say?" he half joked.

"You could start with 'sorry,'" Keyla told him, "and go from there." She encourage with a smile.

"Hey, everything okay?" Heather asked as she poked her head in after a quick knock on the door. "Arron your parents have decided to spend the night in a hotel then go back to Rome tomorrow morning but I have talked them into waiting until you've had a chance to talk—to *apologize* to them before they leave. They are waiting in the library for you," She came fully into the room, prepared to let Arron know that his behavior was unacceptable, that hitting Howard was totally uncalled for, she was ready for a fight—if need be—to get him to apologize but she was surprised when he simply nodded in agreement with her.

"Thanks, Heather." Arron smiled at her before adding, "Could you tell them I'll be right there," Arron said his voice portraying a calm he didn't feel. *One thing at a time.* Reace's words came to him, he nodded. It was easier now that he had shared his emotional burden with his friends, his comrades.

"Sure," Heather said with a surprised expression before leaving the room.

Arron took a deep breath and followed behind her, pausing at the door to glance one more time at his friends, Reace and Keyla, "Thanks," he said.

Reace nodded.

"Anytime," Keyla told him, watching as Arron opened the door and went through it, she waited ten seconds before turning to Reace, the smile fading from her lips as she spoke, "What Arron just told us was big, huge big!"

"I know." Reace replied still looking at the door.

"Malic's going to turn him." Keyla stated.

"I know." Reace agreed.

"Maybe that's what the feeling was? If Zarrick joined Malic then the balance . . ." She broke off frowning as Reace slowly shook his head.

"Zarrick isn't a chosen Guardian. He's not one of the fourteen. He has no sway over the balance besides in your dream Malic was dead right? Everybody was." Reace reasoned.

"Thanks for the reminder," Keyla grumbled. "But your right." Her frown deepened in thought, "So what would Malic gain by turning Zarrick?" She asked.

"I don't know," Reace said honestly then turned to look at her, "but we have to find out."

Keyla nodded in agreement, thinking of Arron she returned her gaze to the door he'd just went through.

# CHAPTER EIGHTEEN

NATE TURNED TO HIS MOTHER; they had just watched Reace and Keyla leave to cool Arron down. Mrs. White and Heather were tending to Margaret and Howard while Jake was cleaning up the broken furniture.

One look at Nate's face and Kittana pulled him into the empty dining room where they could talk; taking a seat at the table she motioned for him to do the same.

Once seated Nate stared at his hands, his thoughts were traveling fast, almost too fast for him to comprehend but one thought keep coming to the surface. He wanted to deny it, but he couldn't. It was his fault—all of this—was his fault. Arron hit someone, his idol had actually hurt someone and he was to blame.

"Nate, this isn't your fault," Kittana spoke reading his thoughts, she wanted to reassure her son but even to her ears it sounded hollow.

"How can you say that?" Nate's gaze swung to his mother's. "Coming here I've put the balance at risk. Dad went to jail and Arron . . . Arron has flipped. He hit someone mom! Don't you think that's totally out of character? It's Arron, by FENTRA!" Nate half shrieked, "I've never seen him get angry before," Nate shook his head, "not like that."

"Arron's anger, your father getting arrested, those things had nothing to do with you, Nate, and they were put into place by our actions before you born. When we left Earth to go to Taysia we didn't tell people where we were going or why, we never thought we'd be back." Kittana started to explain but Nate cut her off.

"Exactly," He agreed. "If I hadn't wanted to come, if I had thought it out better, if I'd just stayed on Taysia . . . none of this would have happened," Nate told his mother and for a second she was stumped, he did have a valid point.

"How did you get here, Nate?" She asked deciding to take a different approach.

"Timelana," Nate answered. "One of her abilities is to open portals so I asked her if she could bring me here, she said, it was my destiny to come here." He looked at his mother with earnest eyes. "I honestly didn't think it through mom, I just wanted to come here so badly . . . ever since Malic showed me, I . . ."

"Malic?!" Kittana jumped on the name, her expression demanded an explanation.

"Yeah," Nate winced, "I guess I should have told you about that sooner." Nate mumbled. "Malic came to me, mom, he showed me Earth in this smooth round crystal sphere."

"You were inside stone mountain?" Kittana was horrified, how could this happen and she not know about it?

"No," Nate hastened to reassure her. "It was . . ."

As Nate told her what happened Kittana's fears increased instead of decreased. Malic had played with her son's emotions—that she was sure of and that made her angry. They had been so relaxed about Malic, lately. Cocky even, as they countered his every evil move or so the seven Guardians had thought, Malic was obviously smarter and stronger than any of them gave him credit for. The only question left was . . . what was he planning now? That question brought fear into her heart.

Nate stopped talking and both he and Kittana looked up as Jake entered the room and sat down beside Nate. "Dude, I thought you said that Arron was a nice guy."

"He is!" Kittana and Nate said in Arron's defense.

Jake huffed then retorted. "Yeah, well, nice guys don't go around attacking old men. Does he have an anger problem or something?"

"Ah, Jake, you don't know where your father was coming from, he and his father, Mr. Price, have a lot of issues. Arron has lived his whole life with parents who totally ignored him. They left him here with a housekeeper when he was only a child and from what I have been told they didn't visit often. Now put yourself in his place . . . How would you feel if your mother abandoned you like that?" Kittana asked, "I'm not saying what Arron did was right or wrong, I'm only saying that we don't really know both sides of the story and until we do how can we judge who was right or who was wrong?"

Jake looked down at his hands, Nate's mother was right, he'd feel the same way his father had . . . he'd want to hit someone too. He just never knew that Arron was treated that way; he never guessed that his grandparents would or ever could do that.

"I . . . I'm sorry, I didn't know." Jake said roughly as emotion swamped him.

Nate put a hand on Jake's shoulder, "How could you have known?" he asked, "You really don't know Arron and no one here really ever talked about him." Nate smiled in sympathy, "but there is still time to get to know him, he really is a great guy—you'll like him, I promise."

Looking at Nate, Jake smiled. "Thanks," he said then glanced around and added, "been a lot of excitement here today, normally this place is pretty quiet."

"We're sorry to bring everything down on you like this . . ." Kittana began but Jake stopped her with a raised hand.

"Don't, I'm glad you came, I'm glad I got to meet to my . . . dad, I'll never be sorry for that or for finding out the truth about myself," he glanced at Nate and repeated his earlier word, "Thanks."

"Okay, boys," Mrs. White announced as she entered the room. "School's still on for tomorrow, so it's bed time."

"Aw," Jake began but cut off at a look from the elderly house keeper.

"Don't you 'aw' me, Jake Price!" Mrs. White said in a no nonsense tone that compelled both boys to get up and leave the room.

"Wow, you are amazing!" Kittana said in surprise and awe at the older women and her ability to make two teenage boys go to bed when they were told. "Can you teach me how to do that?" she asked.

Mrs. White winked and with a smile crinkling up the corners of her eyes teased, "It's all in the tone, child, all in the tone." before hustling back to the kitchen, humming some nameless tune as she went, gathering up the dishes.

*

"Look, mom . . . dad, I'm sorry." Guilt climbed up Arron's back to settle on his shoulders as he looked at the darkening bruise on his father's face. Had he really caused that? Yes, of course his anger did and with him being the Guardian of Death—Howard was lucky that he still had his life, Arron thought. Drawing in a deep breath, being the Guardian of Life as well made Arron want to heal Howard but he fought the urge knowing it wouldn't make things between them any better.

"I'm sorry." He said again, guilt and shame weighed heavily on the younger man, their silence wasn't helping either. "Please, can we talk?" Arron cleared his throat, "I'd like to explain," he added tearing his gaze away from Howard's face.

"I'd like to hear your explanation, but if you don't mind, I think we'll sit over there." Howard steered his wife to the far end of the room.

Arron clenched his jaw, for the moment he stayed where he was by the door. He didn't want to infringe on their personal space and he accepted that his father didn't feel very safe with him—for that Arron couldn't blame him.

He had come here to explain—to say he was sorry and to give them both, him and Howard, another chance to somehow make amends before leaving again for what may be the last time, however, he wasn't about to shout, he thought as he sat in a chair, closer to them.

"I'm sorry," Arron began, "I took my anger out on you. It was just . . . I've had so much going on right now." He wished he didn't have to say this, he wished he were anywhere else. This was worse than being at the dentist.

"I have a wife and a son back home," he paused to let that information settle before adding the part he dreaded.

"You have a wife?" Howard stared at Arron as if wondering how any sensible women would ever marry him.

"And a son—other than Jake, does Jake know?" Margaret asked.

Arron winced at how quickly his mother thought of Jake and his feelings. He didn't want to be jealous of his own son, but he couldn't help it. Right now, he regretted telling Tia not to use her powers on him. Christ! He wished she were here, Arron sighed, before answering his mother.

"Yes," He nodded, "I told Jake earlier." A ghost of a smile graced his face as Arron thought of all the questions Jake had pestered him with about Zarrick and the look on Jake's face when he said couldn't wait to meet him . . . the smile fell from Arron's face and he closed his eyes.

His two boys would never meet, Zarrick would never acknowledge that they were brothers, heck, Zarrick hardly wanted to believe that Arron was his father. Opening his eyes Arron stared at his parents a moment, lost in his own thoughts he almost forgotten they were there waiting.

"Ah . . ." Arron started trying to remember what they wanted to hear. "Zarrick's about a year younger then Jake. Tia is my wife," he looked to his mother before adding, "You'd like her."

"How does having a family make you go crazy?" Howard questioned in a voice that demanded and scoffed all at once.

Arron took another deep breath. This was hard to say, hard to admit out loud. He was glad he didn't have to tell them everything. They'd never understand everything, so choosing his words carefully he began, "Yesterday, I found out that Zarrick isn't really mine, Tia had an affair, years ago."

"Oh, Arron, I am so sorry to hear that, you must be crushed," Margaret turned sympathetic eyes to her son.

"So you came back here thinking to take Jake away from us. You lost one son so you think you can just get another . . . a replacement? We will not let you take Jake; we will fight you on that." Howard's words dripped acid.

"I'm not here for Jake," Arron gritted out through clenched teeth, he was getting frustrated that everyone kept assuming that he had come back to take his son away from them, Were they just not listening to him? Taking a deep calming breath he explained for what he hoped was the last time. "I came back here to help Reace and Kittana find their son, Nate." Why Nate ever wanted to come here, anywhere else he could understand but here?

*Why here?* Arron demanded of Nature in a silent conversation that only he could hear. Glancing at his parents he continued trying to put their fears to rest.

"Finding Heather here and Jake . . . well that was just a huge surprise." Arron paused, "Look, even if I wanted to "take Jake", I couldn't." Arron physically shuttered as he thought of what might happen to Jake if he ever tried to enter Taysia. Jake wasn't a Guardian, would he be turned into a shadow? Arron couldn't take that risk, he wouldn't.

"Don't get me wrong, I love my sons—both of them and I wish I could have been there for Jake while he was growing up," Arron cocked his head, tears shimmered in his eyes, "I wish I could be here now, but the truth is . . . I can't." Arron didn't say anymore for a few minutes. "Zarrick needs me he's going through a rough time lately." Arron shook his head sadly, "I would like to spend more time getting to know Jake but I can't . . . I have to return home very soon."

"How soon?" Howard pushed, sounding pleased, Margaret hushed him.

"Friday morning, early." Arron answered then added, "Don't think that I wouldn't love to have Jake with me but I can't, I won't take Jake away from the people who love him," Arron's eyes and voice hardened, he swallowed the lump of jealously, forcing himself to be happy for his son before adding, "or the people he loves."

*

Reace was sitting in the kitchen, nursing a coke. It was one of the things he missed about Earth—coca-cola, he thought as he raised the can to his mouth and took a long swallow. He savored the acid feeling as it bubbled its way down his throat to pool in his stomach. Lowering the can, Reace glanced at it as he tilted the can a bit before setting it down again. He looked around, his eyes catching the clock on the stove, 12:47 it read. Suppressing a yawn, he ran a hand over his face in an effect to stave off sleep, he was so tired, everyone else had gone to bed hours ago, everyone but Arron, Reace amended silently.

From where he sat in the kitchen he could see down the hallway clear to the front door but right now his sight was focused on the light that shined from behind the closed door that sat in the middle of the hall, the door to the room where Arron was still talking to his parents. Reace wondered what they were talking about for so long. He figured when they were done Arron would need someone to vent too, in all the years they had been friends it always seemed to Reace that Arron had always been there for him, now it was his turn. Reace was determined to return the favor, so here he was trying his damnedest to stay awake and wait for his best friend.

Reace shook his head and smirked to himself as he thought of all that Arron had been through in the last two days, he had to admire his comrade, and Arron was taking it all in stride. Reace didn't think he could have handled it all so well.

Reace looked up expectantly when someone entered the room. He was disappointed when it wasn't Arron and stared down at his coke.

"Hoping I was Arron?" Heather guessed, but at his crestfallen expression she already knew she was right. "Sorry to disappoint you." she added going to the fridge and getting out a bottle of water.

Reace didn't say anything, just continued looking down at his hands resting around his coke can.

Heather watched him from where she stood for a moment, noting his sudden keen interest in his soda can, biting her lip she moved to sit on the stool beside him. It was now or never, she thought as she summoned her courage.

"Hey, Reace," she waited for him to glance at her before continuing, "I wanted to talk to you." She let out her breath, feeling more than a little awkward as the silence continued. Get a grip, she scolded herself, she was less nervous running boardroom meetings with her boss there.

"You do?" Reace asked. Her statement had caught him off guard; except for a couple of weeks when they were thirteen she never *wanted* to talk to him.

"Yeah, I . . . I know we've never really gotten along, I guess that was probably more my fault then yours so I wanted to say . . . I'm sorry."

Reace was surprised, Heather was actually apologizing to him and she seemed really sincere, actually interested in his reaction, so maybe she had changed.

"It takes two," Reace offered seeing the honesty in her eyes then he added, "I'm sorry too." He held out his hand in an offer of peace and friendship, smiling when she took it.

"I've always wondered . . . it probably sounds stupid." Heather ducked her head to hide her heated cheeks, an embarrassed smile twisting her lips. "If I had been nicer then maybe you wouldn't have . . . left. You know, maybe Arron and I would still be together and Jake would have grown up knowing his father."

"Heather," Reace catching her gaze he continued. "Nothing you could have done or changed would have made any difference to Arron or us . . . we still would have left, we had too."

Heather looked down and smiled sadly, "I know. It was just some silly fantasy."

Reace watched her, wanting to make her feel better but he didn't know how; didn't know what to say.

"You know, I've always liked you, Reace, even when I was being a bitch." She glanced at him then holding his gaze steady. "Kittana sure is lucky to have you, you're a good guy, Reace. You always were."

They were silent for a moment each savoring the feeling of friendship that was growing between them when Heather suddenly spoke.

"Well, now that we are friends, I was wondering if I could ask you something?"

"Shoot," Reace nodded his consent.

"Okay," She began slowly, "you know Arron, right—better than anybody. You two have always been inseparable, believe me I know, I've tried, but you know him best right?"

The fear in her eyes made Reace frown in concentration—wondering what she was scared of—he listened intently.

"I was wondering, worrying actually," she took a deep breath before rushing on. "Is his parents' right? Should I worry that he'd take Jake away from me? Jake's all that I have. I . . . I . . . couldn't bare it if Arron took him away. Not that he could, in a court of law I think I have the upper hand. I have raised him and all that, but he is Jake's father and he would be entitled to parenting rights, besides that, Jake is sixteen and can make his own decisions. I guess, I'm scared Arron will take Jake with him when you guys leave to go to tay . . . taysee."

"Taysia," Reace corrected, his eyes widened in surprise as he wondered just how much Arron told her about them.

"Yeah, Taysia." Heather repeated then looked at Reace with all her emotions and worries shining in her eyes.

Reace looked away, damn it! How could he answer this? He inwardly sighed, he had to try though, she was really upset and he could relate. He glanced back at her, his eyes searching her face as he asked. "Does Jake have any special, different marks on him . . . perhaps on his wrists?"

"Arron asked that question too."

Heather stated and Reace almost smiled at how alike he and Arron were.

"Don't tell me you have a piece of glass embedded into your wrist too? God! What is it with you guys and these weird mutilations?"

Reace stilled, Heather's comment made him realize the seriousness of this situation and that he had to be careful. Heather may be close to them through her son but she wasn't one of them.

She didn't seem to notice Reace reaction as she continued talking.

"Jake does have an unusual ability, he was born with it," She hesitated for a moment looking deep into his eyes, seeming to make up her mind she continued. "And if I thought for a moment that you were a blabber mouth, I wouldn't tell you. I've never told anyone before, not Arron's parents, or mine, but we both know, Reace that you can keep secrets."

Reace nodded in memory of some of the secrets he had kept before he turned his attention back to her.

"He can self heal."

Reace was taking this as well as Arron did, Heather thought, almost like they were used to unusual things happening, as much as she wondered why, she was glad for it, with them her son would never be made to feel like a freak, but at the same time she wanted them to freak out a little—like she had when she first discovered her baby boy was special.

"But, he has no mark?" Reace demanded watching Heather closely, he needed to be sure.

"No, no mark," Heather shook her head. "How can there ever be a mark when he heals instantly?" she stated the obvious. Turning a quizzical frown on Reace she demanded. "I don't see what a mark has to do with Arron taking Jake away with him to this home land of yours."

Reace let out a relieved sigh, he wasn't about to explain that the mark didn't come from the outside but from the inside. It couldn't be healed, it was a sign of the power they wield—a symbol of the Guardian they were. He, himself, had been healed countless times, but the mark was as permanent as the blood in his veins—It couldn't be changed. But he could tell her not to worry, Arron couldn't take Jake away with them, he wasn't a Guardian—Starian, but not Guardian.

"Don't worry, Heather." Reace smiled at her. "Arron wouldn't risk it. He wouldn't take Jake from you."

"What do you mean, 'won't risk it'?" Heather insisted, she thought she would feel relieved to hear that from Reace but instead she had more questions.

Reace stared off into space, just over her shoulder and visibly paled as he remembered the shadow creatures, how they were once ordinary Starians, people. He physically shuddered when he thought of Jake turning into one of them. Reace forced the images from his mind as he tried to maintain what he hoped was a reassuring smile. Trying to ease her fears he repeated, "Don't worry about it, it doesn't matter. Arron won't take Jake from you. He can't take Jake to Taysia." He looked into Heather's eyes as he vowed. "I won't let him."

Heather's frown deepened, she was about to say more, demand answers but she didn't get the chance when they heard a commotion in the hallway before it moved to the front door.

Moments later Arron walked into the kitchen, he had seen the light on when he accompanied his parents to the front door and he knew that Reace would be here. Man, he really needed to talk to his comrade. He stopped short of the doorway, seeing Heather and Reace, the two of them with their heads together, talking as if they were old friends. What the . . . ?

"Did hell freeze over?" Arron demanded his gaze locking with Reace as he came fully into the kitchen. His facial expression clearly demanded an explanation. "You two are actually sitting together and talking?"

Reace half smiled and said with a shrug, "Arron, we're not kids anymore. We can behave like adults."

Heather glanced from Arron to Reace realizing they wanted to be alone, to talk. She turned her gaze to the clock.

"It's after one!" she exclaimed in genuine surprise, "I have to get back to bed, I have an early broad room meeting tomorrow," *and a ton of work piled up that I didn't do today.* She added to herself.

"Thanks Reace," she called over her shoulder as she left the kitchen in search of her warm bed.

"Okay, I feel like I've just entered the twilight zone, what going on?" Arron asked after Heather left.

"She apologized." Reace replied, watching Arron standing across from him, as he lifted his can of coke to his lips to take another sip.

"Apologized . . . Heather . . . to you?" Arron questioned in bewilderment. "Now I know I've entered the twilight zone."

"Yeah, guess having Jake changed her for the better." Reace said.

"Having Jake or us balancing the forces?" Arron asked and as Reace raised eyebrow, he explained what he was thinking. "Maybe I'm wrong but coming back here . . . man, people have changed. My parents, Heather," he gave a short laugh and rolled his eyes, unable to believe he was saying this, "even John. I don't know maybe it's just us, maybe I'm reading too much into this . . ."

"You think?" Reace replied sarcastically. He was with Arron right up until he mentioned his stepfather—there was no way he'd believe John had changed.

"I know it sounds crazy, but when I saw John earlier he seemed happier almost like he was a different person and while I was there I saw a picture of him—he's got a new family, Reace, a wife and a couple of kids."

Reace's eyes snapped to Arron's and his face whitened in shock.

"He has a child, other children? You don't think . . ." Reace let the sentence hang in the air. This changed things; unlike Arron, Reace couldn't believe John had changed. Reace knew all too well how his stepfather could fool people. No one had ever, to Reace's knowledge, even suspected what John was really like, but Reace knew. His hand went to his stomach, unconsciously rubbing the spot where John once stabbed him. He knew what his step-father was capable of, he had lived it and now that he knew John had other children—other victims—he couldn't stay away. He had to do something! Reace lowered his eyes so Arron couldn't see, couldn't guess what he was planning.

"I don't know," Arron answered solemnly. He was suddenly sorry he brought it up, "but maybe us balancing the forces changed people, made them nicer . . . maybe John's not drinking anymore? Look at Heather."

"A complete one-eighty, I know but, Arron, she had a child—a life altering event," Reace reasoned, still unwilling to believe that John could change.

"And my parents; Reace if they can change . . . John can too." Arron persisted.

"NO! No way. Arron, I hear what you're saying, I really do, but, when I saw him earlier he seemed like the same old John to me." Reace shook his head remembering how John threatened him. "There is no way he's changed."

"Yeah, maybe you're right . . . I just can't help thinking that . . ." he trailed off.

"Thinking what?" Reace prompted, knowing that Arron wouldn't have said anything if he hadn't thought it all out first. Playing with it in his mind like a kitten with a ball of twine.

"That Earth would be effected by the balance to," Arron leveled his gaze at Reace, "I mean if every other planet, why not?" he finished with a shrug.

"It makes sense," Reace grudgingly agreed, "I just . . . I can't see John changing," Reace said. But as Arron's words, his theory, sunk into Reace's head he began to think about the possibility. He remembered how he wasn't afraid of John earlier today . . . not at first. He had thought that maybe it had been because he had grown up or that they were in a public place—with other people around . . . but now? Maybe Arron was right, maybe it was because John had changed.

Reace didn't want to spend any more time talking or thinking about the man who put him through hell so he changed the subject.

"How did things go in there?" Reace cocked his head toward the room Arron and his parents had talked in for over two hours.

"Actually . . . pretty good," Arron said slowly, he wasn't surprised that Reace changed the subject. Turning his head to look back down the hallway he had entered from earlier, then looking back at Reace he smiled. "They know I'm not staying and after they finally got it through their heads that I'm not taking Jake away from them, things went pretty good,"

Reace yawned, covering it behind his hands as he rubbed them over his tired face.

Arron, seeing the yawn, yawned in response. Glancing at the clock he realized just how late it was, "Why don't we turn in, you look like crap and we can talk about this in the morning."

"Need your beauty sleep, huh?" Reace teased finishing off his coke and putting the can in the recycling bin.

"Well, we can't all go around looking like you." Arron retorted following Reace out of the kitchen turning off the lights as he went.

*

As Reace snuggled in bed, he wrapped an arm around Kittana, pulling her closer to him.

"Arron okay?" She asked, her voice soft from sleep.

"About as okay as he's going to be after everything that happened," He was quiet for a moment then continued, "I've got to tell you, he's taking everything pretty well."

"Uh-huh," was Kittana's only reply.

Reace's eye's narrowed in the dark at her tone, pulling away from her, he demanded: "What does that mean?"

She rolled on her stomach turning her head to face him, "Hitting his father isn't taking "things well". He's holding it all in, letting it build until he exploded. Look, Reace, I know Arron's a great guy, one of the best, but what's happened to him is huge, life altering even." She paused, seeking out Reace's eyes in the dark as she admitted. "I'm worried about him,"

"Me too," Reace quietly agreed, sighing heavily as he pulled her closer to him again, snuggling into the warmth of their bed.

Everything was quiet for several long minutes until Kittana swatted a hand in his general direction and spoke in a loud whisper, "Reace, are you asleep?"

"Not anymore, why?" He replied in a tired voice.

"Do you think we were wrong coming here?"

Kittana waited for Reace's answer, he took so long to answer her that she had wondered if he had fallen asleep.

"No," He finally said. "If Timelana said it was Nate's destiny, then I think it's safe to say that we were meant to follow him. Besides it feels right—in some twisted way—being here, knowing that Arron has a son—not that I want to stay or anything—but I am not sorry that we came." Reace inhaled deeply before continuing, "Arron mentioned earlier that he thought Earth was affected by the balance. He had some good points too."

Reace thought about how Heather and the Prices had changed.

"Heather really apologized to you?" Kittana questioned. Being this close to Reace it was easy for her to read his mind.

"Yeah," Reace replied, "It was a surprise to me too, now I wonder if Arron was right."

"I think he is," Kittana said around a yawn as sleep started to overtake her again.

Reace listened to her breathing even out and knew she had fallen back to sleep. He yawned as his thoughts turned to John and the 'new' family he had. He pondered as his eyes drifted close, could he really have changed?

# CHAPTER NINETEEN

REACE JERKED AWAKE FROM HIS nightmare, opening his eyes he stared into the early morning darkness, calming his racing heart and forcing himself to breathe evenly. He tried to go back to sleep, but every time he closed his eyes he couldn't help the images that danced in front of them, or the fear that ran through him: Nate had taken his place in his childhood memories of the violent times with John—his son took his place and Reace could nothing but watch as John beat and belittled Nate before savagely stabbing him.

As tired as he was, Reace couldn't go back to sleep, fear for his son's safety drove him out of his bed. Quickly and quietly, so not to disturb his sleeping wife, Reace pulled on his jeans and grabbed his t-shirt, than crept silently into the hallway. Living with an abusive parent had taught him how to move without making a sound, with fear and adrenalin running through his veins, he used this skill to make his way into Jake's bedroom.

As his eyes adjusted to the darkness he found his son sleeping on a mattress on the floor. Nate looked so peaceful in his sleep that Reace let out a sigh of relief and smiled. In his mind's eye he could still see the happy child Nate had been. Crouching beside his son, Reace ran a hand gently over Nate's hair, ruffling it.

Satisfied that Nate was alright, Reace stood up, quietly leaving the room, closing the door behind him, he leaned against it. Ever since Arron had mentioned that John had a new family, Reace couldn't get the idea that John might be abusing them out of his mind. It weighed heavily on his shoulders. Reace knew there'd be no sleep for him until he knew for sure.

Running a hand through his hair Reace pushed himself away from the door, turning to look at it one more time before moving down the hallway. Relieved that his son was alright, he had to check on somebody else, he had to make sure they too, were safe.

Reace couldn't get the images, memories out of his head. Arron's words *he's got a new family.* echoed in his mind. His fears drove him out of the house and across the yard.

He had once believed that his step-father only hated him, only hit him because he had deserved it but after learning the truth—that John had once hit his mother and he tried to hit Keyla too, well now, he wasn't so sure. This new 'family' John had what if . . . what if he was abusing them too?

After retrieving the key from where he had hid it years ago, Reace slipped through the back door of John's house, stepping softly into the dark kitchen, quietly shutting the door behind him. He knew what he had to do. A sober John didn't hit, but a drunken John was dangerous.

If Arron was right and John had really changed then he'd have stopped drinking. Reace had to search the house for alcohol, if he found none, then he'd be satisfied that John wasn't hurting anyone and he would believe that his step-father had changed.

He'd start his search in the kitchen. Pocketing the key, Reace turned away from the door and paused . . . the kitchen.

He backed up, leaning against the door he'd just shut, as memories assaulted him. He could still feel the fire in his belly as John viciously twisted the blade . . . Reace shook his head and swallowed the bile that clawed its way up his throat from his nauseous stomach. Pushing away from the door, he forced his mind to focus, he had to search the house, now before John or anyone else saw him.

As quickly and quietly as he could, Reace searched the kitchen, in all the places John used to keep his alcohol. The subtle changes to the place didn't escape his notice—a women's touch. Reace smiled, making his way toward the den and his step-father's mini bar.

He stilled for a moment when he heard a creek, but hearing nothing else he started moving again. Reace was almost to the den when someone slammed into him from the side, taking them both to the floor.

Fighting against his natural instincts to use his powers, Reace took a few well aimed blows. He finally got a grip on his assailant, only to be tossed off him in a slick judo move leaving Reace pinned on the floor.

"Who are you and what the *FUCK* are you doing in my house?" The guy demanded, his brown eyes glaring holes through Reace.

Reace rolled his eyes then looked into the teenagers face, trying to make out his features, his age in the early morning light before finally saying. "I'm your step-brother."

"I don't have any brothers." The guy tightened his grip stopping Reace's struggles.

"Yeah, well, I'm not happy about it either," Reace growled. "Look, I didn't come here to fight you."

"Why did you come here? To steal?"

"There is nothing *here* I want." Reace spat.

It was the way Reace sneered the word 'here' as if the house itself left a bad taste in his mouth, that confused the teen and he loosened his grip, in the dim light he searched Reace's face, then allowed Reace to get up off the floor.

Reace looked nervously at the clock on the wall as it chimed, he figured he had about a half an hour left before John woke up—if he still kept the same schedule—and he wanted to be gone before then. He leveled his gaze back on his new brother. "I don't have much time, I just wanted to know . . . you can be honest with me, I've lived with John before, has he ever hit you or your mother?"

"What? Are you crazy? Dad would never hurt us, he'd never hurt anyone!" The teen exclaimed. Honest confusion and disbelieve showed on his face, reflected in his frown, as he stared at Reace.

He should have been relieved, happy even to know by the boy's reaction that John had never abused him but instead pain sliced through his heart as the words echoed through his body. *He'd never hurt anyone!*

There was so much Reace wanted to say to that: *Can you tell that to my stomach, because every time I enter the kitchen I can still feel that cold blade twisting in my gut? Can you tell that to my tongue that won't spit out the words fast enough for fear they'll be wrong? Can you tell me to stop worrying, wondering when he'll explode?* Instead he swallowed these words. With a snort and a shake of his head he said.

"You really have no idea what John is capable of . . . and I hope to God you never find out."

The teen took a step back at the sheer amount of feeling in the other's boy voice. Those eyes that glittered like shards of ice made him wonder if they were talking about the same man. What the kid had gone through to make his so hard?

Reace suddenly tensed when they were both washed in light as the switch was flicked on.

"WHAT THE HELL IS GOING ON DOWN HERE?" John's voice still gruff from sleep boomed loud in the quiet house, making Reace freeze and Shane turn to face his dad. John paled when he saw Reace standing beside Shane.

"Reace!" He barked the name.

At the sound of John's voice, Reace's body reacted, snapping to attention.

"What are you doing here? I thought we had an understanding."

Reace swallowed hard, refusing to give into the urge to utter 'yes, sir' then turn and leave. He tore his gaze away from John and glanced at the teen beside him, strengthening his resolve, he had to do this. He had to be sure, lifting determined eyes to John's again. "That was before I found out that you had another family."

"Dad, do you know him?" Shane demanded confused. His dad had never mentioned a son, but their body language, the way they reacted to each other, spoke volumes.

Dad? This kid got to call John, 'dad.' Jealousy cut though Reace like a hot knife through butter as he remembered all the times he had been beaten for using the same word.

"Yes, Shane," John's voice sounded tired as he admitted. Even after all this time John couldn't help the lip that curled as he claimed Reace as his child. "He's your step-brother."

Trying his best to reign in his emotions Reace turned to the younger man who had tackled him. He half smiled as he said, "Hi, I'm your older brother, Reace."

"You can't be older than me, you look eighteen. I'm twenty-one."

Reace's half-smile turned into a knowing smirk. "Trust me I am a lot older then I look."

"I'm Shane, and that's my sister, Haley." With a gesture he introduced the thirteen year old girl that came down the steps behind John and stood there watching with interest the family drama unfolding in front of her.

"SHANE!" John's wife screeched, coming down the stairs, moving protectively in front of her youngest while staring with scared, fearful eyes on her oldest child as she instructed, "Get away from him! He's dangerous." When she turned to Reace her eyes changed instantly from worry to hatred as she yelled at him. "WHAT ARE YOU DOING HERE? WHAT DO YOU WANT? WHY CAN'T YOU JUST LEAVE US ALONE?"

Reace was taken aback by the look in her eyes; she looked at him like he was something that crawled out from under a rock. He frowned as he tried to figure out where he'd seen her before.

"You called the cops on me yesterday, didn't you?" He asked but he knew the answer before she nodded. Hers was the face he'd seen watching him in the window as the cops led him away yesterday.

"And I'll do it again! I don't know how or why they released you but . . ." She stopped suddenly when she heard John's quiet voice.

"I dropped the charges." John admitted then repeated in a louder voice. "I dropped the charges."

Both Reace and his wife stared at him in shock.

She couldn't believe he'd be that kind hearted.

Reace was stunned that John was actually standing up for him, almost protecting him from her wrath.

"John?" she said when she found her voice, "John how could you? Why? He's a murderer—he tried to KILL you and now he's back to finish the job! HE'LL KILL US ALL!" At her words all eyes turned to Reace, he squirmed a bit under the sudden attention, and the allegations against him. "Why can't you LEARN from your father's kindness?"

Laughter bubbled up inside of him, Reace couldn't help but let it escape. John kind?—to him?—the thought was ludicrous; the whole situation suddenly just struck him as funny.

Her face a mask of fury, crumbled in surprised mortification when Reace laughed.

Knowing it probably wasn't helping him Reace ran a hand through his hair and over his face in an attempt to calm himself but it was useless he had almost no control over what was coming out of his mouth. "Lady, you have no idea what you're talking about . . . NONE OF YOU KNOW WHAT JOHN . . ."

"Reace! That's enough!" John snapped interrupting Reace's words. His eyes narrowing in on Reace with a deadly serious warning as he growled, "Do you need another lesson in control?"

Reace's face darkened with memories of the past and fear entered his eyes, when he heard John's words and the meaning behind them.

"N . . . n . . . no s . . . sir!" Reace closed his eyes, inwardly cursing himself for stuttering—for being afraid. He was an adult now, a father and a Guardian! He didn't have to be afraid. John couldn't hurt him anymore. Taking courage from these facts, he opened his eyes and glared at John before saying, "I don't need any more 'lessons' from you, but you need one in telling the truth. What you did . . ." he shook his head suddenly not sure who he was angrier at: John or himself. "What I let you do. I let you. I just accepted it, accepted that you were right. But I can't . . . I won't let you do that to anyone else."

"REACE, I SAID THAT'S ENOUGH!" John bellowed, his face turning red in anger. With his eyes glaring a warning at Reace he lowered his voice to ask his wife: "Michelle, would you mind excusing us while we go into the kitchen, we need to have a little chat."

At the mention of the kitchen, at being in there with John, Reace paled.

"Dad, what is he talking about?" Shane demanded he had been listening and watching everything and now he needed some answers. He needed to hear his step-father tell him that what he was thinking was wrong, that this Reace, his new step-brother, was lying. But John didn't seem to hear him he just stared at Reace with a weird expression on his face.

"NO! No . . . n . . . not the k . . . k . . . kitchen," Reace blinked hard forcing himself to get the words out.

"Scared of the kitchen? Can't imagine why," John taunted with self-satisfied smirk on his face as if he shared a private joke with Reace—only Reace wasn't smiling. John sighed then amended, "Okay, Michelle, why don't you and the kids go get breakfast ready, while me and Reace talk in the den."

"John, I don't want you to be alone with that man." Michelle said firmly, letting her contempt for Reace show on her face as she glanced briefly at him.

John looked from his wife to Reace, before settling his gaze on his wife and saying, "It'll be okay, trust me."

"It's not you I don't trust, it's *him!*" she pointed at Reace.

"Reace won't hurt anyone today besides he doesn't have any weapons on him, do you Reace?" John added trying to dispel his wife's fears.

"No sir," Reace replied pulling up his t-shirt as he slowly turned around.

"No! Dad, I want to . . ." The words burst out of Shane when saw his mother's nod of acceptance.

"Go with you mother, Shane. It'll be alright." John cut him off with a firm but gentle voice.

"But,"

"Shane! You heard your father; he and *his son* need some privacy." Michelle spoke firmly as she rounded up her children and pushed them into the kitchen speaking loud enough for Reace to hear, "and I need to call my mother."

Reace nodded, he knew she said that for his benefit. She was smart he grudgingly thought if he were a killer then letting him knew she'd be on the phone to someone would be a smart way to let him know that should anything happen, he'd have someone to point a finger at him. The way she took care of her kids and John—she was a good women, he just hoped John knew that.

They both waited until Michelle, Haley and Shane had gone from sight before turning to enter the den.

John sank wearily into a leather covered chair, he watched Reace hovering by the closed door then he sighed rubbing a hand over his thinning hair and down his face.

"Reace, sit." He ordered and when Reace stiffly complied John continued, "Relax, I'm not going to hurt you . . . the man who could pick up a knife and stab you is gone. I've changed. I'm a member of A.A. I've built a new life after you left. Look around, search the house, if you have to, but you'll find no alcohol . . . anywhere." John had spread his arms out to welcome a search as he leaned back into his chair. "I haven't had a drink in seventeen years," he added honesty.

Reace nodded, he didn't add that he had already searched the house instead he spoke his thoughts as they occurred to him.

"You love those kids: Shane, even though he isn't yours." Jealousy and hurt rose to the surface within him, leaving him weak with it. His mind adding numbers and dates together, he raised tearful eyes to John as he asked, "Why? He's a bastard—like me. Why him and not me?" He shook his head as he continued, "I would have done anything for you . . . I would have worshipped you! Why couldn't you have loved me too?" Reace turned his head away trying desperately to reign in his emotions, blinking back the tears, he sniffed and turned his attention back to John.

John shifted, suddenly uncomfortable in his chair. This was the question he hoped he'd never have to answer. He had asked himself this question when he first met Shane, at the age of four and he was surprised at how quickly he had come to love the boy. He opened his mouth a few times and closed it again before finally saying, "I had thought, that after you were born, it'd just be the three of us—you, me and Carol—a family. But you, you wouldn't let me near you, I couldn't hold you without you screaming and crying." John paused remembering; strong feelings colored his words. "In the middle of the night you'd cry and Carol would leave me to go to you. She spent hours looking at you and talking about you. It was always Reace this and Reace that, Reace, Reace, Reace . . ." John's expression was bittersweet as he remembered his first wife and the baby Reace had been. "You made her smile and laugh, unlike I was able to do for months before you were born. You made her happy."

Reace smiled at that—he liked hearing about his mother—he had so little actually memories of her.

John glanced at Reace then away, ashamed of the way he had felt: jealous of a child—an innocent baby. With a deep breath he continued telling Reace, "It didn't take me long before I realized that she loved you more then she loved me. I tried, I really did, for five years I tried . . . ," John ran a hand over his face, "but I couldn't love you. I was too . . . envious of you."

"Then came that night when I found out you really weren't mine, Carol had an affair before we were married with a man she had known for less than a week." This was hard for John to say—to admit.

"She loved him more than me too."

He looked down at the floor wishing he could have a drink to make this easier, he hadn't wanted a drink in seventeen years, being around Reace being forced to remember his mistakes, made him want to drink, to find forgetfulness in the bottle of booze. Instead he sneered at Reace.

"She knew you weren't mine . . . you were his . . . his bastard!" John paused for a moment trying to control his urge to drink and the urge to take his anger out on Reace.

"She left me, she took you—*her precious son* and left . . . she died that night but *you*, you survived." He raised his eyes to glare at Reace, "A constant reminder of my mistakes; a constant reminder of how I drove her away, how she loved your father and you more than me. How could I love you?"

Reace stared at him, then looked away, that's why John hated him . . . that was why John had hit him so many times growing up, this sick twisted form of jealousy? Jealousy turned into hatred. John's voice drew Reace's attention back to him as he spoke again.

"When you left, when you used your freaky powers to electrocute me, you gave me a new lease on life. It was like you'd killed me—the old hate filled drunk that enjoyed hurting you—and I was reborn. Without you here to constantly remind me of my past mistakes and what I had lost. I was able to move on."

"I have stopped drinking. I have a loving wife. A son who wants my attention, who lets me get close to him and a daughter—a child of my own. A family." John looked at Reace his eyes no longer glaring, but imploring Reace to believe him. "Since you left I have never hit or hurt another person, I swear."

*If it weren't for me, John would be a good man* . . . words Reace had once told Keyla echoed in his mind as what John told him hit home. Arron was right! Earth too was affected by the balance. John had changed. He had become a . . . a good man, the man Reace had always known he could be—if he weren't around. Reace nodded accepting this new John with an inclination of his head.

"Why did you come back?" John's question brought Reace's eyes up briefly to meet his.

"I came as soon as I found out you had other . . ." Reace couldn't keep the emotion out of his voice, jealously turned his lip upward in a half-sneer, "kids. I had to make sure they weren't getting hurt."

"I get that." John said sourly, "I meant, why did you come yesterday? Michelle said you were lurking around before she called the police. What did you want?"

Reace let out a heavy breath before saying, "It's not important now."

"I asked you a question and I expect an answer." Impatience colored John's words and he had to work at controlling the compelling urge to fall back into old routines. "Now, tell me. What did you come back for?"

John's tone made fear dance alone Reace's spine, forcing himself to calm down, even as he stumbled over his words giving into his step-father's demand, "I . . . I was c . . . coming over to s . . . say I was s . . . s . . . sorry."

John's eyebrows shot up in surprise, he'd never expected this. His expression clearly asked: *What for?*

"Sorry for the way I left it; for using my powers on you. I could have killed you." Reace stared at his hands, ashamed of what he had almost done in the past. If it hadn't been for Keyla he had often wondered if he would have killed John and if he had would he be on Malic's side, would he be evil now?

"I know," John said.

Lost in his thoughts Reace barely heard John's quiet admittance, he continued as if he hadn't,

"Killing someone—even you—is something that I wouldn't be able to live with." Reace gave a short laugh as he just answered his own question. "Keyla was right about that too." He mumbled to himself remembering how she had once said something similar to him, turning serious again he went on, "I wouldn't be able to forgive myself so I had wanted to apologize for my actions . . . They were wrong."

"Your actions were a wakeup call. Reace, you have nothing to be sorry for," John said with a sigh as he continued, "If anyone should be sorry . . ." John ran a hand down his face. "Look, Reace, I'm not proud of the way I treated you, but you turned out okay. Your mother would be . . . would be proud of you."

He could tell it was hard for John to say that to him, but it meant the world to Reace to hear it from the only father he had known. Reace swallowed the lump of emotion that threatened to choke him as John continued speaking.

"Look, they—Michelle, Shane and Haley, they don't know much about you or what I did. We both have new lives now, Reace, the past is dead and buried. Let's leave it that way, okay?"

Reace knew that John was asking for his forgiveness and his silence, could he forgive and forget? The answer surprised him, even after all John had done to him, yes, he could forgive and he could keep quiet but he'd never forget.

"As long as you stay sober and don't hurt anyone again, John, I'll stay away and I'll stay quiet about what you did," Reace stared at John as his mark flashed, letting his powers come to the surface, he allowed the sparks to play across his finger tips, in a display of electricity. Reace watched with interest as John's face paled, then he spoke again.

"If, however, you ever have a drink—even a drop and if you ever even *think* about hitting anyone . . . I'll be back and I'll make you wish for a quick death." Reace stood up still watching John, he added, "I may not be a killer John, but I'll make an exception in this case. I won't let you hurt anyone else." Reace closed his fist. Sucking the electricity back inside himself he ended the display of sparks.

With a last look that spoke volumes at the man who had raised him, Reace left the den. John was still staring after him as he walked out the front door of his childhood home, leaving his step-father and his past behind him.

# CHAPTER TWENTY

KITTANA AND KEYLA CAME DOWN the stairs, early Thursday morning, just as Nate and Jake where heading out the front door.

"Hi! Bye!" Jake said with a quick wave of his hand, as he grabbed his jacket and went out the door; Nate following close on his heels.

"Hi mom, Key, bye!" Nate said trying to follow Jake but paused at the sound of his mother's voice.

"Nate! Wait," Kittana said. "Where are you going?"

"No time mom, bye." He called as he slipped out the door.

"Nate!" Kittana was talking to the door that Nate closed behind him. Using her telepathy she spoke to her son. *"Nature, where are you going? And don't tell me you haven't the time to talk."*

Nate, hearing his mother's voice in his head, bent down, pretending to tie his shoe as he telepathed back to her, he didn't want Jake or anyone to see the expression on his face during the silent conversation and think that he was weird. *"Mom, I can't do this right now. I can't talk to you and Jake at the same time—not in public. We'll talk later after school . . . I promise, okay?"*

*"School!"* Kittana used telepathy, alarm coloring her silent words.

*"Yeah, but don't worry we'll be fine,"* Nate replied within his mind then added, *"I'll be careful."*

*"You had better be careful. Nate, using your powers in public can be very dangerous, for all of us!"* Kittana told him, *"We are leaving early Friday, Nate, remember that."*

Nate could almost feel her smile as she added.

*"And I'll be holding you to your promise, we WILL talk after school. I Love you and remember to be careful"*

Nate got up and started walking again, turning his attention back to Jake and away from his mother as they walked to school.

Kittana glanced at Keyla then silently continued toward their earlier destination. As the twins entered the sun drenched kitchen Keyla asked, "So, where did Nate and Jake go?"

"Oh, the boys went to school," Heather answered before Kittana got the chance. "Did you sleep well? No more nightmares, Keyla?" Heather asked pleasantly as she sipped her coffee. Her attention on the hot brew she didn't see the weary look Kittana gave her sister but she noticed the added tension in the air.

Kittana looked at Heather—who was seated eating breakfast in the cozy breakfast nook in the corner of the spacious room—as if to read her thoughts until Keyla nudged her with her elbow, telling her sister with a look to knock it off before Keyla answered Heather.

"Yeah, fine thanks. Is that coffee?" Keyla pointed to the coffee maker on the counter, she could already smell the delicious aroma wafting throughout the house.

"Sure, help yourself. There's also bread in the bread box and the toaster is to the left of the coffee maker." Heather instructed.

"Coffee's fine, thanks," Keyla replied, as she moved around the island toward the coffee. She spotted the mugs in one of the two glass paneled cupboards above the machine and poured herself and her sister a cup.

Kittana watched her sister interact with her former friend feeling torn. Part of her wanted to sneak away and come back later—she'd done a good job of avoiding Heather so far. Yet another part of Kittana wanted it to be like old times when she and Heather were inseparable friends.

Heather's gaze swung to Kittana's face, she was being so quiet that Heather felt like she had to say something. She had practiced what she wanted to say so many times in her mind over the years, daydreaming of the chance to someday say them out loud and now that she had that chance, she found herself scared. Wondering where to start, she opened and closed her mouth a few times determined to speak but nothing came out.

"So, the boys went to school, huh?" Keyla stated looking at the clock, it was before eight in the morning, "Isn't it a little early for school?" she wondered out loud, wrinkling up her nose.

"Yeah, Nate didn't want to be late," Heather replied, then turned to her old friend to ask, "Kittana how do you do it? How did you get your son to love school?"

Kittana just smiled as she accepted a hot steamy cup Keyla handed her. She was surprised to hear that Nate loved school, at home she practically had to hogtie him to the chair and that was after she dragged him into the study room, perhaps it was more than just school work that had him so fascinated, she wondered remembering a time in her youth when she'd have done anything for the chance to go to school and make real friends, she sighed. Maybe the apple didn't fall to far from the tree.

"Are we talking about the same Nate here?" Keyla almost choked on her coffee as surprised look on her face just seconds before it melted into a knowing smile as she added, "There must be a girl involved somewhere." Seeing Kittana's frowning glare she added, "What? Besides being Nate, he IS a ragging, hormonal teenager—there has to be a girl involved to get that boy interested in learning."

"I . . . I suppose you could be right," Kittana grudgingly admitted.

"I'm glad to hear that Jake's not the only one." Heather said with a relieved chuckle that faded into an awkward silence.

"Kittana, Keyla." Heather's voice seemed loud in the quiet that had fallen. Gaining their attention, she took a deep breath and continued. "I'm glad you're here. I've wanted to tell you for so long . . . I'm sorry," her eyes moved from one twin to the other "to both of you . . . for the things I've done and the nasty things I've said." Heather's eyes showed her remorse and sincerity as they moved back to meet Kittana's again. "You were right when you said the only thing that really mattered is liking yourself. In high school I wasn't . . . I wasn't a nice person, I didn't really have much self-esteem—oh, I know I pretended to but, that was more of a cover up, like make-up makes a plain person beautiful . . . anyway, having Jake, well, he was the best thing that ever happened to me." Heather paused, "I like who I am now," she held Kittana's gaze steady for a second before looking down at her half-finished coffee cup, she continued, "I know that we'll never be friends again—not like we were, but I wanted you to know that I've changed and that I am sorry."

Truly touched by Heather's apology Kittana moved to sit across from her, placing her hand on top of Heather's in a gesture of friendship before she spoke.

"Thank-you, that means a lot, really." Then, after a moment's pause, she added. "Heather, we can be friends—just not like we used to be and not because I don't want to but because I . . . we can't stay here. We have to go home."

"I know," Heather said quietly with a sniff, lifting her head to meet Kittana's eyes she continued with a warm, attentive smile. "You know that you'll always be welcome here, when you're in town, right."

"Of-course," Kittana smiled. Taking a sip of her coffee, she made a face, turned toward her sister and said in an accusing voice, "You didn't add sugar!"

Keyla grinned and handed her the sugar bowl, then she sipped her own black coffee. Keyla turned toward Heather she was quite impressed by Heather's apology. It took a lot of guts to do that. From what she'd seen and heard Heather had certainly changed a lot since high school and Keyla briefly entertained the idea that maybe they had something to do with that, then again maybe not, people can change their life around. The way one acted in high school isn't necessarily the way they'll always be. Heather did have a child at a young age, maybe the responsibility that came with motherhood, forced her to grow up and think of someone other than herself. Perhaps having Jake was the nudge in the right direction she had needed.

"You did a great job raising Jake, and he's a wonderful young man." Keyla spoke the compliment as she thought it.

"Thanks, Keyla," Heather said a pleased smile grew on her lips and a pink color rose to her cheeks.

"Is that coffee I smell?" Arron asked as he entered the kitchen, his sleepy voice breaking the relaxing atmosphere that had fallen between the three girls.

"Freshly made, it's good too. I'll get you a cup." Keyla offered already pouring him a mug of the black brew and adding the cream and the two heaping spoonfuls of sugar, just the way he liked it.

"Thanks Key," he replied when she handed him the cup. "Ah . . ." Arron sighed as he let the hot liquid slide down his throat, making him feel more awake—more human, "well, now that I feel alive again I'll say it, good morning everyone!" his gaze fell to Heather's and he returned her smile with an added wink of his eyes before asking her, "Where's Jake?"

"He went with Nate to school. Why?" Heather inquired when she saw the disappointment on his face.

"I was just hoping to spend some time with him, we're leaving early tomorrow." he told her looking at the floor, he didn't want to see the disappointment on her face—that look that called him a horrible father. He wished he could stay and get to know Jake, but his hands were tied. A damned if he did and damned if he didn't situation. He had to go back. Arron raised his eyes to Heather.

Heather surprised him by merely nodding, excepting that fact that Arron had other responsibilities, another life—one that she would never totally understand. She had so many questions that probably wouldn't get answered. It was like reading the first ten chapters of a book but not having the actual book so you could read the rest and find out what happens to the characters. Rolling her eyes she caught a glimpse of the clock on the stove.

"Oh no! I'm late; I have to get to work!" She exclaimed as she rushed out of the chair, placing her mug in the sink, grabbed her keys, brief case and purse, pausing at the garage door to change her slippers for her shoes, giving her guests a final glimpse she added, "ah, make yourself at home, Mrs. White is around somewhere, the boys will be home around two-thirty this afternoon, Arron you can spend time with Jake then, okay? I'll be back by five, bye. See you later."

With a farewell wave she was gone. In the silence that fell in the kitchen after Heather departed, the three Guardians heard the sound of Heather's car as she started it and drove away.

"Arron," Kittana asked. "Where's Reace?"

"Huh? I haven't seen him since last night," Arron replied as he made himself some toast, turning his head toward Kittana he ask. "Why?"

"You haven't? He got up early this morning I just assumed he'd be with you."

"You don't suppose he'd go over . . ." Keyla asked letting the rest of her sentence hang in the air.

"No, not after yesterday," Kittana said but she didn't sound too sure of her words.

"Shit!" Arron breathed, rubbing a hand over his face, silently cursing himself for being so stupid, "Last night I mentioned that John had a new family—kids." Arron admitted, his gaze held Kittana's as he added, "I never would have brought it up if I thought he'd go over there."

"Arron, it's not your fault, he's a big boy; he can take care of himself. You know, . . ." Keyla reassured him as she ran a comforting hand up and down his arm. "I'm not sure we could stop him if he really wanted to go anyhow."

"He's okay and . . ." Kittana said she was using her telepathic mind link with Reace to find out where he was or if he was in trouble, she was just about to tell them where he was when the back door opened and he strolled in, with a mutter she finished her sentence. ". . . He's on his way back."

Reace stopped short, three pairs of eyes seeming to pin him into place and catching the last of his wife's sentence he offered a quick grin before guessing, "You were worried about me?"

"You leave without telling anyone where you're going and we find out that you went over to John's—a man that scares you like nothing else can—Yeah, I'd say were worried about you." Kittana replied exasperated.

"What happened over there anyway?" Keyla demanded. She could see that Reace was shaken although he hid it well and her curiosity was in overdrive.

Reace glanced at Keyla seriously thinking of denying that he was at John's but then his gaze fell to Arron and he admitted. "You were right." Reace ran a hand over his mouth then dropped it as he added in a heavy voice, "he has changed."

"Who? John?" Keyla inquired, but knew the answer before she even asked. John changing was hard to wrap her mind around, but then again, when she first met him it was like John was two different people: one that she couldn't imagine hurting a fly and the one that Reace knew. She had seen both sides of Reace's father: the John with Reace around and the John without Reace. Maybe without Reace he had become the one who wouldn't hurt a fly. She supposed it was possible, stranger things have happened—like Heather apologizing.

"Yeah," Reace answered then explained, "Arron had a theory of Earth being affected by the balance and it appears that his theory is right. John, his parents and Heather . . ."

"Nasty before we balanced the forces of good and evil and afterward they've changed for the better," Kittana's voice took over, finishing Reace's explanation.

"I wouldn't have used the word '*nasty*' but yeah, that's it." Reace agreed.

"Good work Arron," Keyla praised.

Arron's dimples winked when he smiled at her.

Turning her attention back to Reace Keyla asked. "So John's not hurting his new family?"

"No, he's stopped drinking and he . . . he loves them." Reace kept the emotion off his face but he couldn't keep the bitterness out of his voice, he closed his eyes briefly wishing away the ache in his heart as he mentally replayed the conversation with his stepfather.

"Reace," Kittana said, reading his thoughts she could only imagine the way he must feel.

Reace's eyes snapped open, but he didn't look at her, he couldn't, he didn't want to see that look of pity he heard in her voice.

"It's okay, Kit," Reace swallowed, "It's okay." He repeated forcing himself to believe it. Turning to Arron he spoke after appraising him, "Man, you look like crap."

"Thanks," Arron raised his near empty cup in a mock salute to Reace, before adding. "Like looking in a mirror, ain't it? I guess I got as much sleep as you did."

Reace's eyes darkened in concern, one eyebrow quirked in silent question.

"Nightmare," Arron replied to the unspoken question on his comrade's face.

"Nightmare?" The twins echoed at the same time.

"Do you want to talk about it?" Kittana asked.

"Was it anything like mine?" Keyla demanded.

Arron watched himself put the empty cup down, taking a moment to recall the dream trying to remember the details; he shook his head.

"No. Nothing that scary." He finally answered Keyla, then elaborated, "It was just about Tia . . . I felt like she was lost or something." Arron pressed his hands into his eyes and ran them over his face before adding, "It's just everything that's been happening is getting to me . . . I feel like I'm on an emotional rollercoaster." He admitted turning his burning gaze to Kittana he asked, "Reace told you right?"

It was one good thing about having best-friends that were married you only had to tell one of them something for them both to know it. When Kittana nodded, Arron sighed, Reace hadn't disappointed him, for that Arron was glad. He didn't feel like explaining the past few days again. He just wanted to forget it happened and moved forward.

"Hey, I'm right there with you, comrade," Reace said clapping Arron on the back, giving his shoulder a light squeeze before dropping his hand.

"We all are," Keyla added smiling at Arron.

"Don't worry Arron everything will turn out the way it was meant to." Kittana said.

"That's supposed to make me feel better, Kit? What if things aren't meant to turn out good? What if Zarrick turns evil, Malic . . ."

"We won't let that happen," Kittana's stern voice cut into Arron's words, stopping them.

"I hope your right." He said earnestly as he let her words, her self-assuredness wash over him.

Kittana hoped she was right too.

*

Nate walked with Jake and a few of Jake's friends. They entered the school talking and laughing with each other in a familiar way that told anyone watching that they'd been friends for years. Nate played along amazed and beyond happy to be included, to be part of a group. It was something he had always dreamed about and it would never have happened on Taysia.

Nate's wide, innocent gaze took in everything around him, every smell, sound and sight, committing them all into memory. They were leaving tomorrow at dawn, he didn't want to but he feared his parents would insist that he go back to Taysia. He'd just gotten here and every second that he stayed on Earth he fell in love with this world more. Nate knew that going back was the right thing to do but, the truth was, that he didn't want to.

The bottom line was that he wanted to stay but how would he convince his parents that he belonged here? Nate was drawn out of his thoughts by a voice who spoke, not to him but about him, as he passed.

"There is that new kid," One girl said to her friends, looking Nate up and down in a way that made Nate walk straighter as he passed her.

"He's cute," another added.

"Hot! Would be more like it," Corrected a blond girl making Nate blush. He glanced at the group, the girl who had just spoken was standing beside someone Nate recognized, he smiled.

"Hey, Nate," Anna-Maria called to him from the midst of the gawking girls.

"Hi Anna," Nate stopped walking and stood with her. "About tonight . . . did you want me to pick you up or meet you there . . . at . . . at the dance?"

Nate wiped his sweaty palms on his jeans, he was nervous talking to her this morning, he briefly wondered why? He hadn't been this nervous last night when it was just the two of them, maybe the knowledge that she liked him or that he had at least a second chance at gaining her affections made him scared he'd screw it up somehow. It wasn't everyday that the girl of your dreams asked you out, and having no prior experience he was unsure of what to do, how to act. What was expected of him anyhow?

"Meet me there, it'll be easier." She smiled, unable to keep her eyes from eating him up, he truly fascinated her, besides being a hunk, he was different than any boy she had ever known and she found that refreshing.

"Sure," Nate nodded as he stood there still smiling at her.

"Come on, Nate," Jake grabbed his arm and pulled him toward their homeroom class.

"Bye," Nate called looking back at her before disappearing down the crowded hallway.

"You're going to the dance with him?" The blond beside Anna asked in a disbelieving voice as she watched Nate disappear down the hallway.

"What about Cody?" Another demanded.

"What about Cody?" Anna returned the question, watching Nate walk away, looking back at her friends she added, "We're over, Cody and I broke up, remember?"

"But he walked you to class yesterday . . . I thought . . ."

"You thought wrong!" Anna snapped letting her temper color her words, "Cody's history, Nate's now." Anna's face lit up like a Christmas tree when she spoke about Nate.

Her friends didn't say anything more but the looks they exchanged spoke volumes and silently asked the question: *Does Cody know about this?*

"Come on we'll be late for class," Anna suddenly spoke and the group moved down the hallway and into the classroom.

\*

It was just after lunch when Jake's friends had just gotten up from the table calling over their shoulder as they left the cafeteria, "See you in gym, Jake, Nate."

"Gym, what's that?" Nature quietly asked Jake.

"It's playing sports and stuff," Jake answered distractedly as he gathered his trash, piling it up on his lunch tray.

"Sports," Nate repeated, he'd seen something like that in the crystal Malic had. Nate grinned, he couldn't wait to go to gym.

Jake was about to get up and put his tray away when two heavy hands, one on each of his shoulders pushed him back down and held him in place, as the large muscled bodies attached to the hands sat on either side of Jake. He didn't have to look at their faces to know who held him because Cody had just taken a seat beside Nate, across from Jake, and wherever Cody was his two goons were never far behind.

The smile fell from Nate's face, replaced with a glare. The wind picked up speed outside the school; tossing papers around, some of them sticking to the windows outside the cafeteria. Nate clenched his hands into fists under the table trying to keep his new found abilities under control. It was harder then he thought to reign in his anger and control his powers as they fought to surge to the surface.

Cody stared at Nate until Nate growled, "What?"

"You and Anna—not going to happen," Cody stated with a shake of his head, "You are not going with her to the dance or anywhere else. You're going to tell her you've had a change of heart or you've found someone else . . . I really don't care what you tell her, just break it off."

"And if I don't?" Nate inquired his voice sounding calm despite the glare in his eyes.

Cody smirked as he flexed his fingers, putting one fist inside the other. He grinned wolfishly as he cracked a few knuckles before replying, "Let's just say for the rest of your life you'll be walking funny."

"Don't threaten me. Cody, I'm not scared of you." Nate said his steady gaze never wavered from Cody's eyes.

Cody was taken aback for a moment, no one had ever spoken to him like that, but he covered it well, his next words were coated in acid. "When I'm done with you . . . you will be."

Nate was about to say more but he caught sight of Jake in the corner of his eye. Jake was shaking his head in silent warning, one that Nate heeded and cursed at the same time.

Why should he hide the fact that he was powerful? All his life he had always been the weak one and now that he finally discovered some of his powers (Timelana said in time he'd learn to use all of them) he had to pretend to be weak. It wasn't fair! Why should he have to hide the fact that he was powerful? That he had battled others who had powers? Why did he have to pretend to be scared of this stupid jerk?

He didn't bother giving himself any answers to these questions. It was the answers he didn't want to hear right now. What he wanted to do was show Cody the meaning of the word 'fear.' He wanted to beat Cody, take him down a peg or two, the guy was just so full of himself and from everything Nature had heard and seen so far about Cody, everyone else was too scared to stand up to him. Nate wasn't. But instead of giving into his true feelings he heeded Jake's warning—knowing it was the normal thing to do. Nate lowered his blazing eyes in defeat and slowly nodded.

Cody smiled in pleasure at Nate's nod of compliance.

"Glad we see eye to eye!" He clapped Nate on the back as he got up then he turned in a fast, swift movement and slammed Nate's head into the table, holding it there with a hand pushing on the back of Nate's head.

Cody's two body guards grip tightened on Jake until it hurt.

Cody leaned down into Nate's ear, pulling on his hair, as he spoke.

"Don't ever try to take what's mine again!" Then Cody released him. With a motion of his hand, Cody signaled his friends and the three of them strolled out of the cafeteria.

Leaving Nate holding his aching head and glaring at Jake, who glared back.

"What did I tell you? Rule number one, you don't fuck with Cody Marshal and you don't date Anna-Maria. See what happens when you mess with him? And you got off easy. How's your head?" Jake asked genuinely concerned.

Nate's glare intensified.

"I'll be fine," He said in a clipped voice.

"Okay, so, what are you going to tell Anna?" Jake asked.

"Nothing's changed, Jake, I'm still going to the dance with her." Nate stated getting up from the table.

"What? But you heard Cody, he doesn't screw around. He'll hurt you—make you wish you were dead." Jake said following behind Nate, putting away his tray and garbage as fast as he could before trying to keep up with Nature's angry strides.

"Jake, I told Cody I wasn't scared of him and I meant it. I'm not." Nature seethed as Jake walked beside him. "Heck, Zarrick . . ." Nate forced himself to stop talking. Jake didn't know his brother and Nate didn't want to disillusion him.

"What about Zarrick? Nate, he's my brother, I deserve to know. What about him?" Jake demanded. Studying Nate's face he took a deep breath, turned his head away. "Oh, man!" He swung his head back to hold Nate's gaze steady. "He's like Cody, isn't he?"

"I never said that," Nate shot back.

"You didn't have to," Jake replied.

"Look, Jake . . ." Nate began but the loud buzz of the bell broke off any other words.

"We're late," Jake stated curtly. He hadn't even gotten used to the idea of having a younger sibling; he didn't what to hear this now. He didn't want to disillusion himself. "We'll talk about this later," Jake added before breaking away from Nate to go to his class.

Nate nodded, which caused his headache to reinstate itself, as he ran what he told Jake though his mind again. It angered him that Jake thought he'd run from Cody.

Give into Cody's demands? No way! He'd had come too far, put too much at risk. He had a chance to experience life and love and he'd be damned if he'd let some normal earthling-jackass, with a hyped up sense of himself stop him now.

Nate was so involved in his thoughts that he failed to notice the darkening clouds that moved across the sun outside. He stomped to his next class as his thoughts continued.

Nature had never backed down from a fight—even when he knew he had almost no chance of winning. Life with Zarrick taught him about bullies and Zarrick was a lot scarier then Cody—a lot! Cody couldn't even blow things up. Nate couldn't help but smile at the image of Zarrick facing off with Cody.

\*

"Today boys we're going to have a game of basket-ball." The coach announced.

It was last period of the day Jake and Nate were in the same gym class and sat side by side. Nate leaned over a bit to whisper to Jake.

Before Jake could reply the coach's keen eyes narrowed in on them, irritated that he'd been interrupted.

"Do you have any questions . . . Nathan?" the coach directed his question at Nate after checking his name on the clipboard he held. "Something you'd like to share?"

"It's Nate, and yes," Nature corrected, turning his attention on the coach, ignoring the snickers and strange looks from some of his classmates. "I don't know how to play and I was asking Jake to explain the rules of the game to me."

"How dumb do you have to be to not know the game, sissy boy?" Cody's loud remark was a little harder to ignore, Nate clenched his jaw tight and kept his eyes focused on the teacher in front of him.

"You seriously don't know how to play?" The coach asked hardly believing what he was hearing. "Have you ever watched a game on T.V.?"

"No sir, I've never played sports and back home we didn't have T.V . . . ,"

"Shut-up now." Jake muttered under his breath causing Nate to frown and stop talking mid-sentence.

"Okay," The coach drew out the word as he stared at Nate like he had three heads. "Let's refresh everyone's memory of the rules."

After the rules of the game were explained to everyone they started playing, Nate found he had a natural talent for the game, and he thoroughly enjoyed it. He was on such a natural high afterward that even Cody threatening him again didn't bring him down.

"So what did Cody say to you after gym?" Jake asked, bringing up the subject of Cody again on their way home after school. He had seen Cody talking to Nate and he saw his murderous expression when Nate brushed past Cody; totally ignoring him.

"He just reminded me of his earlier threat." Nate answered with a careless shrug.

"And you walked away from him? Dude, you should've seen the look he gave you, you totally pissed him off!" Jake warned "You'll be lucky if he doesn't beat you up now especially after you totally creamed him in b-ball!"

"I'm not scared of Cody," Nate reminded Jake then smiled, "It did feel pretty good to beat him in the game though!"

"You're crazy to not be scared."

"Why should I be, you've seen what I can do, heck I've gone head to toe with Zarrick, when all I thought I could do was make it rain and grow flowers, and he can blow things up—what can Cody do?"

"Zarrick can blow things up? Really?"

"Yeah," Nate nodded.

"What else can he do?" Jake inquired thirsty for any information about his younger sibling.

"Ah, he can play with emotions," Nate started slowly not sure if he should be telling this to Jake but the look on his friends face encouraged Nate to continue, "but not like his mother, Tia, The Guardian of Emotions. Zarrick is the Guardian of War and he can make you feel that 'fight or flight' feeling. He can make you angry enough to fight to the death—to start a war." Nate swallowed the anger he held toward his lifelong rival when he thought about the fairies Zarrick was toying with a few days ago. For the second time, Nate wondered if coming here was a mistake. What was Zarrick doing now, was he hurting the fairies again? What would happen now that Nature wasn't there to stop him?

# CHAPTER TWENTY ONE

## Taysia

AFTER WATCHING ARRON WITH KEYLA, Tia walked slowly back to the crystal mountain, she walked behind Link with her son by her side. All she could think about all the way back to her room was what she had to do to set things right. It would be hard—she'd be giving up so much, but she was consoled by the fact that she was finally doing the right thing.

In her room, staring at the pink crystal pyramid she held in her hand, she thought about what she'd tell Arron when she said goodbye. Tia was setting him free and finally after a lifetime of getting things wrong, she was finally doing something right.

Quietly, when she was sure Link and Awkwade were busy, Tia slipped out of her bedroom, looking left then right before heading down the hallway, down the steps and out of Crystal Mountain.

If Tia had looked behind her she would have seen the yellow eyes that almost glowed with malice in the dim light of her bedroom. She'd have known that her son, Zarrick had been with her the whole time, but Malic had masked their presence from her using his power of the mind. She had no idea that he was there or that he was controlling her thoughts and feelings, but Zarrick did.

He knew what was happening, what Malic was planning and doing. Trapped in his own mind, unable to control his own body, Zarrick was helpless to stop it—to save the one person that mattered the most to him—his mother.

*

"Link," Awkwade called softly from across the room, she was staring into a flat, opaque green rounded crystal that hung on the wall of the top chamber in the mountain made of crystal. Although Link had told her Malic was gone, she had been monitoring Stone Mountain on and off as she went about using her powers to help others through the crystals. What she saw in the colored oval both surprised and scared her at the same time.

"What?" He answered absently. He was staring into his own orange crystal seeing scenes that only he could see unless he linked hands with another Guardian then they would have shared the image.

These crystals that graced the walls were one of the tools the Guardians used to see into the other worlds and to help those who called upon them. There were seven of these crystals equally spaced around the room, nestled in between the bookcases that lined the walls of the top chamber in the crystal mountain. Each oval was a different color; a color that matched the aura of the seven Guardian's powers.: pink, orange, yellow, green, blue, violet and white;

"Link!" Her voice grew more insistent as she demanded his full attention.

"What is it, Awkwade?" Link sighed as he turned to her, waving a hand over the polished orange surface he had been staring at, closing the window into the world Dicot.

"Someone is in Stone Mountain, I cannot see clearly but I know someone is there." Her was voice full of apprehension.

"You're sure?" Link asked in alarm, as he moved closer to his wife. He was worried that somehow Malic had returned. At Awkwade's nod he added, "Okay. I'll go check it out."

"I'll go with you." Awkwade offered.

"NO!" his tone broke no argument, his eyes flashed with worry, "You stay here with Tia, in case . . ." He let his words hang in the air.

"Be careful," Awkwade's eyes spoke volumes and Link nodded at the emotion in them, as he returned her gaze.

*

Link wasted no time getting to the Stone Mountain. Once there he stealthy crept from room to room, finding them all empty. Finally he made his way into the throne room, the main chamber. In the doorway he paused, shocked at what he saw.

Tia was seated, cross-legged on the floor, her hands resting on her knees, palms upward. Her body glistened with sweat, her eyes tightly closed, her lips moved slightly as she chanted, but what scared Link the most was the purple haze that surrounded her, filling the room.

Link's stomach bottomed out, hoping to stop her before it was too late and he refused to believe that it was already too late, he yelled. "Tia, No! TIA!"

Her eyes snapped open at the sound of his voice, they were sad and scarily vacant. Her voice seemed to come more from the purple haze then from her and Link could still hear her chant the Starian death chant even as the mist surrounding her spoke to him with her voice, "I have to do this, it is the right thing to do."

"NO! TIA, NO!" Link shouted but he was too late.

He watched helplessly as the air around them burst into flames. Her body was consumed instantly, the smell of brunt flesh and bone stung Link's nostrils as fire erupted all around him, though it didn't hurt the Guardian of Fire, his knees buckled and he fell to floor, tears streaming from his eyes. It wasn't the heat nor the smoke that made them water but the loss of a friend.

In his line of vision he saw her blackened body, engulfed in flame, explode in a puff of ash. He closed his eyes then, remembering her friendly smile, her wide eyes that no matter how big her smile was, always seemed sad.

He remembered the day they had first met.

*The high council of Fentra (made up of members from all five planets in the solar system) had done research into why Staria died, trying to figure out what happened? The planet had been thriving and healthy when suddenly almost with no warning it just stopped. Life was totally wiped out; the buildings still stood but no living thing, not even a blade of grass, remained. The council members said they had found evidence that the legends of the Guardians were true and the second verse of the prophecy was coming about. They had sent*

157

out advertisements for anyone from the remaining planets in the Fentra solar system, with the mark of the Guardian to come forward and be heroes—they were looking for the four Guardians from the second verse in the prophecy.

Since no one had ever seen the mark—Guardians hadn't been seen in well over four hundred years—they ended up with a lot of hopefuls and fakes. Eventually Link, the Guardian of Fire, from Vanishtar, and Awkwade, the Guardian of Water, from Volairon were discovered. Now, the high council members were searching in the villages surrounding the cities on Vanishtar looking for the next two Guardians. They had already searched the other planets, Dicot and Volairon with no more luck and no one dared go near the exiled planet of Zyled.

The streets were crowded with people hoping to catch a glimpse of these new would be heroes or in hopes of being them themselves. Link was in the midst of the crowd when someone bumped into him and a weird feeling came over him. He scanned the crowd with his eyes but he found them useless so closing his eyes he concentrated on the feeling. He wasn't sure why or how he knew that the weird feeling was another Guardian, a she and he knew she was close, very close.

She was behind him, turning quickly he reached out a hand, grabbing her wrist he opened his eyes and stared into her face—huge violet colored eyes dominated her pixie like features and drew his attention—eyes that looked up at him in fear a second before they narrowed slightly.

Link dropped her hand. Stepping away from her as pure terror flowed through him making him freeze with fear, helpless to do anything more than watch her retreat from him.

He didn't know how long he stood there as he dealt with the emotions flowing through him. When someone tapped him on the shoulder and he spun around, ready to use his power to defend himself, but he paused, flames in the palm of his hand, blinking at Awkwade in confusion.

"Whoa power down, hot stuff! Let us talk about this." Awkwade responded ready to defend herself if need be.

Link shook his head to clear it, glancing at his hand then back to her face in horror. What had he almost done? He turned away from her as he reined his fire power in.

"What happened?" She asked after seeing the look on his face before he turned from her.

"I ah, I think I have just met another Guardian." He said slowly turning back to her.

*"You have found another?" Awkwade was impressed, "Where? Who?" She looked around hoping to get a glimpse but in this crowd it was impossible to pick out just one person.*

*"I am not sure," he admitted raising his eyes to her face, "but I felt her, I saw her and then she . . . well, I do not know exactly what she did, but I . . . I have never experienced anything like that before."*

*"Can you find her again?" Awkwade asked.*

*Link could tell by the way her brow wrinkled that she was worried. Time was running out, the officials said that there were no warning signs, but she thought they were wrong, much to his protests, she had been spending every spare moment in the libraries, studying the weather patterns on Staria before it died, she said the same things were happening here on Vanishtar. They needed to go soon before it was too late, they had to find the other two Guardians and somehow go to Taysia and balance the forces of good and evil.*

*"She could not have gone far in this crowd." Link said his eyes scanning behind him where he had last seen her then he turned his orange gaze to Awkwade's "Do not tell anyone yet, okay? I want to make sure first."*

*With a nod Awkwade agreed, she watched as Link disappeared into the throng of people. She hoped he would find the girl and they would go to Taysia, she didn't want whatever happened on Staria to happen here on Link's home planet or to her own.*

*Link ran in the direction he had helplessly watched the violet eyed girl flee in. Running through the crowd his sharp eyes assessing everyone he saw then dismissing them when they were not the girl he searched for. Coming to the end of the crowd he was about to give up when out of the corner of his eyes he saw her.*

*"Wait!" Link called to the girl. She had been watching him and when she knew he had seen her she took off running. Ten minutes later, after he chased her through several nearly deserted streets, and into a blocked alleyway where he finally caught up with her.*

*Panting he spoke to her, "Please . . . I just . . . want . . . to talk."*

*Hope swelled inside of him when she stopped looking for a way out and slowly turned around to face him, her face a mix of so many different emotions that Link couldn't name then all.*

*"Thanks," Link said after catching his breath, "I am Link and you are . . . ?"*

*She frowned, his manners where more suited to a formal gathering then the middle of an empty street.*

"Okay," Link said when she refused to answer him. "Listen, I have this mark," he showed her the small glass like flame embedded into the skin of his left wrist. "I can do some pretty amazing things with fire and not get hurt . . . back there," he pointed behind them, "you made me feel something I have never felt before—fear. Do you have a mark too?"

The girl just continued to stare at him refusing to say anything, but Link saw something in her face, something that encouraged him.

"The high council members say I am a Guardian like those seven from legends of Deia's prophecy and I think, no, I know you are a Guardian too. Please, come back with me and we will do a test to prove that what I think is true. If I am wrong then you can go home—no harm done, but if I am right and you are a Guardian than its your duty to be a hero, to help those in need, to save this planets life. Please, say yes" Link pleaded holding out his hand to her.

He was surprised by the brilliant smile she flashed him as she nodded placing her hand in his. He breathed a sigh of relief, he was worried that she would say no and run away again. If he were honest with himself he would admit that he was worried she would use that fear power on him again and that was one feeling he never wanted to experience again.

"Tia," she spoke startling him with the sound of her voice, at his confused expression she clarified, "My name is Tia."

She had been proven to be the Guardian of Emotion—by her blood, her mark being totally disfigured. In an accident, Tia claimed, but the way she said it made Link wonder especially after meeting her father. Seeing the way the man treated his daughter made Link want to hit him.

Link shook his head to clear away the direction his thought had taken, forcing them back to Tia he thought of the past seventeen years after coming here and meeting the other four Guardians—the ones of the prophecy. Tia meant so much to him—like that little sister he had never had but always wanted. In the past seventeen years they had all become a close knit family—all of them. He had never seen Tia as happy as when she was with Arron and their son Zarrick. And now she was gone. He couldn't quite believe it.

Why Tia, why now? It didn't make any sense.

Link slowly got up off the floor, sparing one last look around the room, there was nothing left even the fire had died out.

"Tia," he whispered, "why?" He demanded from the empty room. How would Zarrick take this news, he wondered and Arron, what would he tell Arron when he came back?

As Link turned toward the door, ready to leave he was surprised to see his life mate, standing there holding a pyramid shaped pink crystal in her hands.

"Awkwade?" Link spoke her name.

"After you left Crystal Mountain, I started looking for Tia, I thought that if Malic were back then you might need help." She paused looking down at her hands for a moment before looking back to him. Holding up the pyramid shaped crystal she said, "I found this in her room."

"A kyvein crystal," Link stated. Throughout the Fentra solar system kyvein crystals were used to store information, record thoughts, usually the last words of a person who went to Niteon to die. Could Stone Mountain be Tia's Niteon? Yes, the answer hurt Link like a punch to the stomach, raising confused teary-eyes to Awkwade he questioned. "Why would she . . . she has lived through so much, why now, why this?"

Awkwade's heart broke for Link, she welcomed him in hug, he and Tia shared a special bond of friendship. She, herself was never very close to Tia, but being a Volairon she didn't allow herself to get close to many people. Link was an exception—he was her mate for life, her miteon. Tia had been nice, she seemed well adjusted, happy even, Awkwade didn't understand why she would kill herself but one thing Awkwade was sure of was that Arron wasn't going to like this and Zarrick? How would they tell the child that his mother was gone?

# Chapter twenty two

Earth:

Kittana had just told Nancy and David goodbye, this time she did it face to face. She didn't tell them the truth, as much as she wanted too, knowing they never understand or except it, instead she simply said she had to go back home later tonight. Hugging them good-bye with promises that she'd visit again if she could was hard, Kittana wiped the tears from her eyes with her hands as she closed the door and walked down the steps. She pasted a smile on her face when she saw Anna-Maria coming up the front walk after school.

"Hi, Anna . . ." Kittana's happy greeting was cut off by Anna's snarl.

"What are you doing here?"

"I, ah, just came by to say good-bye."

"That's rich!" Anna retorted sarcastically.

"What's your problem?" Kittana demanded.

"My problem?" Anna repeated before she unloaded her emotional anger, "my problem is you. You left them seventeen years ago—without a word. You let them think the worst. Then you come waltzing in here acting as if everyone should kiss your ass! Would it have killed you to pick up a phone and call, just once in the past seventeen years, it would have saved her a lot of pain," Anna looked at Kittana with contempt. She used to feel sorry for her foster sister—a woman who just disappeared, possible murdered. Countless nights Anna lay awake listening to her mother cry with worry. Yet here Kittana was standing in front of her now, like she had never left and she had this wonderful life with her husband and son. It disgusted Anna. How could she do that to the people who loved her, did she just not care?

"It wasn't like that . . ." Kittana began wanting to be able to confide in Anna about their powers and everything but she knew she couldn't.

"It wasn't as if you left the planet! There's a phone on every street corner." Anna shot back, angry at her foster sister and at the fact that her parents placed this selfish woman above their own child.

"Look, I didn't come back here to fight with you. I want us to be friends." Kittana implored her.

"So you can hurt me too when you leave again? No thanks. I've already spent a life time living under your shadow and I don't want to spend another looking for you!" Anna stormed past Kittana and into the house slamming the door behind her.

Kittana stared after her stunned for a moment by the sire volume of anger Anna held toward her perhaps she was right to feel that way Kittana thought as guilt for all the pain she had caused leaving the way she had before flared inside of her. She hadn't meant to hurt anyone, but she had hurt them badly and her pathetic attempt to make amends now was just too little, too late. Sighing, with fresh tears stinging her eyes, Kittana turned around and starting toward the Price's home.

Half way there she gasped as a sharp pain sliced through her heart, squeezing it. Doubling over she emptied the contents of her stomach on the sidewalk. After a few seconds the pain subsided and Kittana was able to breathe deeply.

"What the hell?" she whispered to herself sitting down on the sidewalk for a few seconds, just breathing and wondering what just happened.

Perhaps, it was the same thing that they had experienced last night? And if it was, then she needed to get back home—they all did, something must be happening on Taysia, something serious.

Worry forced her to stand she had to get back to Arron's fast! There were too many people around for her to teleport so she started jogging.

*

"Hi dad," Nate said as he and Jake entered the room. Reace, Arron and Keyla were sitting on the barstools at the counter in the kitchen, talking. Nate sat across from his father, calling over his shoulder when he heard the fridge door open. "Get me one too."

He smiled a thanks as Jake sat the cold can of coke in front of him before sitting next to him at the counter and popping the top on his own can.

"My God! Nate, what happened to you?" Keyla exclaimed when she saw his face. Nate had a little cut on his forehead and a darkening bruise on his cheek from where Cody had pushed his head into the table, the cut was from the tray that was on the table at the time. He still had a slight headache from that incident and he curse Cody for it.

"It's nothing," Nate mumbled staring at his coke can. He didn't want to ruin his chances of convincing his parents that he could handle things by mentioning bullies.

"Nothing?" Jake repeated his tone said he didn't agree. "Two words, Cody marshal." Jake announced as if that was all the explanation he needed to give.

"Who's Cody Marshal?" Reace demanded not liking the look of his son's face—not after the dreams he had last night. He glanced at Arron with a new appreciation at how well his comrade had handled seeing him like that and not doing anything. Right now, Reace wanted to hunt this Cody down and electrify him.

"He's nobody, just a bully at school," Nate grudgingly answered as he glared at Jake.

"A bully?" Keyla asked then offered, "Do you want me to fix him with a spell?"

"No!" Nate said, mortified.

"Yes!" Reace spoke at the same time.

"You can do that?" Jake sounded impressed.

"Keyla," Arron said as he playfully punched Reace's shoulder with a frown on his face. "Let's not blow this out of proportion. Here Nate, let me heal you and then we'll forget it happened, no harm done."

Arron moved to stand beside Nature, placing his hands over Nate's bruise and cut. Concentrating on his power, Arron's mark flashed and his hands began to glow slightly, his vision blurred, seeing the damaged skin up close he guided his powers into healing what was broken. When he took his hands away Nate's face was perfect, like it never had a bruise or cut.

Jake stared at his father in fascination. "Awesome!"

"Thanks Arron." Nate muttered feeling much better now that his headache was totally gone.

"Anytime." Arron smiled pleased with himself that Jake thought his powers were cool and not freaky or scary, but his son didn't know the other power he held, the power of death.

"We have to talk," Reace announced. He wanted to talk to his son about so many things, like this bully, coming to Earth, how or why he wanted to leave Taysia, but right now they had more pressing matters. "all of us. Malic is planning something and we need to figure out what before we end up walking into a trap."

"So, you're taking Keyla's dream seriously?" Nate had suspected that her nightmare was more than just a scary dream and he wondered what her vision was about as he waited for one of them to explain it.

"I think it was more than just a dream, I think it may have been a warning," Keyla admitted.

"We can't just shrug off the whole heart-attack-feeling-thing—we all felt that," Arron looked at Keyla and Reace waiting for a nod to his silent question before adding, "twice."

"Twice?" Nate echoed, his gaze swung to his father's, his expression a demand for answers and a mask of worry.

Reace nodded. "Something's happening on Taysia and we need to be prepared for anything. Now, we don't have much time, we have to go back tonight—before dawn, the sooner the better."

"You're leaving?" Jake croaked turning wounded eyes on Arron, as he continued, "No, NO! You can't . . ."

"I'm sorry, Jake, but I don't have a choice you know what I am. The balance is at risk. We felt it! We have to go." Arron tried to reason with his son, but the truth was he felt the way Jake looked—crushed.

"IT ISN'T FAIR! I've just met you," Jake cried.

"Life isn't always fair Jake, if I could stay, I would. I would love to spend more time with you." Arron responded but Jake wasn't listening.

"I've spent my whole life thinking you were dead; wondering what you were like and now that I've find out your alive and I finally get to meet you—you're just going to LEAVE?!" Jake stood, his eyes blazed with unshed tears, hurt and anger, all directed at Arron.

"YOU'RE NO BETTER THEN A DEAD BEAT DAD! I WISH I NEVER HEARD OF YOU!" He shouted before he left the room, slamming the backdoor behind him.

Arron was off his stool in seconds, he wanted to go after Jake, make him understand how much this was hurting him too, but Reace's hand on his arm stopped him. Arron turned confused eyes to Reace.

"It's better this way." Reace's eyes carried silent messages to Arron. "If he's mad at you, he'll not try to follow."

Arron's expression turned to horror as it dawned on him what Reace was saying, "No," he whispered, "I've got to warn him."

Shrugging off Reace's hand Arron took a step toward the door just as Keyla's voice rang out, soft and musical, causing him to pause.

"Do you really think he'll listen to you right now?"

"No," he answered slowly turning to face her, the wheels turning in his mind, as he gazed at her, an idea formed. "But, he might listen to you, or one of your spells."

"Arron, are you sure this is a good idea?" Reace inquired. He knew that look on his comrades face.

"No," Arron answered with a devilish grin as he grabbed Keyla's hand, "but it's the only one I've got." Turning to Keyla his eyes pleaded with her. "Keyla please, say you'll help me?"

Keyla bit her lip, she, like Reace, wondered if this was a good idea. She glanced at Nate to see what he thought and when he nodded to her, she turned her attention back to Arron. Keyla was helpless to say no; not when he looked at her like that.

Arron's grin widened bringing out both dimples when she nodded.

"Okay, first, we need to find him." Looking from Nate to Reace, before looking back to Arron as she asked, "Any idea's where Jake went?"

When no one spoke she sighed heavily. Holding tight to Arron's hand she called her powers to the surface as she spoke her spell,

"Jake Price is whom we seek,
　　　Show us the path of the one I speak."

Her mark flashed as she waved her hand in the air in front of their eyes. Jake's foot prints glittered on the floor of the kitchen, and led the two of them out the back door, across the yard, over a fence and into the shelter—much to Arron's surprise.

# CHAPTER TWENTY THREE

"JAKE, WE NEED TO TALK . . ." Arron said as soon as he saw his son.

"Great!" Jake muttered standing in the middle of the main room of the shelter, he had been restlessly pacing the length of the room trying to get his emotions under control, having stopped when he heard them enter. "I should have known you'd find me here." He muttered to himself, then turning to them he let his anger and hurt color his words, pointing in Arron's direction he spoke. "I have NOTHING to say to you."

"I have something to say to you, Jake, please just listen," Arron pleaded.

Jake didn't want to listen. He didn't want to even look at his dad. Moving past him, he headed for the door.

"Hold!"

Jake stopped mid-stride when Keyla, who stood beside Arron, pointed at Jake as she spoke the first word from her spell. Her voice rang with authority as she continued her spell,

"Now you will do as you are told.
Sit, on the couch and lend an ear.
What we have to say, you need to hear!"

Arron's expression was one of surprise when Jake compliantly moved away from the door to sit on the old ratty sofa, waiting for them to talk to him. Arron glanced at Keyla, she raised an eyebrow—a signal for him to go ahead. Arron sat on the over turned crate in front of Jake, eye to eye, before he started.

"Ah, I get that you're pissed off at me, Jake. Right now, probably more than before, with Keyla's spell forcing you to listen but what I have to tell you, to warn you about—it's important and we don't have much time," he glanced at Keyla. She nodded encouragingly for Arron to continue, turning back to Jake he went on to say, "I guess you're feeling like I don't want you around but that's not true. I love you, Jake, you're my son. Okay? But I . . . You can't ever follow me into Taysia-no matter what anyone ever tells you. Jake, you've got to promise me that you'll never try to enter Taysia, I'm a Guardian. You are not." Arron knew he wasn't explaining this right and he sighed in relief when Keyla interrupted him.

"Jake, Arron's only trying to protect you. In our world there were things called shades, they were once like you—ordinary people maybe with a special talent, maybe not. They were changed when they tried to enter Taysia, changed into a mindless, faceless," she frowned in memory, "horrible, evil creatures. Not dead but not alive either."

Jake's eyes opened wider in surprise as he listened.

"One came to Earth once" Arron continued explaining, "but even here he didn't change back. He was still a shadow." Arron frowned and averted his eyes, unable to look at Jake as he added, "He hurt your grandmother, I couldn't stand it if you got turned into one them because of me." Arron raised his fear filled eyes to Jake's.

"You're scared I'm going to turn into some kind of monster?" Jake stated his eyes narrowed in disbelief. Now that he was back in control of his body, he didn't move towards the door, instead he stayed where he was, caught there by curiosity and horror that they'd think he was some kind of monster waiting to happen.

"No! yes! Keyla?" Arron turned to her for help.

"Maybe you'd understand where we are coming from if we show you," Keyla offered as she moved toward the wall, taking her finger she drew a large circle speaking as she did.

"In this circle I have cast
        allow us to see scenes from the past."

Jake's eyes widened in fascination as he watched the wall where Keyla had moved her finger over sparkle with bright lights, swirling with colors, a picture forming as she spoke again.

"Show us Yentar, young and free,
Before his face was taken from thee."

Jake was surprised to see a young man who looked surprisingly like his dad, like himself, but he knew the man he saw couldn't be Arron or himself because the image on the wall had blue streaks running through his blond hair and his eyes were a light blue instead of the brown of his and Arron's eyes. Besides the places the young man was were like nothing Jake had ever seen before.

Keyla moved her hand over the scene speaking again,

"Now allow us to see how he was transformed by fate,
Forever a shade, hidden in shadow, formed in hate."

The colors swirled again creating a new picture, it was like watching a T.V. screen only with no sound and for that Jake was glad, he didn't want to hear the scream of pain and terror he could see on the face of the man Keyla called "Yentar" as he got twisted, a blackness covering him, turning him into a monster, a solid shadow with no features, no distinguishing expression—no face.

Yentar, Jake repeated the name to himself, he'd heard that name before. Jake's face paled and his gaze swung to Arron. Yentar was Arron's real father. Was Arron an evil creature? Jake's gaze moved back to the colorful moving picture on the wall created by Keyla's magic.

Magic! Jake could hardly believe any of this was happening, it seemed so surreal yet, so real at the same time.

Lost in his thoughts he barely heard Keyla as she finished the spell,

"This circle I have cast,
Close now; for we have seen the past."

Keyla closed the circle by using her finger and retracing the circle backwards, starting from where she finished and ending where she had started. The swirl of colors faded to a mere sparkle before disappearing as if they had never been there.

Jake stood up and moved toward the wall just as the sparkles disappeared, he wordlessly touched the wall, sparing a glance at Keyla then turning to stare at his father.

"Why did Yentar, look like me?" Jake demanded he needed to be sure that what he was thinking was true, he needed confirmation.

"Because, Yentar was my biological father." Arron grudgingly admitted, ashamed of his parentage. Then Arron's burning gaze pierced Jake as he added, "Haven't you ever wondered why we look nothing like Howard or the rest of the Prices? It's because Yentar raped my mother thirty-four years ago to conceive me."

"So that's why you think I'll turn into a monster, one of those shadow things? You think I'll be like him?" Jake's eyes widened, "like you? Are you a monster?"

"Yes!"

"NO!" Keyla spoke quickly overtop of Arron's hissed answer. She whirled on him and in a firm voice said, "No, Arron your not anything like Yentar. He was evil, you are good and a Guardian." Turning to Jake she told him, "Jake, Arron's nothing like a shade. Nothing!"

Keyla looked from one to the other, hoping to get through to them.

"I have the power to kill, Keyla." Arron stated looking at his hands, at the symbol that marked him a monster.

"But you never use it. Arron, just because you can hurt people doesn't make you evil. It's your actions that determine that."

He wanted to believe her; he wanted to be a good person but the guilt he carried inside swelled to the surface. She was wrong! He had used his power to kill before and he had once attacked his best friend, almost killing him too. She had no idea of his constant battle not to give in and use his power of death. It seeped in, no matter how tightly he tried to shut it out, reminding him that he had to struggle everyday to keep the vow he'd made years ago.

"Jake," Keyla turned to him, imploring to listen to her. "Arron's only trying to protect you. Humans, Starians or anyone who isn't a Guardian can *NOT* enter Taysia."

Jake glanced back to Arron, his face a mix of emotions.

"Are you . . ." He swallowed to get past the lump of emotion that settled in his throat making it dry. His voice cracked as he asked, "Are you disappointed in me . . . for not being a Guardian, like you?"

Jake anxiously waited for Arron to answer, trying hard not to show how important the answer was to him.

"NO! Never," Arron shook his head, "and I don't think you'll be like Yentar either, that's why I'm warning you. As much as I wish things were different, that we could stay or take you with us . . . you can't ever come to Taysia." Arron's gaze never wavered from Jake's proving his honestly.

"It may not happen like that—with my ability . . ." Jake desperately wanted to believe that they were wrong. He had just found his father and now he was being told he'd never see him again, that they had to say good-bye, and there was nothing he could do about it.

"You're right, it may not but I can't take that chance," Arron said then added, "I won't let *you* take that chance. Please, promise me that you'll never . . ."

"Alright," Jake said not letting Arron finish his sentence, his eyes moved to the wall where he had seen Yentar change into a shadow creature. Jake didn't want that to happen to him. His gaze moved back to Arron's, he held it steady as he vowed, "I promise." Watching Arron's face take on a relieved expression, he was compelled to make amends for the things he had said earlier, he really hadn't meant them. "I'm sorry, dad, for earlier, I . . ."

"No, Jake," Arron moved to stand in front of his son, "I'm sorry." Arron gave a small smile and a slight shake of his shaggy hair, "I seem to saying that a lot lately, but it's true, I am sorry I wasn't there when you were growing up and I'm sorry that I have to go now, but I want you to know that I love you."

Jake hugged Arron.

As Arron put his arms around his son he smiled through the tears that clouded his vision. When they moved away, Arron gaze caught Jake's again, with a hand still on Jake's shoulder he added, "I'll come back and visit you when I can, if you ever need me for any reason, all you have to do is call for the Guardian of Life, I may not always be able to come but I will hear you."

Jake nodded not trusting himself to speak.

Embarrassed by the emotions running through both of them, Arron looked around him, clearing his throat he muttered, "This place hasn't changed much."

Arron breathed in the smell of the shelter, an odd combination of rust, mold and stale air. Wrinkling his nose he asked addressing his son. "How did you find it?"

"Ah, a few years ago," Jake answered moving to sit beside Keyla who had taken a seat on the coach, "I guess, I kind of stumbled onto it. I'm surprised that Mr. Stelmen's kids haven't discovered it . . ." Jake rambled then looked at Arron as he remembered something Nate had mentioned, "Why did Reace chose to sleep here, Nate said he'd stay here for days at a time. Why?"

"He and Mr. Stelmen didn't always get along." Keyla answered for Arron.

"Duh! Reace tried to kill him—not exactly a father/son moment," Jake moved his hands as he talked, "What I don't understand is why? Mr. Stelmen is a nice guy."

Keyla looked at Arron when he snorted. She could see by the expression on his face that he was thinking of telling Jake the truth.

"Arron," she spoke to gain his attention, "No!"

"Why not?" Arron snapped. He couldn't stand the thought of John fooling everyone, he was getting away with murder and no one knew it. The injustice of it all made Arron's blood boil. "We're leaving in a few hours, so what does it matter?"

"It matters to me," Reace announced from behind Arron as he, Nate and Kittana had entered the shelter. They had been searching for Arron, Keyla and Jake, Kittana using her telepathy had found them.

"And to John's new family," Reace added as Arron whirled around standing face to face with his best friend. "When I said I want no one to know, I meant *no one*." Reace growled as he glared at Arron, he softened his voice when he added, "besides, he's changed."

"That doesn't mean it never happened. Reace, you can't walk around pretending IT NEVER HAPPENED!" Arron yelled, letting his feelings color his words.

"I KNOW IT HAPPENED, ARRON, I LIVED IT! AND I STILL RELIVE IT EVERY DAMN NIGHT!" Reace shouted back, his voice holding just as much frustration as Arron's.

"Talking about it doesn't help, okay? Can we just leave it in the past and move on." Reace spoke in the quiet that followed his outburst.

"Leave it in the past?" Arron repeated in a tone that said he couldn't believe what Reace wanted him to do. He didn't want to let it go, not yet, the anger in Arron demanded an outlet.

"Reace, that man has another family and you're just going to let him get away with it?" Arron demanded.

"You've convinced me that he's changed. What do you want me to do, Arron, confront him? Use my powers on him? 'Cause that really worked so great last time," Reace retorted sarcastically, rolling his eyes as he thought about the time he had spent in jail yesterday afternoon—not an experience he wanted to repeat.

"No. Reace, I don't know . . . maybe . . ."

"NO! Arron, I don't want to talk about it." Reace growled pushing a hand through his hair in frustration. He and Arron hadn't had an argument like this in years, not since they left Earth.

"Talk about what?" Jake asked looking from one Guardian to the other.

"NOTHING!" Reace insisted in a tone that made Jake sorry he had said anything.

"Why, Arron?" Reace lowered his voice, his eyes narrowed as he continued, "You've kept this for so many years why would you want to betray that now?"

"Yeah," Keyla agreed. "You were always 'don't tell other people's secrets' you even stopped me from helping Reace with a spell once," Keyla reminded Arron only to receive a glare from him.

Reace glanced at her too as if suddenly remembering others were in the room, then looked at Nate and Kittana before letting his gaze land on the floor, embarrassed.

Arron ran his hand through his hair, turned his back on them looking for a reason for his behavior, twisting back to his friends, he gave them the only answer he could—the truth.

"I don't know, man," his gaze landed on Reace as he spoke, "maybe it's that I need to unload it, you said it yourself, I've been keeping this so long. Or maybe it's just that I can't stand the way John is getting away with it all." Arron's face took on a pained expression.

"He hurt you and not just once . . . Now he's free to live another life! He's got happiness with another wife and kids but you . . . you're still afraid of him. You still have nightmares, you just admitted it!" Arron reminded Reace before he could object. "Besides, Jake's family, Reace," Arron pointed a hand in Jake's direction, "and he asked."

"Just because he's your son, doesn't give him the right to know about me and telling him would make him look at John differently, they're neighbors! Arron, they have to interact sometime."

"But if Jake knows then he could watch out for the kids," Arron added.

"Or he might make things worse for them . . . Look, Arron, I promised John that as long as he stayed away from alcohol and didn't hurt anyone then I'd stay quiet. If John found out that Jake knew than maybe he'd . . ."

"Drop his end of the bargain?" Keyla supplied when Reace stopped talking.

"Yeah, maybe," Reace admitted realizing only now how foolish that sounded. "I know it sounds stupid but trust me on this, Arron, telling Jake or anyone would be a bad idea. He has no real reason to know and it might even make things worse." Reace pushed.

Arron nodded in acceptance after seeing the look on his comrades face, "Okay, Reace I get it, I'm sorry."

"And" Reace prompted one eyebrow raised.

"And I promise I won't tell anyone anything about John and you." Arron said feeling like he was ten years old again. The look of relief and the smile Reace flashed him made it worth it and he returned the smile.

"Thanks comrade," Reace's words said it all. Arron was still as trustworthy as always and Reace was glad he could count on and confide in him, they were more than friends—they were comrades.

"Ah, guys, in case you've forgotten, Jake is still in the room, so you might as well just tell him now anyways," Kittana said. Judging from the thoughts Jake was having, she knew he had already figured out most of it.

"It's okay." Jake looked up at the sound of his name he raised his hand toward Reace and his father as he added, "I don't really want to know anymore."

Jake's stomach was turning at what his mind had already put together, based on what he had just heard he figured that Mr. Stelmen had abused Reace in some way, Jake didn't need the details. He was having a hard time associating the nice Mr. Stelmen he knew with the one that Arron, Reace, Keyla and Nate had talked about.

He had heard about situations like this that happened to other people, horror stories of abuse that none of the neighbors knew or even suspected it of happening. Jake had never believed that the neighbors didn't know, maybe they turned a blind eye but he always thought they must have known. How could someone not notice or hear something like that? Now, right here in front of him was proof of that phenomena, and Jake vowed he'd not be naïve anymore, evil things did happen—he just never thought it would happen to him, in his neighborhood, to someone he knew. Today he found out it had happened to two people he knew: Reace and his grandmother. How many more did he not know about, he wondered?

Reace nodded respecting Jake's choice, he was embarrassed that Jake or anyone, he glanced around him, had seen him and Arron's discussion and he certainly didn't want to have to tell anyone about his past, even talking about with Arron, Kittana or Keyla was hard. He just wanted to leave it in the past and forget about it. Reace shrugged as he sat down on the cold floor, his back against the wall, he breathed in the air and felt himself relax. He was in the shelter, a smile turned his mouth and a sigh escaped him, he felt safe here, at home. Relaxed. Comforted.

Arron sat down beside him on the floor, between Reace and Jake (who sat on the sofa next to Keyla). He nudged Reace with his elbow as he shook his head.

"I can't believe you actually like the smell of this place," he teased.

Reace's smile turned into a full grin and he laughed but didn't say anything, he felt contented in here.

"Okay," Kittana spoke sitting on the over turned crate, her son sat on the floor opposite to Reace and Arron. "We've only got a couple of hours to figure this out." Kittana said bring everyone's attention to her and the possible problems at hand.

"I've brought dad's journals here maybe there is something in them that'll help us." Kittana said taking the book bag from her shoulders and taking the books out of it handing them around.

"Kade's journals, they're still here?" Keyla's voice held a note of reverence and her eyes misted with unshed tears as she took the book Kittana held out to her, she thought of the father she had never really gotten the chance to know.

Kittana nodded then said, "but before we start in on the research, I have to know, somewhere between two forty and three ten today, as I was walking back I felt it again—that heart stopping rollercoaster ride. It was worse this time, anyone else feel it too?" Kittana saw the other three Guardians nod then she went on to ask, "Anyone else get sick?"

"You were sick? Are you alright now?" Keyla's response was quicker than Reace's but his eyes narrowed in concern as they zeroed in on her face.

"Yeah, I'm fine maybe my powers just amplified the feeling." She explained more to herself then to anyone else. "Let's get back to the research." She turned toward Jake. "Jake I know you can't read Starian, here is a journal that's written in English, if you want to help we can sure use it."

"If you can figure out the pigeon scratch," Keyla commented. "What?" She demanded receiving a glare from her sister, "I know the man's our dad, and a saint to you, but his penmanship truly sucked!"

Kittana shrugged, she couldn't argue with the truth.

"I'd be happy to help," Jake answered taking the journal from Kittana he looked around him at all the faces he had come to know and care about in the past twenty-four hours. After their talk and Keyla's spell he had a new appreciation for his father. Keyla was cool and her sister Kittana was nice. Reace . . . Reace was everything he'd imagined he would be and more. The only disappointment Jake felt was that Reace didn't know him. In reality they weren't the kindred souls—the best friends they were in his imagination.

Turning his attention back to the old note book he held in his hand, Jake opened it and started to read, a slow smile settled on his features. He was good at deciphering so he could make out most of the words but he had to agree with Keyla, an award for neatness or penmanship would never be given to Kade Messer.

# CHAPTER TWENTY FOUR

ARRON RUBBED HIS HANDS OVER his eyes they had been going over the journals for what seemed like hours and his eyes felt like they were going to fall out of his head and roll away, just to get a break. Turning the page, he paused, his eyes fighting to focus; his brain screamed at him that there was something here, something different. Arron reread the first line on the page, it was the prophecy. What was so different about that, he wondered? He'd read the thing thousands of times. It was engraved into the wall of the Crystal Mountain. Even as he questioned, Arron reread it and this time there was something different.

"Hey, wait a minute!" Arron said his voice loud in the quiet room, causing everyone's attention to snap to him.

"Here, Kittana read this. My eyes aren't working right . . . it seems longer than the one on Taysia." Arron said as he handed the book to her.

"Sure what is it?" Kittana asked as she looked at the writing on the page.

"It's the prophecy," Arron replied with a puzzled frown.

After reading it to herself she looked at Arron and with a smile she spoke, "Your eyes are fine this is longer. I always thought something was missing from the prophecy on the wall—the original one Deia wrote had three verses to it."

"Three verses?" Nate echoed. This was news to him.

"Yeah," his mother answered then began to read it out loud translating it fluently as she went.

> "There are seven times two who guard the life force.
> One will rise to alter the course,
> Against the one the remaining stand
> Balance tipped on Taysia's land
> Until from seven there is one."

She paused to take a breath before reading the second verse:

> "Seven to one through time and space,
> The power of four the one shall face.
> When one and one make three,
> Pleased are the powers that be.
> The balance restored the course is set."

She looked up at everyone before saying, "Here is the third verse:

> Out of the light the dark descends
> Beware a foe who is a friend.
> The one thought dead to be alive.
> Nature divided, only one will survive,
> And all will be as before."

She finished reading and looked up.

"Wait a minute," Nate spoke after listening to his mother read the prophecy he was confused. "The prophecy has three verses, since when? On Taysia there are only two verses, Kade must have been mistaken. Maybe he got mixed up or found more of Deia's prophecies and added them together?" Nate suggested trying to reason what he knew with what he heard.

"It's true, Nate, there are only two verses written on the wall in Taysia but that doesn't mean there are only two verses," Reace told his son, "when we first entered crystal mountain there was only one verse on the wall, the second one didn't appear until we were ready to face Malic, by then half of the verse had come to pass."

"Are you saying that if we were to go look on the wall in Crystal Mountain the third verse would be there?" Nate asked.

"We don't know for sure, but it's possible," Kittana answered then added, "Dad's done a lot more research into all this then we ever could and he had many more resources then we do. When we first found the prophecy we read the three verses. I believe Kade's is right."

"The second verse ended with us." Kittana continued, "Afterward Timelana told us that it was only the beginning that there was more . . ." She trailed off as her sister interrupted her.

"You think she was talking about the third verse."

"Yes." Kittana replied.

"But how can there be a third verse here and not on Taysia?" Nate questioned.

"This is getting us nowhere!" Reace groaned. "Arguing over who is right. Let's just assume that Kade's right: there is a third part to the prophecy and go from there."

"Alright," Arron agreed. "We have to figure out what it means, what's the first line of the third verse again?" Arron directed his question to Kittana.

"Huh? Oh, out of the light the dark descends." Kittana read then looked up and asked. "Any ideas on what it could mean?"

Everyone fell silent, trying to figure out the phrase.

"Out of the light the dark descends." Jake repeated. The wheels turning in his head as he mulled it over then suggested, "Maybe it's describing a time?"

Nate jumped on the theory, exploring it out loud. "Like the line 'seven to one, through time and space' was describing a time when Malic was the only Guardian on Taysia and you four were on Earth." Nate gestured to the four adults in the room. He started to get excited as further evidence to back up this theory occurred to him. "Seven times two who guard the life force' also described a time when all fourteen Guardians were born on Staria, seven good, seven evil—a balance."

"So, every first line of the three verses is describing a time." Kittana summed up. Proud she grinned at her son. "Good work, Nate!"

"Okay, so what time is 'out of the light the dark descends' talking about?" Keyla asked.

"How about now?" Reace answered then expanded, "We've had what sixteen, seventeen years of peace, love and balance—light on Taysia."

"So now it's time for evil to take over?" Keyla didn't like where this was going. It wasn't fair, they had balanced the forces didn't that entitle them to a life of ease and carefree happiness? Now she was hearing that it was all for nothing that evil was going to take over again? She silently fumed. *Maybe they could stop it.* her mind suggested but first they had to decipher the riddle.

"Well, lately it seems everything is falling apart, Arron is having a hard time." Kittana pointed out.

"Thanks." Arron mumbled sarcastically.

"Basically, out of the good times evil comes." Reace re-stated then his expression changed becoming lighter as he added, "It makes sense, when you least expect it, tragedy strikes."

"That's what Malic said!" Arron exclaimed his expression animated, "When we least expect it he'll attack. Man, I thought he was talking about us, years ago. But maybe he has waited all these years for the perfect time to strike." Arron rubbed a hand over his face and through his hair as he stood—to restless to sit any longer he started pacing the room like a caged animal as he berated himself. "How could I have been so stupid—so blind? How could I have missed this?"

"Arron, calm down and stop pacing," Kittana responded, "None of this is your fault. How could you have known what Malic was planning?"

"We aren't even sure Malic planned anything . . . yet," Keyla added. Watching Arron restlessly pace back and forth she demanded in an exasperating tone. "Arron, sit!"

Surprisingly, Arron complied, sitting again on the floor beside Reace, but he couldn't stop himself from moving, he jiggled his knee up and down impatiently as he tapped his foot.

"What's the next line?" He inquired looking intently at Kittana.

"Beware a foe who is a friend." Kittana read the second line then both her and Keyla looked at Arron. He was two Guardians combined into one, the Guardian of Life and Death, could that be about him?

"I'm not a foe," Arron stated seeing the look on the twins faces.

"No," Reace agreed with a shake of his head, adding in Arron's defense, "This is after we balanced the forces, we found out about Arron before remember? Malic already tried using him against us."

"And he failed." Kittana finished, sparing her sister a look before turning to Arron with apologetic eyes, "Reace is right, sorry Arron."

He nodded.

"Sorry," Keyla mumbled.

"One thought dead to be alive," Nate picked up the third line, it had caught his attention the first time his mother read the whole thing, he'd been thinking it over, wondering what it could possibly mean, but he had yet to come up with anything. He glanced at Jake and asked. "Any ideas?"

Jake returned Nate's puzzled look with one of his own as he shook his head.

"That could be talking about you Reace. We all thought you were dead." Keyla suggested.

"No, I don't think so," Arron spoke slowly belying the speed his mind was putting things together. He looked up at them as he explained, "The one throughout the whole prophecy had so far been Malic so I think it's safe to assume that he's still the one."

"He has called himself the one," Keyla added agreeing with Arron.

"So according to this, he'd have to have died or at least made everyone think he was dead." Jake clarified.

"Maybe that's what we felt? Maybe it was Malic, maybe Malic died or at least made it seem like he had." Kittana suggested, putting their experiences together with their theories.

"But that makes no sense." Reace said as he rubbed a hand over his face before saying, "Why would he die now? What would he have to gain by that?"

"Well he'd have . . ." Kittana broke off not sure what she was going to say, "I don't know." She finished with a shake of her head and added, "I'll admit it, I'm stumped!"

"What else does it say?" Keyla asked.

Kittana looked at the open journal in her lap as she read again, "Nature divided, only one will survive."

"Does that mean Malic wants to kill me?" Nate gulped and wide eyed he stared at his parents for answers.

"No, divide and conquer—separate and kill?" Arron guessed.

"Not just divide, it was more specific," Reace continued, "Nature divided . . . Nature separated . . . maybe it's referring to a time when Nate left Taysia—like now. We are all separated, we are all away from Taysia—we left Tia, Link and Awkwade . . ." Reace let his sentence drop, unwilling to continue. His gaze flashed to Arron's.

"You don't think . . ." Keyla didn't finish her sentence either.

"NO!" Arron gasped, the breath left him and the blood drained from his face as his mind reeled from the truth of their unspoken words.

"We felt the disturbance twice now, what if Malic has taken advantage and has killed . . ." Kittana broke off after she said that. This was the important breakthrough that they were looking for but at the same time she hoped to the powers that be that they were wrong because if they were right then that would mean two of their friends had died and that was too painful to think about.

"Kill another Guardian?" Nate questioned in disbelief, his expression clearly demanded, *How?*

"He's done it before, remember the Guardians before us?" Kittana reminded them how Malic got his powers.

"Malic does have the power of the mind and emotion what if he used them to make the person . . . want to . . ." Keyla didn't want to put a name to the horror she was talking about, if they were right then one of their friends could be dead right now and Keyla didn't want to think about who.

"NO!" Arron said forcefully, he didn't want to believe what they were saying, what his heart was telling him.

"He's tried it before . . . on me and Reace. Remember, in our dreams the last time we were on Earth?" Keyla added softly.

Arron closed his eyes as he whispered, "Tia."

"It may not be Tia, we could all be wrong about this." Kittana quickly reassured him.

"No!" Arron surprised everyone with his sharp, firm tone. Opening his eyes he stared into Kittana's with determination. "We are right, it fits—all of it" Arron rubbed his hands over his hair, holding onto his head as he added, "That feeling . . . twice, the dream I had last night about Tia being lost . . . it all fits." He let his hands drop and his head fall back into the wall behind him.

"Including my nightmare," Keyla added softly.

Arron nodded swallowing hard; forcing his words passed a throat that suddenly constricted. "We . . . we have to go back. Now. Sooner than dawn, I know that's the time when magic, moon and sun are balanced and everything, but . . . we have to try."

Keyla nodded, biting her lip as she took in Arron's broken expression, her own heart breaking at her friend's pain.

Nate stared at the floor in front of him, hearing everything they said, his thoughts tumbled around inside his head, a jumbled mess of confusion and he didn't want to sort it out; to do so would be to . . . painful. *What have I done?*

"It's all . . . my fault." He whispered in shame and guilt at what his actions had brought about. "This is all, my fault!" Nature repeated close to tears, tears he stubbornly blinked back.

"Yes, it is!" Arron agreed.

"WHAT?!" Kittana and Keyla whirled on Arron.

"If he wants to be treated like an adult then he'll have to learn to except responsibility." Arron defended his statement at the accusing looks he received from his lifelong friends. Wanting them to understand where he was coming from, he continued explaining, "The truth is that if he hadn't come here without telling anyone where he was going—forcing us all to come searching for him—then none of this would be happening." Blaming Nate only made him feel worse then he already did. Arron looked away from the hurt look on the boy's face. He didn't care right now if his words, right or wrong, hurt anyone. In the back of his mind he was sorry for the look of disbelieve and misery on the young Guardian's face and on the faces of his friends, but Arron didn't care . . . he couldn't let himself think about caring right now, he was too scared of what feeling may turn him into.

"Arron, we don't know for sure if . . ." Kittana began.

"Kit, the balance was put at risk." Arron reminded her, his voice was even, devoid of emotion. "I think it's a safe bet that Malic has taken advantage and Tia, Link and Awkwade weren't strong enough to stop him. They're not the ones from the prophecy, we are. So—yes it is Nate's fault."

"Not entirely," Gaining everyone's attention Reace went on to say, "Arron, you're forgetting the part that Malic played . . . He encouraged Nate, maybe even drove him with emotions to come here. Why would Malic want Nature out of the way?" Reace asked letting that question sink in before adding, "Malic planned this and if anyone's to blame for what's happening on Taysia—whatever that is—it's Malic." Reace paused, "but blaming anyone even Malic, doesn't change anything."

"And we still have to figure out what's happened." Keyla added.

"I'm not going back to Taysia with you." Nate suddenly announced.

"What? Nate!"

"No, mom." Nate's voice was steady and held a note of confidence, sure that he was doing the right thing, he explained. "Arron's right. You all felt it, you four are the chosen Guardians, together you need to go back to fix my mistake. I'm sorry that I let you down. I'm sorry that Malic got to me. I'm sorry for so many things, but coming here . . . I'm not sorry for that. This is my destiny. This is where I belong. Taysia doesn't need me, the balance doesn't need me. I am needed here on Earth. Timelana told me that it was where I am supposed to be." Nate's eyes begged his mother, Arron and Keyla to believe him before settling on his father. "I played sports today, dad, do you know how that feels?" Nate asked, then before his father could answer he went on, "No, of course you don't, you've never played any, but to run . . . to play with kids my own age, to have a date, a chance at a girlfriend . . . I can't . . . I won't give that up. I won't go back with you."

"Nate, you're a Guardian." Kittana tried again to reason with her son.

"Yes, and on Taysia I am useless." Nature stood up as he argued his case, "You think that Malic made me come here, but he didn't. This is what I've always wanted. If Malic did use his powers on me it was only to increase my own desires to a point where I acted on them. Don't you see, coming here was my choice, *it's my destiny*! Here, mom, I can make a difference, here I am needed. And like Timelana said, she's only a call away if I ever need to return home. The only thing I regret about leaving Taysia is . . ." He didn't quite know how to say this to Arron, to any of them, so he settled on saying, "Watch over the fairies, okay?" His gaze locked with Keyla's for a second.

She nodded her eyes filling with tears.

"Nate, you have no idea what Earth is really like, the people here . . . they won't accept you. They'll hurt you." Kittana said as she stood and walked over to her son. Taking a deep breath, tears stinging in her throat, she put her hand on Nate's arm.

At the contact of skin on skin, Nate gasped in surprise as images filled his mind like memories—only they weren't his memories they were his mother's and father's. Nate recoiled in fright at the experiences he was shown through his mother's telepathic mind.

He physically wrenched away from her touch, he was speechless for a moment as he stared at her, his eyes narrowed in an emotion Kittana couldn't read but was surprised at the intensity of.

"You think that'll happen to me?" he accused, "You think I won't be able to handle things? That I'm WEAK, always needing to be protected! Well, I'm NOT weak anymore and like Arron said I am a Guardian—fully grown. YOU CAN'T TELL ME WHAT TO DO ANYMORE!" Nate shouted, the ground beneath their feet trembled slightly and the dark clouds that were building outside exploded with a loud clap of thunder that punctuated his words. "I'M NOT A LITTLE KID, CAN'T YOU SEE THAT? I AM SICK OF YOU ALWAYS TRYING TO PROTECT ME!" Nate, with his mark pulsating with energy, pointed to the door that suddenly blew open on a gust of wind. "I DON'T NEED OR WANT YOUR PROTECTION. I WILL NOT BE GOING WITH YOU, I'M STAYING HERE!" He finished shouting as he stormed out of the shelter, pausing only to lift a hand letting wind he controlled slam the heavy steel door shut behind him.

Silence filled the room.

Jake watched everything with wide-eyed interest, seeing the display of supernatural power made him feel like he was in the middle of a movie, only this was real, he remind himself. And he was somehow, by some miracle, a part of them.

*Shit! This was real!* He spoke to himself spurring into action. Standing, Jake decided to follow Nature and somehow stop him from using his powers in front of others. Kittana was right. People here just weren't ready for people like them—for Guardians.

"I'll go and make sure Nate doesn't do anything stupid." Jake looked to Arron, silently asking him not to leave without saying goodbye.

Arron nodded, watching him leave.

"Well, that went well," Reace stated sarcastically.

"Did you feel that earthquake?" Keyla asked excitedly.

"You don't think . . ." Arron started, he was worried that now that the balance was put at risk, maybe Earth was about to suffer the same fate as Staria had years before, but before he could voice these thoughts, Keyla cut him off.

"And that wind Nate seemed to control?" Keyla added.

"Nature is discovering more of his abilities." Kittana agreed, turning to Reace she added, "Remember at my parents' house that thunder and lightning? It could have come from Nate." She finished as she got up to follow behind Jake, she wanted to get to her son before he made a mistake and used his power around the wrong people.

"Kit," Reace's voice made her pause in her steps, "let him go. Maybe Nate's right, maybe he should stay here."

"Reace!" His wife whirled on him with an accusing glare. "How can you say that?"

He shrugged, "You said it yourself his powers are growing since coming here,"

"Yeah, and you think he can handle them? Reace, you know what can happen . . . how easily . . ."

"Let's get back to figuring this all out . . . let everyone cool down. After we get this prophecy figured out we'll talk to Nate." Keyla's voice broke into Kittana's sentence cutting her off. "He'll listen then," she promised.

"Key's right," Arron agreed. "We only have a few hours left to figure what is going on, before we head right into it."

Kittana frowned, but grudgingly sat, they were right even though she didn't want to admit it.

# CHAPTER TWENTY FIVE

NATE STOMPED AWAY FROM THE shelter—away from his family, from anything that had to do with Guardians, Taysia or the prophecy. He just wanted to be human like everyone else, to go to school, play sports and fall in love . . . to be normal. As he walked, his blood pumping through his veins like liquid fire, he caught sight of his hand—his mark—it was glowing, pulsating with unleashed power. He wanted to scream, to give into the temptation and let it all out, he wanted to unleash his powers, use them for destruction until his anger was gone, but he couldn't. He knew it wouldn't help anything, in fact it would only make things worse.

Nate stopped walking, closed his eyes and inhaled deeply. As he stood there in the dark of night feeling the cool rain on his skin, he could sense every tree, flower, and cloud; every rock, hill and being from the tiniest insect to the mightiest tree. He felt their energy, their life force flow toward him and he knew that same energy flowed from him; they were all connected. He had never felt this way on Taysia—like he belonged.

Exhaling, he relaxed, opening his eyes he glanced down at his mark. When he saw that it no longer glowed he breathed deeply again. Seeing how dark it was Nate realized it was late. The dance had probably already started by now, he guessed. Hearing a twig snap behind him Nate glanced over his shoulder, letting out a relieved sigh that it was only Jake.

"Hey, Nate, there you are." Jake said catching up to him. He was relieved to see that Nate's hand no longer glowed—that was just too freaky! Not that Jake would ever admit it, but Nate's abilities kind-of scared him, Nate was capable of . . . so much and he could use his powers to hurt people, a lot of people.

"I'm not going back in there, and nothing you can say will change my mind. I meant what I said, I'm staying here and I'll defend my decision if I have to." He looked ready for a fight, Nate's eyes glittered with determination and something else Jake that respected.

"I never said anything about going back," Jake calmly stated.

"Didn't they send you out here after me?" Nate asked puzzled.

"No," Jake said slowly choosing his words carefully. "I came out here because I wanted to. Dude, we're friends and I don't know what that means to you, but in my book—friends stick by each other."

Nate studied Jake for a moment before breaking into a grin, changing the subject he asked, "What time is it?"

"Nine fifteen," Jake answered, after looking at his watch then he asked, "Why?"

"Let's go, we're late for the dance."

"The dance? But what about . . ." Jake sputtered.

"I'm going to that dance." Nate's tone of voice discouraged Jake from arguing.

"Lead the way," Jake agreed sparing a glance over his shoulder in the direction he had just come from, at the same time he offered up a small prayer to whatever God was listening that they didn't run into Cody.

They walked most of the way in silence, both of them thinking, replaying the conversations they heard in the shelter through their minds. When they reached the high school, they both sighed—one in relief, the other in resignation as they entered the dance.

Nate paused when he saw how the gym was transformed into a dim lighted, music thumping, dance floor. He was very impressed and a pleased smile blossomed over his face as he watched countless bodies sway to the music. He elbowed Jake giving him an excited grin before heading into the throng of teenagers gathered to dance their stress and general pressures of life out in time with the loud music.

As Jake followed Nate, he kept nervously glancing around. He was worried about what could happen if Cody and his goons found them and their abilities were discovered? After the display in the shelter, if it came down to a fight could Nate keep his powers under control? If Cody chose to take out his frustration on him, would Cody see how fast Jake could heal? Would Cody tell everyone what a freak he really was? Spurred on by these worries and the bad feeling in the pit of his stomach, he grabbed Nate's shoulder.

"Nate," he began when Nature turned with a questioning look, "I don't think this is a good idea."

"Don't worry it's just a dance; I know what I'm doing." Nature reassured Jake with a pat on his arm. "There's Anna," he announced, his face lighting up when he saw her. "See you later." Nate left Jake staring after him, looking worried.

"Nate, hi!" Anna smiled her greeting when Nature walked up to her. "I was beginning to think you weren't coming."

"I had some . . . family issues to work out first. Sorry I'm late."

"That's okay, I'm just glad you're here now," she said wondering what family issues he had. Had Kittana told Nate what she had said to her earlier? Trying not to show how nervous she was as she took Nate's hand and started leading him toward the middle of the dance floor, as she spoke. "Let's dance."

Half way there Nature suddenly stopped and when she turned with a confused expression he admitted. "I don't know how to dance. I have never heard music like this before."

Anna looked at him for a moment in disbelief. He had never danced before, she heard that part but did she hear the rest? *He hadn't heard music like this before?* His words echoed in her mind, it fit with what she was starting to suspect—that he was from another world. Giving her head a shake she mentally scolded herself what was she thinking, that was crazy, like something strait out of a comic book. It was impossible, just because he didn't know how to dance didn't mean that he was an alien, she told herself. Lots of people didn't know how to dance and lots of people may not have heard this song before, she must have been mistaken she couldn't have heard that he had never heard music like this, he must have meant that he'd never heard this song before just because it was her favorite didn't mean it was everyone else's. Embarrassed by her own foolishness she smiled brightly at him as she said, "Then I'll teach you, come on, it's easy!"

He returned her easy smile with one of his own as he allowed her to lead him onto the dance floor.

"Okay, just feel the music and move your body to the beat." She told him starting to dance herself.

Nate watched her, then glanced around him at everyone else and tried to follow them but he couldn't feel this beat she mentioned.

After watching him struggle for thirty seconds she stopped him. Anna had never really had to teach anyone to dance before, it was harder then she thought.

"I'm not doing well, am I?" he asked feeling like a fool. "I've never heard music like this before and I can't find the beat."

"Just come a little closer and," she tactfully suggested, "look into my eyes. Try to feel the music, let it move you, sway with it," she said pulling him closer to her, her hands around his waist.

Looking into her eyes, Nature relaxed. The rest of the world dropped away until it was just the two of them and the music. Unconsciously his body responded to the music, swaying into hers, following her movements as if answering them. He pulled her closer until their bodies were touching, sliding, shifting against one another as they moved in rhythm with the beat.

Nate licked his lips, staring into her eyes he saw a flare of heat grow inside them and suddenly he wanted to do more than just dance with her. Dipping his head as she moved hers up to let him have better access to her lips.

Before their lips could meet a heavy hand on his shoulder shoved Nate away from Anna-Maria.

Cody appeared in his line of vision.

"Nate, I am very disappointed in you. I thought we had an agreement. I thought we saw eye to eye." His face had a pleasant expression but his eyes sparked with malice. "Now, you've made me mad."

"I'm not afraid of you, Cody." Nate said refusing to be intimidated.

"So you've said," Cody smirked then challenged. "Let's take this outside and see what you've got."

"No!" Anna started pushing her way between the boys. She looked from one to the other. She didn't want Nate to get hurt and she knew what Cody was capable of. Turning hard eyes on Cody she added, "Cody! I am not your girlfriend anymore. I can date or dance with anyone I want too. You have no right to be jealous."

Cody glanced at her but didn't say anything he just inclined his head and looked behind her.

Before she knew what was happening strong arms encircled her from behind, forcing her into a dance she didn't want, dragging her against her will away from Nate and Cody to the other side of the room.

Blissfully unaware of the drama unfolding around them, dancing people filled in the space she vacated, blocking even Anna's view of Cody and Nate.

"Let her go." Nate growled his eyes narrowed on Cody.

"Don't worry, Brandon won't hurt her, he doesn't know what to do with a girl anyway." Cody said then turned on his heal and strode off the dance floor in the opposite direction.

At first Nate was confused but he soon realized why Cody looked so confident his two body guard buddies were behind Nate prodding him to move, following their leader.

# Chapter twenty six

"Okay so we're agreed on our theory of what the prophecy means?" Kittana stated her eyes passing over everyone making sure they were all in agreement before adding, "And we go back tonight ready for anything."

The four of them left the shelter searching for Nate and Jake outside. Coming up empty, they decided to expand the search into the house.

Thirty minutes later Arron, Kittana and Keyla met in the kitchen.

"My, my, you all look like you've lost the battle and the sky is falling, sit and tell me what happened?" Mrs. White gestured to the chairs at the breakfast bar when she saw them enter her domain wearing identical worried expressions.

"Nate's missing . . . again," Kittana answered then continued, "And Jake is nowhere to be found. We've asked Heather, but she doesn't know where he went either. She hasn't seen him since this morning."

"Have you seen them?" Arron asked.

"No, but I know they come home after school 'cause the brownies I set out are gone, their books were piled by the front door, and two cans of soda were still on the counter when I started supper." Her warm gaze moved from Kittana and Keyla to Arron then she added, "Don't worry they'll be back when they get hungry. They've probably just gone to the dance; Nate was so excited about it yesterday, he couldn't stop talking about it. You know if I didn't know better I'd swear that boy's never been to a dance before but handsome boy like that . . ." she broke off, a twinkle in her eye as she added. "I bet he's got lots of girlfriends back home."

"Dance? What dance?" Arron asked.

"Boy, get your head out of the sand, a high school dance." The warm expression on her face belied the tone of her voice and made her words seem like a mother's caring caress. "Don't tell me that you've forgotten about some of the dances you've been too. 'Course those high school dances couldn't hold a candle to the wild parties you used to throw." Mrs. White gave Arron a knowing smile as she admitted. "You didn't think I knew about that did you?" she nodded her head as she added, "Well, I know a lot more then you think I do." Her grin broadened at the question in his eyes.

Her gaze made Arron feel warm inside.

"Well, if they've just gone to the dance, then what time do you think they'll be back?" Kittana inquired.

Mrs. White's gaze moved over Kittana as she answered, "Jake's curfew is eleven and he's never been late, so I suspect they'll be home by then and they'll be mighty hungry too since they missed supper. You look like you're hungry too, want me to fix you up a plate? Won't take but a few minutes and there are plenty of leftovers."

"Not right now, Miss. White, but thanks." Arron answered for the group, too worried to even think of food.

"I think we should find Reace and let him know what's going on—that we at least know where they went." Kittana said and as one they got up and left the kitchen.

"So we are just going to stay here and wait for them?" Keyla hissed at her sister as they moved into the hallway. She was confused by the sudden change in her sister's attitude. In the shelter Kittana was ready to chase her son down and now she was content to just sit here and wait.

"Yeah," Kittana replied, "I've been doing some thinking. Nate has gone to a lot of trouble to come here just to experience school and life, what's the harm in letting him have this one dance? We're still leaving as soon as he gets back." she finished.

Keyla didn't say anything more she just bit her lip and slowly shook her head behind her sister. Nature was sixteen—the same age they were when they had made adult decisions about their lives, their destinies. Her sister wasn't seeing that her son had grown up and was making his choice. Kittana was blinding herself and in her fear of letting go, she couldn't see that she was pushing Nature away. Keyla just hoped that when her sister finally realizes what she was doing it wouldn't be too late.

\*

"Heather, can I ask you something?" Reace's voice tentatively broke the silence. He had purposely stayed behind while everyone else left the living room after asking Heather if she'd seen the boys.

Heather nodded, she had been watching him and she knew he had something on his mind by the way he acted: nervous energy that refused to allow him to relax, pretending to be interested in the little knickknacks around the room while his mind worked up the courage to talk to her. She waited with curiosity, wondering what was on his mind, what his question was.

Reace sighed, frowned and licked his lips before speaking, "This isn't something that's easy for me . . . I haven't even talked to Kit about it yet, or Nate. I'm not sure if I'll have time later through so . . . I thought I'd talk to you first."

Moving closer to her, he took a seat in front of her, on the newly replaced coffee table. He knew it wasn't polite, but he didn't have time for pleasantries he needed to see her eyes, her face when he asked her.

"Nate really likes it here."

"Thanks, I'm glad. Your son is . . ." Heather began, but Reace didn't let her finish.

"He wants to stay." He blurted out then rushed on. "We can't. I was wondering . . . I know this is a lot to ask of you, given our backgrounds and all, but Jake and Nate—they seem to really hit it off and they are both *special* boys." Reace emphasized the word special, hoping Heather would catch on to his meaning and she didn't disappoint him. He continued, "I wanted to ask you if you'd watch out for Nate, look after him for us . . . just until he finishes school. We wouldn't be able to pay you much and we would come as often as our . . . work allows." Tension crawled up Reace's back and settled on his shoulders as he finished speaking and waited for her reaction.

He was prepared for the worst, he expected her to laugh or yell at him saying he was crazy. He was ready for anything but her softly spoken question.

"You're asking me to be his legal Guardian, while you and Kittana are away?" Heather asked. She had never suspected this. It meant a lot to her that even after all of the nasty things she did and said about him in the past, he'd trust her with his most precious gift—his child. She swallowed the lump of emotion that clogged her throat, smiling past the tears that shone in her eyes, she gazed at him.

"Yeah, I guess so." Reace answered with a nod of his head, "Look, I know we've had our differences in the past, but you've done such a great job with Jake and you know about us—more than anyone . . ."

"Okay," Heather answered him tentatively, cutting into Reace's nervous words. "If it's alright with Kittana and Nate, then I'd love too. And I think Jake would love to have the company." Heather said then as her corporate mind worked fast she added, "But you'd have to sign and witness a document saying that you have given me the legal right to act in your child's best interest well you are away."

Reace nodded, he looked relieved as he wiped his palms on the knees of his worn jeans before smiling at her and standing.

"There you are! Reace, we have been looking everywhere for you. We figured out, well mostly Mrs. White, that women is a wonder! She figured that Nate and Jake went to the dance." Keyla said as the three of them entered the room.

Arron frowned at the guilty expression on Heather's face.

Kittana looked from Reace to Heather and back again her eyes narrowed slightly as she read their minds before she exclaimed.

"YOU DID WHAT?"

"Kittana . . ." Reace began moving toward her as he spoke but she cut him off with the hand she held up, stopping his forward progress as well.

"NO! No, no, no, I can't believe that you'd do something like this." Kittana said in disbelief with a shake of her head.

"Kittana whatever you think we did . . . let me assure you that you are wrong." Heather began she didn't want Kittana to think she had any designs on her husband—that was ancient history. And she didn't want to ruin their budding friendship over misconceptions.

Kittana's eyes snapped to Heather, the intensity of her gaze made Heather shrink back for a second,

"Do you mean to tell me that Reace didn't just ask you if our son could stay here and finish school? Didn't you just accept to be his legal Guardian on Earth?" Kittana demanded, but she didn't need Heather's confirmation to know that she was right. Turning her attention back to Reace she was about to say something but Heather's whispered words halted her, making her forget what she was about to say.

"How could you possible know that?"

"Kit, look," Reace said gaining her attention, "Nate came here for a reason and if he feels that strongly about being here than maybe he should stay."

"NO!" Kittana shouted.

When her dark blue eyes met his lighter turquoise-blue ones, he asked her in a voice that was gentle and coaxing. "What are you afraid of?"

Kittana took a deep breath and let it out slowly before she admitted. "What if Nate is right? What if Malic is out to kill him? Here he'd be vulnerable . . . he wouldn't even know it was happening."

Horror showed on his face for a second before he shoved that feeling behind a mask of resolve. "We won't let that happen," Reace told her then added as his mind formed a plan, "We'll go back and stop Malic . . . once and for all."

"How?" Keyla demanded. "We can't kill him, not with all the power we possess."

Reace looked at Keyla then at Arron.

"Arron can." he stated nodding in his comrades direction.

"No, Reace." Arron said firmly, "I won't do it. I won't use my power of death."

"What? Why not? Arron, it's my son's life we are talking about here."

"I know and I'm sorry but I promised myself I'd never use that ability again—no matter what and I mean to keep it." Arron held Reace's gaze steady.

He was scared that if he used it once, if he gave into that temptation, he'd not be strong enough to stop himself from using it again. Would he be able to turn it off or would he kill those he cared about whenever he got angry at them? Would he turn into the monster Malic said he was? Would he turn evil?

His fears must have shown on his face because Reace nodded and didn't push the issue. Feeling bad for letting his friend down Arron offered: "There has to be another way to stop Malic."

"You're talking about destroying the balance. We can't do that!" Keyla said gaining Reace's attention.

Reace turned a defiant expression on her. "I'll not stand by and let that monster kill him!"

"No, no we won't." Kittana agreed with him then sighed, "Nate really wants to stay here, doesn't he?"

"Yeah, but . . ."

"Okay," Kittana turned to Heather as she gave her consent. "He can stay." Turning back to her husband she added, "We will just have to make sure we know every move Malic makes, his every thought."

"Kittana?" Suddenly worried as she blocked him out of her mind, turning off their telepathic connection—he hadn't even been aware that she could do that—Reace demanded. "What are you suggesting?"

She didn't answer him. She didn't want Reace to know what she was planning. She should have done this years ago, but she hadn't wanted to see the horrors that Malic had done to other people. She didn't want his memories in her mind. She wanted no part of Malic's evil, but now in order to protect her son she was willing to do anything . . . even mind melding with Malic. It was the only way to know his every thought, his every move. It was the only way to protect both the balance and her son. She'd do anything to keep Nature alive, anything!

Luckily Kittana was saved from Reace's probing gaze and his answer demanding silence, by Heather's voice.

"So you're all these Guardian beings? You're all the same as Arron, right?" Heather asked. "You all have powers like Arron and Jake, don't you? God, why didn't I see it before?" She asked herself more than them. Heather put her head down and covered her face with her hands for a second before raising her head again to look at them. She didn't have time right now to freak out, she'd do that later—after they all left.

"Yeah, ah, how much did Arron tell you?" Keyla inquired carefully.

"Not enough," Came Heather's quick reply. "Nate too, he's like you." She asked more for confirmation than anything else. Reace had already told her as much, but she just needed to hear it again.

"Yes, he is." Kittana confirmed then added, "It's not like we're any different now than before. Heather, we have always had these powers . . . you just didn't know it in high school."

"High school?" her voice squeaked and her eyes widened.

"Guess we were good at hiding it, huh?" Reace smirked when Heather's gaze moved from Kittana's to his, before moving to Arron's. He was surprised at how well she was taking it all.

"Okay, well, ah . . . what can you do? What powers do you have? Does Nate have? Do you all have those glass mutilations too?" Heather asked trying hard to understand everything. Her first instinct was to laugh, call them crazy and search for a rational explanation but after raising Jake and seeing firsthand the miraculous healing his body did and then witnessing how Kittana knew without being told what she and Reace had talked about; she had no choice but to believe them. And if she was going to be looking after Nate for them then she needed information, especially if she had to hide his powers from the rest of the world, like she did for her son.

"Glass mutilation?" Keyla repeated, trying to figure out what she was talking about, "oh, our marks. Yes, we all have one it's the sign of a Guardian, a symbol of the power we wield. Each one is different, mine is a crescent moon, Kit's a star, Reace's a lightning bolt, Arron's you've already seen and Nate has one too, it looks like a leaf. He's the Guardian of Nature."

Heather nodded her eyes wide as she took it all in, wondering how she could possibly believe all this, then again how could she not, the voice in her head argued with her, her son was a part of them.

"You all have different . . . different abilities." It was more of a statement then a question.

"Yes, look, the less you know about us the better. All you really need to know is that we are only a call away." Reace spoke looking at Heather as he added, "we will hear you."

"What about Nate? What powers does he possess? If I am going to be looking after him I need to know as much about him as I can." Heather's gaze moved from Reace to Kittana, "You can trust me. Kittana, in the past I've done things I'm not proud of but I will take good care of him, as if he were my own son. I promise."

Kittana nodded, not trusting herself to speak—how could she? They were talking about leaving her child behind.

"Nate's powers are those of Nature. Back home," Keyla said answering Heather's question, "all he could do was grow flowers, trees and things and it rained whenever he was sad or upset but since coming here we think his powers have grown."

"Before he was born, we were told he'd be the most powerful Guardian ever to be created." Arron added, glancing briefly at Reace and Kittana before turning his gaze to Heather and finishing. "We aren't entirely sure what he is capable of," he paused, "but Nate's a good kid and he normally has a good head on his shoulders . . . What I am trying to say, Heather, is that he won't willing hurt anyone. He won't use his powers that way, okay."

"Okay."

"Did you want us to sign a paper or something?" Kittana asked Heather and then when everybody looked at her Kittana shrugged as she sat in a chair. "We might as well get that over with now, if we're hanging around here waiting for Nate and Jake anyway."

"Yeah," Heather said with a frown, she was caught off guard again by the way Kittana seemed to just pluck information out of thin air; information she had no way of knowing. On second thought, she didn't really want to know how her friend did it. Heather got up and left the room in search of paper and a pen, thoughts of what the letter should contain filling her mind.

*

After they had agreed on a contract and everyone sighed and witnessed it Kittana glanced at the clock, it was only quarter after ten. They still had another forty-five minutes to wait, Kittana sighed.

"How do I call you?" Heather suddenly asked, "Reace, you said before that all I have to do is call you and you'd hear, but how? I'm sure you don't have cell-phones on Taysia, besides the reception is probably pretty crappy. So how do I call you?"

"You simply call us by our name: Kittana, Guardian of the Mind." Standing, Kittana introduced her true self to Heather. Her mark glowed, pulsating with an inner power that made her skin shine bright for a moment before receding, leaving Heather to wonder if she had really seen that or if she had imaged it.

Keyla smiled brightly as she spoke next, "Keyla, Guardian of Magic,"

Heather's eyes widened as she watched Keyla begin to glow with an inner light.

"Reace, Guardian of Electricity." Reace added with a nod of his head as he, in turn, introduced himself with a flash of his wrist.

"Arron, Guardian of Life," Arron said when it was his turn.

Thunder rumbled, shaking the house just as Arron's glow diminished.

"You can stop showing off now." Arron said to Reace, sounding annoyed.

"Thirty seconds ago." Reace retorted then clarified, "that wasn't from me."

"Thunder?" Heather muttered, a confused frown on her face as she remembered the weather forecast she had been watching before Reace interrupted her earlier, "but, it's supposed to be clear tonight."

"Maybe waiting *here* for Nature was a bad idea." Kittana and Keyla spoke at the same time.

"Yeah, let's go." Reace agreed and Arron nodded.

The four Guardians turned toward the door, ready to search out and help one of their own when Heather's determined voice halted them.

"Wait! I'm coming too!" She announced.

"But," Arron sputtered.

"No buts, if Nate is in trouble, Jake is with him."

Arron gave Heather a look she couldn't read before nodding his consent.

"Great! We can use my van." She grinned as she pointed a small device she held in her hand at the window. At the push of a button her van parked outside roared to life.

"Cool!" Keyla said, impressed by technology.

# CHAPTER TWENTY SEVEN

As CODY LED THE WAY, Nate followed, having no real choice as he was flanked by Cody's bodybuilding friends who nudged Nate.

Using an entrance that had no teachers around it, they made their way outside but before they could move down the stone steps of the courtyard and toward the back of the school, Jake appeared in front of Cody blocking him.

"Jake, this has nothing to do with you, get out of my way!" Cody growled.

Jake put a hand on Cody's chest and pushed him back a little as he spoke, "See, that's where you're wrong, Nate's my friend. What are you going to do? Beat the crap out of him then what? And what about the next guy Anna dates, are you going to beat them up too?"

"Move!" Cody demanded angrily he didn't like what Jake was saying.

"No!" Jake said forcefully "Cody this is . . ."

Jake words were interrupted by Cody's fist as it flew into his face. Unprepared for the punch Jake stumbled backwards then unbalanced he teetered on the top of the stairs before he fell backward. Tumbling down until he came to a rest at the bottom with a sickening thud as the back of his head collided heavily with the cement.

"JAKE!" Nate yelled as he pushed passed Cody, ran down the steps, kneeling beside his friend. For a moment he was startled by the red liquid that was spreading below Jake's head. It was several seconds before he remembered that Jake could heal himself.

Cody, came down the stairs, standing behind Nate, he made a sound that was half-chuckle/half-snort as he uttered, "Maybe you should learn to pick better friends."

Nate wasn't sure if Cody was talking to him or Jake but it didn't matter. The cruel words and lack of compassion made a rage grow inside of him; a rage that spurred Nature into attacking Cody.

Above the frenzy of punches volleyed between the rival boys, above the hustling of feet and clothes, dogs could be heard barking. The collective sound of excited animals reminding anyone who heard that they were once a wild breed that although mostly tamed, could still remember their savage side, but the teenagers, intent on their own personal battle didn't notice the barking getting closer or the thunder that sliced through the chilly damp air of night.

Nate was winning the fight; he had gained the upper hand and was sitting on top of Cody, pinning him down as he threw several punches into Cody's face before he was dragged off him by Cody's friends. They held Nate tight between the two of them while Cody slowly got up off the ground and wiped the blood off his face. Nate watched with angry eyes as Cody spat out a stream of bloody mucus on the ground inches from where Jake still lay, motionless.

Seeing Jake made Nate angrier, how could they not care that they may have killed another person? Nate knew that Jake couldn't die—he'd self heal, it may take time but Jake was Starian and with his ability he'd be fine, but they didn't know that. Cody and his friends, they just didn't care!

Nate struggled against the tight hold the two overly muscled guys had on him. He wanted to hit Cody again. To hit him until he did care, but Nate was no match for their combined strength and he remained trapped, helpless to stop himself from being dragged away from the school's door where at any moment the night guard or a teacher could come out and interrupt them.

*

After Heather parked the minivan in the school parking lot and everyone piled out of her vehicle they figured the easiest way to find the boys would be too spilt up.

"Arron, me and Heather will go into the dance and see if we can spot them in there, you and Reace circle around the school." Keyla organized.

As she, Heather and Arron left the parking lot they heard Kittana talking to Reace. "Okay, Reace you go that way, I'll go this way and we'll meet in behind the school."

Inside the school gym, Keyla was surprised at how well it was decorated; transformed from an ugly gymnasium to a cozy, music thumping dance hall. Nodding her head in time with the beat of the loud music, she smiled as she glanced around, searching the faces of young teenagers, looking for someone familiar but the only familiar face she saw was Arron, standing beside her.

Arron's eyes were flicking over the crowded dance floor and into the shadowy corners, his gaze was drawn back to the dance floor when he thought he heard Jake's name shouted over the music. Arron frowned maybe he just imagined it, the music was too loud to hear much of anything and he seriously doubted anyone could shout loud enough to be heard over it.

Heather who stood alongside of Keyla elbowed her, leaning in toward Keyla's ear she spoke and inclined her head at the same time, "That girl's not enjoying the dance, look at the way the guy is holding her it's more like . . ."

"He's restraining her." Keyla finished for her.

"What do we do?" Arron asked.

"Look for Jake or Nate, I'll handle this." Heather told them leaving Keyla's side before she had a chance to argue. As Heather approached the struggling teens she thought she recognized the boy, going with her hunch she tapped the teen on the shoulder calling him by name.

"Brandon Murphy! That is no way to dance with a woman. Here let me show you." Heather's voice was the voice of a mother and had the desired effect of startling the teenagers into compliance.

Brandon immediately let go of Anna who gave Heather a grateful look before scurrying away toward Arron. The guilty expression on Brandon's face turned quickly to embarrassment as Heather took Anna's place and started giving the young man a much needed lesson in slow dancing.

Arron and Keyla stood where they were watching Heather with astounded expressions, only turning away when someone grabbed Arron's arm and shouted just as the music ended.

"JAKE! DON'T JUST STAND THERE, NATE'S IN TROUBLE! CODY'S TAKEN HIM OUTSIDE, THEY ARE HAVING A FIGHT! Oh my god, it's all my fault." Anna moaned with an unbelieving shake of her head as she wondered how she could have been so stupid? How could she have forgotten about Cody! She should never have asked Nate to the dance then he'd be safe. If only . . .

"Don't worry about Nate, he'll be fine. We'll make sure of that!" Keyla's words brought Anna back to the problem at hand. She had overheard the girl's words—she couldn't help it, half the school had overheard. Keyla chewed her lip and after a quick glance at Arron who nodded, she grabbed his hand before muttering the words to a spell.

"Everyone in this room and near,
     What Anna spoke you didn't hear."

The last thing they needed was an audience when they found Nature.

"Kittana? Thank god you're here! I'm sorry for what I said earlier, if you can help Nate . . . I'll take it all back and I swear I'll never . . ." Anna's words halted when Keyla shook her head, Anna's expression instantly changed from sincere to confusion.

Keyla rolled her eyes at the look on Anna's face and letting go of Arron's hand to use her hands as she explained.

"Kittana and Reace are outside looking for Nate. I'm Keyla, Kittana's twin." She gestured toward Arron introducing him to Anna. "This is Arron, Jake's father."

"You're not Jake." Anna stared at Arron in disbelief then added with a flush of pink on her cheeks, "I'm sorry I thought you were, you look . . . ah, I mean he looks amazingly like you." Turning her attention back to Keyla, Anna took her hand. "We've got to go help Nate and Jake. Cody's got them, I just know it! Nate's parents probably don't know where to look, come on, please." Her eyes moved from Arron to Keyla imploring them to come with her, at the same time she tugged on Keyla's hand.

After nodding to Anna, Arron glanced back toward Heather for a second before following. Leaving Heather on the dance floor, he and Keyla followed Anna out the side door.

*

Reace headed around the school in the opposite direction from his wife, Kittana. Half way around the side of the large grey brick building Reace paused. He thought he heard a low growling sound coming from the side of him. Slowly he took another step forward and this time he heard the growling sound again, only it was coming in two directions one to the left of him and the other behind him. Slowly Reace turned his head to look over his left shoulder.

Two large dogs, both with their teeth bared growled menacingly at him. Reace rolled his eyes, *This trip just keeps getting better and better!* He thought sarcastically. He was about to use his powers to lightly stun the dogs, but before he could even summon his electricity to the surface, the dogs who looked ready to eat him, or at least use him as a giant chew toy, suddenly laid down on the ground, yawned, then fell asleep.

*"Kit"* Reace called to his wife using his mind, knowing his telepathic wife could hear him. *"There were two dogs here ready to eat me then just like that they went to sleep. You have anything to do with that"*

*"You only had two? I had about six over here. It was the oddest thing to it was like they were on guard or something . . ."* Kittana paused, *"Wait, there's someone coming."*

Reace quickened his pace he didn't have time to think about why these dogs were behaving strangely, but he briefly wondered if his son had something to do with it. He had to find Nate. Then help Kittana. Reace came around the corner of the building, behind the school and paused, his eyes widened before narrowing in anger at what he saw.

# Chapter twenty eight

"Hold him tight boys," Cody instructed. Cody had his friends drag Nate behind the school, out in the football field where nobody would stop them, where nobody would hear Nate's cries for help.

"This is going to be fun!" He told his friends who laughed and grinned wickedly.

Watching Cody with heated eyes Nate was oblivious to the rain and loud clap of thunder, anger was in control of Nature now, he taunted. "You think hurting me will make Anna stop liking me? It'll do nothing but make you a coward!"

Hearing the truth in Nate's words Cody lost control and moved to punch Nate.

He was ready for him and kicked out with his foot catching the surprised Cody in the chest and propelling him backwards.

Cody landed on his back in the mud, glaring at Nate with hatred as he got up.

"You can't even beat me with two guys holding me back!" Nate smirked.

"Come on Cody, you can take this little wimp." The guy on Nate's left encouraged, tightening his grip.

Dogs barked and growled menacingly around them but Cody didn't hear, he was too intent on his goal of teaching Nate a lesson.

Cody came at Nate again, determined to punch the stubborn smirk off his face. This time when Nate kicked out, Cody caught Nate's foot, holding it in a vise like grip as Nate struggled to release it.

He grinned viciously as he twisted the foot he held, relishing in Nate's grunt of pain, and the satisfaction at hearing Nate yelp as he tore ligaments.

As the blinding pain exploded in his leg Nate's mark flashed, and before Cody could twist it farther breaking the bones, a loud rumble of thunder boomed overhead, flashes of lightning streaked through the sky snaking their way toward the four boys on the ground.

"NATE!" Reace yelled as he ran forward. He crouched beside the three bodies sprawled on the ground around his son. Checking to make sure they were still alive, Reace sighed in relief when he could feel their study pulse beneath his fingertips.

Nate stood there watching his father, letting his anger boil over. The ground shook, trembling in Nature's outrage. The wind whipped the hair on his head and it swirled around him as the wind picked up speed. He stood tall, despite his injured leg, glaring at his father with adolescent rage.

"I DON'T NEED YOU TO STAND UP FOR ME! I DON'T NEED YOUR PROTECTION!" Nate shouted as thunder rumbling in the sky above them and lightning flashed around them.

Reace slowly stood.

"Calm down, Nature." He cautioned looking around at the angry weather.

"NO! I will not be calm. You can't control me!" The rain around them turned to hail as the temperature suddenly dropped to below freezing. "Why do you think that I can't fight for myself? WELL, I DON'T NEED YOU ANYMORE!" The wind, cold now, whipped toward Reace.

Directed at him by his son, the bitter wind hit him in the face and pushed him backward a step then two before Reace regained his footing, he frowned against the ping of hail hitting him.

"I CAN DO MORE THEN GROW FLOWERS AND MAKE IT RAIN. I CAN DEFEND MYSELF."

"AND YOU CAN HURT PEOPLE TOO, NATE, INNOCENT PEOPLE IF YOUR NOT IN CONTROL." Reace shouted above the wind as he struggled to remain standing. "PEOPLE LIKE ANNA." Reace pointed to where Anna-Marie was standing.

Nate glanced in that direction and he saw her staring wild-eyed at him, behind her stood Arron, Aunt Keyla and his mother, Kittana. Instantly the wind calmed and the hail turned to back rain, warming as it lessoned. The ground stopped trembling as Reace took one step then another toward his son.

"Nate, you are not the same as everybody else. You're special because you were born the most powerful of all Guardians . . . the Guardian of Nature. Your emotions, your powers, your strength is tied to the elements." He paused catching Nate's gaze and holding it with one of his own. "Simply put, you are Nature and Nature is you."

"I know dad, but sometimes I just get so tired of always having to be controlled, hiding myself. I have only been here for three days, how did you live a lifetime here and not show your powers?" Nate asked.

"I didn't." Reace admitted. "Once I got angry at some bullies, much the same as you did tonight, and I accidentally shocked them too."

"Wait a minute, are you saying that I did that? That I shocked them." Nate looked around him at the three bodies on the ground then back to his father. "You didn't . . . ?"

Reace shook his head. "Your powers are growing Nate, thunder storms are a part of Nature, so is lightning."

"That was me," Nate said again. His mind putting together all the times in the past two weeks when he got mad and had heard thunder, he had thought that his dad had been the one responsible for it but it wasn't his dad. It was him!

"I understand how you feel, I felt that way once too, but I promise you, Nate, it will get easier. The older you get the more you'll realize how your life influences another. You have more power than any of us," Reace shook his head and added, "I don't envy you that, but the powers that be knew that when they created you, and they wouldn't have given you something you couldn't handle."

"You really think I can handle it?" Nate looked up from under his lashes at his father. He heard the truth in his voice and he wanted to see the belief on his face.

"I know you can." Reace laid a hand on Nate's shoulder as a smile flashed on his face, "and your mother knows it too."

Nate smiled back, but his smiled faded replaced by a worried frown when they heard a groan come from one of the bodies on the ground. "Do you suppose they'll be okay?" he asked raising questing eyes to his father.

"Yeah, we'll take care of it," Reace said then added, "You'd better go talk to Anna."

"If she'll let me, I guess she'll think I'm a freak now." Nate muttered sulking a bit.

"It's a good sign that she stuck around." Reace shrugged watching Anna, "maybe she'll understand more than you think she will."

Kittana, Keyla and Arron came forward as Reace watched his son carefully make his way toward the girl he liked, Reace hoped, for his son's sake, that he had read Anna right and she'd understand everything Nate had to tell her.

Nature sure had grown up fast. It seemed like yesterday that Reace held a tiny infant in his arms for the first time. He could still feel the wonderment at the tiny miracle he had help to create. The worry he had about being a good father, a smile lit his features as he remembered the joy and awe of childbirth and fatherhood. Now here they were—back where it all began, seventeen years ago—only this time it was his son instead of himself facing huge life changes.

Reace looked on as Arron bent down to heal the three teenage bullies on the ground then he raised his gaze to his wife who stood still her face expressionless as she manipulated the minds of the three boys. It was Keyla who caught Reace's attention when she spoke.

"Where's Jake?" She asked a frown of confused worry on her face.

Reace glanced around, his eyes quickly, carefully scanning the area before turning his gaze back to Keyla, "I don't know, I haven't seen him."

"From what I gathered," Kittana's voice interrupted them as she came out of her trance, "Cody," she sneered the name as she nudged him with her foot. From her brief visit inside his mind she didn't like the kid, looking back to Reace and Keyla, she continued telling them, "After pushing him down the stairs, they left Jake, by the door of the high school."

"But Jake wasn't there when we got here." Keyla reminded them, "Do you think someone found him and took him to the hospital?"

"No," Arron said standing up, "let's get out of here before they wake up then I'll explain." Arron looked at Kittana before taking her hand and Keyla's. Keyla held Reace's hand as he closed the circle by taking Kittana's outstretched hand.

*'Nate, we'll meet you back at Jake's house.'* Kittana telepathed to her son before closing her eyes and using her teleporting talents, she moved them in the blink of an eye and a flash of her wrist to Jake's fenced in back yard.

"Okay, why do I get the feeling that I am the only one who doesn't know something?" Keyla complained letting go of her friends hands. "Why wouldn't Jake be in the hospital? Did Heather bring him home?" she asked them then answered her own question before anyone else could, "No, she couldn't have because he hadn't been there when we arrived. So where do you think he is?" she turned her confused expression to Arron. "Is he hurt? Arron, we've got to find him!"

"Keyla, Jake isn't hurt, he can self-heal." Arron told her then added, "I haven't witnessed it myself but Jake told me about it and Heather confirmed it."

"So, Jake's okay. Right?" Keyla asked.

"Yes, at least I think so. My guess is that he left the school probably to come back here to get us." Arron said and pushing a hand through his hair his eyes reflected his worries. "I just hoped no one witnessed his ability."

\*

Nate nodded as he limped toward Anna having heard his mother's words in his mind.

Anna wasn't looking at Nate, her eyes were riveted on the Guardians, she had watching as they used their powers of healing and then teleporting, before turning her wide-eyed gaze to stare at Nate who now stood in front of her. Before she could speak or even from a coherent thought, he spoke. She frowned at what he said, it didn't make any sense, who or what was Timelana?

"Timelana," Nate called softly again. When she appeared beside him it was as he had hoped—time had stopped. He turned to the Guardian of time and sighed with relief before admitting.

"Timelana, I'm scared. I want her to like me as much as I . . ." he paused, "I have never told this to anybody, but I used to dream about this place, about her." He glanced away from Timelana to look around him. His eyes lingering on Anna's frozen features in front of him before going back to Timelana as he continued talking, "This probably sounds crazy, but I knew what her laugh would sound like before I heard it."

"That doesn't sound crazy to me." Timelana said softly.

"I just don't want to blow this," Nate continued as if she had never spoken, "I've never had to explain what I am before . . . not when it really mattered. How . . . what can I tell her to make her see that I'm not a freak; that I am a person—just like her, not just some alien from another world."

"You're a Guardian, Nate." Timelana said in a commanding voice that made Nature lift his head and look at her. "That isn't something to be despised."

"I know but she doesn't, how do I make her see that? What do I say?" he beseeched her.

Timelana ached to help him, to tell him what she knew of his and Anna's future but she couldn't, it went against the rules of time and she'd not risk changing the outcome of future events. Nate's future and the future of his children were too important to risk. Drawing a shaky breath Timelana could do nothing more then watch him struggle and offer this advice:

"Nature, I am sorry I can't give you the words to say . . . those have to come from you. Just speak to her from your heart and be honest."

The expression on her face meant a lot to Nate, it was a look that sympathized, encouraged and hoped all at once and it made Nature feel like he wasn't alone; that he could do this. Turning his attention back to Anna's features frozen in time, he nodded. "Alright."

By the look on his face Timelana knew he was ready for time to restart. She thudded her staff softly on the ground, but before she disappeared in a swirl of bright colors, a smile brightened her face when she heard Nate's muttered words.

"I hope I'm ready for this."

"Nate, are you okay? What's going on? Was Cody really struck by lightning? We've got to call an ambulance. Where's Jake? And who or what is Timelana?" The questions flew out of Anna's mouth as time restarted.

"I'm fine. Cody's fine too. Arron's a . . . a doctor, he has already . . . checked them over." Nate stumbled over the half truth as he tried to answer her questions.

"Doctors don't disappear." Anna frowned at Nate. "And speaking of disappearing where the hell did they go and how?"

Nate sighed, "You saw all that, huh?"

"Nate, I need some answers. What the hell is going on?" Anna demanded.

"Look, Anna, I can explain, I promise. But right now, I'd like to find Jake, make sure he's okay first."

The image of the last time he'd seen Jake, unconscious and bleeding from the back of his head swam before his eyes.

Anna nodded, not sure what else to do.

"Your hurt!" She exclaimed watching him take an awkward step forward, "We need to get you to a doctor."

"I'll be fine . . . Arron will take care of it." Nate told her with confidence. "Right now, I just want to get away from here before Cody wakes up and we've got to find Jake."

"Okay," The look on his face made her agree with him, it was a mixture of worry, dread and hope. "Jake's mother is inside maybe she's found him." She suggested as she moved toward Nate grabbing his arm and swinging it over her shoulder at the same time as her other arm encircled his waist, supporting him and helping him to walk faster. The look he gave her was one that she couldn't read and he glanced away quickly, looking forward as they made their way across the field and around the school to the front entrance.

They were just about to go inside when they saw Heather coming out.

"Nate, there you are! Have you seen your parents? They are worried sick about you! You've scared them and me. We are just going to have to set up some rules if you're going to be staying with me. I won't tolerate this kind of behavior from Jake and I won't take it from you either. Is that understood? From now on if you want to go somewhere you will have to tell me where you're going, who you're with, when you'll be home and I want a phone number so I can reach you if something happens."

"Yes, ma'am," Nate nodded when she took a breath. "Have you seen Jake? Is he inside?" He wanted to ask her if he was okay but he didn't want to alarm Jake's mother, by the sound of her voice she was mad enough at him already.

"No, Jake isn't inside and neither is Keyla or Arron. Have you seen them?"

"Arron, Aunt Key and my parents went back to your place they asked me to tell you they'd meet you there. I think Jake went back there too." Nate ignored Anna's quizzical expression as she stared at him, wondering when this conversation had taken place, she hadn't seen anyone talk to him (expect his father) and she wondered how he knew where they had gone?

"Okay, well, my van's over here, why don't we head on home?" Heather suggested. She started walking toward the parking lot, starting up her van with a push of a button.

If Nature was surprised by the car that blinked its lights and started by itself he hid it well.

"Do you need a drive home?" Heather directed her question at the girl beside Nate as they moved with her toward the running car.

"No, I'm going with Nate, I want to make sure Jake's okay too and that Nate gets the help he needs." Anna spoke firmly. In the privacy of her own mind, she added, *and I want to hear the answers that Nate promised me,* as she helped Nate into the mini-van.

When they were all settled Heather started to leave the parking lot. Easing out into traffic she glanced at Nate in the rear view mirror. "What happened Nate? You look like you've been in a fight."

"Yeah, something like that." Nate mumbled turning his head to look out the window.

Heather frowned she knew Nate was trying to tune her out and she wondered what she could say to make him see that she was on his side.

"Listen Nate, if you're going to stay with me you're going to have to learn to trust me," she paused gaining eye contact through the mirror, she hoped her eyes conveyed the message she wanted as she continued, "I told your parents I don't mind looking after you while they're away but . . ."

"Wait!" Nate demanded stopping Heather's flow of words. "Did you just say that my parents are letting me stay here on Earth; in Springfield, while they go back to Taysia without me?" Nate needed to be sure he heard that right; his eyes never left Heather's face in the mirror.

"Earth? Taysia?" Anna repeated, "Nate, you talk as through . . ." She trialed off.

Heather nodded to Nate and with her expression she cautioned him to be careful.

Nate nodded back accepting her caution and the friendship he read in her expression. He was still surprised by his parents letting him stay, but he'd wait until he heard it from them before he got his hopes up that they had actually listened to him.

Glancing at Anna he knew he promised her the truth and now was the time to come clean with an explanation. Once they got back to Jake's, Anna-Maria would witness things that she'd freak-out over if he didn't inform her now. The longer he waited the more time was running out. Nate inwardly sighed and turned to face her.

"Anna, I have to tell you something but first you have to promise not to freak out until after I'm done." He waited until she nodded before continuing, "You've read Kade's journals—the books in Kittana's storage box—remember the strange language I spoke when I read them to you?

That language was Starian, from a planet called Staria. A planet my grandfather was born on. Anna, the journals are true."

"So, what you're saying is that you're an alien?" Anna clarified.

"I wish it were that easy," Nate muttered and at Anna's confused expression he admitted, "I'm more than that, I'm a Guardian."

"A Guardian?" she repeated a question in her voice.

"Yes, Nate is short for my real name, Nature. Anna, I was born Nature, the Guardian of Nature."

Anna's eyes widened as the mark on his wrist suddenly pulsed with light and his skin shined brightly for a second.

After the show of power he continued as if it never happened.

"Basically it means that I was born with all the powers of Nature. I can control the weather, the ground, grow flowers and trees . . . all of Nature."

"Okay, so you're telling me that you're a Guardian and that you're from a different planet?" Anna said with an expression of disbelief on her face. She glanced at Jake's mother to see if she believed this too. The look on Heather's face was one of incredibility, but not disbelief. Anna turned her attention back to Nate when he spoke.

"Yeah," he agreed.

"Okay," Anna drew out the word, frowning and biting her lip. "So, you're a Guardian and you have powers." she stated having a hard time believing him.

"Yes," Nate answered watching her expression carefully.

"You're a Guardian and you have powers," Anna repeated she knew she sounded dumb but she just couldn't help but repeat that phrase, like she was trying to get comfortable with this information and hoping by repeating it, that he'd tell her it wasn't true, that it was some kind of joke.

"Yeah, look, can we get past that part. I'm a Guardian and I have powers, I can control Nature but I am still a person, Anna, just like you." He shrugged before continuing, "It's just that I can do things that you can't."

"Like control the weather," Anna said almost sarcastically then her voice changed, sounding more accusing as she demanded. "Did you make Cody and his friends get struck by lightning?"

"Not on purpose." Nate grudgingly admitted. "Anna, I am still learning what I can and can't do, like that lightning, but I swear to you that I'd never try to hurt anyone on purpose." The honesty in his eyes compelled her to believe him. "At first I thought my father, who's the

Guardian of Electricity, did that and I got pretty mad at him . . ." Nate paused, his checks colored in memory, "but he told me that it was me, not him and that makes sense too, lightning and thunderstorms are a part of nature. Anna, I am sorry that I lost control and I hurt someone but he's okay now, Arron healed him. Look, hurting someone, even Cody isn't something I set out to do and all I can do to make it better is promise to keep tighter control over my abilities in the future." Nature and Anna where so involved in their conversation that it took words from Heather to realize that the car had stopped.

"Okay, we're here." Heather announced as she got out of the van, they followed suit.

"Anna, are you okay? You are taking this . . ." Standing beside the now parked minivan, Nate began, but broke off when her eyes focused on his face.

"I'm fine," she lied, "let's just find Jake and get you fixed up, you really shouldn't be walking on that foot." Focusing her attention on him rather than thinking about everything he had just told her made her feel better . . . more in control.

# Chapter twenty nine

They walked into the house and slowly made their way toward the voices they heard in the kitchen.

"HOLY CRAP! Nate, are you okay?"

Jake's voice brought everyone's attention to the arrival of the newcomers. As one, the five people in the kitchen turned to face Nate, Anna and Heather.

"Yeah, I'll be fine after Arron heals me." Even as he spoke, Arron was moving toward him leading him to a chair, which Nate gratefully sank into. His foot was really throbbing now. He winced as Arron lifted the leg, took off his shoe, and pulled up the pant leg of his jeans.

"I'm sorry," Arron said, making Nate wonder if he was talking about earlier in the shelter or the injury. Arron's eyes searched Nate's face for a second before placing his hands on the injured leg and foot.

Jake, Heather, and Anna watched in fascination as Arron called his power to the surface, channeling it into healing Nate's leg.

Arron's hands glowed, a soft yellow and he closed his eyes seeing past his hands into the broken muscles of Nate's leg and foot. In his mind Arron saw the torn tendons and broken ligaments. Using his power Arron healed them, restoring them to perfect health before easing out of the newly repaired knee and ankle. He shifted his position moving to heal the bruises and broken skin on Nate's face and torso.

Afterward when Arron glanced up he was surprised and a little embarrassed to see so many pairs of eyes watching him.

Nate smiled, flexed his foot, his grin widened.

"Thanks Arron." His expression conveying the message that thing's between them were great. Arron smiled in return.

"That was so cool!" Jake cooed.

"Wow," Heather said on a breath. "Did you always know how to do that?" she asked referring to their high school days.

Nate looked at Anna; she was still watching everything with a wide-eyed stare. His face darkened with a frown as his hope that she'd understand and not freak out disappeared into the realm of reality. She thought he was strange. He had blown any chance he had of being with her. Jake's voice snapped Nate out of his depressing thoughts.

"What happened, with Cody?" Jake asked then with down cast eyes he added, "I'm sorry I couldn't stop him."

"It means a lot that you tried." Nate countered then to lighten the mood he added, "You think I look bad, he took the worst of it. And that was before he got struck by lightning"

"Nate! You shouldn't be happy about that. You could have seriously hurt someone." Kittana cut in.

Nate rolled his eyes at his mother's words before continuing to talk to Jake.

"I'm just glad your okay, you took a nasty fall down those steps. Thank the powers that be for your ability."

"Anna! Hi, do you need a ride home?" Kittana spoke in a loud voice, hoping to drown out Nate's last words.

Before Anna could answer Kittana's question, Nate spoke for her.

"I'll walk her home . . . later. It's okay, mom, she knows."

Anna nodded, not trusting herself to speak just yet as she tore her gaze from Nate and Arron and as Nate's words sunk into her head she looked with concern at Jake.

"Stuck by lightning?" Jake eyes went meaningfully to Reace then swung back to Nate when Reace shook his head and glanced at his son. Nate's smile broadened as he watched Jake's expression change. "YOU did that?" Jake stated surprised, impressed and at the same time, a little scared.

"Yeah, apparently," Nate admitted after a brief glance to his father.

"Whoa,"

"You fell down the stairs, are you okay?" Heather asked, her eyes asking her son if anyone saw him. Arron turned concerned eyes to Jake as well, carefully scanning his body looking for any sign of discomfort or damage.

Jake smiled, a little embarrassed but pleased at his father's obvious concern then he gave his head a little shake that was almost unnoticeable, but Heather saw it and she relaxed and let out a sigh of relief, Jake's secret was still safe from the outside world-at least for now.

"Yeah, I'm fine." He answered his mother's question. Feeling Anna's eyes on him he added with a conspiracy twinkle in his eye and a shrug of his shoulder, "maybe a little sore, but I'll heal."

"She knows?" Kittana repeated then looked at her son, "Nate, you can't just go around telling people about us."

Nate winced, as a sudden headache pierced his brain when his mother accidentally broadcast with her telepathy at the same time as she spoke.

"Come on mom, after what she witnessed, even dad said it was alright to tell her."

"Reace!" Kittana turned toward her husband.

Reace shot his son a mock glare before defending himself. "If he's going to stay here he's going to need a few friends." His words got a double take from Arron and Keyla, who gave Reace a funny look that he ignored as he continued. "Take it from a guy who has been there. It's hard to keep it all inside, under tight control." He glanced briefly at Heather, Jake and Anna, shrugging as he added, "They'll help."

Anna's gaze swung from Nate to Kittana then to the others in the room and her brow furrowed as she spoke, her voice sounding almost accusing, "You're all like Nate. You're all aliens, aren't you?"

"I never said I was the only one, Anna. I am a Guardian, so are my parents, Aunt Keyla, Arron and there are others too . . . back home on Taysia."

"Taysia? Is that like some . . . some space ship full of aliens waiting to attack Earth, colonize the planet and make us your slaves?" Anna's voice held a note of panic she couldn't hold back any longer. Even though she knew she sounded stupid she couldn't seem to help what came out of her mouth, even if she didn't really believe it.

"Anna, don't be silly, that only happens in the movies." Heather told her as she moved to comfort the scared girl but stopped when Anna backed away, recoiling from her touch.

"Really cheesy movies," Jake added.

"No one is going to hurt you Anna," Reace offered his assurance hoping she'd believe him.

"There is no space ship, we aren't exactly aliens." Keyla paused "We're Guardians, we help people."

Anna's gaze flicked to her foster sister as her mind reeled from what she had heard and witnessed and knew to be true.

"Taysia is the world where the Guardians live, where we have lived for the past seventeen years." Kittana started to explain than stopped when Nate took over.

"Guardians are beings chosen by the powers that be, God, fate—whatever you want to call it—for whatever reason they are granted special abilities or powers to protect the things they are chosen to protect. Like a gardener who tends the flowers, keeping them growing, protecting them from frost, weeds, bugs and other creatures. Making sure everything stays in order, and things happen the way they are supposed to, according to the grand design."

"Anna, there are Guardians who govern everything, from all walks of life, from every planet in the universe." Nate went on explaining, "There are Guardians of animals, birds, fish; fairies who look after the flowers, nymphs to watch over trees and forests with the help of other creatures too. There are even Guardians for the elements but out of all these Guardians there are only fourteen who must stay on Taysia. These Guardians are the balancing forces, seven good, seven evil—a balance."

Jake looked with pride to his father, before his eyes moved to Keyla, Kittana and finally Reace as he continued to listen to Nate explain to Anna.

"The balance they struggle to maintain affects the level of good versus evil on all the planets in the universe. If evil tips the scales then more evil dominates others worlds, like Earth. More violence, wars, powers struggles, gangs, slavery, corruption . . . you get the idea, right?" Nate glanced at her making sure she understood him, before he continued, "It's the same if good tips the scales, people would have more compassion toward each other, love would rule their hearts instead of bitterness and anger. But the thing is Anna; balance is the key to having peace and life. When Malic took over Taysia in the time before my parents, Keyla and Arron—the chosen four from the prophecy . . ."

"Prophecy? What prophecy?" Anna demanded finding herself caught up in Nate's story, wanting to know the details. His voice made it sound so possible that she found herself believing him.

"It is Deia's prophecy," Arron spoke, answering the question. "She was a famous prophet on Staria thousands of years ago. She predicted the coming of the Guardians to Staria, but they have been around since the beginning of time, even in Earth's own history: the Greeks, the Vikings and countless other civilizations called them Gods but they were really Guardians."

"When Malic took over Taysia, killing the seven who opposed him, Staria died." Nate continued.

"Staria's the planet Kade, your grandfather, came from, right?" Anna asked.

Nate nodded, "Yes, a whole planet of life was wiped out and others were next."

"That's why you had to leave?" Anna gaze moved to Kittana, "Isn't it?" Kittana nodded.

"We had to stop Malic, we had to balance the life forces." Reace added.

"And we did," Keyla said, "We saved Vanishtar."

"So you won, you defeated the evil guys. Why do you have to go back?" Heather asked.

"That's just it, we didn't defeat Malic, there isn't a winner or a loser . . . it's not a contest, it's a balance." Kittana clarified then explained further, "in order to live, to have life, you must have both good and evil. You have to know that evil exists in order to appreciate the good."

"Balance, that sounds very Chinese, you know like the yen and yang symbol." Heather commented.

"Guardian means protect life in Starian." Nate added.

"So is everyone here a Guardian?" Anna asked her voice less panicky and accusing than before. After hearing the whole story and it fit with everything she had known, everything she had wondered about since reading Kade's journals and seeing her foster sister again. It was like watching a TV program with a fuzzy picture that suddenly came into focus, matching what she heard with what she saw—forming a complete picture. She still had questions, lots of them, but she understood now better than before. Kade's journals finally made sense to her.

"I'm as normal as you are." Heather's eyes moved to her son, she was about to say that Jake was normal too when he spoke up.

"I think it's obvious that I'm not normal but I am not a Guardian." He held up his left wrist. "I'm just a quarter Starian," Jake confirmed surprising himself saying that out loud—to admit his father's heritage—it was something he was proud of. He smiled reveling in the feel of it.

Anna wondered what his hand had to do with proving his statement then she caught a glimpse of Arron's wrist and Keyla's, they had something on it, a mark of some sort that at this distance she couldn't make out. Lifting her gaze back to Jake's face she realized that she didn't really want to get a closer look.

"Speaking of the balance we should be getting back," Keyla said after glancing at the clock on the stove. Her words were like a weight that hung in the air around them, sobering them to the realization that this was good-bye.

"You're really going to let me stay here?" Nate watched his parents closely. He needed to hear it directly from them.

*"He's happier here than he ever was on Taysia."* Reace sent a telepathic message to his wife's mind.

*"Listen to yourself, Reace, of course he was happy on Taysia it was his home!"* Kittana telepathed back to him.

*"No, Kittana, look at him. You know I speak the truth."*

Kittana turned her attention to her son, who lifted his eyebrows waiting with hope filled eyes for her answer. Tears blurred her vision as she nodded. "If that's what you truly want."

Nate's smile told Kittana that Reace was right, he did belong here on Earth. It was time for her to let him grow up.

"What about Malic, he may try to hurt him here?" Keyla asked giving voice to Kittana's fears.

"And like us, Nate will stop him." Arron answered. Raising eyes full of pride to Nature, he added, "He is more powerful than any of us."

Kittana nodded then added in her mind. *"Yes, but he's my baby!"*

*"He was our baby, now he's a full grown Guardian and we have to let go, let him make his own choices."*

She was startled for a second when Reace answered her; she hadn't meant to broadcast her thought.

*"You're right. And if this is what he really wants then we can't stop him, can we?"* Kittana replied telepathically.

Reace smiled that slow smile that lit up his eyes, made her stomach flip over and her heart skip a beat.

The look on Nate's face made Arron's chest feel uncomfortably tight, he spoke fondly when he said, "I'm going to miss you, kid."

Nate swallowed the tears that suddenly clogged his throat. He knew he was right to stay here but he just hadn't thought it would be hurt to say goodbye.

"I'll miss you, too, but this isn't goodbye, I'll visit and you can visit too, Timelana will help. She's just a call away." Nature reassured Arron then he turned to Keyla when she spoke.

"Yes, we'll stay in touch, but that doesn't mean we won't miss you, Nature." Keyla said engulfing her nephew in a hug.

"And I'll come up with a spell to visit so we won't always be bothering Timelana, she's a busy woman." Keyla told Nate, but the truth was that the Guardian of Time intimidated her.

Jake looked at Arron, he wasn't ready to say good-bye to his father—he'd just met the man and he wanted more time to get to know him so he offered, "I'll . . . I'll drive you."

"Ah, no," Heather countered his offer not feeling comfortable with her son, who had just gotten his license, driving in the dark. "I'll drive."

Heather stood and put on her jacket and her shoes, car keys in hand she headed for the door.

"Nate, are you sure you want to stay here?" Kittana asked one more time as she too got up and prepared to follow Heather and Jake out to the car.

"Yeah, I'm sure." Nate glanced at Anna then turned back to his mother as he added, "You go on, I'll walk Anna home."

"So this is goodbye," Keyla interrupted, her eyes filling with tears, she engulfed her nephew in another tight hug.

"No, Aunt Key, this is I'll see you later." Nate's voice was muffled against her shoulder. Moving to look into her face, a smile played at his lips as he continued, "Until you figure out that spell, Timelana is only a call away."

"So are we," Reace added taking Keyla's place, hugging his son. "Remember that. If you ever need us for any reason, we'll be here. We're proud of you."

Reace moved away so his wife could hug him too.

"Behave yourself and mind Heather, she's your legal Guardian here. As soon as we deal with this mess on Taysia—whatever it is—we'll visit, I promise." Kittana said staring into her son's face she continued, "Don't tell anyone else about us, don't use your talents to show off and don't get into any more fights, please. Arron's not here to heal you and . . ."

"Mom, I'm not an idiot!"

Kittana smiled sadly at him, tears filling her eyes clouding her vision, she blinked them back. "I know, Nature. This is just . . . hard to say goodbye."

"Then don't say it. Mom, this isn't goodbye . . . we'll keep in touch, I'll visit and you'll visit. We'll be okay, trust me." Nate hugged her then. It was hard for him to say goodbye too; harder than he expected it to be.

When they parted his mother touched his face, cupping it as she looked at him with pride and naked love shining in her eyes.

"When did you get to be so smart? When did you grow up?" not waiting for an answer she hugged him again and kissed his cheek. "I love you and we will all miss you, but you are right you do have to fulfill your own destiny and if staying here is where you feel you need to be than that's where you should be. I am so proud of you, you know that don't you?" Her eyes, wet with tears searched his face.

Nate only nodded unable to trust his voice, he spoke with his mind.

*"I know mom."* He kept his arm around her as they all moved toward the front door.

Mrs. White intercepted them at the front door. After hearing their concerns about the boys she hadn't been able to sleep and when she heard the commotion at the door she came running. Her eyes taking everything in, searching out Arron's face and with a crestfallen expression she stated.

"You're leaving?"

"Yes," Kittana answered. "There are some pressing matters back home that need our immediate attention. I want to thank-you for everything you've done. Heather said it was alright for Nate to stay here with Jake, please look out for them the same as you did for Reace and Arron."

Mrs. White nodded, her eyes shone with the tears that clogged her throat. Arron took her by the shoulders and he spoke when she looked into his face.

"You've been more like a mother to me than anyone; thank-you for that and thank-you for always being there for me and now for my son, Jake." Arron engulfed her in a tight hug whispering in her ear he added, "I love you."

When they parted she patted his shoulders saying, "Don't be a stranger, come back and visit."

Mrs. White's throat pumped with the effort of swallowing the lump that threatened to spill over into tears, Arron was having a hard time leaving already—that much was evident in his eyes and she didn't want to add to that. But hearing those whispered words from him had been music to her ears and she'd hold them in her heart forever.

"That's a promise." Arron said with a teary smile before turning away and heading out the door.

Reace's throat clogged with emotion as he watched the exchange between the housekeeper and his comrade, he too had the same feelings as Arron about the old woman, but he didn't say anything.

Mrs. White looked at Reace with a fondness she always felt for the boy, stepping forward she grabbed him to her in a hug that surprised the Guardian of Electricity and warmed him at the same time.

"Don't go getting yourself into trouble! You're a good boy, Reace, always were." She chuckled as his checks reddened.

Embarrassed Reace kissed her cheek before slipping out of her embrace and ducking shyly out the door.

After briefly hugging Nate again, Kittana hugged the dear old housekeeper, before she and Keyla followed closing the door behind them.

"Come on Anna, I'll walk you home." Nate said as he handed Anna her jacket.

Anna slipped it on and after glancing at Nate she hurried out the door.

"Kittana wait!" she called as a confused Nate hurried after her.

Kittana was just about to climb into the running minivan when she heard Anna's shout and paused, turning to face the younger woman as she came to a stop beside her.

"Kittana," Anna breathed, "I just wanted to tell you that . . . I am sorry. Sorry for earlier . . . I shouldn't have said those things to you, I shouldn't have blown up at you like that . . . it's just that I . . . I . . ." Anna looked at her foster sister with sorry eyes, eyes that conveyed so much more then she could say.

"You didn't want to see your mom get hurt again," Kittana finished for her, her heart softening for the girl. "It's okay, Anna I understand. I don't want to see Nancy or Dave get hurt either, I love them too."

"Yeah," Anna-Maria nodded and quietly added, "I know."

Kittana's eyes watered as she held out her arms in a hug which Anna accepted briefly hanging on tight before letting go.

Kittana climbed into the waiting van and then glanced at her son, who stood slightly behind Anna. "*I love you Nate, be careful.*" she telepathed to him and with a flash of her mark the sliding door closed.

"*I love you too, mom.*" Nate spoke in his mind knowing his mother would hear him. A tear fell down his cheek as he watched them drive away.

"Be careful" He whispered.

# CHAPTER THIRTY

NATE WATCHED AS THE CAR drove off down the street with everybody he knew inside of it. For a moment he wanted to run after them begging to go home with them. He was a stranger in a strange land and he was alone. He'd miss Taysia and all of the friends he had left behind, but more importantly he'd miss his family.

Glancing at Anna he reminded himself that this was right, this was where he was supposed to be, this was what he wanted. And he could always go home; that door would always be opened to him.

"You're going to miss them, aren't you?" Anna asked watching Nate.

"Yeah," Nate replied softly returning his gaze to the empty street and after wiping his eyes he looked at her, his expression turned into one of resolve as he added, "Come on, I'll walk you home, now."

They walked in silence for a few blocks, Nate wasn't sure where to start or what to say to her—there were so many things to say he didn't quite know where to start.

"Oh, look! It's a porcupine." She suddenly exclaimed. In the light from the street lamps you could just make out the roly-poly waddle of little legs and prickly fur as it crossed the street and continued onto the grass a twenty feet in front of them. "It's so cute, I love porcupines! I did a class report on them in grade school." Anna added babbling a bit—she too was nervous.

"Do you want to hold it, pet it?" Nate offered. They had stopped walking to watch the night creature.

"Oh, come on, they're wild, we couldn't get within two feet of one without getting seriously hurt." Anna scoffed in a whisper.

Nate raised one eyebrow as if to challenge her statement then he turned toward the wild animal, his mark flashed as he started to make chirpy-grunting sounds then squatted down and held out his hand.

When Nate made the noise the porcupine stopped and looked at him, at them, for a second before it answered Nate with the same type of chirpy-grunting sounds and to Anna's astonishment the porcupine came forward nudging his nose into Nate's hand as if he were a familiar pet looking for an affectionate pat.

Nate made another sound and it was answered.

Anna watched both Nate and the wild animal in amazement. It seemed like they were having a conversation with each other, through body language and those noises Nate was making. Then, as Anna watched, he nodded and he passed his hand over the ground and closing his eyes in concentration. There was a flash on his wrist again just before tiny white salt rocks appeared to come up out of the ground. With a look of adoration at Nate the porcupine bent his head and starting eating the white rocks. Nate, seemingly out of breath, chuckled a bit before turning his smile on her.

"You can pat him if you want to, he'll let you now."

"How? What did you do?" She asked. As she tentatively knelt beside the furry rodent and carefully ran her hand lightly over his quill filled fur, surprised to be able to do so without being hurt.

When the white salt rocks were gone the animal lifted his head looked at Nate again before grunting and at Nate's answering grunt the animal looked sad for a moment before it moved away, turning to go toward the back of the houses that lined the street.

"That was amazing!" Anna breathed.

"Yeah." Nate agreed watching the rodent waddle away.

"How did you do that?" Anna asked. "I've never seen anyone do something like before."

"I am the Guardian of Nature, Anna." An aura of power surrounded him but he continued to speak. "I can control all of Nature; the ground, the wind, weather . . . even animals." Nate's voice held a note of awe as he realized just how powerful he could be.

"So that's why there was a ring of dogs at the school," Anna interrupted him, remembering the events of the night.

"Ring of dogs?" Nate questioned bewildered.

"Yeah, there were at least twenty dogs around you and Cody, in a semi circle about twenty feet from you, growling but not moving any closer. Then suddenly they all just fell asleep. It was . . . odd." Anna glanced at Nate searching for answers.

Nate was shocked, he didn't remember any dogs and he was sure he hadn't summoned them on a conscious level but one thing he knew was that his mother or Keyla had something to do with them all suddenly going to sleep.

"Guess I must have summoned them without realizing it, Anna, I am still learning what I can and can't do. I've always been able to talk with animals, but I didn't know I could control them."

"It must be pretty scary having all that power inside of you . . . I mean, if you wanted to, I guess you could use it to your advantage."

Nate looked down, a smile playing on his lips, he shook his head before looking back to her and saying, "No, there are rules. The more power you have, the more rules to follow."

Nate thought about Timelana, she had infinite knowledge of everything and everyone in the universe. If she wanted to she could do almost anything but she followed the rules allowing things to happen as they were meant to, helping only where needed to further the grand design along. Knowing that if she put so much as a toe out of line disastrous things could follow.

He glanced at Anna, as he continued to try and explain what he was just coming to understand. "Nature has to follow rules or else . . . consequences. It's kind of hard of explain, but if I tried to use this power for my own pleasure—say if I wanted to make it sunny all the time, then there'd be problems like drought. If I allow my emotions to rule me and I'm sad, it'll rain . . . too much rain isn't good either." Nate paused as he realized something, "That's why Timelana had to tell my mother she was pregnant with me, she was tapping into my powers. She thought my dad had died—but he didn't, he'd just disappeared for a while. She was sad—devastated really—and it wouldn't stop raining, not just on Taysia but on every planet."

"I get it," Anna said when his expression asked if he was explaining it right. "Like a working adult that gets paid can't just go out and blew the money. They have to pay the bills, buy groceries . . . make the money last until next payday. Even though you have amazing powers, you still have to use them responsibly."

Nate grinned, "You're amazing!"

"Me? How?" She demanded, a confused frown wrinkled her forehead.

"After everything you've seen and heard, you're not freaked out, why?" Nate countered giving her a question at the same time he answered hers.

"I don't know," she shrugged his question catching her off guard. "You're different from every other guy I know maybe that's why I like you." Anna paused then added, "I liked you before, you know. Maybe I sensed that you were different . . . I don't know but I do know that . . . that I still like you." She paused again running what she had just said in her mind wondering if it made any sense or not.

"You do?" Nate asked as hope swelled inside of his heart, maybe he still had a chance with her.

"Yeah, and I'm not all freaked out about this, . . . well," Anna started then changed her mind and truthfully told him. "Maybe I am freaked out, but I did read your grandfather's journals when I was little," her cheeks reddened as she admitted, "I used to daydream that . . . that it was true, and that someday I'd meet . . ." She glanced at him then away in embarrassment.

"Does that mean you'll want to see me again?" Nate asked half scared of her answer. What she'd just told him gave him hope though and it showed in his eyes.

"Definitely," She answered, glancing at him again than she rolled her eyes as she added, "If I am ever allowed out again."

"What does that mean?" He asked in confusion.

"I'm late, I was supposed to be home hours ago, my parents will be very mad at me and I'll get into trouble . . . probably grounded—that's when they make me stay home and I'm only allowed out to go to school, but," A slow smile brightened her face as she stared into Nate's eyes, "but I think it was worth it."

"I'm sorry that I made you get into trouble, I'll talk to them if you want," he offered, not really sure of what he'd say and he tried to hide his relief when she shook her head.

"That's okay, they aren't that bad. Actually, as parents go they're pretty cool." Anna defended realizing at the same time that she meant it.

They started walking again and after a few minutes of silence Nate glanced at her, he hated to say this but he had to make sure, "You know you can't tell anyone about me right?"

"Duh," Anna replied then added, "Who'd believe me anyway?"

"So you're really going to be okay with . . . everything?"

Anna glanced at Nate catching his gaze she said thoughtfully. "I think . . . I will be," then speaking more to herself then Nate, she repeated, "I will be."

The look she gave him he couldn't quite understand but it made his heart expand.

*

After the chosen four had set up the candles in a large ring, they were in the same place they had been before—the clearing in the woods just outside of the city. The place had all of the elements: air, earth, water (from a nearby brook) and now Keyla called her magic to her, bringing the element of fire.

"In this circle candles stand,
　　　Flare to life as I command."

With a flicker of light shinning from her wrist and an upward motion of her hands the candles they had placed in the wide circle sparked, then flared, settling seconds later to a small lick of flame that danced above each candle.

This was the place they had opened the portal to Taysia seventeen years ago and again two days ago, and Keyla was more than certain that they'd open it in the future, now that one of their own was here. She was going to miss Nate, but she thought as she sniffed back tears. *This is what he wants.*

Standing in the middle of the circle of lit candles she turned to the others, motioning them to enter and begin the spell to take them home—to whatever fate waited for them.

Panic rose inside of Keyla, swelling up from the dream she had, she breathed slowly, deeply, trying to calm down as she mentally told herself that it was only a dream not a premonition. It wouldn't happen like that.

Arron watched Keyla motion to him, he wanted to go back home—he had wanted that since they first came here, he wanted to make sure Zarrick and Tia were okay. God, he hoped so! He hoped they were wrong about the prophecy, but he couldn't shake the feeling in his gut—and now that it was time to go he found his feet unable to move forward. This was harder then he thought it would be. He was torn between wanting to stay with one son and needing to go to another son. Cursing, Arron ran a hand though his hair and stormed a few feet away.

Jake looked from the circle of fire to his father, now was the time for goodbye. Jake swallowed hard, clearing his throat and when Arron spun away, Jake followed a perplexed frown on his face.

"Christ! I hate this." Arron suddenly spoke spinning around to face his son, staring in a face that mirrored his own and eyes that looked so much like his, yet so different. "I've just meet you. I wish I could stay . . ."

"It's okay, Dad," Jake said watching the way Arron's expression softened, matching the warm fuzzy feeling inside of him at the pleasure of calling Arron 'dad', he continued, "I understand you have to go back. It's where you belong."

Arron blinked at the truth of Jake's statement surprised by how grown-up it sounded. He nodded in acceptance, holding his son's gaze steady he spoke, "I promise I'll be back as soon as I can, I swear."

"I know," Jake replied roughly.

Arron gripped Jake on the shoulder and pulled him into a tight hug, holding him for a moment before letting go. Arron sniffed, lowering his tear filled eyes for a second before snapping them back to Jake's, memorizing the boys face—every detail.

Reace nudged Arron when he paused on his way to join Keyla. Looking at Jake, Reace extended his hand, a smile on his lips and truth in his eyes, he said, "Thanks for everything, Jake. I wish we had more time."

"Yeah, me too," Jake replied his voice cracked with emotion before Reace could turn away Jake added, "Hey! Don't worry about Nate I'll make sure he stays cool."

"Look after each other," Reace said, a touch of sadness entered his face. He turned toward Heather, as she and Kittana moved closer to them his eyes held a warm thank-you for her.

"Heather, I don't know what to say," Kittana paused then continued, "Thank-you so much for everything you've done for us and for looking after Nate. He's a good kid, but he's still learning his powers, so, if you have any problems remember we're just a call away. Don't let him have any alcohol—it's like a poison to Starians but he's already found out that much, so I don't think that'll be a problem."

*"Kit, let's go!"* Keyla spoke to her sister without words.

The only indication Kittana gave that she received the telepathic message was a slight annoyed frown as she continued to talk to Heather, "After the balance is restored we will visit. Remember we're just a call away and thanks again." Kittana quickly hugged Heather adding when they parted, "You've been amazing." Kittana quickly turned away taking Reace's hand they stepped together into the circle.

Arron, following Kittana, moved to hug Heather, "Kit's right," he said. "You have been amazing. You've done a great job with Jake, you're a wonderful mother. Nate's in good hands."

Heather and Jake watched with mixed feelings and expressions of sadness and awe; sad at the parting of friends and family and awe at what they were witnessing.

Arron stepped into the circle, joining hands with Reace and Kittana. Without looking back he nodded to Reace to begin. If he did glance behind him Arron was scared that he wouldn't have the strength to leave. He closed his eyes, leaning into the feeling of power that ran through him at the contact of his friends—his fellow Guardians. It was like an adrenaline rush only sweeter and more intense, picking up speed as it flowed from one to another, around and around their enclosed circle of clasped hands.

"I am the Guardian of Electricity," Reace began the spell. It was a spell they were all familiar with by now. An aura of blue light shone, surrounding him, reaching up into the sky above them.

"I am the Guardian of Magic," Keyla spoke next, turning the sky a bright pink.

Arron opened his eyes, it was his turn now, taking a deep breath he spoke.

"I am the Guardian of Life." In his mind he couldn't help but add *and death.* The air around him glowing yellow before rushing upward to meet with the two colors already there.

"I am the Guardian of the Mind," Kittana finished the first part of the spell as a white light blasted from her joining the others high above their heads.

"Now let out our powers combine,"

At Keyla's words the colors, suspended in the sky, swirled together, creating a rainbow, spinning faster and faster, picking up speed as they chanted

"Through time and space,
Taysia's the place.
The power of four
Will open the door."

Keyla's voice rang above the chant, strong and commanding as she finished the spell.

"Powers that be heed our plea.
The path is the same,
Take us home the way we came.
Through time and space,
Taysia's the place.
The power of four,
Will open the door."

A warm breeze blew inside the circle of candles picking up the hair on the heads of the chosen four, silver sparks rained down on the Guardians as the colors of their auras swirled together at a mind boggling speed.

"Through time and space,
Taysia's the place.
The power of four,
Will open the door."

The chanting voices rose above the dark mist that appeared from nowhere, swirling around them like a thick cloud, enveloping them and extinguishing the candles. When the strange mist dissipated the four Guardians were gone.

# CHAPTER THIRTY-ONE

"KEYLA, OPEN YOUR EYES," REACE's voice urged.

She could hear the smile in his voice as his hand tugged on hers. Keyla slowly blinked open her eyes and looked around, they were back on Taysia. They had made it! Her smile broadened as she slowly breathed then with a squeal of delight as she ran to Arron and engulfed him in a hug. "You're alive!"

"This place looks the same; if the balance had been tipped shouldn't something look different? Shouldn't it be as dark as before?" Kittana frowned in question, could they have been wrong, she wondered?

Her words were like a bucket of ice water after a day in the sun and spurred them all into action. The four scanned the area around them then started moving at a fast pace toward their home, crystal mountain.

They hadn't gone far before they were met by Link and Awkwade.

Arron's breath caught and his heart heavy. Tia wasn't with them.

"Where's Tia?" He didn't have to wait for an answer, one look on their faces confounded his worst fears.

"No, NO! TIA!" He screamed pushing past them he ran home, calling her name as he searched through every room of Crystal Mountain.

Standing in the middle of their bedroom, willing her to be here, he was startled by his son's voice. He hadn't even noticed the boy was in the room with him.

"She's gone." Zarrick waited until Arron turned to him before continuing, "Dead." He spit the bitter word out of his mouth; his eyes glittered with hurt, anger and pain. It tore at Arron's heart to see his son like this then Zarrick's next words slammed into Arron, "And It's all your fault!"

Arron stared at Zarrick in a haze of guilt as Zarrick continued, "If you had stayed here, where you belong . . . none of this would be happening! SHE'D STILL BE ALIVE!"

"This isn't Arron's fault, Zarrick, he . . ." Keyla spoke in Arron's defense as she entered the room ahead of her sister, Reace, Link and Awkwade.

"You're right. It's not entirely his fault, you're to blame too." Zarrick's face twisted in hatred. His mark flashed at the same time he flicked his fingers at her meaning to blow her up or at the very least hurt her, but Arron came to her rescue his shield came up fast, protecting her from his wrath.

"No." Arron said firmly then in a controlled voice continued, "You want to hurt someone, blame someone, blame me; Keyla has nothing to do with this."

"I do blame you. You're supposed to be the Guardian of Life, why didn't you stop this?" Zarrick demanding turning back to the man who raised him, his lip curled in a sneer as he continued ranting, "It's because of her!" he pointed to Keyla. "You wanted to be with her instead of my Maya! Don't!" He warned as Arron took a step forward, about to say something. "Don't try to deny it. You love her, you care more about Keyla then my mother . . . you always did. I HATE YOU!" Zarrick shouted before running out of the room.

Arron stared at the door until Link blocked his line of vision. "He's just angry, Arron. He didn't react when he first found out about her . . . I think he was holding it in."

"He's just trying to deal with his grief." Awkwade added, "Let him have some time, he'll come around and realize that it's not your fault."

"Give him time," Link echoed.

"So it's true then?" Arron's voice was hoarse with grief. "Tia's really . . . gone." He whispered as he closed his eyes.

He couldn't believe this was happening, this was real. He had held on to the hope that they were wrong and now his hope was gone. His heart was broken, smashed into a thousand pieces, he couldn't breathe. Arron slowly sank to his knees on the floor. *Why Tia? Why did you have to leave me? How could you do this to me?* Arron silently demanded, but Tia couldn't hear him, she couldn't answer him, she was gone.

"TIA!" Arron screamed as tears streamed unnoticed down his face.

"Arron, I . . ." Reace started then stopped, he didn't know what to say. The look Arron gave him—the broken emptiness of it—stunned him.

"Go, just go away." Arron whispered needing to be alone, as alone as he felt.

Reace nodded and as he ushered everybody out, Awkwade stepped forward moving away from the doorway.

"Here, Tia left this for you." She pressed the pyramid shaped pink crystal into Arron's hand before she left the room giving Arron the privacy he needed.

Arron stared at it for a few seconds before hurling it across the room in an angry outburst. The crystal was the last thing Tia left him and he didn't want it. If he accepted it, it would be like accepting that Tia was dead. The word echoed in his mind, dead.

She was gone, she was gone and he wanted her back. Jumping up Arron tore the room apart in search of the pyramid he threw—his last link to her.

When he found it he clutched it close to his heart, sank into a fetal position on the floor. He didn't know how long he sat there staring into nothing, reliving the past memories of Tia—that was all he had left. He hardly noticed the tears that ran down his cheeks nor the crystal softly starting to glow, caught up in his grief, he didn't feel the crystal grow warm. When Tia suddenly appeared in front of him floating in a light pink mist, he was startled.

"What the . . . ? Tia?" Arron gasped, dropping the crystal he held as he reached out to her, but his hands went through her as though she were a ghost. The crystal made a ting sound as it landed on the floor and Tia disappeared.

Arron shook his head, wondering if he was going crazy. Picking up the pink pyramid holding it in his hand again he stared at it then at the place Tia had appeared. His eyes going back to the crystal as he thought about

Tia, why would she leave him this? What was it about the crystal that was so important?

When the apparition appeared again, he stayed still watching her and then she spoke.

"My whole life I tried to do what was right, but no matter how hard I tried everything always came out wrong, even loving you, Arron. Zarrick, is the only good thing I've ever accomplished, the only thing I've ever done right . . . until now."

"Fitca, Arron don't be sad, don't be angry or mad, be free. Free to be with the women of your heart. I know you'll always think that you loved me and maybe I did own a piece of your heart, but now it's time for you to move on. I know if I were alive you'd never go to her, so I set you free—to fix the wrongs I've done—I set you free. This is the right thing to do. Rayla vinex ce, Arron, rayla vinex ce." After she whispered the words again she faded out, disappearing forever from Arron's life.

\*

"Tia is really gone? I can't believe it!" Keyla said, her voice breaking the heavy silence that descended as the five Guardians made their way downstairs and seated themselves around the table that boar their marks. "Why would she suddenly want to end her life force?"

"Tell us what happened," Kittana asked turning to look at Link and Awkwade.

"Just after you left," Link began, "Zarrick was attacked."

"Zarrick?" Keyla asked confused. Why would Malic attack his own flesh and blood?

"Is he alright?" Kittana demanded, alarmed by the news.

"He's fine," Awkwade laid a comforting hand on Kittana's arm as she reassured her that the young Guardian was okay.

"He recovered quick enough to go with me and Tia into Stone Mountain to confront Malic, but he was already dead." Link said.

'Dead?' Keyla echoed in the stunned silence that followed Link's last word. "Malic gave up his life force? Why?" She demanded.

"Are we sure Malic is dead?" Kittana asked wanted to make sure, at the nod from Link she sighed with relief. Her son was safe and she didn't have to mind meld with her nemesis.

"Are you sure it was Malic who attacked? If he was dead, how could he have?" Reace questioned. Wondering if there was some unseen force at work here, something they needed to find out about especially if it was powerful enough to take out Malic—the Guardian of all evil.

"I really don't know what happened, Reace, all I know for sure is that it wasn't natural." Link held Reace's gaze steady for a few seconds before continuing his tale, "Malic's body was left behind."

"His body?" The twins spoke at the same time.

"Yeah, but don't worry I took care of it." Link told the girls, "Tia tried to tell you what happened with the help of Malic's crystal sphere. Did you get the message?"

"You must have because you came back, and without Nate, did you find him?" Awkwade asked.

"Yeah, we found him. He's on Earth. He chose to stay behind." Kittana answered.

"My dream, that's how she told me, it was through my dream." Keyla exclaimed suddenly relieved now that she knew for sure it was a message from Tia and not a premonition of things to come.

"Your dream? What dream? Was it a premonition?" Awkwade asked. Although she found it interesting that Keyla sometimes had dreams about the future, dreams that came true, she didn't envy her.

"At first I thought it could be, but now I understand, in my dream I saw dead bodies, everyone—including Malic, Tia was trying to tell me that Malic was dead."

"Wait a minute! If Malic is dead then the balance is tipped—good this time instead of evil." Reace said suddenly, bringing everyone to the awareness of the seriousness of the situation.

"Do you think that'll mean Vanishtar's in trouble again?" Awkwade asked fearing the answer.

"Until seven new Guardians appear." Keyla's voice gave hope. "When Malic died he had to release the powers he's stolen giving them to new Guardians." Keyla suddenly stood and walked toward the far wall of the cavern, the wall where Deia's prophecy was engraved. The others followed her wondering what she was doing. Bending down she parted the tall flowers and different grasses that grew up from the dirt covered floor, covering the last verse that had magically been carved deep into the crystal.

"Out of the light the dark descends,
Beware the foe who is a friend,
The one thought dead to be alive.
Nature divided, only one will survive
And all will be as before."

Kittana read the newly added verse to the poem over her sister's shoulder.

"Maybe we were wrong about the prophecy?" Keyla suggested, standing to face the others. "The one thought dead to rise again. Instead of a person it could have referred to powers, instead of Malic 'The one' could have been referring to evil throughout the whole thing. The old Guardian of evil is dead, so until new ones appear, maybe we're the ones that conquered? Without Malic the balance is tipped, when the seven new Guardians come we will be balanced again and this time more evenly."

"So we wait here for the new ones?" Link asked, his voice giving away the uncertain feeling he had about that idea.

"Malic dying must have been the first disturbance we felt." Kittana gave voice to her thoughts.

"And Tia the second," Keyla added, turning to Link she was about to ask him something but her sisters voice interrupted her.

"So it might stand to reason we'd feel more disturbances, we may feel the new Guardians before they come."

"How did it happen? Why did she do it?" Keyla asked Link after her sister had finished talking.

Link was about to answer her but fell silent as he watched Arron approach them.

"What is this?" Arron demanded, holding up the pink pyramid crystal Awkwade had given him earlier. He came forward placing it on the table, in the midst of them as everyone again gathered around the table taking their seats and looking at the object but no one touched it.

"Oh, Arron, I keep forgetting that you're not from our solar system." Awkwade spoke, "That's a kyvein crystal otherwise known as a memory crystal. It's used to store memories or messages, usually those of a person choosing to go to Niteon to give up their life forces." She supplied the explanation and then added, "It works by holding it in your hand and thinking of the person who made the memory."

Arron nodded having already figured out that much. He turned his attention to Kittana as he asked, "What does 'rayla vinex ce' mean? Tia spoke some of her message in Starian I could translate most of it but that phrase . . . I have no idea. I've never heard it before."

"Rayla vinex ce," Kittana repeated she hadn't heard that one in a long time . . . not since her father was alive. "It means look forward. Forget the past, and look to the future. It goes hand in hand with laymar van zyon, they are often quoted together. rayla vinex ce tos laymar van zyon—Look forward and walk with courage."

"Tia wants you to more forward, not wallow in the past or grieve in the present," Awkwade added, "look to the future, follow your destiny."

Arron's gaze swung from the Guardian of Water to the one of Fire, he asked, "How did it happen, was it Malic?" He cringed at whatever he was about to hear but he needed to know.

"No, Malic was already dead by then," Link and Awkwade filled the fourth Guardian in on what they had already told the others.

"Afterward Tia said she was tired and went to lay down. Arron, I swear to you if I had known or even suspected . . . I would have stopped her . . . somehow." Link paused for a moment then finding his voice again he continued his account of what happened. "Awkwade saw something—some presence in Malic's mountain so I went to check it out."

"That's when I discovered that Tia wasn't in her room." Awkwade added giving Link time to collect the courage to tell them the rest.

"I . . . I found her, in Malic's throne room . . . she . . . she was surrounded by a purple haze." The words were difficult for Link but he forced them out, past a throat that constricted in memory, his nostrils flared as he tried to suck in enough air to continue. "I tried to stop her," he raised his tear filled gaze to Arron's "but I was too late."

"This isn't your fault, Link. It was Tia's choice." Reace couldn't stand to see the look of guilt on Link's face. After the hell he'd gone through half of his life thinking he'd been the one responsible for someone's death—it wasn't something he wanted anyone to experience. The self-loathing, anger and overwhelming depression weren't Link's to own . . . not this time. "There was nothing you could have done."

Link looked at Reace, heard his words and a part of him knew the truth of them, yet another part of Link wanted to believe that it was his fault and as crazy as it sounded, he wanted to hurt himself as much as he was already hurting.

"Rayla vinex ce," Arron's whispered voice carried in the quiet that descended.

Link wasn't sure if Arron was talking to him or just repeating the last words Tia told him, but he took comfort in the phrase, look forward. It lessened his guilt, it sounded so much like something Tia would tell him that for a moment it was like she was still here, still a part of them.

\*

Eight months passed quietly on Taysia as they waited for the new Guardians to appear, but on Earth eight years passed. Jake had finished school and wanting to do something good with his abilities had become a cop. Nate too, had finished high school and spent four years in college earning himself a job teaching English at the high school in Springfield. He kept in touch with his parents via Timelana and they had all attended his and Anna-Maria's wedding a year and a half ago (Earth time). Now, Nate was waiting until the birth of his first born before calling on them again, but things don't always go as planned . . .

# PART TWO

# Chapter One

## Earth: Springfield Memorial Children's Hospital

"I'M DYING, AREN'T I, MOM?" The boy rasped through dry lips. From where he lay on the hospital bed he looked up at his mother, his voice weak.

Danielle closed her eyes for a second holding back her tears. It hurt to hear her child ask that because she had to answer it. Not able to look him in the eye and tell him the truth, she lied.

"No, no honey, you're not going to die." She forced herself to meet his gaze as she added, "I promise." Looking up she saw the doctor as he entered and motioned to her that he needed to talk to her. Smoothing a hand over Bradley's hairless head she told him, "I have to go now the doctor wants to discuss something with mommy. Go to sleep sweetheart, you'll be getting better soon."

Bradley closed his eyes, the morphine making him sleepy, he quickly fell into a deep sleep. Danielle turned away from her only son after smoothing the blankets over him. She followed the doctor to his office.

"Miss Cameron, please, come in and have a seat," Dr. Ryan Summers said, holding the door to his office open for her he followed in behind her. He was a middle aged man with kind eyes and lots of degrees hanging on the walls of his hospital office. He sat down behind the desk only after she took a seat.

"I don't know quite how to tell you this," Dr. Summers said. To himself he added, *No matter how many times I've had to speak to parents, family members, or significant others. It never gets any easier.* With a sigh and a deep breath he rushed onward. "Miss. Cameron, your son isn't responding as we had hoped to the treatments. Instead of shrinking, the tumors are growing . . . It's my professional opinion that your son, Bradley, isn't going to live to see his next birthday. Now, I'm not god, things can change. His condition could improve, but frankly there isn't much hope of that."

The doctor looked at the patients' mother with compassion, he had a child himself and he couldn't imagine what he'd feel if someone told him that his child was dying. This was the hardest part of his job—the part he hated—he couldn't save everyone.

In high school before he had saved the life of Reace Stelmen he hadn't know he had this passion inside of him, back then his whole life had been football but after saving someone's life, Ryan discovered a whole world of medicine and football became something of a pastime. His dream of becoming a doctor was born and he loved it, but this part of the job when he couldn't save a child—he took it hard.

He had tried everything he could think of, called every specialist he knew, but still the boy just wasn't getting better, in fact, he was getting worse.

"You're telling me that my son is dying?" she demanded in disbelief. "No. NO! There's got to something you can do . . . money is no object. You find something. My son isn't going to die. HE'S NOT!"

"I'm sorry, Miss. Cameron, I really am." His eyes held a look of pity mixed with sincerity.

She hated that look and at this moment she hated the doctor, this hospital, and everyone who had healthy children while hers was wasting away . . . dying.

The pager on his belt bleeped and Dr. Summers excused himself from the office leaving her to her feelings in private, but she hardly noticed. Her mind was frozen by the doctor's earlier words.

How could her son die, she wondered? She couldn't lose him. He was all she had left. All the family she had in the world. Ever since he had been born, Bradley had been her whole world. It had just been the two of them and now he was dying and there was nothing anyone could do. She didn't know how long she sat there her mind and body refusing to move as she took in and processed this heartbreaking news.

Her eyes fell to the papers that cluttered the doctors desk, on top there was a flyer. Her eyes stared blankly at it for a few minutes before the words sunk into her head. 'Come see the power of the gods' the flyer's bold lettering caught her attention, snapping her out of her trance. An idea forming in her mind she quickly scanned the rest of the information then hastily she gathered up her purse and jacket and left Springfield Memorial Children's Hospital.

An hour later she found herself at the museum staring into a glass case of jewelry from ancient Greece. A bracelet had caught her attention. It was gold with a large yellow stone in its center. It was gaudy and huge but there was something familiar about it and she found she couldn't tear her gaze away from it.

'The bracelet of life' the card in front of it read.

Where had she heard that before she wondered? She turned her gaze back to the card to read more about it.

'Part of a legend that claimed the wearer of this bracelet had the power of a god and could heal the sick, give life back to the dying.'

Her eyes flickered to the bracelet. Could it be true? Could this bracelet really heal the sick?

Her father believed these tales to be true. He was James Cameron, a great archeologist. A better archeologist than a father, she thought with a snort as she went back, inside her mind to a time when she was eighteen.

*Danielle had been so excited. They were planning on going on a family trip just her and her dad, no work, no school, just the two of them. She had her bags all packed and had just carried them downstairs when she saw her father coming out of his study. He had that look about him. That look that said he was excited about something and he wasn't alone. Her spirits plummeted. They wouldn't be going anywhere after all.*

*She nodded and smiled politely as the man, with her father, waved and said good bye. Danielle waited until her father made it back toward her before saying anything.*

*"What's going on daddy? We aren't going are we?"*

*"Now, don't say that sweetie, we will go, I promise. It's just that this thing has come up and it's a once in a life time opportunity I can't pass it up. But*

I'll make it up to you, I promise." James said then added, "When I get back, a week at the most, we'll go then. You can pick it—anyplace in the world."

Danielle looked at him, at the happiness on his face and give in, "Any place?" she asked, "With no complaints from you at all."

"Deal! You're the best, sweetie." James smiled at his only child then kissed her forehead and went whistling into the study to get ready for the expedition.

Danielle waited for a week, planning her trip, shopping for new clothes and telling her friends all about this great trip she was planning. A week turned into a month and still her father hadn't come back but Danielle wasn't worried this usually happened, expeditions were always unpredictable. Sometimes they last longer than expected. Her birthday came and went. Not a word or a card from her father, but that made her more angry than worried.

The night her father finally came home, she was ecstatic and so was he. His face had the look of someone in love.

"Danielle!" He rushed forward engulfing her in a hug that she returned with just as much force. When they pulled away he spoke, "I've got something for you; it's a belated birthday present."

He held up a blue jewelry box with a white ribbon around it.

Excited Danielle tore open the box, expecting something brilliant and beautiful with diamonds or rubes, but what she got was a surprise. Inside the box there was no glint of gold or shine of silver. It was just some fake-looking, gaudy bracelet. It was blue, the whole thing was blue, even the medal. The stone in the center was huge and unlike any stone she had ever seen, but it wasn't exactly pretty. Danielle hated it instantly, her face fell from happiness but her father's shined brighter when he gazed at the bracelet.

"It's the bracelet of the gods." He gushed on not even aware that his daughter wasn't as excited about the find as he was. He didn't even notice that she was disappointed in her gift.

"Legends say it holds the power of the almighty Zeus—the power of lightning. If we could figure out how it works—harness the power . . . oh man, that would be amazing, wouldn't it? I've had it tested the metal and the stone in the center are unlike anything on Earth. Don't you see, that's proof that the gods really existed."

"Or proof of aliens," Danielle muttered. Looking up into her father's face she saw how excited he was and she sighed, then lied. "It's beautiful, thank-you daddy."

In his enthusiasm, James went on almost tripping over his words as he told her the tale of how the bracelets where made and the legend that lost them.

Now she wished she had paid more attention to what he had said but at the time she was too disappointed to think beyond her pain. They never did get to take that trip, Danielle thought sadly. Her father had gone back into his study . . . more research followed by another expedition—one he wouldn't come home from. Through his research he had discovered that there were more bracelets—seven to be exact, and he had a lead on a second one.

She had never known if he was right or not . . . until now. She was staring at the second bracelet. Her father believed the bracelets held powers. Could he have been right? The one thing she knew for sure was she had to try.

Even though she had hated that bracelet, she had loved her father and out of love for him she couldn't bring herself to throw away something that meant so much to him. She had kept the hideous clunky piece of jewelry. It was in the back of her jewelry box. Danielle was positive that it matched the bracelet in front of her. It was just as gaudy, held the same kind of rock the only difference was this bracelet was golden not blue; that was an improvement, she thought. If her hunch was right then it would help her to save her son and that was all that mattered to her.

James Cameron had not been good at keeping his promises but she wasn't going to follow in his footsteps. If this bracelet could heal then she would do everything in her power to get it—she had to keep her promise to her son. Taking out her cell phone Danielle snapped a few pictures of the bracelet. She had research to do and she had to be sure.

*

Parking her car, Danielle glanced up and paused, looking at the large house in front of her. It was the only home she had ever known. Her father may not have been there for her but he had provided well. She and Bradley were still living off his seemingly endless supply of wealth. But all the money in the world couldn't help her save her son from death.

All the money and doctors couldn't save her son, but maybe she could. That thought spurred Danielle to leave her car and run up the front steps made of stone. Opening the door, she rushed in. Walking swiftly toward the study—her father's favorite room in the sprawling house, a room hardly used anymore.

She didn't feel sad that the room still held the faint smell of her father. She didn't have time to dwell on the past. Her eyes quickly scanned the shelves finding what she was looking for Danielle took down the ancient book and the journal beside it.

One good thing about her father was that he took excellent notes. He recorded everything he thought, found or read about when he was on a hunt. First she flipped through the old text finding what she hoped too, she carefully laid open the brittle book across the desk and sat down heavily on the chair. She grabbed her cell phone and flipped it open, finding her stored pictures of the bracelet at the museum. Staring at the pictures on the page before her, she grinned, her first real smile in days.

She was right! The bracelet at the museum was the same bracelet. One of seven that, according to the ancient Greeks, held the power of the gods and even though they all connected and looked similar, each bracelet was a different color and each bracelet held a different power.

Picking up her father's journal she read further about an Athenian man who had gathered all of the mystic bracelets and used them to destroy his enemy—the king of Atlantis. This story strongly suggested that the Athenian man caused Atlantis to sink below the sea. He threw the bracelet of Poseidon, the God of the sea, in after the king, the bracelet lost forever. Afterward the Athenian man grew too powerful and later was betrayed by his wife and killed, his body thrown off a cliff into the sea. The bracelets, deemed too powerful for one person, were taken and separated then buried in different parts of the ancient world.

Her father had found one of the bracelets (the one he had given to her) in a temple of Zeus, inside a cave at the top of a secluded mountain, hidden for years from view. The cave was revealed after an earthquake.

Another of the bracelets, her father suspected, went to the grave with Edward Leedskalnin, James reported seeing one on the wrist of the builder of the coral castle in a photo of the man. How or where Edward Leedskalnin found it was as much a mystery as how he moved the coral.

Danielle's eyes misted for a second, her father had given her the power of the Gods and she had been ungrateful at the time. Now she silently thanked him for giving her this chance to save the life of her child.

Blinking away the moisture from her eyes she read on, learning that James Cameron had extensive scientific testing done on the bracelet before he had given it her. It didn't surprise her; her father had always been very thorough. What did surprise her was the results, the metals and stones of the bracelet she had were not from Earth, giving truth to the legends that they came from the God's home: Mount Olympus.

Her father had also written down a poem that he had translated from the wall of the cave where the temple of Zeus was found. This poem, he thought, was the key to unlocking the powers of the bracelets and it had to be said seven times by the wearer of the bracelet.

That gave her hope a boast, she sat back and thought. She didn't need all seven bracelets, she wasn't a greedy, power-hungry person. All she needed was the bracelet at the museum. The power to heal and give life to her son and if it couldn't be bought then she knew who could get it for her. One way or another she'd have the power of the Gods, but first she she'd have to make sure it worked.

Danielle left the journal opened to the page that translated the spell on the desk as she went to her bedroom, rummaging through the bottom drawer of her jewelry box, she sighed in triumph as her hand curved around the trinket she needed.

Returning to the study she put on the bracelet, she didn't think it as ugly as before, not now that she knew its power. She hoped her father was right and that chanting this poem seven times while wearing the bracelet activated the dormant powers within. Taking a deep breath, she spoke out loud the rhyme:

> "With this bracelet in my hand,
> All of your powers, I do command.
> From immortality you shall fall,
> Guardian of Electricity, heed my call.
> Our destines to entwine,
> Your powers become mine."

# CHAPTER TWO

## Taysia

REACE WOKE WHEN HIS WIFE suddenly gasped and sat up in their bed. Closing his tired eyes he heard her get out of bed then dress and slip out of the room. He had meant to follow her, to get up and go with her, giving her the support he knew she needed. Unfortunately he had fallen asleep again and didn't wake up until several hours later when sunlight hit his face. Sunlight that came from a thinner place in the crystal wall of the mountain they lived in. Acting like a window it allowed the light to enter and illuminate the interior.

Now realizing how late it was he rushed to get showered and dressed. He wanted to talk to Kittana, somehow make her tell him what was wrong. He could tell she was worried—upset even. She hadn't been sleeping or eating lately. Reace suspected she was having nightmares. About what, he didn't know, but he was determined to find out.

"Kit, there you are," Reace sighed in relief at finding her beside the lake. Just as Zarrick had said she would be. On the way out of their mountain home he had seen the young Guardian of War and he had asked the boy if he had seen Kittana, and Zarrick told Reace where to find her.

"Kit!" Reace called again as he neared her, but it was as if she hadn't heard him. She just stood there staring out at the beauty around her, but judging from the expression on her face she wasn't seeing it.

"Kittana?" Reace tried again this time reaching out a hand to touch her shoulder.

She jumped, yelping in surprise at the touch. Placing a hand over her racing heart she demanded. "Reace! You scared me. Why are you sneaking up on me like that?"

Reace frowned, she must have been doing some pretty deep thinking to not have noticed his approach—he hadn't been quiet. He didn't tell her that, instead he asked, "What were you thinking about?"

"Nothing," she said quickly.

Too quickly, Reace's frown deepened with worry as he looked critically at the dark circles around her eyes.

"Damn it, Kittana! Stop lying to me." Reace said, running a hand through his hair in frustration. "Look, I care about you, I love you and I can see that something's been bothering you. Something is keeping you up at night." He cupped her cheeks, framing her face with his hands and rubbing his thumb on her cheekbone beside her eye. Staring into her deep blue eyes he spoke again, "Whatever it is . . . tell me. Please, just tell me."

Her eyes searched his worried face, she wanted to tell him, wanted to tell someone about the dreams she'd been having. Dreams of another life, of being locked up in an insane asylum back on Earth. Dr. Drake, the psychiatrist she had once gone to at the urging of her foster parents, had been there. He told her that this life she was living was all a dream. A place her brain created to hide from the harshness of reality. He said she couldn't handle the tragedies of her life and retreated into a world her mind created. Dr. Drake told her that her father and mother and twin sister had all died in a fire when she was five and he had proof too. Newspaper articles of the fire and the people she thought were real, people she thought she knew: Arron was a rich playboy who lived in Rome with his loving parents and he had never been to Springfield; Reace had died at the age of five in the same accident that took his mother's life.

Kittana had tried to deny it, tried to tell him and the other doctors with Dr. Drake that he was wrong that they were all wrong, but memories of life at the asylum and at the Macdonald's house when she was little infiltrated her mind. She remembered the fire that took her families lives. She remembered being in the hospital afterward how it hurt to talk—the smoke had made her throat sore. She remembered being with Nancy and going to the store to buy red shoes when she was six. She remembered the first day of school—it was Nancy who took her and then came to get her when she had an episode, freaking out when the teacher asked the kids to draw a picture of their family.

It was shortly after that, Dr. Drake had said, that she had come to live at the asylum. She was seven and David and Nancy just couldn't help her anymore. Dr. Drake had told her that she had been in her dream state most of her life. This was the first time in years that he's seen her break away from it. He smiled at her, patted her knee and told her that the new experimental drugs must be working and then he left her alone in her room staring at four white walls, just before Reace appeared beside her, tapping her on the shoulder.

Looking around herself she was once more in Taysia, and Reace was standing before her demanding answers. How could she tell the man she had a child with, the man she loved more than anything, that he might not be real? She couldn't.

She was scared to tell him, or anyone, scared that the dreams were more than just dreams . . . what if they were true? She was so confused. Every time she closed her eyes lately, she was awakened by a memory of this other life. These dreams seemed so real, but so did this, her mind told her, as she stared into Reace's teal colored eyes. She couldn't deny that he felt real but she was unsure if this—Taysia, being a Guardian, Reace—wasn't just a beautiful dream. She wasn't sure anymore what was real.

Reaching up she touched his hands, taking them away from her face she held them, needing to feel him, to know that he was real.

"I'm sorry Reace, I can't tell you . . . not yet. I need more time." *Time to think,* she added in her mind. She hoped that with a little time she'd figure it all out. When she had, she mentally promised, she'd tell him.

"Reace," Kittana spoke his name when he started to mentally pull away from her.

Reace shook his head trying to clear the slight buzzing sound he heard. Feeling dizzy he staggered backwards, letting go of Kittana's hands. His eyes widened in surprise when the scenery around him flickered.

"Reace?" Kittana spoke in alarm at the way he was acting. What was wrong, she wondered? Reaching out to him she screamed when her hands passed through him. "NO!"

He watched, in shocked horror as her hands passed through him like he was a ghost. Then his eyes found hers.

"KIT!" He screamed her name, but no sound came from him. All he heard was the buzzing in his ears, and over top of it he could make out a woman's voice.

"With this bracelet in my hand,
All of your powers I do command.
From immortality you shall fall,
Guardian of Electricity, heed my call.
Our destinies to entwine,
Your powers become mine."

Kittana saw Reace mouth her name again. He looked like he screamed it but she couldn't hear any sound. She reached out her mind to speak to him telepathically, but he wasn't there. She watched helpless, as he faded from her sight. She stared at the place he had last been. For a moment not knowing what to do then she found her voice.

"KEYLA! ARRON! LINK! AWKWADE!" she screamed. Sinking slowly to the ground and locking her arms around her knees, she rocked back and forth muttering, "Reace, come back, please, come back." Then she screamed, "REACE!"

\*

"Keyla," Arron spoke coming up beside her in the attic room of the crystal mountain. "Can we talk?"

"Sure Arron," she smiled her answer, giving him her full attention as he sat beside her.

"About what Zarrick said, when we came back here . . . about it being my fault that Tia . . . that Tia died."

"Arron, it wasn't . . ." Keyla began her heart going out to her friend.

"Let me finish, please." Arron said, not looking up from his hands. This was hard to say, he couldn't look at her too. What if he was wrong? He wouldn't be able to take the look on her face if he was. Taking a deep breath he continued, "He was right and so was Tia. Do you remember back in high school when we were sixteen and seventeen? We kissed at your apartment and you wanted to be friends?"

He looked at her then, he had to see if she really remembered. When her face brightened slightly and she nodded and Arron let out a sigh of relief . . . she remembered.

"Well, I accepted that and I buried my feelings for you. I thought I had moved on, I loved someone else, but you were always in my heart. Tia was right about that. It's just taken me so long to see it." He paused to rub his hands over his face as if he was trying to scrub away the past and the guilt he felt. "She was the Guardian of Emotions . . . she was right about so many things . . . I do love you, Keyla. If you still just want to be friends—that's okay, but I want us to be more . . . I won't pressure you. I just . . . I just want you to know that you're more to me than just a friend."

Keyla couldn't believe Arron had just said that to her, she gave herself a pinch to see if she was dreaming . . . she wasn't.

"Arron," she said, reaching out and taking his hand. Holding it in hers, she continued, "When I told you that I only wanted to be friends, it was because I was scared. Everyone I had ever loved left me. I took a chance on friendship with Reace and he didn't let me down, but when you and I . . . when we kissed . . . it scared me. The feelings I had for you . . . I wasn't ready." Keyla took a deep breath. She hoped she was saying this right. She had wanted to tell him this for so long. She had cursed the day she told him she just wanted to be friends. It was the stupidest thing she had ever done and she was working up the courage to take it back when he had met Tia, after that it was just too late. Now that he had come to her and asked again she was tripping over her words.

"I am ready now . . . to be more."

He looked up at her startled for a moment by what she said then a slow smile spread over his face bringing out both of his dimples. His hand tightened on hers.

Their heads moved slightly closer to one another, Keyla closed her eyes, her lids to heavy to stay open on their own. They were about to kiss when they heard Kittana scream their names.

Keyla's eyes flew open in alarm and stared into the worried brown eyes of Arron. Holding tightly to his hand, she muttered the words to a spell,

"Magic in me,
Heed my plea.
From inside these four walls
Take us to the place from where my sister calls."

\*

"No!" His voice finally left him in a desperate plea, followed seconds later by a scream. Reace barely registered it as coming from him. Pain seared through him, burning like liquid fire through his veins. A pain like he'd never experienced before—it was like someone was peeling his skin off, leaving him raw and numb; to numb to speak or even think.

Reace was on his hands and knees when the pain ebbed, receding enough for him to breathe and glance around. He was in a room—a library by the looks of it. And a few feet away from him stood a woman, a look of surprise, surprised mixed with pity, on her face.

"Well, at least now I know that legends are true and if this bracelet works than so will the other."

"What?" Reace rasped out between breaths. Trying to understand what was happening. Where was Kittana? Where was he? And why?

Her eyes hardened and she raised an arm, Reace frowned trying to figure out what she was doing. He didn't have time to notice anything more than the bracelet that flashed seconds before electricity flew from her fingertips racing toward him as he staggered to his feet.

Reace welcomed the lightning like a long lost lover and he opened his arms wide to receive it. knowing it would renew his energy, make him feel more complete—like when he was a child, he knew that it would take away any hurt, any pain, making him whole again.

He was surprised however, when the striking bolts hit him. Instead of making him feel better, pain exploded again throughout his body, dancing along his spine until Reace fell to the floor closing his eyes and lost consciousness.

After checking to make sure he was still alive, Danielle spared a glance for the stranger sprawled on her floor as she moved toward the desk. She wasn't sure what she had expected, but that there were still Gods around wasn't something that even crossed her mind. Behind her eyes, she could still see the look of pain and disbelief on his handsome young face, but she wasn't sorry. Her son needed the help of a God and if they weren't going to help then she'd do it herself . . . with their powers.

Her eyes lit up, her father had provided her with a way to save her son.

"Thank-you daddy," she whispered. The bracelet she wore was only one and not the one that held the power of life, but she knew where to find the one she needed to save Bradley's life. Picking up the phone she dialed the number of an old family friend.

"Derek, hi! Yes, this is Danielle. Listen, I need you to do me a favor . . ."

As she hung up the phone Danielle smiled. It would be done. She was relieved. This time tomorrow her son would be healthy.

Now, what was she going to do with the strange man in her house? Danielle pondered that for a moment. She could call the cops on him saying there was a burglar in the house. That would get him away from her and keep him busy so he couldn't take his powers back; couldn't try and stop her, not until she had saved Bradley. If he told the police the truth . . . well, Danielle shrugged, who would believe him? It was perfect. No, better than perfect. It was fool proof.

She'd call the cops on him. That decided, she grabbed her purse and keys and headed out the door. She couldn't call the police from here that might look suspicious. She'd say an alarm was tripped and the company called her first about a possible intruder. Yes, that might work.

Danielle paused by the door, she couldn't get the look that crossed the god's face out of her mind. She glanced back toward the room where he was still laying on the floor. On impulse, she pulled some bills from her purse and placed them on the table in the hallway. Maybe he didn't deserve what she had done to him, a small voice in the back on her head whispered.

In her defense, she argued with herself, she hadn't known there were still Gods and she needed to save Bradley. Pursing her lips together in resolve, what's done is done, she told herself. She'd give him a few hours to find the money and get out of her house. She decided, easing her guilt ridden mind by giving him a chance at least.

She was doing the right thing, she reminded herself, as she opened the door and left. She'd call the cops in the morning she thought as she slid into her car, started the engine and drove off in the direction of the hospital and her son.

# CHAPTER THREE

## Earth

REACE WOKE UP WITH THE sunlight shinning in his face. Blinking his eyes open, he shut them quickly as light pierced his skull and started a chain reaction that had him rolling over as his stomach heaved. After spilling its contents he waited until his rioting stomach stilled, then he opened his eyes again, focusing on the Persian rug beneath him. He frowned in confusion wondering where he was and why? How did he even get here?

The events that led to his current condition came rushing back to him, making him dizzy. After emptying the contents of his stomach on the expensive carpet a second time, he sat back and tried to figure out what happened. His thoughts and memories were moving around in his head too fast for him to comprehend, at the moment. Reace drew in a ragged breath before gagging at the smell of his vomit beside him. He needed to move before he got sick again. He stood on unsteady legs, his eyes scanning the room looking for a bathroom, an exit or the woman whose face swam before his eyes.

Who is she? He wondered, not having an answer for himself. After realizing that she was a memory and not actually there with him, he moved to the exit he found across the room.

Cautiously, he turned the knob on the door. Unlocked? He was surprised but shrugged before opening the door and carefully looking around.

Entering the hallway of the large house, he quickly and competently searched every room, pausing every now and again to listen. Satisfied that he was alone in the mansion—at least for now—he went into a bathroom on the main floor to rinse his mouth and wash his face and hands.

It was as Reace washed his hands that he noticed his left wrist. There was no mark. No jagged outline of a lightning bolt, no sparkle of tiny crystals embedded into his skin. Not even an impression or anything to say he'd ever had the mark of a Guardian—nothing but smooth skin.

Reace stared at his wrist, traced the spot where the mark of the Guardian had always been. He looked at himself in the mirror as if making sure he was still the same person. His mind was in a whirl, like in a dream the words he heard before came back to him.

'With this bracelet in my hand,
All of your powers I do command.
From immortality you shall fall,
Guardian of Electricity, heed my call.
Our destinies to entwine,
Your powers become mine.'

He remembered the woman whose face he couldn't place earlier, she had said those words then Reace remembered the pain.

What did she do to him? Did she . . . No, she couldn't have. It wasn't possible . . . was it? Did she somehow take his powers from him? He glanced at his wrist again before scanning the room with his eyes, searching for a power source. He had to make sure—had to see for himself if it was true.

Drying off his fingers carefully Reace placed them on the outlet he found not far from the countertop. He closed his eyes, concentrating on calling the electricity to him. When nothing happened, Reace tried harder. Still, nothing happened. He opened his eyes to glare at his fingers then at the outlet before trying one more time. This time he jammed his fingers into the socket and jumped back in surprise, hitting his back against the wall, as the painful shock traveled up his arm into his shoulder.

It was true! He wasn't a Guardian anymore. The truth of that stunned him and he let his legs buckle under then, slowing sinking to the floor.

*I'm not a Guardian.* his mind echoed in disbelief but the proof was in front on him. He drew up his knees and resting his arms on them as he studied his wrist.

"I'm not a Guardian," he whispered, tears burned behind his eyes and fell unnoticed down his face. He would never be able to go home, he'd never see his wife or Arron, Keyla or any of the others. He could never enter Taysia again.

Reace didn't know how long he sat there staring into nothing, lost in his despair. Where did he go from here, he wondered? He couldn't go home. Nature's? He thought of his son. NO! He couldn't face his child now, couldn't tell him that . . . that he wasn't a Guardian . . . that he had lost . . . Reace let out a ragged breath as he let the thought drop.

Could he go to the shelter? It wasn't his anymore, it belonged to Jake now and if Jake found him there then Nate would know. He didn't want his son to know what a failure his father was turning out to be, so the shelter was out.

That left only one option, but before he could go anywhere he needed to figure out where he was. Standing Reace turned and left the bathroom avoiding the mirror as he went, he didn't want to look at himself right now.

For a second time Reace searched the house, this time he was looking for information. He found some mail on the table and picking it up he read the address; west side of Springfield, in a wealthy suburb. Reace smirked, of all the places he could have ended up, it was a weird coincidence that he was again on Earth and in Springfield.

From here, it was only a few miles . . . he could walk. With a destination in mind Reace made his way to the front door and paused when he saw the money on the small table. Now that he was human, he'd need money. Reace quickly grabbed the bills off the table and shoved them into his pocket.

He continued out the door and down the walkway to the gated driveway. When he heard sirens he ducked, hiding in the shrubbery beside the four foot stone wall topped with iron rails. Seconds later several cop cars came up to the closed gate. Reace watched as they entered the driveway followed by a small gray car.

She must have called the cops on him, Reace figured when he saw the same woman from his mixed up memories of last night step out of the gray car and move with the police into the house. He didn't wait around for them to come out and search the grounds, finding him. Instead he looked up, searching the area around him before hoisting himself up on the wall and climbing over the iron fence. Jumping down into the street, he turned left and started walking.

\*

Approaching the front door, Reace noticed the weed infested, long grass of the lawn and frowned, John never let the grass grow higher than five inches. Reaching the door he knocked before he noticed the chipped paint around the door. He was starting to wonder if his step-father still lived here when he heard the click of a lock turning.

John opened the door. Seeing Reace his blood-shot eyes narrowed and his lip curled into a sneer, as he demanded. "What are you doing here? Bastard!"

Reace frowned as apprehension settled in his stomach, but he didn't have time to do anything more as John grabbed him, pulling him into the house by the shirt he wore. Letting the door close on its own, he slammed Reace against the wall before growling.

"I asked you a question."

John's breath was close to his face, he reeked of alcohol—days worth of alcohol, but Reace didn't register that, his mind was still reeling from the events of the day past. Fear of his step-father filled his body and only left room for reaction.

"I've n . . . n . . . nowhere else t . . . t . . . to g . . . g . . . go. I've lost everything." His eyes filled with water.

Reace's face looked the way John felt—broken. He loosened his grip on his step-son but his voice was still gruff as he demanded, "What do you mean, you've lost everything?"

"I . . . I've lost m . . . m . . . my powers, I c . . . can't g . . . g . . . get home. I'll never see my wife again or any of my friends."

A tear slipped down Reace's face, startling John. He hadn't seen Reace cry since he was seven.

Reace didn't seem to notice the tears as he went on to say, "I . . . I can't go to my son . . . not like this." He sniffed blinking back the tears before anymore could fall.

"I've lost everything." He whispered turning his face away from John, trying to compose himself. His eyes scanned the room around them seeing how unkempt it was.

"W . . . w . . . wait a m . . . m . . . minute." Reace closed his eyes for a second, cursing his stuttering mouth. It only happened when he was scared. He forced himself to stop stuttering, stop being afraid. He wasn't five anymore, he could fight back, he told himself. Opening his eyes, he glared at John.

"Where's your wife? Your other children, Shane and Haley? I thought you had turned over a new leaf?" he questioned, finally registering the reek of alcohol coming from John and what it meant.

Reminded of his family—his wife and kids and how he lost them, John saw red and he tightened his grip on Reace, slamming him hard against the wall again. John grinned in satisfaction when he heard Reace's head connect with the wall.

Reace winced as pain erupted in the back of his head, colors blurred before his eyes and he blinked to clear them.

"They left me because of you!" John hit Reace in the stomach and felt adrenalin pour through his veins at the groan Reace gave.

"Me?" Reace squeaked when he got his breath back. "How can you blame me? I wasn't even HERE!" Reace's voice rose in volume as he pushed John back, away from him.

"After you left that last time, they wanted to know what you were talking about so I told them. I told them everything—everything about my childhood, Carol, my drinking and you. What I did . . . then Michelle left me. She took the kids and left. That was eight years ago." John's voice was rough with hurt, anger and unshed tears. He focused on his anger and directed it to Reace.

"Because of you I've lost two wives. YOU'VE RUINED MY LIFE!" He yelled as he launched a fist into Reace's face.

Reace took the punch square on his left cheek. His head and body twisted with the force of the blow and using the natural law of physics, Reace's body twisted back hitting John's surprised face with a fist of his own.

"Stop blaming me for your mistakes!" Reace said, breathing hard as he glared down at John. His step-father was on the floor where Reace's punch had landed him. "You're a coward, dad. You don't have the guts to admit you've made a mistake."

John, surprised by Reace's attack stared at him as his words sunk into his head.

"Don't call me that I am not the father of a freak like you." John demanded as he got up off the floor.

"You're the only father I've known, so whether you want to be or not you're my dad."

John charged toward Reace but Reace was ready, catching him, he used John's forward motion and turned them so he held John pinned against the wall.

"If you want to change your life, you can. Just stop blaming me and except that you've made mistakes." Reace loosened his grip a bit as he added, "Get sober, get cleaned up, be a better man."

"Why do you care, bastard?" John sneered trying to hold onto his anger. "Why would you want to help me . . . after all I've done to you? Huh, why?"

"Because you're the only father I have and you don't turn your back on family." Reace said then added, "If you want your wife back than fight for her. Show her you've really changed."

John swallowed hard as the fight—the anger—went out of him and he nodded then asked when Reace released his hold on him. "So why are you turning away from your son?"

"I'm not . . . it's different . . . I can't . . ." Reace's throat pumped working hard to ease the lump that constricted it. His emotions where to close to the surface and he strove to bury them, he didn't want John to see his pain.

John nodded in understanding as Reace turned away from him. They stood in silence for a moment before John suddenly asked, "D . . . do you think Michelle will take me back?"

Reace was surprised by the sudden change in the older man. Had he heard that right, John was asking him for reassurance?

"If I can forgive you . . . she can too, but I've got to tell you it may take a lot of work, she's been gone for eight years. She may have met someone else."

"She hasn't," he said quietly, remembering when he saw last her. They had bumped into each other at the supermarket about a month ago, she looked sad and lonely and from what Shane (the boy still came over to visit him every few weeks or so, probably without his mothers knowledge) had told him she missed him. He missed her too.

It may take some work, like Reace said, but it would be worth it and he was willing to do it for her, for them. Maybe he could make it up to her; show he'd really changed. For the first time in eight years, hope swelled inside of him and for that he had Reace to thank. But instead of saying the words thank-you to his step-son John offered, "You . . . you can stay here."

"I can clean this place up for you, help you get sober again." He offered, to proud to except charity.

John nodded.

*

Reace made John and himself dinner spending as little time as possible in the kitchen. They ate in an awkward silence in the dining room after which, Reace tided up the house. At first he didn't mind the work of cleaning it took his mind off his own problems and gave him something to do, but the more he worked, the more he cleaned, the more he was reminded of his earlier years with John. Reace's anxiety grew, even though the first thing he had done was to watch John pour all the contents of every bottle of alcohol down the drain earlier, he couldn't help but wonder: How long would it be until John's next attack? Would he survive it? He couldn't heal himself anymore, and Arron, Kittana and Keyla couldn't help him either.

Reace wasn't even aware of when he had stopped sweeping, leaned the broom against the wall and started pacing. The more he thought about it the more he didn't feel like he could stay here. He was too anxious—too many bad memories for him to relax.

Turning on his heel he left the house.

He had to get out of there. He couldn't breathe in that house. Everywhere he looked, everywhere he cleaned, painful memories clouded his mind with things he didn't want to remember. Pushing them from his head, he tried to clear it as he walked down the street with restless energy.

He turned right, walking down the sidewalk leading him toward the old downtown area of the city. Reace didn't really care were his feet took him he just needed to move his body—to rid it of the anxious energy coursing through his veins.

He tried not to think at all but his mind wouldn't let him, it kept bringing up what not having his powers meant. It meant that he had lost his family. He was alone now . . . and normal. Reace took a ragged breath, it was funny how things worked out, he thought. While growing up he hated his gift and wished he could be like everyone else. Now that he'd finally gotten his wish—it wasn't what he wanted anymore. Not now.

He had spent the last thirty years learning what he could do with his powers—his gift. Reace's lips quirked up at the corners as he thought of his comrade. Arron used to refer to Reace's powers as a gift when they were kids but all through his childhood and into his teens he only thought it a curse, a curse that made him different, that made him the freak that his father hated. Now he realized that Arron was right. It had it taken meeting Kittana and Keyla, traveling to other worlds and helping many other beings, becoming a Guardian and raising a son, but he finally agreed with Arron, it was a blessing—a blessing that had just been stripped from him.

His face fell into a frown and his jaw quivered as he thought of how he'd never be able to see Arron or Kittana, Keyla—anyone he had come to love—again. Clenching his jaw in an attempt to stop the quiver and hold the tears at bay, he shook his head slowly, silently cursing his bad luck.

When Reace walked passed a bar, he paused, turning to look at the darkened door. He was human now, he thought with a shrug and he had some money. Reace fingered the bills he stole from the woman's house he still had them in his pocket of his jeans. *Why not?* He thought, as he reached for the door handle. He'd never been inside of a bar before.

Reace entered the darkened interior of the bar and for a moment he stood there, just inside of the door wondering what to do next. Even though early, by bar standards, the bar was not empty, people milled about, some playing pool at one of the two pool tables in the back of the room and others sat at tables washed in the atmosphere of the tavern, tapping their feet as they watched a local band play.

Reace turned as two people came into the bar behind him forcing him to move forward. He walked up to the long counter of the bar where several patrons were seated on stools. He watched the other people in the room for a moment, not really knowing what was normal in a place like this. When the bartender looked expectantly at him, Reace had no idea what to do then he heard the guy next to him order a whiskey on the rocks.

Reace waited until the bartender looked at him again then he ordered the same.

Drink in hand, he lifted it half way to his mouth then stopped and looked at it. Staring into its amber deeps he admitted he was nervous. Would he really be able to drink this without his body reacting?

Catching the flesh of his left wrist within his sight, he remembered with bitterness that he was normal now. Taking a deep breath Reace raised the glass to his lips and took a sip. He almost chocked but settled for wincing as the liquid burned a path down into his belly. It wasn't bad, in a weird way he almost liked it, the pain in his throat now matched the pain in his heart.

He took another sip.

Reace sat at the bar for a while, he didn't noticed as the crowd increased nor the time that he wasted just sitting there ordering one whiskey after another, wallowing in self pity and alcohol. When he finally moved off the bar stool he stumbled backwards, holding on to the bar for support. His confused gaze connected with the bartender and he asked her.

"I can't feel my feet. Why can't I feel my feet?"

"Because you're drunk." She answered him with a bemused smile.

Drunk, the word echoed in Reace's mind, he grinned grabbing a glass off the bar, he spun around.

"Drunk!" He repeated then he threw back his head and laughed. "DO YOU HEAR THAT WORLD, REACE STELMEN IS DRUNK!" He yelled, then feeling the coolness of the glass in his hand he threw it across the room with enough force to smash it as it hit the wall. Glass rained down on the floor and Reace watched it fall with a satisfied look on his face.

When he heard someone scream he raised his head wondering what the commotion was about.

Two burly bouncers grabbed Reace's arms and forced him toward the door. While the bartender called the cops, a bar employee cleaned up the broken glass.

Outside Reace's eyes widened, he saw a shadow move on the side of the building,

"SHADOWS!" He yelled struggling to break away from the hold the two muscled men had on him. "We have to stop them." He told them, "Shades! You don't understand, we have to stop them before they hurt someone. AUGH! LET GO!" Reace shouted in frustration, finally breaking away from the bouncers when they heard the wail of the police sirens. He rushed to the wall feeling and touching all the shadows searching for what he thought he saw.

Could he have been wrong?

"It's only a brick wall." He muttered, frowning in disbelief. Maybe the shadows he thought he saw were only the shadows of him and the other men. Reace stood facing the wall, touching it when other shadows appeared and grew beside his own. He turned, seeing two policemen had joined the guys that had brought him outside. His first thought was to run, thinking the cops where after him, but he stayed where he was wondering why would they be chasing him, he hadn't done anything wrong had he? He couldn't remember and he didn't feel like trying.

"S'only a shadow." Reace slurred to the cop as the officer came up to him. Turning Reace around and leaning him against the wall as he cuffed Reace's hands behind his back.

"Sure it is," the officer spoke as he led the drunkard to the parked car with its flashing lights.

"Not a shade, Kit killed all the shades." Reace rambled on, "The only way to kill a shade is too burn it. Did you know that? Kit killed them all with a psychic blast, white light. There are no more shadows left." His words did little to comfort him and his eyes looked wildly about as if to reassure himself that there were no shades left.

"Come on buddy, let's sleep it off in the tank," The other officer said, opening the back door of the police cruiser. It was when they were helping Reace into the backseat of the car that he suddenly yelled.

"WAIT!" Reace stopped half in and half out of the police cruiser, burping loudly before saying, "I don't feel so . . . good."

Reace doubled over and threw up before passing out.

"Great," The police officer muttered as he looked down at his shoes and wrinkled his nose at the smell.

# CHAPTER FOUR

## Taysia

AFTER ARRON AND KEYLA CALMED Kittana enough to find out what happened to Reace. They called the other life force Guardians to a meeting held in the bottom floor of their mountain home. Currently Keyla, Arron, Kittana and Link sat around the table that held their marks, waiting to start.

"Where is Awkwade?" Kittana's impatient voice questioned Link. She, Arron and Keyla had called all of them together to explain what happened to Reace and hopefully come up with some kind of solution to get him back.

Keyla had already tried every spell she could think of to locate him and bring him back. She and Arron had used the colored crystals attached to the library walls to locate him, but with no luck. This meeting was their last hope maybe together the five of them could come up with something.

"I don't know where she is, but it's not like her to be late especially when it's something this important." Link replied feeling an uneasiness settle in his gut.

"With Malic gone, we have to make sure that the surrounding planets are safe, maybe she's busy on a call." Keyla suggested. "I'm sure she'll be here soon." Keyla added hoping to ease the worry she saw flicker across Link's face.

"There's been no real change in the balance." Link stated.

"How can that be?" Arron questioned, "Malic is dead . . . gone and until new Guardians arrive—the balance is tipped."

"Good this time instead of evil, maybe that makes a difference?" Kittana suggested.

"It shouldn't matter you can't have life without both good and evil." Arron argued.

Link was quiet, thinking. Something had been brothering him about the way Malic passed on. He'd been running the scene over and over in his mind for the past few months, and he kept coming up with the same answer: something wasn't right. Voicing his suspicions, he spoke. "What if Malic isn't dead?"

"What?" Everyone at the table said, turning to stare at him in disbelief.

"Well, when we found him, his body wasn't burnt . . . just lifeless. And he was inside a circle of melted wax, what if he was performing a spell to take on another shape or form? It would fit with the third line from Deia's prophecy: *The one thought dead to be alive*."

"Did Malic have the power of magic?" Keyla asked.

"He must have had," Kittana answered focusing her mind on something else besides Reace. "He had taken the powers of the five other evil Guardians and I think in order for us to balance, for there to be seven times two, they must have had similar powers to ours.

"So if there is a good magic . . . white magic there'd have to be an equal, dark . . . black magic," Keyla nodded in understanding. She turned to Link. "You think Malic took another form like the lady in the crystal, Zaylar?" Keyla asked. When they had first come to Taysia they had met the old Guardian of magic. Instead of dying and giving Malic the option of wining, she gave up her magic to those who came next—to Keyla—but instead of giving up her life force she had put herself into one of the crystals that graced the study room walls choosing to wait for the four Guardians of the prophecy—Keyla, Kittana, Arron and Reace.

"But she could no longer use her powers so what would Malic gain by doing that?" Kittana reasoned.

Link sat back and thought for a second. Remembering how odd that it was that Zarrick got attacked just before they discovered Malic's body. It was Zarrick who suggested using the crystal in Malic's chamber and

Zarrick who helped Tia use it—almost as if he knew how or had used it before.

"Maybe," Link said slowly, "maybe Malic willed his powers to someone else?"

"Zarrick?" Kittana said in shocked surprise as the name floated to her from Link's mind. Her eyes flashed to Arron. He had paled and the look of anguish flashed on his face but when he reminded quiet, Kittana spoke for him, "No, he's not evil."

"Besides Zarrick's not 'the one', in the prophecy. Malic is." Keyla added, smiling inwardly when she heard the sigh of relief that Arron gave.

"What if Malic had found a way to possess somebody, to become a part of them?" Link suggested not willing to give up on the nagging sensation that somehow Zarrick was involved.

"You mean switch bodies? But that's impossible isn't it?" Arron finally spoke glancing at Keyla and Kittana.

"No, it's possible," Keyla said slowly turning scared eyes to Arron. "However that person would have to be related to them."

Arron's eyes widened in alarm, an expression that was the mixture of guilt and horror flicked over his paled face.

"Well, there goes that theory. Malic doesn't have any living relatives." Link turned to Arron when he heard Arron's horrified gasp.

"Link," Arron began, finding it hard to get the words out. "Malic does have a son . . . Zarrick." He paused, looking away from them as he continued, "Zarrick is Malic's biological child." Arron was going to be sick, he had failed Zarrick. He had left when his step-son needed him the most.

"Arron," Kittana spoke gaining his attention. "If Malic did use Zarrick, I'm sure it wasn't voluntary. Zarrick may have had his share of issues—we all have, but he's a good kid. He's your kid—you raised him and if Malic used him for whatever sick reason I'm sure Zarrick wouldn't willingly help him . . . he wouldn't."

Arron lowered his gaze and nodded letting Kittana know he heard her words, but they did little to make him feel better.

Link was surprised by Arron's admission that Zarrick was Malic's son. Did that mean that Tia . . . ? Link couldn't even think it instead he focused on the problem at hand—the balance. "There is only one way to find out for sure . . . we have to confront him."

"But how can we tell if he's Malic?" Keyla asked, "We've been around him for the past eight months and he's seemed normal—like himself."

"When we found Malic's body his marks were gone, nothing left of them but a faint imprint. I suspect if Zarrick is Malic then he'd have the marks." Link suggested, avoiding Arron's gaze. They were Guardians and they had an obligation to the balance—worlds were depending on them.

Arron nodded, he had wondered why Zarrick who had always wore sleeveless tees had suddenly taken a liking to long sleeved shirts after Tia died. Could it have been to hide something?

Arron wondered how he could have missed this? He was trying to rebuild his relationship with his son and to get them both past Tia's death. How could he have not taken the time to notice a change in Zarrick especially one this big?

"And the powers." Kittana added with a shake of her head at their stupidity. How could they have once again underestimated their evil nemeses? "What if he did something to Reace? Sent him somewhere? We have to find out?" She turned worried eyes on Arron and Keyla looking for reassurance. "We have to confront him, now!"

Link was about to ask what happened to Reace, but something caught his attention: A whisper that called to his soul. Link's head tilted, listening with a sinking feeling in his gut, before turning fear filled eyes at the others in question and demanding, "Do you hear that?"

"Hear what?" Keyla asked.

"Fire!" Link replied standing and moving quickly to the steps, horror in his voice as he told the others what he heard. "It's coming from upstairs, one of the bedrooms!"

Running, he took the stairs two at a time, reaching the second floor ahead of the others. He rushed into the flame engulfed room.

Arron, who followed close behind Link, stopped in the doorway to Awkwade's room. He wasn't the Guardian of Fire and walking into the room he'd get burnt. Arron could feel the heat as it raised blisters on his skin.

They needed away to contain the blaze, keep it from spreading, Arron thought, as he raised both his hands letting his protective shield come. It shimmered golden in front of the door. Arron concentrated, moving his hands apart a bit and the golden shield spread along the walls of the bedroom enclosing the fire and the Guardian of Fire within.

Link stood in the middle of the room, fire surrounding him and he closed his eyes. It was like watching Tia burn all over again only this time it was worse. It was Awkwade.

"Awkwade!" Link screamed in agony at his heart shattering.

He opened his eyes to see Arron's golden shield surround the room and he knew the Guardian of Life couldn't hold a shield that size for long—not in this heat. Pushing his grief aside Link called on his powers of fire, holding out his arms wide, he called the blaze into himself, controlling the fire until it was gone. Nothing left but the smoke. Link fell on his knees to the floor. He was numb, he couldn't think. Awkwade was gone and that was all he knew. Lost in his grief he didn't notice Zarrick in the corner of the room, watching with an excited gleam in his golden eyes.

"Awkwade, where is she?" Keyla demanded in the hallway behind Arron.

Arron dropped his shield and turned to her, his mouth opened to say something but a sudden wave of dizziness overtook him and he stumbled backwards. A loud buzzing sound filled his ears. He covered them with his hand in an effort to stop the ringing, but it was futile. Looking wildly about he could see Keyla saying something but he couldn't hear her.

Arron reached out his hand to try and touch Keyla but his hand went through her. He stared wide eyed at his hands, then looked at Kittana standing behind her sister, as he faded away.

"NO!" Kittana yelled running to where Arron was, searching for him with wild eyes. "No, Arron, come back!" She sobbed.

"What . . . what just happened? Kit where's Arron? Where did he go?" Keyla demanded her fear rising.

"He's gone!" Kittana cried, "Just like Reace, there all gone: Reace, Arron, Tia and Awkwade." Kittana paused, tears streaming down her face. "Everyone is gone."

"Kit?" Keyla said reaching out a hand to her sister, she'd never seen her like this—so hopeless.

"NO. DON'T TOUCH ME! DON'T . . . DON'T COME ANY CLOSER. YOU'RE NOT REAL!" Kittana shouted. "YOU'RE GOING TO LEAVE ME TOO! YOU'RE NOT REAL. NONE OF THIS IS!"

"What? Kit I . . ." Keyla started wondering what Kittana was talking about who wasn't real?

"NO! YOU'RE NOT REAL!" Kittana raised a hand, her mark flashed and Keyla was thrown through the air.

She landed hard, her head connecting to the wall first then her body followed sliding silently to the floor but Kittana didn't see she had already run into her room.

# Chapter five

## Earth

When Arron woke up a few hours later, it was dark. Looking around him, he shook off the fog surrounding his memories. *How did I get here?* he asked himself. *Where was here anyway?* He wondered as he slowly got up, pushing himself to his feet. He ignored the nausea feeling that swam in his stomach and the dizzy way the darkness spun around him. Right now, he needed a clear head, he needed to figure out where he was and then he needed to leave. He was pretty sure that whoever brought him here would be back and Arron didn't want to be here when they came.

Now that the room had stopped spinning, he made his way toward the crack of light he could see coming from under what he assumed was door. Feeling his way in the dark Arron stumbled over what he was surprised to find out was a metal chair.

*A chair? Where the hell am I?*

When he got to the crack of light, he felt around for a way to open the door, finally his hand closed around the cool metal rod of the door leaver and Arron was stunned to find it unlocked as he pushed it and the door opened.

*Why bring me here then let me go?* He silently asked of his kidnappers.

Arron stumbled out into an early morning lit parking lot. A parking lot like those on Earth, he paused looking around as he tried to gain his bearings. He saw several signs and all of them indicated that he was at Springfield Memorial Children's Hospital.

"A hospital?" Arron spoke the word like a question then it dawned on him that he'd read the signs and they were in English. He must be back on Earth, but how? Why? And what was he doing in a children's hospital? He'd been left in a darkroom and looking down at his attire, Arron assumed he wasn't a patient. Maybe he could find some answers inside—at least they'd have a pay phone. He walked around to the front of the building and taking a deep breath he re-entered.

Arron glanced to the front desk, everything he ran through his mind made him sound like a mentally unstable patient so instead he crossed to the pay phone he spotted on the opposite wall and dialed 411 for information. He pushed one for English and waited.

"Hello, you've reached information, how can I help you?" A pleasant sounding female voice asked over the phone.

"Yeah, ah, could you tell me the phone number and address of a Jacob Arron Price?"

"One moment please." There was a sight pause then the operator came back on. "Sorry, sir but I can't give you that information. It must be unlisted, I have no Jacob Arron Price in the system. Is there anything else I can do for you?"

"Unlisted, great!" Arron muttered then answered her question, "Yeah, how about Nate Stelmen?" Arron could hear the clicking as she typed in the name. "S-t-e-l-m-e-n," he supplied without being asked, he wanted to make sure she had the right person. He couldn't afford to waste time going to the wrong person's house.

"Yes sir, there is a Nate Stelmen. Do you want his address as well as his phone number?"

"Yes, please," Arron answered committing what she said to memory. He thanked her and hung up the phone. If memory served him he had a lot of walking to do, Nate lived on the other side of the small city. It could be worse, Arron mused, he could have been in another country or another city; it was luck that he had been brought back to Springfield.

*

After hours of walking, he was exhausted, his feet hurt, he was hot and his legs were sore—everything ached. Arron frowned as he briefly wondered at that, why hadn't his body rejuvenated itself?

Looking up at the building in front of him, he had finally arrived at the address the operator had given him. Arron's relieved expression changed as his face screwed up into a frown when he opened the door and saw the stairs. Nate and Anna lived on the sixth floor of an eight floor apartment building and judging from the 'out of order' note on the elevator he'd have to climb the steps.

"Fuck!" Arron muttered as he turned his tired and sore body and started climbing.

Arron made it to the door and congratulated himself on not falling flat on his face, as he knocked on the door. He almost passed out with relief when Anna opened it seconds later—a smile on her face.

"Jake," Anna said. She was about to ask what happened but changed her mind when she saw the shake of his head. "Not Jake?" She questioned, confused for a second. Her brain worked fast to figure out who could be at her door looking so much like Jake Price, her husband's best friend then it dawned on her, "Arron?"

He nodded almost falling forward with the effort.

"Arron!" she said again with a brilliant smile. "Come in, come in, this is a surprise. Does Nate know you're here? Or Jake?" she asked moving aside to let him enter.

Arron stumbled forward into her apartment, falling into a chair he croaked out the only word his parched mouth could form, "Water."

"Ah, sure, I'll get you a glass," Anna said then moved into the kitchen to pour him a glass of water. Her mind whirled wondering what was going on, why was only Arron here and looking half dead on his feet? The last time the Guardians had been on Earth it was at her and Nate's wedding and there were four of them she had the impression that the Guardians traveled as a group, so to see Arron alone made her wonder and worry about the rest of them. Something must have happened because judging by the worn-out look of her unexpected guest this wasn't a social call.

"Okay, now tell me what's up. You look beat to hell," Anna demanded after Arron had downed two glasses of water and was working his way through a third.

Off his feet, resting and refreshed by the water he had drank he felt good enough to talk—to explain, but how . . . where did he start? He wasn't even sure what happened to him.

At Arron's cautious look she added, "Arron, I know all about you and the Guardians. God, I'm Nature's wife and carrying his child," she pointed to her hugely expanded middle just in case—by some miracle, he had failed to notice it before. "I'd think he'd tell me everything, don't you?"

Arron smiled and opened his mouth to tell her what he knew and what he thought happened to him and Reace.

*

As Nate navigated his way through the traffic on his way home, he chewed his bottom lip in worry. He had left work early—canceling his afternoon classes at the high school, when his wife called. He had told his coworkers that he needed a few days off—a family emergency he had said, letting everyone believe it was the baby, but the truth was he didn't know what was going on. All Anna would tell him over the phone was that the baby was fine and Arron was with her.

"The baby is fine, Arron is with her," Nate repeated out loud the phrase his wife had said. He was relieved that Arron was there, if there was any problem with his child then he'd be forever grateful to the Guardian of Life healing the baby and Anna—if she needed it, but if the baby was fine then why was Arron there? Why Arron and not the others?

"What the hell was going on?" Nate growled as he quickly and sharply pulled into the parking lot and parked his car. He mechanically got out, and locked the car with the push of a button. His only thought was in making his way to his apartment and seeing his wife, seeing for himself that what she said was true—they were fine. Then he'd be able to breathe and focus on Arron.

Nate's eyes, when he walked through the door sought out Anna's, his face held the unasked question that hung in the air.

"I'm fine and so is Jr." Anna answered, Nate nodded. The air in the room seemed to lighten in response to Nature's sigh and smile of relief.

"Arron, is that really you?" Nate said as the older man stood up from the table, and came toward him. Arron engulfed him in a hug.

"In the flesh." Arron answered. His smile slowly vanished from his face as he thought of the answers he knew Nate would want.

"What . . . what are you doing here? Is dad and mom with you? Are they okay?" Nature asked when they had broken apart and he waited, watching as the older Guardian took a seat at the table. The apprehension inside of Nate increased at the expression on Arron's face, he had hoped this was a social call, but his senses were telling him that something was wrong.

"Your mom and Keyla are on Taysia," Arron started answering Nate's question carefully, then with a bewildered expression and a shake of his head he just said it. "Nate, I don't know . . . I don't know what I'm doing here or how I got here . . . or where Reace is."

"What do you mean you don't know? Where is dad? How . . . how did you get here without the power of four? Did you ask Timelana for help? Are your powers growing?" Nate demanded. He didn't understand what Arron was telling him.

Arron looked away from Nate, letting his own frustration come to the surface. He got up from the chair in the kitchen and started to pace the space between the table and the stove.

The phone rang and Anna went to answer it leaving the two Guardians alone.

"Arron, you've got to tell me, what's going on? Where is my dad?"

"I don't know." Arron stopped pacing and turned anguished eyes to Nate. "Kit said he just disappeared—faded. The last thing I remember was the look on her face when I faded too. Nate, my hands . . . they went right through Keyla, it was as if I were a . . . a ghost!"

"And you ended up here?" Nate asked, trying not to give in to the panic rising inside of him.

"Basement of a children's hospital." Arron replied.

"Maybe you're here to help someone, like dad did before I was born?" Nate suggested hoping it just that simple.

"I don't think so," Arron said with a shake of his head. "Reace didn't just disappear like this then . . . it was different and I've seen your father blend in with the electrons, heck so have you."

"In a flash of light, yeah," Nate sighed his agreement.

"But this wasn't like that, it was different, he—we both just faded . . . like ghosts. We had no control . . . no warning . . . it just happened." Arron sat at the table again, pushed his hands through his hair. With his head down he added. "I don't know what else to do . . . where to go." He sounded like a lost kid. His head came up fast and his eyes focused on

Nate's face as a thought occurred to him. "If I ended up here then there is a chance that Reace did too. Nate we have to find him. I promised your mother, we'd find him."

"We will," Nate assured. If he found it odd or weird that he had to reassure the older Guardian, Nate didn't show it. "First though, I need to get changed then we can sit and figure this out." Nate's eyes moved to Anna's when she reentered the room.

"Jake just called, he's at the precinct, they have a guy in the holding tank that he thinks is Reace." Anna paused, her eyes going from Nate to Arron, "Jake wants you to go Id him. He can't hold him much longer—guess this guy was picked up last night for a minor infraction at a bar. He was drunk."

Arron eyes widened and a confused expression covered his face. "Can't be Reace, we can't drink."

"He sounded pretty sure. Why don't you two go see. If it is Reace then bring him back here and we can figure everything out then, Okay?" she suggested her tone discouraging any arguments. "If not at least you know where he is not, no harm done."

Arron smiled at her. "You are going to make an unbelievable mother; you know that?" He said then turned to Nate, "You heard the woman, let's go!"

"Yeah," Nate said still trying to take everything in, with this new information a change of clothes was the last thing on his mind. What was his father doing in jail? And why was he drinking? It made their powers go crazy, maybe that's what happened, but that didn't explain why Reace had gone into a bar in the first place. One thing was for sure—he'd get no answers to his questions standing here.

"Nate," Anna's voice spurred him into action.

Grabbing his jacket that she held out to him and kissing her on the cheek, as he led Arron out the door and down the steps, into the parking lot behind the apartment complex. Getting into Nate's car they made their way to the police station, to Jake and Reace and hopefully some answers to what was going on.

# Chapter six

"Nate, thank-god you're finally got here. I've had a hard time thinking up reasons to keep him here. I'm pretty sure it's Reace but . . ."

"But what?" Nate demanded. "What would he be doing in jail?"

"He was picked up at a bar. He was drunk . . . caused a disturbance. It's luck that no one was hurt. Then he threw-up over Ricky's shoes. Thankfully, I've managed to talk Ricky out of pressing charges over that one."

"Can't be Reace." Arron said in disbelief as he came up beside Nate.

"Dad!" Jake's voice held a note of surprised happiness as he engulfed his father in a hug.

"Hey, Jake! It's good to see you."

Jake just stood there after they parted, taking in the sight before him. The beaming smile slowly fell from his face as he took in the expression on his father's face and the fact that Reace was in the holding tank. Jake frowned.

"This isn't a social call is it? What happened?"

"A lot." Arron replied. His eyes telling Jake that he couldn't talk about it here.

"I'll get someone to cover my shift." Jake announced.

Arron nodded. "There must be some mistake Reace can't drink, he can't be drunk."

"No mistake. We finger printed him. You can see for yourself," Jake replied as he led them both toward the holding cell.

"Reace Stelmen, you've been sprung. Come on, let's go!" A guard called out.

Reace got to his feet walking unsteadily toward the door of the jail cell. He kept his eyes down as he followed the guard he assumed that John had gotten him out.

"Reace! Christ! Man, it's good to see you." Arron moved forward putting a hand on Reace's shoulder, pulling him into a hug. Arron's nostrils flared as he took in the smell of his comrade, he had definitely been drinking. "We weren't sure what happened to you. Kit's beyond worried. I'm glad you're alright."

"Arron?" Reace's eyes rose to meet his smiling face. Then he latched on tight to Arron as he admitted his fears out loud. "Arron! I thought I'd never see you again."

"Yeah, it's me, comrade." Arron said clapping Reace on the back and pulling away a little embarrassed and at the same time curious about the way Reace was acting.

Reace's bright smile suddenly turned downward and he frowned, "How . . . how did you get here?" He demanded, than his eyes widened in terror and he stuttered, "D . . . d . . . did she g . . . g . . . get to you too?"

"Later man," Arron replied giving Reace a look that spoke volumes before lifting his hand off Reace and turning to Nate.

Reace nodded at the silent message in Arron's eyes. They'd talk later in a place more private. Reace swallowed his growing fear and his concern—how were they going to get out of this? How were they going to get their powers back?

"Dad?" Nate asked not quite sure what to say or what to make of the condition his father was in? What happened to land him in jail? To make him drink—Nate could smell the alcohol. "Are you okay?"

"Nate!" Reace stared at his son, his eyes narrowed in anguish for a split second before he hid that emotion behind an overly bright smile he directed at both Nate and Jake. "Jake! That uniform looks good on you."

Nate got the impression that his father wasn't happy about seeing him and he frowned at that thought. Why wouldn't his father want to see him? What happened to him?

Nate didn't ask any of these questions, not yet. He'd have to wait until they got back to his place. In the privacy of his home they'd talk. He wrinkled his nose at the smell, after his father had cleaned up, he amended silently.

\*

"You were really in a bar . . . and drunk?" Arron demand when they had gotten in the car. He really didn't have to ask, Reace reeked of alcohol, vomit and stale air, but he was having a hard time understanding how or why Reace, who never drank would suddenly change, especially after growing up with an violent alcoholic? What happened to drive his comrade to drink?

"Yeah," Reace quietly admitted not looking at them, he wasn't proud of his actions.

"How? You're a Guardian. What about your powers?" Nate demanded from the front seat as he maneuvered the car through traffic. The three of them were in Nate's car, on their way back to his apartment; Jake was following them in his car. "Did they go crazy? Is that why you ended up in jail?"

"I . . . I don't have any powers." Reace mumbled still looking down at his knees.

"What?" Arron exclaimed, he couldn't have heard that right.

"I said, I don't have any fucking powers anymore!" Reace repeated, than continued in an angry, irritated voice, "Look, I went into a bar and got drunk then I threw a glass at the wall. That's how I ended up in the slammer, okay? Are you satisfied now?" Reace, rubbing a hand over his aching head, was still feeling the effects of being hung over for the first time in his life and he wasn't happy about it. "Fuck! This sucks!"

"Get over it!" Arron growled back and then demanded, "What do you mean, you have no powers? Reace what happened?"

"One minute I was standing on Taysia talking to Kit and the next . . . I don't know . . . I was in a house on Earth." Reace closed his eyes for a second remembering. "Somehow she had my power and she . . . she electrocuted me."

"You're sure it was your power? She could have shot you with . . ." Nate trailed off when Reace spoke again.

"Trust me, it was my power."

Silence filled the interior of the car and lasted well after Nate had parked the car, and the three of them made their way to the eighth floor, each of them digesting this news and the ramifications that went along with it.

Anna-Maria met them at the door when the three men entered the apartment.

"Reace," she said a relieved smile on her face with a mixture of welcome. "We're glad you're safe!" She came closer to him but stopped inches from him and wrinkled up her nose.

"You're pregnant?" Reace announced in surprise when he saw her extended belly. He turned to Nate with a genuine smile on his face as he exclaimed, "You're going to be a dad!"

Reace moved to hug Nate but Nate's hand on his chest stopped him.

"You can hug me when you smell better," Nate said then added, "You really need a shower."

"Yeah," Reace agreed, then turned back to Anna with a sheepish expression.

"It's down the hall, first door on the left. The towels are on the shelf above the toilet." She pointed the directions to him, then as she moved away from the door going toward the bedroom she shared with Nate she added, "And I'll get you some of Nate's clothes, you're about the same size."

"Thanks," Reace muttered as he followed her, making his way to the bathroom and a hot shower.

# CHAPTER SEVEN

WHEN REACE CAME OUT OF the bathroom wearing clean clothes twenty minutes later, showered, shaved, and smelling better, he noted that Jake had arrived and was seated at the table in the kitchen. Beside Jake sat Arron and to the right of Arron was Nate and Anna.

Reace breathed deeply inhaling the delicious smell of pizza that sat on the counter. He grabbed himself a plate—that Anna directed him too. After putting two slices on it and picking up a can of coke he took the empty seat at the end of the table. He got one bite of his pizza before Arron spoke. Reace was surprised that he had waited that long.

"What happened to you?" Arron demanded, "You must have been here for a few days, why didn't you contract Nate or Jake?"

"I've been staying with John." Reace admitted and closed his eyes in anticipation of Arron's retort.

"John? Why?" Jake demanded. He thought Reace had been abused by John in some way, so why would he willingly go back to him?

Reace opened his eyes and glanced at Arron with disbelief, the scowl was there and directed at him but Arron hadn't said anything and that surprised Reace. Turning to Jake, he answered him.

"I didn't have anywhere else to go." Reace turned his eyes to his son as he added, "I couldn't . . . I couldn't face you, Nate."

"What? Why?" Nate wanted to know, "You're still my dad that hasn't changed."

"No, but I have." Reace's face crumbled, "I'm not the same person I was . . ." his voice trailed off.

"Reace, why did you go into a bar? After what John did to you, after seeing the way alcohol changed him, why would you even want to go there? What were you thinking?" Arron demanded his voice loud in the quiet room—everyone was waiting for answers.

"I don't know, man, I . . ." Reace turned tear filled eyes on Arron, "I . . . I just wanted to forget that I . . . that I wasn't a Guardian anymore." He looked down at his plate, suddenly he wasn't hungry. He sniffed, blinking back the tears that threatened to spill, swallowing them. He just wanted to go home and wake up in his own bed beside his wife—pretend this was all a dream . . . just a really bad dream, but he couldn't go back.

"Whoa—what?" Jake questioned, "You're not a Guardian, what do you mean? Is that even possible?"

Reace sighed, pulled up his sleeve on his left wrist and showed everyone.

Arron's eyes widened in horror, "Wh . . . where's your mark? How?"

Jake nodded in agreement with Arron. He wanted to know too.

Nate just stared at Reace's wrist in stunned silence. All his life his father had always had the mark of a lightning bolt on his wrist, but now it was just . . . gone; his skin was smooth—like it was never there. What could do that?

His eyes searched his father's face, he could understand the pain and horror Reace must be feeling. Nate tried to imagine how he'd feel. Suddenly not being himself, thrust into a mortal world—cut off from everyone he knew. It must be hell for Reace, especially for him to go back to John's house.

"She's taken my powers . . . everything." Reace whispered. A tear he couldn't hold back slid down his face.

"Oh, Reace," Anna said in sympathy.

"She's done it to you too, Arron." Reace's head came up, he grabbed Arron's left wrist and turned it over, forcing his comrade to look at his own mark.

It was still there, but Reace was right, it was different. Instead of a solid circle in the center of a plus sign, it was just four lines, in the east, west, north, south configuration but the center was empty. It was the symbol of death. Arron's face crumbled into a frown as it dawned on him.

His worst fears founded: He wasn't the Guardian of Life anymore, just the Guardian of Death.

"How did you know?" Jake asked, judging by the expression on his father face, Jake assumed that Arron hadn't known about his mark so, how did Reace?

"Because you're here." Reace answered Jake his eyes never leaving Arron. "And she said, *'If one worked then so will the other.'* Arron I swear I didn't know what she was talking about. I didn't even remember until I saw you or I would have stopped her."

"How?" Nate demanded and when Reace looked at him, he added, "Dad, this isn't your fault. You couldn't have stopped her. She took your powers didn't she?" He didn't wait for Reace to confirm it—he didn't need to, "She used them on you too." Nate knew he was right not only had his father already confirmed it in the car ride over but also in his actions. His dad wasn't acting like the normally quick thinking Guardian of Electricity. He was confused, which followed the pattern of a person struck by lightning.

"Yeah." Reace's frown deepened as he nodded.

"A woman," Arron said, coming out of his trance, his eyes snapped to Reace. "A woman did this to you . . . to me?" When Reace nodded Arron continued, "It was a woman . . . so it wasn't Zarrick. Zarrick didn't do this." Arron breathed a sigh of relief. "Tarine lye Thayia de Mar!"

"Zarrick? Why would Zarrick have anything to do with this?" Nate wondered.

"Yeah, why would you think Zarrick is involved?" Reace echoed. He glanced at Nate before his eyes searched Arron's face for answers.

"Just before I disappeared from Taysia we had called a meeting and well waiting for Awkwade, Link started talking . . ."

"You had to wait for Awkwade?" Nate interrupted. He didn't like the uneasy feeling in the pit of his stomach. "That's not like her, is she okay?"

"What did Link say?" Reace pushed. He had a feeling that whatever Link had to say was pretty important.

Arron's eyes moved from Nate to Reace, he didn't really want to answer Nate's question, not yet, so he answered Reace's.

"Ah, he had this theory that when Malic died he passed his powers to Zarrick. Or that he somehow possessed him."

"That's not possible . . . is it?" Nate demanded looking from Arron to Reace. "Okay, what don't I know?"

"Key said it was possible with magic, but they'd have to be related," Arron turned to Nate as he told him, "Nate, Malic is Zarrick's biological father."

"So, Zarrick's not really my brother is he?" Jake questioned.

"No, not by blood, anyway," Arron admitted.

"Zarrick is Malic?" Nate asked hardly able to believe it.

"We haven't confirmed anything . . . yet. It's just a theory, but we were going to confront him . . ."

"They may have already. Time does pass differently there than here." Nate reminded them.

"We have to get back. We have to get our powers back. We have to stop Malic and we have to save Zarrick." Arron stood suddenly and started to pace the length of the room. He passed the table twice before he stopped and turned to face them.

"The last thing I remember before waking up in that hospital basement was Awkwade." He locked eyes with Reace. "There was a fire, in her room."

"Are you sure . . . it was . . ." Reace didn't finish his sentence, he couldn't.

"Yeah," Arron answered closing his eyes briefly. He remembered Link shouting Awkwade's name—the raw pain in it mirroring his own when he thought of Tia.

"Awkwade's gone." Arron clarified for Nate, Jake and Anna-Maria. For a few moments there was nothing but silence.

*Who is next?* The unspoken words hovered in the air.

It was Anna who broke the silence when she turned to Reace and spoke, "What else do you remember about the woman?" she asked and feeling everyone's eyes on her she explained, "If we can figure out who she is and how she took your powers maybe we can reverse it and get your powers back. Then you guys can go and stop Malic and help Zarrick."

Nate's hand closed around hers and he gave her a light squeeze. Anna turned to see the look of pride and love on his face.

"Good thinking Anna," Jake praised before turning to Reace. "Arron said he woke up in the basement of a hospital."

"Springfield Memorial." Arron supplied the detail.

"Springfield Memorial, that's a children's hospital." Anna added.

"I didn't wake up in a hospital, it was a house—a private residence." Reace replied pushing his grief at the loss of another friend away. Anna was right they needed to focus on getting their powers back. It was the only way to go back; he just hoped they could do it. He hoped they could help Zarrick, for Arron's sake.

"Do you remember the address? What the exterior or interior looked like? Any outstanding details that may help us locate the house?" Jake asked. His police training kicking in, he pulled out a police notepad and a pen out of his inside beast pocket, ready to record the important information.

"Yeah, it was 522 Sycamore Drive and the woman's name was . . . Danielle, Danielle Cameron." Reace remembered seeing her name on the mail he'd picked up from the counter earlier yesterday morning.

"Jake can you use your contacts at the station to find out as much about this woman, this Danielle Cameron as we can." Arron asked and at Jake's nod he added. "Find out what connection she has to Springfield Memorial?"

"Dad, what else do you remember? Anything at all would be helpful." Nate inquired watching Reace carefully.

Reace frowned in concentration, "I remember," he said slowly, "hearing a rhyme . . . like one of Keyla's spells. And a bracelet, it flashed just before she shot lightning from her hand."

"A bracelet? That's interesting." Anna commented then added, "On the news this morning there was a report of a theft at a museum; they were showing ancient Greek artifacts, some were reported to possess the powers of the gods. Do you suppose . . ." She let the sentence drop.

"Anything is possible," Reace responded. "We're living proof of that."

Arron turned to his son. "Jake, can you find out exactly what was reported stolen? Pictures would be helpful too."

"I'll get right on that," Jake spoke as he got up from the table. Taking out his cell phone, he moved into the quieter living room to make a few calls.

Moments later Jake came back into the kitchen.

"Okay, so far I've got a disturbance at the address you gave me, 522 Sycamore Drive. A Miss Cameron called in yesterday morning about a possible break and enter but no suspects were apprehended."

"Yeah," Reace nodded in agreement, "the police showed up just as I was leaving. I jumped the fence and left before they saw me."

"Okay," Jake said slowly looking down at the notes he took, he flipped a page then spoke again, "I ran her name and this is what I got: Danielle Cameron, age thirty-seven, a single parent of a sickly male child who sadly passed away last night, after a difficult battle with brain cancer." Jake paused looking at his father before saying the rest. "Died in Springfield memorial, where he had spent the last few months," he waited a second before adding, "Danielle's father was James Cameron."

His cell phone rang and Jake answered it, moving back into the living room to talk.

"James Cameron, James Cameron," Anna repeated the familiar name then it clicked. "Wasn't he an archeologist?" She didn't need to see Nate nod she knew she was right, "Yes, he was famous for his belief that the Greek mythical Gods were real. He believed that he had found proof too, but he died before he could show that proof and whatever that proof was went with him to the grave."

"Sounds like she's our girl, let's go!" Nate stood.

"Wait!" Arron cautioned. "We can't just go and confront her we need a plan of some sort."

"You'd better hurry." Jake said closing his phone and putting it away as he walked back into the kitchen.

"Why, what happened?" Nate demanded, the hairs on the back of his neck rising in alarm.

"There was a family—North end of Springfield, a doctor who worked at the children's hospital, he and his family—including a seven year old child, have all been found dead. Police and coroners are stumped as to how. It appears they have all been struck by lightning—inside the house." Jake turned sorry eyes to Reace as he added, "That was your power, right?"

Reace nodded, stunned that the woman had actually killed people with his powers. He had to get them back before more innocent people got hurt. He raised his gaze to Arron. "What's the plan?"

Arron was about to speak, he opened his mouth to do so, but all that came out was a groan and he suddenly doubled over as a sharp pain stabbed into his heart.

"Arron! Are you okay?" Nate and Jake suddenly exclaimed.

"Arron, Arron can you hear me? Nod if you can," Anna's calm voice rose above the others.

Arron nodded breathing deeply as the pain ebbed.

"Balance?" Reace inquired catching Arron's eyes.

"What?" Anna and Jake exchanged puzzled glances.

Nate let out a breath.

Arron nodded again, his eyes agreeing with the words Reace spoke.

"We need to get our powers back. We need to get back home."

"And fast," Arron added, worry spurring his mind into action, he told the others the plan as it formed in his mind. Reace adding details as he remembered them.

# CHAPTER EIGHT

Taysia:

"THIS ISN'T REAL," KITTANA SAID repeating it over and over, willing herself to wake up from this nightmare her life had become. She laid on her bed and closed her eyes. She didn't want to be confused anymore. She just wanted to know what was real and what wasn't, which world did she live in? If Taysia was a dream then she wanted to wake up.

Opening her eyes Kittana looked around, she was still in her bedroom inside the crystal mountain.

"No," She whispered closing her eyes tight again. "This isn't real, wake up!" This nightmare couldn't be real. Her breathing evened out and Kittana fell into a deep, dreamless sleep.

*

Keyla woke with a headache, pushing herself up off the floor where she had landed when her sister had used her powers against her—something she was still having a hard time believing.

*You're not real!* Her sister yelled at her. She frowned wondering what Kittana was talking about? She glanced at her sister's closed bedroom door.

She wanted to ask her, but with the throbbing in her head she rethought that idea. She had to find Link and Awkwade maybe together they could find some way to help Kittana and bring Reace and Arron back. Sparing a glance at her sister's closed door she hoped it was soon.

Thinking of a spell to use to get rid of the headache she walked past Awkwade's room and paused, gasping in horror at what she saw, the spell she was forming forgotten.

The room was torched—everything was burnt. In a flash, she remembered that there had been a fire in Awkwade's room. She's gone, Keyla knew and sorrow filled her.

Arron too, he was gone . . . he'd just disappeared, the same as Reace.

"What happened?" Keyla's voice a hoarse whisper was loud in the eerie quiet.

"I've got to find Link." She quickened her pace.

In the top chamber of their mountain home, the place they had all called the library she ran into Zarrick.

"Zarrick!" Keyla breathed, startled for a moment. She hadn't expected to find him here. There was something about him that she was supposed to know but at the moment she couldn't remember what it was. All she did know was he made her feel uneasy so she moved herself across the room as she spoke.

"You scared me, have you seen Link? There was a fire in Awkwade's room earlier and I . . ." Keyla trailed off, Arron was Zarrick's father and he was missing now. How was she going to tell Zarrick that? Keyla opened her mouth to try and tell him but her words never made it past her throat.

"Oh, I wouldn't worry about Link or Awkwade, they are together now."

Zarrick's voice slithered across Keyla's skin raising goose bumps and she had the impression she had heard that tone before.

"If I were you I would be worried about myself." Zarrick flicked his fingers and a chair beside her blew up.

"Zarrick! What the hell! Why did you blow up the chair? You could've hurt someone." She scolded lightly trying to hide the feeling of panic that rose inside of her.

"Then I'll aim better next time." Zarrick said with an eerie smile as he flicked his fingers again.

Keyla ducked and the shelf behind her blew apart.

"Why are you doing this?" She demanded as she tried to come up with a spell to protect herself but she couldn't seem to think of the words.

All that filled her mind was the look in Zarrick's golden eyes. A look of pure evil, full of malice and hatred, it took her breath away.

"Why? Oh Keyla, Zarrick has so many reasons to hate you it's hard to just pick one. You have always been a barrier between his parents, always making his mother feel sad and worthless because she could never be as good as Keyla. Arron has always loved you more than Tia. Even under her enchantment he always put you first."

"It was your fault that Tia died. Did you know that? She saw you and Arron together after your little nightmare. I must take credit for that, it was pretty clever of me, you see I gave you that nightmare." He pulled up his sleeve and pointed at the curling Z on his left arm. "The power of the Dream Guardian is very useful if you know how to use it. You were so scared!" A twisted smile of pride settled on his face as he slowly carefully made his way toward her.

"You . . . How?" The idea that someone had been inside her head made her feel uneasy. And the way Zarrick was talking . . . something wasn't right.

"Keyla, Keyla, Keyla always the last to know. Haven't you figured it out yet? I'm not Zarrick . . . not really. I'm . . ."

"Malic!" Keyla finished for him, horror and revulsion showed on her face.

Malic gave her a mock bow as he said, "The one and only!"

Her eyes widened in surprise at how close he was to her and just as he touched her, she saw the twinkle of triumph light his eyes.

*"Poor little Keyla. Poor little unloved, unwanted Keyla."* The words echoed in her mind and Keyla felt hopeless, lost and alone. She wanted to get away but she found herself unable to move, unable to do anything but listen and feel whatever he wanted her to.

"You are just a reflection of her, your twin, Kittana's the one everyone loved. Everyone wanted her. You are just a pale reflection, an afterthought. Without her you're nothing! Even your father loved her more then you. He took her with him, didn't he?"

Using his power, Zarrick made Keyla nod.

"Your own father couldn't stand you. That's why he left, he took your sister—a child he could love—and left you alone. Even your mother didn't love you enough to want to live with you. She willed herself to die when she found out her precious Kittana wasn't coming back. The thought of living with her cold, unwanted child was too much for her." Malic spoke through Zarrick's lips, his mark of a diamond and that of a star glowing brightly as he used his powers of emotion and mind to twist Keyla's emotions, her memories to suit his purpose . . . revenge.

"Kittana didn't want you in her life either, did she?" Malic asked.

In Keyla's mind flashed the memory of a high school bathroom. *'Key, . . . I have this life now and I don't want any reminders of my past.'* Kittana had said that years ago when they were first reunited, but then she changed her mind, Keyla told herself. The scene changed to the second floor hallway inside Crystal Mountain and Keyla saw her sister slam her against the wall. *'Don't touch me!'* Kittana's voice sounded loud in her memories.

Keyla wanted to tell Malic that this wasn't true, that he was twisting everything—her sister loved her, but the words wouldn't come. Her heart hurt, at her sister's words, like it was breaking. Knowing the feelings weren't real didn't lesson the pain as Malic shoved the emotions onto her.

"And Arron, he's still pinning away for poor Tia. She was wrong you know."

Malic's voice was close to her ear, Keyla could feel his warm breath on her skin as he spoke. It made her want to shiver but her body wouldn't move. She was forced to listen to him.

"She was Arron's true love not you. He's just using you Keyla: he wants a warm body to hold against the chill of the night. A whore is good for that and when he closes his eyes he only sees Tia . . . not you, never you." Malic eyes gleamed with pleasure when he saw her tears spill over and fall down her face.

Betrayal, heartache and the anger and hurt that came with the knowledge that you've been used washed over her. Even though she knew that Malic was twisting the truth to hurt her, using it against her, she felt herself weaken under his over whelming assault of emotions. She found herself starting to believe his lies.

"Reace," Keyla's voice whispered; as tears streamed down her cheeks; confident that Malic couldn't twist their friendship against her.

Malic threw back his head and laughed at her pathetic attempt to grasp for straws. Then with amusement still in his voice he told her, "Reace can't stand you. He's snapped at you so many times in the past, haven't you ever wondered why?" Malic didn't give her time to answer. "He finds you annoying. He only puts up with you because he feels sorry for you. A poor little whore with no friends. It was you who begged him to be friends. It was you who kept badgering him—forcing yourself into his life, forcing your pathetic friendship on them all. They'd all be so much happier if you'd just leave them all alone . . . if you didn't exist."

Malic watched the expressions on her face, "You think I'm lying, but why would I lie, Keyla, when the truth is always much more painful?"

Malic stepped away from her, moving his arms in a wide arch disguising the spell he placed that would ensure no one heard her voice outside the room they were in. With a satisfied smirk he challenged.

"If you don't believe me, go ahead call to them. Call for Reace see if he comes to your rescue?" He raised one finger at her as he added, "If he doesn't then you'll know I speak the truth."

"KITTANA! ARRON! REACE!" Keyla shouted. Finding herself suddenly free to move, she twirled around her eyes searching the area for the people she loved. She yelled again, calling for them to come, "REACE! REACE! ARRON! KITTANA! REACE! PLEASE, HELP ME! SOMEONE! ANYONE! KANDA LYE THAYIA DE MAR! REACE! ARRON!" She screamed his name as sobs bubbled up from deep inside.

They waited but no one came, no one heard her. Malic was right, no one cared.

After a few moments of listening to Keyla cry her friend's names, he spoke.

"They don't care. A Guardian can always hear when they are called. Reace hears you . . . he just doesn't care. None of them do. You're worthless to them. Malic smirked using Zarrick's face. He was enjoying watching her hope crumble and seeing the utter despair on her face. It made his revenge all the more sweet. "See Keyla, the truth is always more painful, but I can fix that . . . I can take away your pain, make everything right again".

Keyla looked up, from where she lay sobbing on the floor, with hopeless eyes to Malic. Scalding tears racing down her face, she whispered, "How? How do you fix this? How do I make this right?"

"There is only one way to stop the pain." The mark of the star flashed as he forced Keyla to say the words of the Starian death chant.

"Sek keylie zo ion kelaze ze decia avada vol rina.
Sek keylie zo thayia ze decia avada vol rina."

"It's the right thing to do Keyla. The right thing to do." Malic smiled at her as the mark of a diamond shined brightly making her feel the devastating despair that would give her the desire to end her life.

*

When Kittana woke it was dark and she was surprised to find herself in bed then, in a flash, everything came back to her and she gasped.

"Reace," she choked on a sob. "Arron, Awkwade, oh my God! It's real!" Her hand flew to her mouth in alarm. "Keyla! What did I do?" She demanded of herself as she jumped from the bed. She ran into the hallway, to her sister's room, calling for her as she searched. Keyla needed her, Kittana felt a sense of urgency something was happening to Keyla and she needed to find her.

Coming out of Keyla's room she raced up the stairs to the library, meeting Zarrick on the steps.

"Zarrick have you seen Keyla?"

"Yes, she's up there." He pointed behind him toward the study room.

"Thanks," she answered pushing past him in her hurry to reach her twin. She ran into the top chamber of the mountain and stopped short.

"NO!" She gasped in horror when she saw her sister sitting on the floor a haze of pink surrounding her. Kittana knew she was too late when her sister turned vacate eyes toward her.

"This is the right thing to do." She spoke in a weirdly detached voice.

"NO!" Kittana shouted at her then ran from the room.

"Zarrick!" She found him in the hallway of the second floor.

"ZARRICK!" She yelled his name again. The young Guardian in front of her didn't turn around; in fact he didn't even seem to hear her. Kittana frowned, her thoughts swirled fast inside her head and she remembered what Link had suggested earlier, in a whisper of horror she spoke his name, "Malic?"

The young Guardian turned slowly to face her, she sucked in a breath. Zarrick's eyes glowed a bright yellow. It wasn't the hazy golden gaze of the angry adolescent Zarrick, but the bright golden intensity of Malic that stared back at her.

"Malic." Kittana said again. Then swallowing her fear, she demanded, "What did you do to her?"

"The same thing I did to Tia, Awkwade and Link. The same thing I'll do to you, Reace and Arron. You can't stop me, not now!" Malic raised Zarrick's left arm, the mark of a flame flashed seconds before a stream of fire shot from his fingertips.

Kittana saw the flash and was more than ready to take him on. Using her power of telekinesis she easily deflected the fire away from her. The smirk on her face and a witty remark on her tongue died when in a blink of the eye he vanished.

As she had been busy deflecting the fire power he shot at her Malic teleported behind her placing his hands on the sides of her head.

Kittana gasped in surprised pain before falling backwards into Zarrick's waiting arms as Malic entered her mind taking her to a place he had spent months creating.

*"Kittana, Kittana, can you hear me?" Dr. Drake said snapping his fingers and shinning a bright pin light in her eyes. When he saw her pupils dilate and eyes blink he sat back and breathed a sigh of relief.*

*"Kittana, I'm glad the new treatments are working, we were starting to give up hope but you've come back to us." The doctor said to her, a smile stretched his leathery face.*

*"Huh?" Kittana replied, her voice sleepy as if she had just awaked from a nap. "Where am I?" She demanded, glancing around the room in confusion. The last thing she remembered quickly falling out of her reach and the more she tried to remember the more elusive the memory became until she knew only the moment she was in.*

*The old psychiatrist turned to his colleagues with a pleased smile as if to say 'the experimental treatments were working. She was actually coherent.' Turning his attention back to the patient he answered her.*

*"You are in Spring Meadows Asylum. It's been your home now for more than thirty years."*

*"NO! My home is on . . ." Kittana's brow wrinkled in confusion and her voice trailed off—her sentence unfinished.*

*"Kittana we've had this conversation before, do you remember?" Dr. Drake asked carefully. "Tell me what you remember?"*

*"I . . . I remember you told me that I've been here all this time. Keyla, my twin sister, my mom and dad died in a fire when I was little. My foster parents, David and Nancy MacDonald brought me here, to you, when I was seven." Kittana answered, her voice sounded automatic and far away.*

*Dr. Drake nodded encouragingly, "What else do you remember?"*

*"Reace, he died too, in . . . in a car accident when he was five."*

*"Yes, go on," Drake encouraged pleased with her progress.*

"And Arron, I've never met him, did I?" Kittana turned her gaze to the psychiatrist for conformation.

He shook his head, "That's right, Kittana, how could you have? He lives in Rome."

"And I've been here the entire time." She finished his sentence.

"Yes," Dr. Drake agreed, his whole face shined with positive pleasure at how well she was responding to the new medicine.

Kittana's eyes moved around the room could this be true, she wondered? Could she have imagined it all? It must be, she told herself as memories flashed in her mind. She did remember this room. Her eyes fell on a doll in the corner.

"What is that?" she demanded pointing to it, her voice held a note of panic and horror. She knew what it was even before the doctors voice reached her ears.

"Oh, that's Nate. Kittana, you named the doll Nate as soon as you saw it and you've spent hours just rocking it and holding it. Anyone who walked by you, you would tell them about your son." The doctor's face held the look of fond memories as he told her this crushing news. He didn't realize his mistake until his eyes moved back to her face.

"NO!" Kittana whispered a look of revulsion on her face.

"Kittana, listen to me, calm down, breathe." Drake cautioned then to his colleagues he spoke as he got up from the chair. "This patient has been through enough for one day, we'll pick this up tomorrow, but as you clearly see the treatments are working." Standing by the door he turned to Kittana as he checked his watch. "Kittana, would you like to go to the common room, watch a little TV? I hear they are serving ice-cream there right about now."

Kittana didn't answer him, she just sat there in her chair, staring straight ahead, but not seeing anything.

"I'll take that as a yes, I'll have one of the nurses take you in," Dr. Drake said then left, closing the door behind himself and his colleagues.

A few moments later the door opened again and a male nurse walked in wheeling an empty wheel chair in front of him. he smiled at her. "Okay, Kittana. How are we doing today?"

Kittana's eyes widened when she saw him he had his back to her and his shoulder length brown and blond streaked hair tied back in a ponytail but she'd recognize him anywhere.

"Zarrick!" She hissed at him and when he turned to look at her with his yellow amber eyes she knew she was right.

"Yes, Aunt Kit." He spoke in a hushed tone, leaning close to her he continued, "I know what Malic's done. There is a way to get you out of here, take you back home Kit, but you have to work with me, trust me." He glanced behind him then back at her before speaking in a loud voice, "Let's get you into this chair they are having ice-cream in the main room, don't want to miss that!" He exclaimed in a false excitement as he helped her out of the chair she was sitting in and into the wheel chair he'd brought.

At his touch Kittana seemed to come alive snaking her hands in his shirt, balling it up in her fist as she demanded answers. "I don't care about ice-cream, how can you help me? Is Taysia real or am I going crazy?"

Zarrick gripped her arm, trying to undo her grasp on him, but she held firm. Glancing around almost as if he was worried someone would over hear them he turned back to her,

"No, you are not crazy. Taysia is real. This . . ." He gestured around him to indicate their surroundings, "This is all Malic's doing. He is inside your head, but you can escape this. All you have to do, Kit, is say this spell." He handed her a small folded piece of paper.

"I can't do magic," Kittana informed him.

"Malic can, you are linked now. Call on his powers—use them as you chant this. It'll work I promise." He nodded to her then in a normal voice he spoke as he helped her into the wheel chair, this time with less resistance. "Okay we're all set. Ah, can you hang on a minute I have to go to the bathroom."

Kittana nodded and watched as he left the room before she unfolded the piece of paper Zarrick had given her. Could she trust him, she wondered?

Did she have a choice, she asked herself? No, the answer came to her. She had to know what was real and what wasn't. Besides everything Zarrick had said made sense, taking a deep breath she read the rhyme from the paper.

"From me to you our powers flow,
        As from this world into the next I go."

It sounded a bit like the Starian death chant, Kittana thought, then shrugged. One way or another, she told herself, she'd find out what was real. She'd end this tonight, one way or another. She read the rhyme again.

# CHAPTER NINE

Earth:

DANIELLE SAT IN THE DARK living room of her home waiting for them. Even through her grief she knew what she did was wrong. She hadn't been careful, left lots of clues and possibly eye witnesses, but at the time she hadn't cared . . . she still didn't. The police would find her and take her away and if she was lucky she'd get the death penalty for what she had done then she'd be with her son again, Bradley.

She hadn't been with him when he'd passed away, she didn't get to tell him good-bye. She had been busy acquiring this trinket. Danielle twisted the golden bracelet on her left wrist, it moved the blue one too—they were connected now, but Danielle didn't notice, she was too caught up in her thoughts. *This useless bracelet was supposed to heal Bradley.* She thought bitterly. She knew it worked, just as the other one did. She had read the rhyme and had taken the power from the God, but it was too late. She was too late and even with this bracelet she couldn't heal the dead.

After she had said the rhyme seven times, substituting life for the word electricity, she had taken the God's power. Excited she had left him in the basement of the hospital to go to her son; she couldn't wait to heal Bradley. She couldn't wait to see him open pain free eyes and talk to her with the strong voice of a healthy child. She wanted to see him run and play again like he had when he was four, before cancer had taken so much from him.

On her way to Bradley's room she was greeted by Dr. Ryan Summers. He blocked her path as he awkwardly told her that her son was dead. Confident that she could bring him back she had pushed her way past him.

She vividly remembered picking up her son's cold lifeless body, cradling it in her arms as she tried to heal him—give him back his life. She had the power now and she tried to save her son, but it didn't work. He didn't wake up. He stayed cold, lifeless . . . dead. She screamed his name crying as she rocked him back and forth.

It was hours later when she left the hospital to returned home, but on the way she had made a little stop at the doctor's house. If her son was dead then he would pay.

Danielle didn't remember exactly what happened next, she didn't remember exactly what she had done but she knew when she left that house that she left no one alive—not even the child.

*What have I done?* She silently cried.

Now she sat here in the dark house, like she had for hours—waiting, just waiting; expecting the police to come, but she was surprised when three men sunk past her window. Hearing them break into her home Danielle stood and quietly made her way across the room.

She waited in the dark by the wall until the three intruders entered the room then she spoke from behind them turning on the light at the same time. "You've picked the wrong day to steal from me!"

Reace, Arron and Nate turned around to face the women with surprised expressions on their faces as they were bathed in light.

"It's not theft to take back what is yours." Reace said recovering first.

"You!" Danielle's eyes widened when she recognized the dark haired man in front of her. He was the same God she had first taken the powers of. "I should never have left you alive."

"You weren't a killer then," Reace told her, remembering the look in her eyes.

"Well, things change and I never repeat a mistake." A twisted smile graced her face as she stepped forward, away from the wall. Remembering the blond as the God she had left in the hospital, she addressed all three of the men in front of her she added. "You think you can beat me? I have your powers now! You're human, you can die and I will gladly send you back to heaven—the mortal way."

As she talked, Reace glanced at Arron giving him a slight nod, with his attention off her he didn't see it coming even Nate's shout wasn't fast enough to avoid getting struck.

Lightning hit him square in the chest, knocking him backward.

"DAD!" Nate yelled as he knelt beside Reace. "Dad, dad, are you okay?" He pleaded. Reace groaned and Nate sighed with relief, knowing that he was still alive.

"Dad?" Danielle echoed, "You have a son?" She sneered at Reace looking down at him as he lay on the ground several feet back from where he had stood a moment ago. "Then you shall know what it's like to lose him."

Danielle raised her arm to shoot a bolt of energy at Nature.

Nate moved, diving out of the way, the lightning bolt crashed into the wall behind him shattering the glass cabinet. Nate realized then that this woman wasn't playing around—she was dangerous and she needed to be stopped.

Thinking of what he could do to slow her down and help until Arron got into position, Nate stood. He moved his hands at his sides, palms downward. His mark flashed as he slowly moved his arms up until they were level with his shoulders. A thick fog appeared along the floor and rose up, covering them until it was level with Nate's shoulders.

"What, what is this?" Danielle demanded before it dawned on her, "You're . . . you're a God too?" She half asked, half accused.

"Not a God, a Guardian. We are all Guardians. We protect the life forces—that is the meaning of the word Guardian." Nate told her, keeping her attention focused on him so she wouldn't notice Arron slipping through the fog making his way behind her.

Reace's eyes flickered to where Arron had been. Could he really do it, Reace wondered? He hoped so, they were counting on him, but Reace couldn't see anything more than shadows in the fog. He slowly gained his feet this time the electricity wasn't as high a voltage as before when she shot him he didn't feel so confused and sick.

Arron was more than halfway across the room. His objective was to get behind Danielle while Nate and Reace distracted her. He was making good head way too, he thought to himself, as he took another careful step toward the woman.

The fog covered all but the top of Danielle's head, luckily they were taller than her and could see each other above the thick fog. Reace watched as Arron took another step toward her closing the ten foot gap but when Arron suddenly gasped in pain and ducked—gone from view—Reace's stomach bottom out as he worried that something happened his comrade.

Arron fell to his knees when a stabbing pain sliced through his heart, stealing his breath away. He looked down at his chest, expecting to see some sort of knife or sword sticking out of him or a bullet hole . . . something to give the sudden pain a reason. But there was none, nothing was there. He raised a hand to his heart just to make sure; the pain was intense for a few seconds that seemed like a lifetime before leaving as quickly as it had come.

Suddenly, the reason for it dawned on the Guardian and his eyes widened in horror at what it meant before narrowing in determination. He straightened, uncoiling his long body as he glanced around him. Arron breathed a sigh of relief that Danielle hadn't noticed him yet, she was still intent on attacking Nate and Reace through the fog. Hoping luck would be with him Arron took another step closer, than another until he had maneuvered his way behind the lady.

When Reace saw Arron stand again understanding dawned on him—he knew what that pain was. Closing his eyes tight Reace refused to think about it right now they had to focus on the task at hand . . . getting their powers back. Suddenly an idea flashed in Reace's mind and he shrugged, it was worth a try.

*I am the Guardian of Electricity.* Drawing strength and purpose from that phrase he starting chanting it in his mind, *I am the Guardian of Electricity.* He didn't have his powers anymore but he was still Starian and that meant he couldn't die unless he wished it. And if he could will himself to live or die then maybe he could will himself to be a Guardian again.

"I am the Guardian of Electricity." He whispered with feeling. In his heart, more than anything, he wanted to be himself again. When a spark jumped between his fingers it gave him confidence and he chanted a little louder. "I am the Guardian of Electricity!"

"Why are you showing up now? Why couldn't you have come earlier and saved my son?" Danielle demanded of Nate. She couldn't see him anymore . . . she couldn't see anything in this thick fog.

"If you had just asked us instead of attacking and taking our powers, then we would have been more than happy to help." Nate's voice carried easily through the fog.

"NOW IT'S TOO LATE! HE'S DEAD JUST AS YOU WILL BE!" She yelled, raising her hand and blindly shooting another bolt of energy, in the direction she heard his voice coming from.

"In order for a Guardian to help we must first be asked, called." Nate explained, easily avoiding the bolt of electricity she shot wildly in his direction.

"Called? That's an excuse! You didn't come because you were too selfish. I will not be so selfish, I will save other . . ."

"Like you saved the doctor and his family?" Nate asked cutting off her words. In an accusing voice he reminded her of the wrongs she had done. "Like you saved that little girl? She was innocent, a child and you killed her anyway! The powers of the Guardians are not meant to be used that way—not for revenge!" Nate paused before adding, "We have come to take them back."

"NO!" she shrieked raising a hand she tried to use her power of electricity but it wouldn't work. With a frown on her face she glanced at the bracelet on her wrist, straining to see it in the fog.

A smile appeared on Reace's face he didn't need to look at his hand to know, he felt it, that familiar rush of adrenalin running through his veins.

"I AM THE GUARDIAN OF ELECTRICITY!" His voice boomed through the fog.

Danielle's eyes widened in astonishment as she saw his body glow, burning away the fog surrounding him. She could make out the triumphant glare shinning from his face.

"You can't take away someone's destiny." Reace spoke then he raised his hands and lacing his fingers together with his first fingers pointing at her, he directed the energy running threw his veins toward Danielle. He reveled in the feel of it as it moved from deep inside of him, carried by his blood to the surface of his skin, it traveled down his arms and out his fingertips.

Danielle's eyes closed when she saw the bolt of lightning speeding toward her. Surprised by the turn of events she acted purely on instinct and raise a hand to fend off the energy streaking toward her. She never thought she'd survive this attack, but she opened her eyes in shock when all she felt was a tinge in her arm.

A smirk appeared on her face when she saw a see-through golden tinted shield in front of her. Danielle opened her mouth to taunt the

Guardians when a strong hand clamped around her forearm. She gasped and turned her shocked expression to Arron.

"You may have taken the Guardian of Life from me, but I am still the Guardian of Death." He told her and watched her with an expression on his face that was a mixture of resolve and pity as he concentrated on allowing his powers to come to the surface.

Her eyes rounded in fear when she saw his mark of death begin to glow on his wrist. The bracelet she wore also flashed as she fought him using the power of life to heal herself.

Arron let himself think of the horrors she had done, killing a man, an innocent woman . . . a child. His mark glowed bright as he let his will overtake hers. His eyes went out of focus as he called on every angry thought he had and willed it into his power of death. Drawing strength from every fiber of his being his mark glowed brighter, and the bracelet of life around Danielle's wrist dimmed under the assault.

When it dawned on her that this was the end, this was what she really wanted anyway—she didn't want to live in a world without her son—she stopped fighting Arron and a smile of peace settled on her face. Her last thought was that she could be with her son again.

Reace breathed through the pain as his mark of a lightning bolt reformed on his wrist, but for once he was glad for the pain. Proud to be marked a Guardian, he rejoiced in it. He was back! Relief flooded him, cradling his left wrist, he looked up to see Arron. He watched in stunned silence Arron's power of death.

Arron's face hardened with bitterness as he watched, willing himself to be the monster he had always feared he could be. He held on tight to her wrist even as her skin, soft with health and life turned dry and rough. Nothing left but the bone and still Arron didn't let go, not until the bone turned to dust and there was nothing left to hold on to.

"How did you do that?" Nate asked his father after dissipating the fog. "How did you get your powers back?"

"I willed it," Reace said simply, moving away from his son, he approached his lifelong friend and asked. "Arron, you okay?"

"In a land through time and space, the hand of death, life must embrace." Arron mumbled. "Another of Deia's prophecies." He added not looking up from the pile of dust at his feet, dust that used to a woman.

"From Deia's book of prophecy, that one's about you I take it." Nate spoke as he came up beside his father and Arron. Bending down he picked up the bracelets, or what was left of them. The once bright, shiny metals were now tarnished and flakey. The brightly colored stones were now cracked and blackened. Nate turned to Arron his eyes going to his mentors left wrist. The symbol had changed back to the one of life and death—a plus sign with a solid circle in the middle. His gaze moved to Arron's face.

"You're the Guardian of Life again, you've got your powers back." He had hoped to make the older Guardian happy by telling him that but when Arron's face remained stony and sad, Nate returned his gaze to the old bracelets in his hand. He stood saying, "I'll see that these are kept somewhere safe."

Arron's vacant looking eyes flickered over Nate before making contact with Reace, he whispered. "I killed her."

"You had no choice. She wasn't innocent, Arron." Reace replied but he could tell that his comrade had the weight of guilt on his shoulders, Reace knew what that felt like—he used to carried it to.

Arron's gaze returned to the pile of dust at his feet. What Reace said was true he had no choice but that didn't stop Arron from hating himself for what he had done. He killed a woman and he broke the vow that he had made to himself years ago to never use his power of death.

Tonight, he had used it; he had watched as he took the life from her. They had no choice, he knew Reace was right. They had to get back to set the balance right again . . . somehow, but was it worth it—the life of an innocent? *She wasn't innocent, Arron.* Reace's words came back to him, maybe she wasn't, but did he have the right to judge? It was her life and like a monster he had taken that from her. How could he ever forgive himself?

"Come on," Reace nudged Arron's arm as he moved toward the door. "Let's get out of . . ." Reace's voice was cut off by a sharp pain that pierced through his heart. His gaze sought out Arron's, who was experiencing the same feeling.

"Dad? Arron?" Nate turned worried eyes from one to the other as he heard their gasps and watched them still their movements. "Shit! It's the balance isn't it?"

"Yeah, that was the third time," Reace spoke as he breathed through what was left of the sharp ache.

Arron nodded, the pain pushing all aside but the need to get home, the need to protect those he cared about. "How are we going to get back, we don't have the power of four?"

Reace turned to Nate and demanded in an urgent voice, "Call Timelana!"

Nate glanced from one Guardian to the other, seeing Arron nod his approval Nate opened his mouth, then shut it again as he turned his attention back to his father when he heard him speak.

"I'm sorry Nature, but we don't have time for goodbyes. We have to go now!" Reace said his eyes carrying unspoken worries that were mirrored in his son's.

Nate nodded.

"Timelana!" He called then in a voice that was filled with worry he told his dad, "Make sure mom's okay." He gripped his father's arm pulling him into a tight hug and as they pulled apart he added, "I'll call you when the baby's born."

Reace was about to say something but closed his mouth when a swirl of colors caught his gaze.

Timelana materialized beside Nate and when the bright colors faded she turned to Nature, the smile on her face didn't reach her eyes. It was the kind of smile that spoke, *Sorry for your loss.*

"This is a hard time for you Nate—for all of you," her gaze moved to take in Reace and Arron. "What happens next will be the hardest thing any of you have ever been up against, for some of you it will be what you were born for." Her gaze fell on Arron and stayed there for a second before moving back to Nature, she added, "What is about to be done cannot be undone," She told them. When the three Guardians nodded in agreement, even though she knew they didn't understand what she was trying to tell them, she held out her hand to Reace.

After a brief hesitation, Reace grasped the soft hand of the Guardian of Time then he held out a hand to his comrade.

Arron looked at the hand Reace held out to him then he glanced at Nate, "Tell Jake good-bye for me," he said and placed his hand in Reace's before added, "and tell Anna not to worry everything with the baby will be fine."

Timelana raised her staff and thudded the floor with it three times. Smoke and swirling pinpoints of brightly colored lights rose up around them and they vanished, Timelana's parting words were all that hung in the air where they had been.

"See you soon, Nature."

After Nate watched his father and Arron leave with Timelana, he turned and walked through the house. He hadn't realized until now how much he missed his family . . . how much he missed Taysia. He only hoped that everything would be okay when he called on them again, he hoped with his whole being that they'd all be there, but with the pain they had experienced three times since being here, he wasn't so sure what to expect. Nate clung to the hope that the feeling was new Guardians arriving in Taysia, but no matter what he told himself, he couldn't shake the grief that claimed his heart.

Once outside, Nate ran to the cover of the bushes beside the stone wall—bushes his father had hid in only a day earlier—he turned back to the house.

"Time to cover our tracks." He said calling his power to the surface, his mark flashed brightly and a second later, thick, dark clouds rolled in. Thunder boomed loudly overhead.

Nature watched with satisfaction as lightning struck the sprawling mansion in several different places simultaneously starting fires that would level the house and cover the fact that the Guardians were there.

He didn't know how long he stood there watching the flames but the sound of sirens woke him from his trance and spurred him into moving. After scaling the wall, he jumped down and calmly strolled the two blocks to where he parked his car, pretending he had only been out for a walk.

*

With heavy feet Nate climbed the six flights of stairs to his and Anna's apartment and as he climbed the wheels turned in his mind. He hadn't realized how much he missed being around his dad and Arron, until they had left. They had too, he knew that, but would Jake understand when he told him that Arron had left without saying goodbye? And with the pains The Guardians of the Balance were feeling Nate wondered if they'd ever be seeing them again. They had left only three Guardians behind and they'd felt that pain three times.

As much as Nate wanted to deny it—he couldn't. He knew what it meant—three Guardians had died. It hurt him to think it, but his mother, Aunt Keyla and Link were dead. Hot tears blurred Nature's vision and he paused on the steps.

Someone had killed three Guardians and his dad and Arron had gone back . . . What if they died too? How would he even know? He wasn't a Balance Guardian so he wouldn't feel anything. He wasn't a

Balance Guardian, but he was still a Guardian and he could help them fight . . . whatever it was. With a nod, Nate raised his head in resolve.

"Timelana!" He called her name for the second time that night. He would go back to Taysia, he would stand with his father and Arron against whatever foe they faced.

# CHAPTER TEN

Taysia:

"THANKS TIMELANA," ARRON SAID LETTING go of Reace's hand when his feet touch solid ground again.

"Yeah, we owe you one." Reace agreed. He tried to look around him, but his eyes hadn't yet adjusted from the bright lights to the darkness they were in now, was it nighttime?

"Goodbye Guardians and good luck," Timelana said. Reace and Arron turned to her in time to see her thud her staff on the ground and they both turned their heads away shielding their eyes, as she disappeared in a blinding swirl of brightly colored lights.

It was several long minutes before their eyes adjusted and the two looked around them. What they saw made their mouths open in shock, and their eyes widened in disbelief and horror.

"What happened here?" Reace recovered first and spoke.

"I don't know, but whatever it was it isn't good," Arron replied.

The place was dead—the lush green grass he remembered from only a day ago was yellowed and brittle. It crunched under their feet like frost in the fall. The trees that were full of life and leaves, ripe with fruit, were twisted, brown and dark. The stench of rotten vegetation hung limp in the air catching both half-Starians off guard and they wrinkled their noses at the smell.

"You know this could only mean one thing," Reace said with a sour look on his face.

"NO!" Arron didn't want to believe it.

"I don't want to believe it either, but we know it's true. Look at this place Arron, they're gone! Everyone, Link, Awkwade, Keyla . . . Kittana—We're all that's left." Bright tears glistened in Reace's eyes.

Arron shook his head in denial, he couldn't speak, his throat was constricted with emotion and his face was wet with tears that leaked out unnoticed.

In silent agreement they made their way slowly through the dead forest. They walked in silence, each deep in thought, in grief. Neither noticed the eerie quiet of the world around them. If they had looked behind them they would have seen the path of green they made with each footstep, but lost in a world of grief—of devastating loss, they barely even saw the path in front of them let alone their tracks behind. The two comrades relied mostly on memory as their feet carried them home, toward Crystal Mountain.

Once inside Reace and Arron didn't quite know what to do, even the Crystal Mountain seemed to have lost its light. Without words the two men made their way up the stairs barely glancing around at the charred remains of the bedrooms. Reace climbed the stairs to the top floor of the mountain leaving Arron behind on the second floor. He said he wanted to search the bedrooms, but Reace suspected he just wanted to have some time alone, he understood.

Feeling hollow, Reace stood in the attic library, his eyes taking in the scene before him, the blackened crystals.

"Soot," he said, smudging it with a finger. The whole room was nothing but soot and ashes. Books that had lasted throughout the centuries now nothing but ashes; People he had loved, laughed with and been through so much with, now nothing but soot.

Tears, hot and fast ran down his cheeks. He heard footsteps behind him, but Reace didn't turn around. If the voice that spoke startled him, he didn't show it.

"If it's any consolation Reace, Kit was the biggest challenge—being a telepath and used to mind games, I had to work extra hard to break her. It took months to make her so confused that she didn't know what was real or fake . . . after that, it was easy to kill her, just as this will be." Malic said reaching out a hand he touched Reace on the side of his head.

Weakened and devastated by loss Reace went quickly into a trance. He didn't see Arron come up the steps, he didn't hear Arron speak.

"Zarrick! Thank-God, you're alive! What happened here? How did they . . . die?" Arron demanded when he saw his son beside Reace. A flash high up on Zarrick left forearm drew Arron's gaze and he reacted, throwing a protective shield around Reace.

Arron's shield pushed Zarrick's hand away from its victim but it was too late, the damage already done.

Wearing his son's face, Malic turned to Arron.

"Malic!" Arron whispered in horror, how could this be Malic and not Zarrick but at the same time he questioned, he knew he was right, Zarrick was Malic. He sucked in a breath, his eyes widening in surprise as it dawned on him.

Suddenly everything was so clear. Malic had used Tia to father a child so he could take over that son's body and destroy them all before they even knew who or what was happening.

Malic was *the one* from the prophecy, he had used Zarrick—he was the foe who was disguised as a friend. The one thought dead to be alive, Nature divided, only one will survive and all will be as before. How could they have been so blind?

Arron's gaze flew to Malic when he threw back his head and laughed, seconds before Reace began chanting.

"NO! REACE!" Arron screamed in desperation. He tried to run toward his friend, wake him from his trance or whatever spell Malic had used, but he found himself helplessly lifted into the air, twenty feet to the ceiling.

"NO!" Arron screamed again, still trying to gain Reace's attention even as Malic waved his hand causing Arron to crash hard into one wall then another before dropping helplessly to the floor. When his head collided with the unforgiving crystal tiles of the floor, Arron lost consciousness. Blood mixed with a yellow fluid trickled out of his ear.

Nate and Timelana materialized in the crystal mountain library and glancing around, Nate saw Arron out cold on the floor from a wound that would have killed a mortal, but Nate wasn't worried. Arron was a Guardian and he would heal and with his powers of life, probably faster than most. Then Nate saw his father and his eyes widened in alarm.

"NO!" He yelled and time stopped.

Reace was two seconds from bursting into flames. Around his body floated the blue cloud of his life force, flames were starting to form around the outside edges of it.

"Your powers are growing, Nature, you are learning fast." Timelana stood beside him as she spoke. "You are the most powerful of all Guardians born. Nature ties into so many things . . . even time. You will find Nate, that you can use a lot of the same powers of the other Guardians. Like the fairies, the Guardians of the flowers and trees, you can grow them too and those who Guard the animals; they to obey you and you have the powers of the elements: earth, air and water—to some extent. Even time bends to the will of Nature, but the Guardians you come from, the Guardians of the prophecy, they are beyond your powers. You cannot interfere."

"Why?" Nate demanded, "Why do they have to die?"

"It is their destiny. A destiny they chose when they came here. They are the Guardians of the prophecy and they must fulfill it. They have lived as Guardians, Nate, let them die as Guardians."

"NO! No, I won't let them die." Nate turned anguished eyes bright with unshed tears to Timelana and pleading he said, "Timelana, you've got to do something . . . rewind time . . . something! You've got to stop this, change it! THEY CAN'T DIE!" Nate's voice gained in volume when she just shook her head sadly.

"Your mother is gone, Keyla is gone. Nate, do you really think that your father would want to still be alive here without them?"

Nate saw in his mind the shattered look on Reace's face at the police station, with a heavy heart he knew she was right, but still he didn't want to let his father go. In so short a time he'd lost everything, everyone, how could he stand back and lose his dad too?

Although her heart was breaking for him, there was nothing she could do to lessen it.

"I am sorry Nature. What is done cannot be undone." Timelana repeated what she had told him before. "This is the way things are meant to be. Nature, death is a part of life, it's a part of the natural order . . . nature even, you cannot have life without death—it is a balance."

"NO! DON'T TELL ME THAT . . . NOT NOW!"

"I am sorry Nate. I cannot stop this. It is the way it is meant to be."

"They're just supposed to die? THEY ARE GUARDIANS!" Tears fell freely now, tears of grief and frustration.

"Yes, Guardians of the prophecy," Timelana said. "And like those who came before they have to give up their powers to those who are next. Nate, how can there be new Guardians if the old are still here?" She asked.

"You're still here. You've lived for more than two thousand years." He pointed out.

She smiled sadly, "The time will come for you to say goodbye to me too, in a few years will be born a new child of time."

The way she looked at him—something in her eyes spoke to him.

"One of my children?" Nate asked, knowing the answer before she nodded.

"Yes, and you will have to teach that child all that I have taught you about the rules of time. We cannot interfere in this, Nate." Timelana gestured to the room they were in. "In order for there to be a balance of seven times two again they must pass on their powers, they must die. The prophecy must be fulfilled."

"Then Malic wins?" Nate said in disbelief.

"Watch and see Nate, The Powers That Be have a plan. It will work out I promise you." Timelana raised her staff then and with her arm held straight out she turned her wrist until the staff lay across them at waist height. She held it steady, "We are unseen, unheard as times moves forward." Her mark flashed a second and her staff glowed as she made them invisible. Then to Nate she spoke, "Release them."

At Timelana's words Nate realized that it was he who had stopped time and it was he who had to restart it, for a second he wondered how and then his father's words came back to him, *I willed it.* With anguish on his face and pain in his heart, Nate willed time to restart.

As hard as it was he had to let go, let fate—destiny happen. Nate's heart thudded painfully in his chest, he slowly breathed as he watched his father die with tears streaming down his face.

*

Arron awoke to the crackling sound of fire and an intense desire to protect himself. Before he was even fully aware of his surroundings or fully awake he had his shield up against the blistering heat and encroaching flames. Seconds later Arron lifted his head as everything came quickly and painfully back to him. His eyes frantically searched the area for Reace, he didn't want to believe what his mind said was true: the flames around him the only remains of his lifelong comrade.

"REACE!" Arron screamed closing his eyes against the pain of loss.

When he opened them moments later they blazed with hatred at the face he had once loved—Zarrick. No, not his son Zarrick, but Malic. Malic used Zarrick's face to murder everyone Arron had loved and for that he would pay.

Anger poured through his veins, red and hot. He trembled with rage—a rage like he'd never felt before. He stood to face Malic, lowering his shield as the flames died down.

"What did you do to my son, Malic? Where is Zarrick?"

"You mean my son, Zarrick. He is here within me. We are one now." Malic's voice was calm. Confident in his victory he took his time.

"NO!" Arron shook his head, refusing to believe him, "Zarrick would never have let you kill everybody . . . Tia."

"Well, he did not exactly have a choice. I am in control now." Malic said, then he frowned looking like he was about to throw up and put his head down on to his chest.

Arron watched wondering what he was going to do—whatever it was he was ready, but when Malic raised his head and looked at him, Arron gasped. He knew those eyes.

"Zarrick?" He whispered half scared to believe it.

"Dad!"

That one word said it all, Arron knew that Zarrick was sorry for the things he's said to him, with one word Zarrick acknowledged that Arron, the man who raised him and loved him was his true father. Arron nodded, tears making his eyes bright as Zarrick continued speaking.

"I can't fight him for long. Dad, you have to finish it. You're the only one who can stop him—stop me. I can't live like this . . . Fitca," He pleaded.

The look on Zarrick's face broke Arron's heart. He was about to deny it, how could he kill his son? Then Zarrick's face changed and Arron's resolve hardened as he heard laughter bubble up from inside his son's body. He knew that Malic had once again taken over.

Just as Malic flicked his fingers toward Arron using Zarrick's power of war, Arron instinctively put up a hand, his golden shield protecting him from the destructive blast.

"You cannot win against me and you cannot save my son. I have finally won and my revenge will be complete with your death!" Malic couldn't resist taunting the younger Guardian.

Anger flowed through Arron, hot and energizing. His powers rose to the surface and with it he realized that Zarrick was right; he could end this. Letting his rage take over Arron released his power of death. A power that he had always kept locked deep inside of himself. Freed from its restraint Arron practically vibrated with the urge to kill.

He took a step forward then another until he was close enough to touch Malic.

Before Malic could do anything, Arron wrapped his hand tight on Zarrick's forearm in a grip that wouldn't let go; his mark of death glowing brightly.

Out of the corner of his eye Arron saw the marks that ran up Malic's arm flare as Malic tried to use his powers against Arron, trying to combat the overwhelming power of death.

Distracted, his mark dimmed and for a moment—a fraction of a second—as he wondered if maybe Malic could truly win then he thought of everyone he loved. In his mind's eye Arron saw them all die just like Reace had: Keyla, Kittana, Awkwade, Link and Tia and the countless others that Malic had ruthless killed before them. A renewed rage built inside of Arron, it poured through his veins into his powers and miraculously his mark shined brighter than ever.

The grin that had covered Zarrick's face, twisting it into an evil smirk that resembled Malic's features, changed to surprise then horror as the marks on his arm disappeared. One by one, in a wisp of colored light that flowed out of him like smoke from a freshly extinguished candle.

"I can stop you and I will save MY son!"

With a final look of disbelieve on his face Malic stared at Arron then he was gone. Arron wasn't sure how he knew it but he knew the peaceful look that settled on Zarrick's face was Zarrick—his son. Malic had gone, dead yet Arron didn't let go—he couldn't.

Zarrick's hand gripped Arron's holding him there. Arron watched unable to stop himself as Zarrick whispered a final. "Tarine-ak."

Arron stared, watching as the life left Zarrick's eyes and they stared back at him for a moment, lifeless, like glass marbles used in wax figures. His son had just thanked him for ending his life. When Zarrick's body crumbled into dust Arron stood there, lost, staring at the pile of dust at his feet until he sank to his knees.

Timelana's words came back to him, *It will be what you were born for.* Arron finally understood why the powers that be had made him two Guardians: Life and Death. It wasn't because he was a monster; it was so he could stop one.

As the tears rolled down Arron's cheeks, now that it was over he could give into his grief. He remembered Keyla's dream, it had been a premonition after all. Malic was dead, everyone was dead and now it was his turn.

"I give up my powers to those who come next.
I give up my life force to those who come next."

# Chapter eleven

Nate didn't look away until he saw Arron consumed by fire, the smell of burning flesh and bone filled his nostrils for the second time with their acid smell. His legs buckled and Nate slowly sank to the ground, hardly noticing that outside the balance was restored. The sun shone brightly for a moment and the grass and trees returned to life, fragment and fresh just before it clouded over; thunder rumbled and lightening sliced the sky, the ground shook and it began to snow.

For a long time he sat there stunned and sobbing as he came to the realization that his world—everyone he had known and grew up with—his whole family were gone.

"Nature," Timelana said, sitting on the floor beside him. His pain she understood, but that didn't stop her gasp at the naked emotion shining in Nature's eyes when he raised them to her.

"The prophecy's fulfilled." He spat bitterly.

"All but the last line—that'll happen the next time you come here."

He glared at her all but sneering the words. "Then it will never be fulfilled! This is the place they all DIED. I NEVER WANT TO COME HERE AGAIN!"

Timelana watched at him with sympathy, not offended by his anger. She knew that when the time was right he would be back. That would be the last of the prophecy. What started with his parents would end with his children. Suddenly her expression changed, her brow furrowed and her eyes turned urgent.

"Nate, we have to go . . . your wife . . . there has been an accident . . . I'll take you there." Timelana held out a hand to Nate as she stood.

Shocked out of his grief by her words Nate wasted no time in gaining to his feet and grabbing her hand.

\*

Seconds later, although to Nate it seemed like an eternity, they materialized on the side of a hill, not far from the highway just outside of Springfield. It was the scene of an accident, a car had gone off the road, breaking through the rusted metal medium it had gone over the embankment coming to a stop with the assistance of a group of trees.

It took Nature a few seconds to recognize the smashed piece of metal and plastic as his and then he started running toward the car.

He could see Anna-Maria: she sat lifeless with a weird expression on her beautiful face. Nate was hardly aware that he had started chanting "Please be okay," but he didn't stop as he reached in the broken window on the driver's side of the wreck to touch her neck in search of a pulse.

At the feel of warm skin, her breath on his fingers and a pulse beneath his fingertips, he breathed a sigh of relief. A smile of incredibility shined from his face when she turned her face to him.

"I should be hurt, I should be dead. I should have hit my head, but I didn't . . . this golden . . . shield protected me," She wrapped her arms around her expanded belly, hugging it as she glanced down, amending her words, "us." Then she looked at Nate and added, "I think Arron must have saved us."

Nate slowly, sadly, shook his head.

"It couldn't have been Arron . . . he's . . ." Nate opened his mouth to say it, but he found he couldn't.

"Prepare yourself, Nature, you'll have to deliver that child now." Timelana spoke just as Anna gave a scream of pain—her labor reinstating itself; her child impatient to be born.

Nate looked from Anna to Timelana and back to Anna who spoke. "She's right, Nate. We'll never make it to the hospital in time. The baby is coming . . . now!" she gritted her teeth as another contraction hit. Breathing through it she looked with a scared expression to her husband.

"What if there are complications?" He turned to Timelana, worried.

"There won't be," she said knowingly.

"But I can't heal and Arron . . ." he trailed off again unable to say it. It would make it too real and Nate wasn't ready yet to face that.

"Trust me," Timelana said, giving Nate a look of confidence and a slight nod, just as Anna screamed through another contraction.

"Okay." Nate took a deep breath, what he'd learned at Lamaze classes running through his mind. "Are you okay? I mean can you move?" he asked his wife. When she nodded he helped her from the car, making her as comfortable as possible on the green grass.

\*

Anna gave birth to a happy healthy baby girl, because of the solid circle on her left inside wrist, they named her Aireona (Air-e-on-a), in honor of Arron in whose footsteps she would follow as the next Guardian of Life. As the newborn, wrapped warmly in daddy's jacket and held against mommy's skin, suckling at her breast Anna and Nate basked in the miracle of their first child. They turned as one when Timelana spoke.

"I hope you understand now, the cycle of life. If Arron hadn't died, Anna and Aireona couldn't be."

Nate's eyes misted and his throat pumped, there were so many things he wanted to say but his body wasn't co-operating. Timelana seemed to know what he was trying to convey and she nodded.

"Nate, the Guardians are not gone forever they will live on in your children and in you. Keep them alive, remember them. Talk about them with your kids—write their story down. Tell it to your children. When the time is right they and others will need to know about Taysia, Staria, and their destiny as future Guardians." She paused looking at the tiny baby held lovingly by her mother.

"She is beautiful Anna, the first of many." Rising her eyes to Anna's Timelana thudded her staff on the ground three times, then she was gone.

It seemed to Anna as if with her disappearance, the rest of the world reinstated itself. The noise from traffic on the road above them, and the wilderness around them was heard and Anna noticed how quiet it had been. Had Timelana stopped time around them to let them have a few moments alone with their newborn, she wondered? Then what Timelana had said came to her and she turned questioning eyes to Nate.

"What was that all about? Did she say Arron died?" Anna demanded. Her eyes that searched his face, filling with sorrow at what she read there before he even spoke a word.

Nate opened his mouth to tell her, his eyes filled with water, he couldn't get the words out. He couldn't say it yet, not out loud, not without feeling the overwhelming grief that threatened to bury him. What was he going to do without them? He didn't want to think about it yet, he wasn't ready. When Nate finally managed to get any words out past his throat it wasn't to answer her question, but to ask one.

"Why did you go off the road? What were you even doing out here in the middle of nowhere?"

"You've been gone for three days, Nate, I was worried so I thought if I went to the place where Jake and Heather said the Guardians opened the portal before, that maybe I'd find some clue as to what happened to you. While I was there my water broke, and I was driving back to the hospital. I thought I'd have lots of time—the Lamaze instructor said labor usually took hours, but I guess not in our case." She smiled fondly at the soft black hair on her daughter head before returning to her husband's bright green gaze. "A labor pain hit me . . . hard and I guess I lost control. The next thing I knew was I was staring through a golden shield . . . then you were there . . . What happened, Nate? We heard about the fire. Did your father . . ." Anna trailed off as a passerby came up to them.

"I couldn't help but see the accident, are you folks alright? I called 911. Help should be here in about five minutes." The pleasant looking middle-aged man said.

"Thanks," Nate replied accepting his offer of help, truthfully he was glad for the distraction, it was a good excuse not to have to answer his wife's questions. He just needed more time to process it all himself, then he'd tell her, he mentally promised himself, looking at his child happily nursing.

*

It wasn't until later in the evening, after both mother and baby were safely tucked into their hospital beds—Aireona in her crib on wheels beside her mother's bed and Anna snuggled beside Nate on the narrow hospital cot—that Anna remembered what Timelana had said before she left. Whatever happened on Taysia, to the Guardians, Anna would be forever grateful if it meant saving the life of her child. Her precious little girl, she thought, looking fondly on the sleeping babe.

At first they were scared to bring Aireona to the hospital but saying no would only raise suspicion so they went. Hoping they could protect her. Nate was amazing, Anna thought her heart swelling with pride for her husband as she remembered how he stopped time to exchange the blood samples and he way he covered the mark on Aireona's wrist with his thumb every time someone came near until the hospital bracelet was placed on her wrist.

Anna couldn't help but wonder what the future had in store for her, Nate and the start of their new family. *The first of many* Timelana had told them and judging from the solid circle on her tiny newborns wrist, the future would definitely be interesting.

Feeling Nate move on the other side of her, she shifted so she could see him better. She had missed him in the past three days that he'd been gone, it scared her how much. She had been so happy to see him after the accident that at first she wondered if she had died. With everything happening so quickly she hadn't paid attention to what he had said, now it came back to her and Anna asked.

"Why couldn't Arron have saved us?"

Nate looked away from her, he knew she needed answers and he couldn't put it off any longer, he had to face it. He had to tell her and then he'd have to tell Jake later tonight when he got home.

Taking a deep fortifying breath Nate told Anna what happened at the mansion with Danielle and afterward. What he had found on Taysia, how hard it was to watch them all die.

Holding Anna, he felt better . . . stronger somehow.

Glancing with love at the child he had help to create and bring into this world. He thought about what Timelana had said, was she right? Would he only have to look to his children to see impressions of his past? His mother's voice, his father's eyes and quiet strength, and Keyla's encouraging smile, would he see those things in his children too? The thought lessoned his sadness maybe his parents weren't totally gone. He could keep them alive, just like Timelana had said. He would write their stories down and they would live on in his heart, in his memories and in his children.

# Epilogue

Seven years later,

WALKING HOME, FROM HIS JOB as a high school english teacher at Springfield high Nate could feel the late afternoon sun on his back warming him against the sight chill in the May air. His footsteps slowed as he fingered a bud from the tall hedge surrounding the roomy backyard of his house.

Shortly after their second child, Kaden, was born and his first book, *Guardians,* was published they had moved into the five bedroom, two story old Victorian home. A smile lit his features as Nate remembered planting the hedge late August a year after they moved. Three year old Airy hadn't wanted the flowers to die so she had used her power of life to bring them back.

Thankfully none of their neighbours noticed it and afterward Anna told him they would need to build a high fence for privacy.

He smiled in memory of how he had bulked at the idea of a wooden fence so they had compromised with a hedge. He remembered going to several garden centers and buying all the bushes they had; A mixed bunch of straggly, half-dead bushes. He'd brought them home and planted them all and as he placed each one in the earth he talked to them.

In his mind's eye he could still see the way the leaves perked up and the branches swayed—uncurling themselves and relaxing as if they were sighing, finally free and at peace. With a little help from him, the Guardian of Nature they grew fast, healthy and strong until they were as tall as he was—six feet. Not many of the bushes matched and the effect was stunning: flowering all spring and summer bathing their backyard and the sidewalk in a riot of colors and different scents.

Nate felt a certain amount of pride as he walked through the front door of his home, the home he shared with Anna and their four young children. With the money he'd made off his second book, *The Prophecy Fulfilled*, the sequel to *Guardians* Anna was able to be the stay at home mother she had wanted to be.

The success of his books surprised him he hadn't penned them to sell. He'd just written the story of his parents as a way to reconnect with them. To remember them and as a way to help with the grieving process but after reading it Anna and Jake urged him to send it to an agent and from there it was well received in the publishing world as Timelana told him it would be.

"Daddy! Your home! Come and see what I did today. I planted a garden. It's beautiful, daddy, wait till you see it. Come on! Come see!"

Elexa tugged on his hand as soon as he came through the door. He felt the familiar electric shock travel up his arm from the tiny four year old Guardian. It reminded him of his father. Smiling down into the excited bright blue eyes of his daughter Nate felt his heart expand, Timelana was right. To see the faces of the past he had to look no further than his own children. Elexa was the spitting image of his father, Reace.

Putting down the briefcase he carried, he ruffled her inky black hair. Her face was aglow with excitement and pride and Nate found that he could deny her nothing. Nodding to his daughter, he let go of her hand. His eyes moved off her to take in the sight of his wife as she neared them. His breath caught in his throat, Anna-Maria was as beautiful and as youthful as the day they first met in high school, even after having four children.

"El, let your father come in first." She gently scolded before turning a welcoming smile on her husband. Stepping into his embrace and kissing him briefly on the lips before she asked, "Hi honey, how was your day?"

"Not as exciting as yours. A garden huh?" He replied.

"Yes, you should come see it. It's quite remarkable—a true sign of brotherly love."

As Nate puzzled over her words he was startled by the small jolt of electricity that traveled up his arm when Elexa slipped her hand into his again.

Her impatient tug spurring him to move through the house, following his youngest daughter, Anna close behind them. Out the back door and into the yard, they came to a stop beside a fully grown beautiful garden in carefully straight rows of tall peas; lush tops of carrots and full, plump, red on the vine tomatoes.

"Look, daddy! I tried so hard to make the rows straight. Mommy helped." Pride was evident in Elexa's voice. She pointed at each one as Nate knelt closer to see. "We planted peas, carrots and tomatoes."

"It's perfect honey, you did a wonderful job!" Nate said admiringly.

Two year old Ty toddled over to them a grin on his face.

"Hi da-dee!" He spoke as he leaned into him in a half hug before turning his attention his older sister. "El come ide with me."

"Okay." Elexa took his hand and the two of them ran towards the swing set to play on the slide, leaving the adults alone beside the garden.

As Nate stood it hit him that it was only May—the beginning of the growing season and that his wife had said they planted the garden today—How . . . what?

"We planted it this morning." Anna explained seeing the questions on Nate's face. "Elexa sat there all morning waiting for it to grow." She pointed to a spot beside the garden. "By the afternoon she was quite upset that it wasn't growing so Ty helped her out."

"Ty? He's . . ." Nate was speechless.

"The future Guardian of time." Anna finished for him.

"But . . . but Timelana's still here. I spoke to her this morning. Ty couldn't have his powers yet." Nate frowned as he tried to figure this out. On one hand he was happy for his son but on the other . . . he didn't even want to consider what it meant.

"Apparently he has some. He aged the garden and with it a mouse. Airy was devastated about the mouse when she came home from school. She brought it back to life."

Lost in his thoughts Nate was only half listening to Anna but the phrase *back to life* reached out and grabbed his attention.

"Back to life?" He repeated stunned for a moment. "Incredible" he added. Arron could never heal the dead and Timelana had told him that Tazok the Guardian of Life before Arron didn't have a shield. Could it be that with each generation the Guardians got stronger? Or perhaps it was that each Guardian tapped into different abilities as they needed them? Like his mother Kittana, the Guardian of the Mind, she didn't know she could do a psychic blast until she did one and even Malic with all his powers didn't really know what hit him.

Music suddenly blared.

"That's my phone. I left it on the kitchen counter. You stay here and watch the kids. I'll be right back." Anna spoke as she left.

Watching his two youngest children play around the swing set, Aireona his eldest daughter moved closer to the garden showing her five year old brother, Kaden, the mouse whose life she had saved and hearing the low murmur of his wife's voice in the house only a few feet away, Nate felt content—almost. With a sigh he called her name.

"Timelana."

He was worried about her. Ty using his powers could only mean one thing and Nate didn't want to think about losing her too. He'd already lost everyone he had grown up with. Over the years he and Timelana had grown close. She was his bestfriend, his last link to his past and Taysia. What he'd do without her he didn't want to contemplate.

"Timelana" he said again his voice giving away the panic he felt. When out of the corner of his eye he saw the swirl of telltale colors and sparks of light that marked her arrival he breathed a huge sigh of relief. Time had stopped around them at least for the moment. Nate turned to the beautiful woman beside him and without words he moved to envelop her in a crushing embrace.

"Nate! I'm glad to see you too." She returned the hug then added a few moments later. "You can let go now. Can't breathe!" She gasped out.

Nate instantly loosened his hold on her but unwilling to let her go completely kept his hands on her shoulders.

Seeing the amount of emotions in his eyes as he stared at her brought a shine of tears to her eyes. Concerned she demanded, "What is it, Nate? What's wrong?"

"Timelana, thank the powers that be! I thought . . . when Anna told me that Ty had used his powers . . . I thought . . ." Nate couldn't bring himself to say it and thankfully he didn't have to as Timelana nodded in understanding.

"Don't worry Nature. We have a life time of friendship ahead of us."

"You're my best friend, Timelana. You, Anna, Jake and the kids, you're all I have. I couldn't stand to lose you too." Nate admitted with a fond look on his face and tears shinning openly in his eyes.

"I have lived for more than two thousand years, Nate. I will not die unknowingly. I will tell you and come say goodbye first. I promise."

Relief flooded him at her words, the calmness and familiarity of her voice soothed his frayed nervous as it washed over him. He dropped his hands from her shoulders as he smiled at her.

"Ty hasn't received his powers yet and he won't until he is ready. He has a lot to learn and when he is ready I will teach him as I taught you. He is the next Guardian of Time, Nate, and like you he is a very special Guardian. He can tap into his future self's powers especially if there is a strong need."

"A garden isn't exactly a strong need, Timelana"

"This wasn't about creating a garden." She gestured towards Ty and Elexa's handiwork as she spoke. "It's more about the love between siblings and a desire to help make someone happy. Your son didn't just randomly tap into his future powers to see a garden grow fast. He did it to please his heart broken sister; to cheer her up and make her happy. Do you understand now?"

"Sort-of?" Nate was quiet for a moment then changed his mind, "No."

"Nature. You still have so much to learn! There is no greater purpose than love and the desire to make someone else happy."

"You sound like he passed some kind of test."

"With flying colors." Timelana agreed a blooming smile on her face. "Take a deep breath, Nate your world is about to expand."

With that encoded message she thudded her staff on the ground and disappeared in a swirl of sparks and colors. With her the quietness passed too. As the noise of the outside world reinstated itself he stood there puzzling over Timelana's words when suddenly someone appeared at his side.

He jumped, startled and then after taking a deep breath to calm his racing heart he laughed at himself. It was only Anna.

"That was Holly, on the phone." Anna clarified when he seemed puzzled. "Something happened today to her girls, Jade and Breann. Thankfully, she called Jake first before going to the hospital."

"Hospital?! What happened? Are they alright?" Nate interrupted seeking answers. He was worried for Jake's children they weren't much older than Elexa and Ty. If anything happened to them he'd . . .

"They're both fine, at least I think they are or will be."

Nate visibly relaxed at Anna's words.

"Ummm . . . Holly thinks this is strange: but Jake told her NOT to go to the hospital and just to bring both girls here. He said he'd meet her here." She paused for a moment before adding, "He hasn't told her anything has he?"

"No. I think he thought that was for the best."

"In other words he was scared she'd leave him."

Nate grinned at her please that she was so insightful. He had come to the same conclusion.

"I'm glad you never left me." Nate said slipping an arm around her.

"That's because you trusted me enough to tell me the truth. Honestly though, I think Jake made a mistake not telling her. After what she saw a little knowledge would have helped."

"What did she see? What happened?"

"Jade fell into the pool. She can't swim. Breann, saw her mother panicking and did what comes naturally to Guardians, she made the water pick her sister up and put her safely on the deck. I don't know what else happened but Holly mentioned something about smoke and a broken arm. I am not sure exactly . . ."

"A mark forming." Nate supplied the explanation. "It's a good thing she called Jake first. If she took those kids to the hospital . . . Kandle Lie Thayia Demar! Who knows what would have happened."

"Yeah, they are on their way over here. Ah, why don't you go and see if you have a copy of your books around for her to read before Jake gets off work." Anna suggested thinking the best way to understand everything was to read *Guardians* and its sequel.

Nate nodded then started for the house. He could hardly believe it, Jake's youngest daughter Breann, the Guardian of Water. He wondered if Jade was also gifted?